The
Golden Couple

By Stephanie Karpinske

The Golden Couple
By Stephanie Karpinske

CONTENTS

1. Wake Up — 1
2. Message — 10
3. Flash Drive — 20
4. Surprise — 30
5. Dana Point — 43
6. Silent Treatment — 55
7. Paul's House — 66
8. Decryption — 74
9. Orgin — 84
10. Options — 97
11. Waiting — 105
12. College Tour — 116
13. Side Effects — 126
14. Luke's Journal — 135
15. Directions — 145
16. Reunion — 155
17. Reykjavik — 165
18. Room 402 — 176
19. Interviews — 188
20. Dinner Date — 202
21. Waltz Lesson — 213
22. The Tour — 223
23. Champagne Toast — 234
24. About Last Night — 251
25. Revelation — 263
26. News — 273
27. Lab Visitor — 283
28. Preparations — 294
29. The Globe — 302
30. Secrets — 313

1. WAKE UP

I gazed out the window of the van at the long stretch of road before us. Tall grasses speckled with wildflowers lined the highway. Colin, the boy I'd grown up with and the boy I loved, rested quietly in the back of the van. I sat in the seat in front of him, keeping an eye on his condition. Erik sat in the second-row seat, my sister Brittany napping on his shoulder. Erik's dad, Jack, was up front, hunched over the wheel of the van, listening to public radio.

We'd been on the road all day and had made it to the western edge of Texas. We had another day of driving ahead of us before we would reach California. There we would gather the belongings of Erik's twin brother, the brother he just recently learned existed but who was now deceased. DNA samples from his brother and my sister would hopefully slow the timer ticking away in Erik and me.

The timer was a piece of software designed to kill us when we turned twenty. It was placed there by GlobalLife Genetics years ago as a safeguard in case we ever escaped from them. GlobalLife could stop the timer and save us. But we refused to go back there. We had to find another way. We didn't know why the timer was set to go off on our twentieth birthday, but it didn't matter. The deadline was closing in fast. I had just two years left. Erik had only a few months.

"Sam?" A voice softly called out my name. I looked back to see that Colin was up. I rushed to the makeshift bed we'd set up for him on the floor of the van. The van was a large work van, like the type floral delivery companies use. Jack had a couple rows of seats added so we could use it for travel. Behind the seats were boxes of supplies and Jack's computer equipment along with the small bed he made for Colin. It wasn't ideal but it was the best we could do given our circumstances.

"Colin, what's wrong? Are you in pain? I can give you more medicine." Colin's face and body were badly bruised and he had a deep gash in his forehead that I'd cleaned and covered in gauze.

"No, I just wanted to see you. Make sure you're really here." Colin's voice was scratchy but stronger than it had been earlier in the day.

"I'm here. And I'll stay right next to you, okay?" I couldn't stand to look at his injuries knowing I was the cause of them. It wasn't me directly, but the people who were after me. The horrible people working for GlobalLife Genetics.

"I thought you were gone forever, Sam." Colin squeezed my hand with what little strength he had. "I thought I'd never see you again."

"I know. And I wish I could have left you a message or—"

"I tried to find you. I looked everywhere. And then weeks went by and I didn't know what to do."

"We don't need to talk about it now. You should rest." I gently moved his hair away from his face to keep it off his wounds.

Colin closed his eyes. "Don't leave me."

"No, I'll stay right here."

He opened his eyes to look at me again. "No, I mean, don't leave me like you did before."

"I won't. Never again." I lay down next to him, pulling the blanket over us both.

I wasn't sure how much Colin knew about what had happened to me the past few weeks. Being captured and held prisoner at GlobalLife Genetics. Escaping and making it down to Texas.

Meeting Erik, a guy with enhanced genes just like me. Finding out about my twin sister, Brittany. Colin probably didn't know about any of it.

When GlobalLife took Colin, I was sure they'd made up lies about me. Maybe they told him I'd run away. Maybe he'd believed the voice mail they faked with me saying I didn't want to see him anymore. Eventually, I would tell Colin everything, but this wasn't the time. I closed my eyes and fell asleep next to him.

"Hey, Sam." The voice woke me up. It was Erik leaning over the seat in front of me. It was dark out now and I could barely see his face.

"My dad's stopping to get gas and Brittany needs to use the restroom. Can you go with her?"

I rubbed my eyes, wondering how long I had slept. "Sure, just a minute." I slid out from under the blanket, trying not to wake Colin.

"It's a few miles ahead," Erik said, "but I thought you might wanna get up."

"Yeah, okay, thanks." I crawled over the seat and sat next to Erik. Brittany had moved up front with Jack.

Erik turned his back to me and looked out into the darkness. I could feel the tension between us. With Colin back in the picture, Erik wasn't sure how to treat me, and I wasn't ready to address the issue. In the short time that I'd known Erik, we'd become close friends, and had started to become more than that. We shared an attraction that couldn't be described. We'd felt it the minute we met. But I fought it, not wanting to betray Colin, even though I was sure I'd never see him again.

Now Colin was back and I had to put my feelings for Erik aside. But part of me couldn't do it. I couldn't pretend my feelings for Erik never existed. They were still there. And all I could do was try to suppress them.

We rode in uncomfortable silence until we finally reached the gas station. It was an old run-down station with just one gas pump. The building next to it was more like a small shack. I started to think it might be better for Brittany to relieve herself in the grassy fields rather than in whatever type of restroom facilities this place had. But it was pitch black in the fields, so that wasn't an option.

I got out of the van and opened the passenger door to let Brittany out. She moved slowly, still in shock after killing the GlobalLife guards who had held us prisoner at her trailer. The scene had played out earlier that day; she hadn't spoken more than a few words since. I was still amazed at what she'd done. But they had killed her mother. And I, more than anyone, knew what a need for revenge could make a person do.

Revenge had driven my actions ever since I'd discovered that GlobalLife killed my parents. The more I learned about GlobalLife, the more I hated them. At Brittany's trailer, I'd killed Alden Worthings, a top executive at GlobalLife Genetics who had ordered my parents' deaths. And I'd killed one of his guards. I didn't mean to kill either one of the men. In fact, I still wasn't sure how it had happened. But I was sure that we were all safer with them gone. At least for a little while.

"Brittany, come on." I nudged Brittany to the shack entrance. She stared straight ahead. "Okay, just wait here."

I went inside to find a small, leathery-skinned old man running the cash register. "Is there a bathroom somewhere?" I asked him.

"Round back. You gotta use a key. It's unisex." He tossed me a wooden stick that had a key hanging from the end of it. I cringed as I touched the dirty stick, trying not to imagine its history.

"Brittany, let's go. It's around the back."

Brittany followed me to a rusty metal door that had the word "bathroom" spray-painted on it. I opened the door to find swarms of flies and a horrible smell. A single lightbulb lit the small room that contained a yellowed toilet and a rust-stained sink.

"I'll wait right out here," I said.

Brittany went inside the disgusting bathroom without even making a face. After a few minutes, I got worried. "Brittany, are you done? We need to go. Brittany?"

I tried the door, but it was locked. I still had the key, so I quickly unlocked the door. I opened it up to find Brittany hunched over the rusty sink, quietly sobbing.

"Brittany?" I went over and put my arms around her. "Brittany, talk to me. You haven't spoken all day. Please say something."

She continued to cry softly. I heard a knock on the door, which I'd left open. Erik poked his head in. "Hey, can I help?"

I shook my head, motioning him to leave.

"No, wait." Brittany turned back toward Erik. "I wanna talk to him. Alone."

I looked at Erik, then back at Brittany. "You want me to leave so you can talk to Erik?"

She nodded like a child.

"Um, okay." I walked away, leaving Brittany and Erik standing by the bathroom door.

Jack was reading the map when I got back in the van. "Where are those two? We need to go."

"It's Brittany. I found her crying in the bathroom. When I tried to talk to her, she wouldn't say anything. Then she asked to talk to Erik."

After a few minutes, Erik came back with Brittany. She had stopped crying and looked a little better. They sat together in the seat in front of me, Brittany leaning up against Erik as she went back to sleep.

I felt bad for Brittany, but seeing her all over Erik was difficult for me to watch. I knew she liked him but I didn't want her using her grief to win him over. It was wrong of me to think that, but I couldn't help it. Brittany played the ditzy cheerleader role well, but deep down I knew she was smarter than that. If she wanted something, she would find a way to get it. And I knew she wanted Erik.

"Erik, what went on back there? What did she tell you?" I thought to him.

"Oh, now you want to mind-talk? After I've been trying to talk to you all day?" Erik kept his face forward, staring out the front of the van.

"I'm sorry, but I've been a little busy back here," I thought back.

"He's slept almost the whole day, Sam. I think you could have spared a minute or two."

I didn't like his tone. It wasn't the Erik I was used to.

"Okay, that's fair. I'm sorry, Erik. I should have listened to your thoughts earlier. Now can you stop being so mad at me?"

He didn't respond, which I assumed meant he was still mad.

"What did Brittany say to you? Was she crying because she killed those men at the trailer?"

"No, Sam." Erik's tone was critical, like I was being insensitive toward Brittany. *"She was crying because of her mom. She feels bad because we just left her mom there on the floor of the trailer."*

"Well, what were we supposed to do? Take a dead body with us?"

"She wanted us to say something before we left. Some final words. She said her mom doesn't have anyone. That no one will even show up at her funeral."

I kept my mind quiet. I didn't know enough about Brittany's mom to know if that was true. But Erik knew her. And from his tone I sensed that Brittany's estimate for funeral attendees wasn't that far off.

"She asked me to say a prayer with her, asking God to take care of her mom. So we did. And I think it really helped her. I think she needed that."

I instantly regretted thinking bad things about Brittany. I didn't know why she chose Erik to confide in over me, but it didn't matter.

She was grieving and it wasn't my place to decide how she did that or who she asked for help. I, of all people, should have known that because I was still grieving the loss of my parents.

"So where are we?" I asked, this time talking out loud.

Erik finally turned back to look at me. "Somewhere in New Mexico. I told my dad I'd take over driving in an hour or so. He denies it, but I know he's getting tired."

As Erik talked, I felt my strong attraction to him again. I imagined us back on the porch swing at his old farmhouse, looking out at the fireflies in the field. It was there that we first kissed, a kiss so incredible that part of me ached to do it again, even though I knew it was wrong.

"Hey, what's wrong, Sam? You got so quiet all of a sudden."

"It's nothing," I lied, relieved that he hadn't been reading my thoughts.

Erik reached over and put his hand on my shoulder. I felt his energy the second he touched me and I knew that's why he did it. It was his way of keeping us connected. Reminding me what we shared.

"Are you okay? I mean, that whole thing with Worthings this morning was pretty traumatic. And you haven't said anything. Do you wanna talk about it?"

"It's weird, but I haven't really given it any thought. I think I'm trying to block it out."

"Guess I shouldn't have brought it up." He took his hand away.

"It's okay. I can't pretend it didn't happen. I killed a man," I whispered, glancing over the seat to make sure Brittany was still asleep. "Actually, I killed two."

"It was them or us, Sam. And you chose us. It wasn't even a choice. You did what had to be done."

"I didn't even mean to do it, though. My abilities just kind of took over. I wasn't trying to kill them."

"Well, however it happened, you helped us get out of there alive. You and Brittany saved us all."

"Yeah, who would've thought, right?" I shivered just thinking about it.

"Sam, if you ever want to talk about what happened, I'm always here."

"I might just take you up on that," I said, wondering how the morning's event would affect me once I'd had more time to think about it.

There's some other stuff we need to talk about. Erik was communicating with his thoughts again.

What stuff? I asked, even though I knew what he meant.

We need to talk about us. *About where we go from here now that Colin is back.*

I paused before responding. *It's not the right time, Erik.*

I get that, but we still need to talk about it. He turned back toward the front of the van.

"So how's Colin doing?" Erik spoke out loud again.

"He's sleeping. He's been sleeping a lot. I hope that's not a bad sign. It seems like the drugs they gave him wore off, but he's still really out of it."

"When we stop, my dad can check on him. It's probably just his body trying to recover."

"Yeah, I hope so."

Erik lowered his voice and turned his head back slightly. "Did he tell you anything yet? About what happened to him?"

"No," I said quietly. "But I probably don't wanna know." I knew from experience that GlobalLife was capable of doing horrible things, so I didn't even want to imagine what they had done to Colin. "I should go check on him."

I crawled behind my seat and kneeled down near Colin. He was still asleep but his body was shivering. I pulled the blanket over him and tucked it in around him. He looked so helpless and sick. He didn't seem to be getting any better. In the dim light, I could see his hair had fallen over the cuts on his face again. I brushed it aside and noticed his hair was wet, like he'd been sweating. I put my hand on his face. It was burning hot with fever.

"Colin?" I tore the blanket off him, trying to cool him down. "Colin? Wake up. Talk to me. Colin?" He wasn't responding. "Colin! Wake up!" I said it even louder but still got no response.

"Jack! Jack, stop the van!" I called out, startling Erik and waking up Brittany. Erik jumped out of his seat and made his way to the back of the van.

"Sam! What is it?" But as soon as he looked at Colin, he knew. "Dad, pull over! Now!" Erik was much louder than me. This time Jack heard.

"What's wrong?" Jack asked. "What's going on back there?"

"It's Colin," Erik called back. "He's sick. He's really sick. He needs help. You need to get back here."

I could feel the van slowing. Colin was still not responding. "Colin, please wake up. Please, I'm begging you. Wake up." Tears were streaming down my face.

Erik watched me, not knowing what to say. I could see the worry in his face as he looked down at Colin, who seemed to be getting sicker by the second. Neither one of us knew what to do, but we could both feel it. The feeling that it might be too late.

2. MESSAGE

Jack pulled over to the side of the road and got out, racing to the back of the van. He burst through the back doors to get to Colin.

"When did this happen?" Jack's urgent tone confirmed that Colin's condition was as serious as we thought. "Sam, how long has he been this way?"

"I—I don't know! I came back here to check on him and noticed that his hair was wet. Then I felt him and he was burning up. And now he won't wake up!"

Jack ripped off Colin's shirt. He grabbed a towel from a nearby box and tossed it to me. "Here, dry him off."

"Why? What are you doing?" Jack didn't answer, so I quickly patted Colin's sweat-soaked chest with the towel as Jack checked his pulse. The color was starting to leave Colin's face and body as his breathing became more labored.

"Jack, he's getting worse! Help him!" I begged. "Colin, if you can hear me, please just hold on, okay?"

"Erik, get the defibrillator. Now!" Jack ordered.

Erik, who had been sitting silently next to me, suddenly burst up. "Where is it? Which box?"

"It's marked 'medical equipment.' Should be on the top." Jack took out a stethoscope from a small metal box on the floor.

Erik crawled over Colin and started searching through a box. "Got it!" Erik said, pulling out the AED machine.

"His pulse is very weak," Jack muttered, "but his heart is racing. Skin is pale. He's unconscious." Jack seemed to be going through a checklist to determine a diagnosis.

"What is it? What's wrong?" I demanded.

Jack started attaching electrodes to Colin's chest. "Ventricular fibrillation. His heartbeat's too fast. His body isn't getting enough blood. We don't have much time. Erik, go up front. And take Sam with you."

"Wait. Let me help!" I pleaded.

"Erik, get her out of here! Now!" Jack's voice filled the van. He turned on the defibrillator.

Erik grabbed me, pulling me up to the second row seat. Brittany had moved to the front seat, unable to handle the commotion going on in the back. It was too much for her, given what she had experienced earlier in the day.

As I tried to crawl back, Erik held me down. "Sam, stop! We need to stay out of the way." Erik kept a hold on me but I positioned myself so I could still keep watch on what was going on in the back of the van.

Jack pushed a button on the AED machine, causing Colin's chest to heave into the air. Then he went back over to Colin and immediately started CPR.

"What's wrong? Tell me!" I begged, but Jack wouldn't answer.

"Sam, just let him do what he needs to do." Erik turned me away so I couldn't see what was happening.

We waited in silence as Jack continued to work on Colin. Finally Jack spoke. "His pulse is getting stronger. Erik, start driving. Hurry up! Find the nearest hotel, motel, whatever."

Erik went up front. I crawled back over the seats, crouching down next to Colin. "Motel? But Jack, he needs a hospital."

"There *are* no hospitals out here, Sam. And even if there were, we couldn't risk him going there. It would alert GlobalLife and if they found him, he'd have no chance for survival."

As the van took off, a box tumbled down beside Jack. He got up to secure it in place.

"Can I touch him now?" I asked.

"It's best if you don't." Jack kneeled down across from me. "The machine is continuing to monitor his heart. He may need another shock."

The light in the van was poor, but I could see that Colin didn't look any better. He was still pale and seemed to have trouble breathing.

"Jack." I paused, trying to hold back tears. "I can't lose him. I've lost too much already. And I've already lost him once. Please tell me he'll be okay."

"I'm sorry, but I can't tell you that, Sam. I'm doing my best, but I'm not a doctor. His condition is very serious."

It wasn't the answer I expected. I was sure Jack would at least pretend that Colin would be fine. But he didn't. And that meant Jack was preparing me for the worst possible outcome.

"Why did this happen? I don't understand. He has cuts and bruises and they're pretty bad, but not bad enough to cause this."

"I don't know. When we get settled somewhere, I'll do some blood work. See what I can find out. His fever is likely due to infection. We've got to get some strong antibiotics in him."

"How can you do blood work at a motel?"

"I have a special device. Erik calls it the dipstick because it looks like those sticks you use to check the oil in your car. Anyway, you dip it in a blood sample, then connect it to the computer and it gives you a complete breakdown of what's in the blood, just like a lab would do."

"Where did you get something like that?"

"It was developed by GlobalLife years ago. When I discontinued my employment there, it just happened to leave with me, if you know what I mean."

"So why aren't doctors using that instead of waiting for weeks to get test results?"

"Companies like GlobalLife dole out technology on a schedule, Sam. A schedule that they determine. They know that they always have buyers, looking for the latest and greatest technology. So instead of selling them the most advanced technology, these companies build multiple versions, each one just a fraction better than the last. People buy one version and then companies like GlobalLife dole out the next one. That dipstick device I have is so advanced, they probably have five or 10 other blood analyzing tools in the pipeline ready to launch before it. That's just how it works."

"Dad, there's a motel ahead. I'm stopping, okay?" Erik yelled from up front.

"Yes, go ahead," Jack called back.

It was a single-story roadside motel. Only five cars were parked in the small parking lot. Jack went into the main office while the rest of us waited in the van.

When he came back, he handed me a key. "We have two rooms, so you girls get one and we'll take the other."

Brittany and I went to our room. The motel must have been renovated recently because everything looked new. The room had two double beds, a side table, a small desk, and a dresser with a TV on top.

"I'll take this one," Brittany said, sitting on one of the beds. It was the first time she'd spoken since leaving the gas station.

I went back outside to help Colin, but Jack and Erik had already taken him to the other room. Colin was lying on one of the beds. Jack was checking his heart again. "Sam, you should wait in your room. I'll come and get you later."

"No, I need to do something. I can't just sit over there and wait. I can help. Just tell me what to do."

Erik came in, carrying boxes of medical equipment from the van. "Erik, Sam's going to help me with Colin. You should go stay with Brittany. She shouldn't be alone after what she's been through."

"Yeah, okay. If you need anything, just come over and get me."

Erik left and Jack starting digging through boxes. "Sam, I need you to find the antiseptic solution. I'll find the IVs."

"IVs? You seriously have IVs?" I asked as I searched through a box.

"I've had this stuff for years. I wasn't even going to pack it. But when we went back to the farm today to drop off the truck, I grabbed all of my medical supplies because Colin and Erik were injured. But I never thought we'd need them."

I located the antiseptic and handed it to Jack. "What are you putting in the IV?"

"I don't know yet. I need to test his blood first. I'm hoping that this was all caused by an imbalance of electrolytes because I can fix that. If he has a heart condition, I can't help him."

"Colin doesn't have a heart condition. He's an athlete. He's in really good shape. He works out all the time."

"Undiagnosed heart problems do show up occasionally in high school athletes. But let's hope that's not it." Jack cleaned Colin's arm and drew some blood. He took the sticklike device he had mentioned earlier and put it into the blood sample. "Sam, can you set up my laptop over there?"

I went to the desk and got the computer ready. Jack came over with the device. It had a port on one end that plugged right into the laptop.

"It will give us the basics right away, like electrolyte levels, glucose, blood count, that type of thing," Jack explained. "Then it will continue to analyze his blood and give us more information over the next hour."

I went back over to Colin and held his hand, wishing he would respond somehow.

"Okay, I'm getting some results," Jack said as he looked at the laptop. "And it's what I suspected—an electrolyte problem. His potassium levels are dangerously low."

Jack returned to Colin and began preparing the IV solution. "We'll pump him up with electrolytes and get his levels back to normal. We'll get some antibiotics in him, too, to get that fever down."

"So he'll be okay?" I asked cautiously.

"He'll need some recovery time, but yes, I think he'll be okay."

The news was good, but it released all of the emotion I'd been holding in. Tears flowed from my eyes. "Did you hear that, Colin? You're gonna be okay." I kissed his cheek and noticed that his skin was still fiery hot.

Jack finished the IV setup, then brought the desk chair over so he could sit next to Colin's bed. "He's not out of the woods yet, Sam. We'll need to keep a close eye on him."

"I'll do it. Let me stay with him. I'll stay up all night." My tears slowed as I committed myself to helping Colin recover.

"You need to get some rest. I can watch him."

"No, I have to do this. Colin would do the same for me. He wouldn't sleep a second if it was me in that bed."

"Okay, but we'll take turns. You need at least a few hours of sleep." Jack went to check something on the laptop, then sat down across from me again. "So how long have you two dated?"

"For about a year. But I've known him forever. We've been best friends since we were kids."

"I see. Well, it's clear that you really care for him."

"Jack, why were you asking me that?"

"Oh, no reason. I just wasn't aware of how serious you two were. That's all." Jack got up to check Colin's vital signs. I wondered if Jack's comments were out of concern for his son. I was sure he had noticed his son's attraction to me and mine to him.

Just then Erik walked in. "Hey, do you need anything? It's been so quiet over here. Is everything okay?"

Jack looked up. "Yes. We've got Colin on an IV. Once his electrolytes are restored, he should be all right."

Erik came over and put his hand on my shoulder. "See, Sam? I told you my dad would help him."

"I know. He's amazing. I can't thank you enough, Jack. Really, if you weren't here—" I didn't need to continue. Everyone knew what would have happened.

"Well, his vital signs are starting to improve," Jack confirmed. "But it may be a while before he's alert again. Erik, how's Brittany?"

"She's quiet. Right now she's watching TV. I tried to get her to talk, but she won't do it. It's like she's trying to pretend that nothing happened."

"I'll go talk to her," Jack said, getting up to leave. "Sam, if you're going to keep watch on Colin tonight, maybe I'll stay in the other room and keep an eye on Brittany. Erik, you can stay over here."

Erik and I looked at each other. I knew we were thinking the same thing. The idea of Colin, Erik, and me in the same room all night was too strange.

I could tell that Jack sensed our discomfort. Our reaction only confirmed that his son and I had feelings for each other that we were trying to hide.

"Jack, I'd feel better if you slept over here," I said, "in case something happens to Colin. Plus if we're taking turns staying up with Colin, it'd be easier if you stayed here."

"Okay, then I guess you'll stay with Brittany, Erik." Jack gave us both an odd look. He left and Erik stayed behind.

Erik sat down across from me near Colin's bed. *"I think my dad senses something's up with us."*

"Well, that's over, Erik. He doesn't need to worry." The words came out before I had time to think. I kept my head down, not wanting to see Erik's reaction.

"So that's it? You're just deciding for both of us?" I could hear the anger in Erik's thoughts.

"I don't know what you want me to say, Erik. Things have changed. When we were back at your farm, I didn't think I'd ever see Colin again. But now here he is. And you and I can't continue whatever it was we started."

Erik crossed his arms over his chest. *"I can't just shut my feelings off like that, Sam. I don't think you can either. We share this connection that I can't even describe. And I know you still feel it."*

"Of course I do. And I can't explain it. It doesn't make sense. We just met."

"It doesn't matter how long we've known each other. I was drawn to you the second I saw you. And you were drawn to me. You said so yourself."

I couldn't deny it. My connection to Erik began the instant I met him, just as he said. It was like nothing I had ever felt.

"Sam, don't you wanna at least see what that means? See where this could go? Because whatever this is that we have going between us, I know you don't have it with him."

Erik waited for a response, but I wouldn't give him one. I kept my thoughts quiet and focused on Colin again, still holding his hand.

"I guess that's it then." Erik stood up. *"I won't bother you anymore."* He headed to the door.

"Erik, this isn't the time, okay? We can talk about it later, but I have to take care of Colin now."

"Yeah, and when he gets better, you'll have some other excuse. So just forget it, Sam." He left, shutting the door hard behind him.

I hated rejecting Erik like that. But I was also mad at him for making me discuss our relationship when I needed to be there for Colin. Deep down, I knew Erik was right. I would never find a good time to talk to him about us. Because I didn't want to think about it. Since Colin had come back, I'd been trying desperately to ignore the intense attraction I had to Erik. The desire to be close to him. To re-create the kiss that I couldn't forget.

As I looked at Colin lying there, his weak hand in mine, I was overwhelmed with guilt. How could I possibly have these feelings for Erik? Some guy I just met! Colin and I had a history together. Years of memories. Great memories. I loved Colin. He was my very best friend. And the last remaining piece of my old life.

About an hour later, I felt his hand moving in mine. "Colin?" I whispered anxiously. "Colin? It's Sam." His hand moved again and his eyelids peeked open.

"Sam?" Colin's voice was weak.

"Yes, it's me. I'm right here."

"I don't feel so good." Colin's words were somewhat slurred from the drugs.

"I know. But you're gonna feel better soon." I bent over and lightly kissed his cheek. The bruises on his face were starting to swell and get darker.

I looked up when I heard the door open. "Sam, how is he?" Jack had returned.

"He's awake. And he's talking."

"That's a good sign." Jack came over to check Colin's vital signs again. "Hey there, Colin, you gave us quite a scare."

"What happened?" Colin asked, turning toward Jack.

"I'll let Sam tell you everything. But the IV seems to be helping. You'll be feeling better before you know it." Jack smiled at me, his assurance that Colin was indeed showing improvement.

Jack went to the laptop that was still analyzing Colin's blood work. "Well, that's no surprise," he muttered. "I should have known that."

I walked over to Jack. "What is it? Did you get more results?"

"We shouldn't talk in here, Sam." He motioned me to leave the room.

I glanced over at Colin, then back at Jack. "Okay, but quick."

Jack and I went outside. "The lab values aren't all in yet, but so far it shows several drugs in Colin's system. One of the drugs affects the central nervous system. That's why he was so out of it at the trailer, barely able to walk and unable to speak. The other one, well, it's a common diuretic but when given to someone who doesn't need it, in the amounts given, it can be very dangerous. It can disrupt the heart rhythm."

"What are you saying, Jack?"

"GlobalLife gave him that drug. They knew it would kill him. But not right away. It would be unexpected, hours later. If you had refused to go with Worthings back at the trailer, you would have had to watch Colin die. It was message for you, Sam. To say that you can't beat them. They'll always win."

3. FLASH DRIVE

"But I didn't refuse," I said. "I went with Worthings. And then he ordered his security guards to kill all of you."

"Precisely. It works either way. Once you agreed to go with Worthings, he had his guards secure you and Erik with handcuffs and guns pointed at you. You were his prisoners and he didn't think either of you could do anything. So that was the time to show you who was in charge. To show that he wouldn't make deals with you. The deal you made with him meant nothing. And he proved that by sending the guards into the trailer to kill Colin, Brittany, and me. But if you had refused to go with Worthings, you would have had to watch Colin suffer and eventually die."

It was exactly Worthings' style. Kill another one of my loved ones, but this time make me watch.

I felt rage building in me again but calmed myself remembering that Worthings was dead now. "Jack, do you think we're still in danger now that Worthings is gone?"

"I hate to say it, but we'll always be in danger, Sam. There will always be another Worthings. GlobalLife will send someone else after us. Probably a whole team of people. Now that they know that Erik is alive, there's no stopping them. They'll do everything in their power to get you two."

"But they don't know about Erik. Worthings and his guards were the only ones at the trailer, and they're all dead."

"The guards wore listening devices. I could see them on their jackets. The communication on those devices is instantly recorded and sent to GlobalLife, kept on their corporate servers. I guarantee they know about Erik."

Before I could respond, the motel door behind me opened. It was Erik. "Dad, I'm going to bed. Brittany's already asleep. You need anything else? Is Colin still okay?"

Jack nodded. "He's doing much better. You can go to sleep. We'll see you in the morning."

"Okay. Night, Sam." Erik didn't sound angry anymore, but he wouldn't look at me.

"Night, Erik," I said, hoping Jack wouldn't pick up on the tension.

But he did. Once Erik was back in his room, Jack spoke up. "What's with him? You two have a fight?"

"I'd rather not talk about it."

Jack paused. "Sam, I need to tell you something, just between you and me."

His tone was making me nervous. "Okay, what is it?"

"Erik is not one to . . . what's the word?" He stopped to think. "Well, he's not one who easily opens up to people. And he's never really been one to show emotion. And while he's had some experience with girls, he's, well, he was never serious with any of them. I probably don't need to tell you all that but—"

"What exactly *are* you trying to tell me?" I asked, begging him to hurry this along.

"Just be honest with him, okay? I don't know what went on with you two, or what was said, and I don't need to know. But in the brief time that he's known you, Sam, he's changed. He's happier than I've ever seen him. He lights up when you're around."

I stood there in silence.

"I can see that you have strong feelings for Colin, maybe even love him. But if you have any feelings for my son, which I think you do, then he deserves to be told. And if you don't have feelings for Erik, then he deserves to be told that, too. I'm sure you would feel the same if the tables were turned."

Jack sensed my discomfort. "Well, I'll go check on Colin again and then get to bed. Or I can stay up first if you want to get some sleep."

"Um, no, I'll stay up with him," I offered, relieved to be off the topic of Erik.

We went inside to find Colin more awake. "Hey, there you are," Colin said softly.

I hurried over to him. "Jack and I are both here. We'll be keeping watch on you all night." He held my hand and I could feel a little more strength in his grip. "You already look like you're feeling better, Colin." I gently hugged him, trying not to hurt his bruises.

Jack stood there waiting. "Let me check him once more, Sam, and then he's all yours."

"Are you a doctor?" Colin asked Jack.

"No. I just know a little about medicine."

"He's being modest. He knows a lot about medicine," I said, glancing up at Jack. Despite the lecture he'd given me, I couldn't be mad at Jack. He *had* saved Colin's life. "Jack is also a genius with computers. And genetics."

"Just like your Uncle Dave," Colin said to me.

Jack smiled. "Dave and I actually attended MIT together."

"Really? But how did you—"

"It's a long story," I told him. "I'll explain later."

"Everything still looks good," Jack said. "Sam, you wake me up if you need anything. Any change in his condition, even if it seems small, you come get me, okay?"

"Yes, absolutely. Thanks, Jack."

Jack went to sleep. I lay down next to Colin and listened to him breathe. He was finally breathing normally again. But in my head, I kept hearing the sound of the labored breathing he had earlier in the day. He's better now, I told myself, moving closer to him. I felt his head rest gently on mine as he dozed off. I tried not to fall asleep, but the day's events had wiped me out.

"I've got some mail for you, Dr. Fisher." A young man wearing a lab coat brought a small white envelope to an older man sitting at a desk. He, too, was wearing a lab coat.

"Thanks, Brian. Hey, did you run those samples yet?"

"Yes, I'll have the report to you soon. I'm just finishing it up now."

"Great. I look forward to seeing it," Fisher said as the young man left.

The professor picked up the envelope. "No return address. That's odd," he said to himself. He ripped open the envelope and pulled out a piece of paper and the tiniest flash drive I'd ever seen. Fisher held the flash drive up in the air. "I haven't seen one of these since—" A panicked look came across his face and he started scanning the room, as if searching for hidden surveillance cameras.

He placed the drive in his shirt pocket and focused on the piece of paper that came with it. It was a note from someone and as he read it, he spoke some parts aloud. "Samantha Andrews. Make sure she gets . . . on the flash drive. Tell no one. Sincerely, Dave Osterman."

"What the hell? Is this some kind of joke?" Fisher was talking to himself again. "I need to call Dave. But the GlobalLife offices had to relocate after the explosion." Fisher began typing on his computer. "There we go, temporary offices are at—" He got a piece of paper and wrote down some numbers, then picked up the phone.

"Yes. I need to speak to Dave Osterman, please." Pause. "What? He doesn't work there anymore? But I just got a—" Pause. "No. Never mind. I don't need to speak to anyone else. Thanks."

Fisher hung up, looking even more concerned. He nervously fished through his desk for a lighter, then took the piece of paper and a metal trash can down the hall and to the outside. He placed the paper in the can and lit it on fire, watching until it burned to ashes.

He went back inside with the trash can, racing toward his office. "Hey, Dr. Fisher." Brian, the young lab assistant was following Fisher down the hall. "Dr. Fisher? I have that lab report ready. Do you want to go over it now?"

Fisher stopped abruptly. "No. Not now, Brian. I don't have time. Something urgent came up."

As I lay in bed, still half asleep, the dream played out in my head again. If my dreams really did foresee past or future events, what did my dream about the professor mean? Was Dave trying to get a message to me? If so, I didn't understand it.

I looked over to find Colin sleeping soundly beside me. Jack was snoring in the other bed. I rolled over to see the clock on the nightstand. 7 a.m.! How did I sleep that long?

My movement woke Colin. "Sam, did you sleep here?"

"Yeah," I whispered. "I meant to sit up in that chair all night, but I was so tired I fell asleep. How do you feel?"

"Better," he whispered back. "Still not great, but a lot better." He turned on his side to face me.

"Colin, you're so bruised. You shouldn't lie on your side."

"I don't care. Come here. I want to give you a real hug. I've missed you."

"I've missed you, too." I hugged him lightly, trying not to hurt him.

A loud beeping noise broke the silence in the room, startling us. It was the alarm clock next to the bed.

Jack sat up, turning to see the clock. "It's after 7! I set that thing to go off at midnight!"

I got up to turn on a light.

"Sam, you should have woke me up." Jack put on his glasses and went over to Colin. "Tell me how you're feeling. Any better?"

"Yeah." Colin tried to sit up. "But I'm sore, especially my chest."

"Well, you might have some bruised ribs." Jack gave me a concerned look. Colin had been so out of it that we really didn't know the full extent of his injuries. My hatred for GlobalLife flared again as I imagined what they might have done to him.

"Colin, do you think you could tell us what happened?" I asked. "Or if you don't want to talk about it yet, that's okay."

"I don't really remember a whole lot. They drugged me with something and after that I was pretty out of it."

"When did they drug you, Colin? Back in Minnesota?"

"Yeah. It was after school. I was on my way to talk to someone who said they knew where you were. I got some cryptic text message saying to meet at the park by Crane Lake."

I glanced at Jack. "And who sent the text? Did you get a name?"

Colin held my hand. "No. And I didn't care who it was. I was desperate to find you, Sam. Nobody knew anything. It's like you just disappeared."

"So you went to the park, and who was there?" Jack asked.

"I never made it to the park. On the drive over there, I had some car problems so I pulled over. As I was checking under the hood, this SUV came up behind me. These guys got out and started beating up on me. I tried to fight back but these guys were huge. Way bigger than me. I didn't stand a chance."

"Is that when they drugged you?" Jack asked.

"No. The fight knocked me out. I woke up in the SUV with the guys who beat me up. And there was this other guy there—tall, dark suit, really blond hair—and he said that he was from GlobalLife. He said something about Sam being their property? It didn't make sense. Maybe I heard him wrong. But he said they needed me in order to get to Sam. I started fighting, trying to get out of there. Then those guys beat up on me again. I don't remember much after that. That's when they must've given me the drugs."

"I'm sorry you had to go through that, Colin," Jack said. "But we're going to get you healed up and back to normal. Are you feeling hungry yet?"

"Yeah, actually I am kind of hungry."

"Sam, help me get some food from the van." Jack went to grab his jacket.

"Sure. We'll be right back, Colin." I put a coat on over my sweats and headed outside where Jack was waiting.

"That text message," Jack said. "It had to be from GlobalLife, luring Colin to the park."

"I don't know, Jack. I'm thinking GlobalLife was following Colin, waiting for the right time to take him. Colin always takes the back roads to that park and those roads are pretty isolated. When his car broke down, that would have been the perfect time and place for them to get him. I don't think GlobalLife would attack him at the park. There are too many people there. I think the person who texted Colin was actually trying to help him find me."

"Who would do that? Who would take that risk? Unless you think it was Dave."

"No, it can't be Dave. GlobalLife has him. Or at least they did when I left. It had to be someone else."

"Who else would put their life on the line like that?"

I thought for a minute. "Jack, I didn't tell you everything about my escape from GlobalLife."

"You said you found an escape tunnel near the underground room where they held you."

"Yes. But I only made it into that tunnel because of Hannah, the lab assistant. She was working in my room that day. She did something to knock out the guards. And then she gave me her badge, which opened the doors."

"What? Why did she—"

"I don't know," I interrupted. "I only know that she was involved in a larger plan to get me out of there that day. And I'm sure she never made it out of the building."

"Why do think there was a larger plan?"

"She said if I didn't escape, it would have all been for nothing, like there was some big master plan that had been in the works for months. And then when I got out of that tunnel, there was a backpack waiting for me with clothes in my size and a pair of shoes."

"I thought Dave was the one who helped you. But you're saying there were other people involved in your escape? Sam, why didn't you tell me this before?"

"There's been so much going on that I didn't even think about it."

I could see Jack's mind working. "What are you thinking, Jack?"

"I'm thinking that there must be other people who want to take down GlobalLife as much as we do. And they seem to be organized. At least organized enough to carry out an attack, like they did at the lab in Minnesota. They're acting as some type of rebel force out to destroy GlobalLife, or at least limit their power. That woman, Hannah, was working from the inside. There must be others on the inside as well."

The door next to us opened. Erik walked out, already showered, dressed, and looking perfect as always. Sandy blond hair, tan skin, stunning blue eyes. I tried not to stare but I couldn't help it. "What are you guys doing out here?" he asked. "How's Colin?"

"Colin's much better," Jack answered. "Sam and I were just talking. We're going to get some food from the van. Are you hungry?"

"I am." Brittany walked up behind Erik. She was wearing his gray hooded sweatshirt which was so big that it hung like a dress on her. I was instantly jealous, thinking of her in a room with Erik all night. And the sight of her in his clothes was making it even worse.

"Brittany, what happened to your pajamas?" I asked.

"I couldn't find them so Erik let me borrow his sweatshirt." She grabbed his arm and smiled up at him. Now that she didn't have her straightener, her hair was naturally wavy like mine, making us look even more identical.

"How are you feeling today, Brittany?" Jack asked.

"I didn't sleep well. But it helped to have Erik there with me." Brittany inched up closer to him, making my skin crawl.

Jack shot Erik a look, unsure what Brittany's comment meant.

"She was having nightmares about what happened," Erik said. His vague response left me wondering what had really gone on over there.

"I'll sleep in your room tonight, Brittany," I offered, not wanting her alone with Erik again.

"So we're staying another night?" Erik asked his dad.

"We have to. I want to see how Colin does today. If he keeps progressing like he has overnight, then we'll leave tomorrow. We'll get an early start."

"I'm gonna go clean up," I said, not able to take another second of watching Brittany hang on Erik.

I went back in the room to find Colin sitting up and watching TV. He looked so much better. His skin had color and his warm brown eyes had life to them again.

"Hey, gorgeous," he said, smiling at me. I loved his smile. I always had. It was sweet and sexy at the same time. And whenever I saw it I couldn't help smiling back, even if I wasn't in a smiling mood.

"I'm gonna go take a quick shower. I'll be right out."

His eyes followed me. "I need a shower. Mind if I join you?"

"Colin!" I went over and kissed him. "Now I know you're feeling better."

Later that morning, Jack went over our plans for the following days. Our next stop would be Dana Point, California, where we would get a DNA sample from Erik's now deceased brother, Luke.

Then we would travel north to Stanford University, where Jack's professor friend would loan us his lab. There Jack would use DNA samples from Luke and Brittany to slow the timer in Erik and me.

Colin didn't hear about our plans, but that was intentional. We talked while he was asleep. I didn't want Colin to know everything that was going on. At least not yet. I hadn't told Colin about the timer or anything else that had happened to me since I left Minnesota. All that could wait. He needed to get better first.

I spent the rest of the day at Colin's side while Jack continued to monitor him. Erik hung out with Brittany, who still refused to discuss what had happened at the trailer.

After dinner that night, Erik, Jack, and I went into the van to talk. Jack told Erik my theory about a rebel group trying to take down GlobalLife and how Colin might have encountered someone trying to help as well.

"Sam, it's got to be your Uncle Dave," Erik insisted. "He's got to be the one who texted Colin. Who else would it be?"

"No, it can't be Dave. Back at the trailer, Worthings said that Dave wouldn't be going back home. That means they took Dave somewhere. He's probably not even in Minnesota anymore."

"Even if Dave's being held somewhere, that doesn't mean he isn't able to send someone a message," Erik said.

His words reminded me what I'd forgotten to share with him and Jack. "Wait. What you just said. I had a dream last night. It was one of those dreams I get. Like a premonition. It was about Dave. I think he was trying to tell me something."

4. SURPRISE

"What happened in this dream?" Jack asked.

"I saw this guy getting a note from Dave. The guy looked really familiar. Anyway, he had an envelope and inside there was a piece of paper and a flash drive. The flash drive was weird. I've never seen one like it. It was super thin, small, and oval-shaped."

"A finger drive," Jack said. "We used those when I worked at GlobalLife. It's meant for files that are only to be seen by one person. That person's fingerprint is the only way to access whatever's on the drive. It's one of those delayed technologies I told you about, Sam. You probably won't see that on the market for five or 10 years."

"Well, I wasn't able to actually see the note, but the guy reading it said a few parts out loud. He said my name and something about the flash drive. And it was signed with Dave's name."

"Your dreams show past and future events, so did you get the feeling that this had already happened?" Jack asked.

"Yeah, I think it just happened." I imagined the guy in my head again, certain that I knew him somehow.

"As in yesterday or—"

"Sorry to interrupt, Jack, but that guy from the dream. I do know him. He was at my parents' memorial service. I remember him now. After the service, everyone came to my house and it was so overwhelming that I went in my dad's office to get away. Then this guy followed me in there, saying he wanted to talk. He told me how my dad got him a job at the university. Dr. Fisher. That's his name. He's a genetics professor. In my dream, he was in his office at the university."

"Why would Dave send something to a university professor?" Erik asked. "Does he know this guy?"

"Dr. Fisher told me that he used to work for Dave's company. When GlobalLife took it over, the guy lost his job and then his family died in a car accident. He said that he really owed my dad for helping him out back then. He offered to help me if I ever needed it. Maybe Dave knew that. I don't know."

"Let's call the guy," Erik suggested, "see if he knows anything. Ask him about the flash drive."

Jack shook his head. "No. He won't share what's on that flash drive over the phone, Erik. If Sam thinks her dream is real, then I think we'll be heading to Minnesota after we go to Stanford."

"Jack, no. It's too dangerous," I said. "That place is crawling with GlobalLife people. We can't go back there."

"It's risky, but it might be our only option. Dave wouldn't try that hard to get a message to you, Sam, unless it was absolutely necessary."

Erik didn't offer his opinion, but I knew he was against the idea.

"Maybe there's another way to contact the guy," I suggested, hoping to relieve Erik's worry. "We can talk more about it tomorrow. I'm gonna go say goodnight to Colin."

"I have one last analysis running on his blood," Jack said. "If everything looks good, then we should plan to leave early tomorrow morning, around 5."

Jack and Erik stayed outside, while I went in to see Colin. "I'll be over with Brittany if you need me, okay, Colin?"

He reached out and took my hand, pulling me down next to him on the bed. "Do you have to sleep over there?"

"Yes. But you'll be okay. You look a lot better." It was a total exaggeration. His face was badly bruised and the gash on his forehead was swollen. "How's your chest?"

He cringed as he tried to sit up. "Still sore. But nothing I can't handle. I've been beat up on the football field a thousand times. This is nothing."

I knew he was lying. I could tell he was in a lot of pain. His injuries were far worse than any he'd had from playing sports. I slid his t-shirt up to reveal dark bruises all along his stomach and chest. I wasn't expecting to see so many. I felt a lump in my throat knowing the bruises wouldn't exist if it weren't for me.

"Sam, what are you doing?"

"Um, nothing. I was just checking out your six pack abs." I gently outlined the definition in his muscles with my finger. "It looks like you were you working out a lot while I was gone."

"That's what I do when I'm stressed. I always head to the gym. And when you were missing, I was really stressed. I couldn't sleep. I couldn't concentrate at school. I didn't know how to find you, Sam."

Guilt consumed me once again as I considered what Colin had gone through because of me. How could I even think of being with Erik when I had a boyfriend like Colin? What was wrong with me? Colin was caring and thoughtful. He was funny and smart. Every girl in my high school wanted to date him. He was the hottest guy there, and a star athlete. He could have had any girl and he chose me.

I scanned his body again and noticed a massive bruise along his lower left side. I moved his jeans down to see it better.

"Hey, you better stop that unless you're planning to take this somewhere," he teased.

"What? Oh, I wasn't doing anything." I carefully pulled his t-shirt back down and noticed him smiling at me. "You're not at all ready for that, Colin."

He laughed. "I'm just joking, Sam."

"Yeah, I know."

"Is something wrong? You seem upset."

"Colin." I felt tears forming and bit my lip to stop them. "I'm so sorry this happened to you."

"You don't have to be sorry. It's not your fault, Sam."

But it was my fault. And I felt sick about it.

"I guess I should go. I need to spend some time with Brittany. We haven't really talked since leaving Texas."

"Are you ever gonna tell me the story of how you ended up with a twin sister?"

"Yeah, but not tonight. I have to get over there before she goes to sleep."

"Maybe you could talk to her in the van tomorrow. That way you could stay here tonight. I might have a relapse if you go next door."

"You'll be fine. Jack will take good care of you. I'll see you in the morning."

"Okay, but can I at least get a kiss goodnight?" Colin was trying to sit up, but his sore ribs were stopping him.

"Yes, but I don't want you breaking a rib for it. Lie down." I leaned over and kissed him just as Erik came through the door.

"Oh, sorry," Erik said, turning away. "I was bringing my stuff over. I can come back later."

I felt myself blushing. "No. I was just leaving. See you tomorrow, Colin."

"Goodnight, Sam. I love you."

"I love you, too." I whispered it in his ear so Erik wouldn't hear. I didn't like him standing there watching me with Colin. I gave Colin a kiss on the cheek, then quickly left, passing Erik on the way out. "Goodnight, Erik." He seemed uncomfortable and didn't respond.

When I got to Brittany's room, she was still up. I sat next to her on the bed and turned off the TV.

"Hey, I was watching that," she protested. Brittany had somehow found her pajamas now that I was sleeping in the room instead of Erik.

"I need to talk to you." I hesitated, not sure how to approach the topic. "Brittany, I just wanna say how sorry I am about your mom. And everything that happened at the trailer."

"Can I just watch my show?" She reached around me, attempting to get the remote that I'd set on the nightstand.

"I know you're trying to pretend it didn't happen but you have to deal with this."

"Bad shit happens, Sam. That's life." She crossed her arms, staring at the blank TV screen.

"Listen. You can put on an act for Erik or Jack, but I'm your sister. You don't have to hide your feelings from me. I just went through this myself when my—our—parents were killed. And I'm still not over it. I relive that night over and over again in my head. And I think about them constantly. Every day. Even though it's been months now."

She rolled her eyes at me. "Well, I guess I'm stronger than you. 'Cause I feel fine."

"You're not fine, Brittany. I know you're not because I tried telling people the same thing when Mom and Dad died. I told everyone to just leave me alone and give me time. Ask Colin. He'll tell you how stubborn I was. But Brittany, all that did was make me more lonely and more depressed. It wasn't until I started talking about it and letting people help me that I started to feel better."

"Well, good for you. But I'm not like you. I told you. I'm fine. My mom and I didn't get along that well anyway."

I reached over and forced Brittany into a hug. She tried to fight me, but I wouldn't let her go. She finally gave in, resting her head on my shoulder. I could tell she was doing everything possible to keep from crying. I kept quiet. Brittany wasn't ready to talk about it. Just like me, she had trouble letting people in.

Eventually she got up and I headed to the bathroom to get ready for bed. "Jack said we're leaving at 5 in the morning, so I guess we should get to sleep."

"Why didn't you stay with Colin again tonight?" Brittany asked.

"Because I thought we should spend some time together. Besides, that's how it should be. Girls in one room, boys in the other."

"Yeah, if you're in summer camp. I don't think it matters at our age."

I didn't respond. I wasn't sure where she was going with this.

"I miss Erik." I came out of the bathroom to find Brittany staring dreamily at the ceiling. "Sam, you don't care if I date Erik, do you?"

The question caught me off guard. Since we'd left, she'd been very aggressive in pursuing Erik. I was starting to wonder if latching onto guys was Brittany's way of dealing with all the sadness and loss in her life.

"I don't think you should be worrying about dating right now, Brittany, especially after everything you've been through."

"Just answer me. You don't care, right? I mean, you have Colin now, so why would you? I know you kind of had a thing for Erik, but that's over, right?"

"Let's not talk about it. We need to get to sleep."

Brittany turned off the light. "Well, you can't have both of them. So I guess that's my answer."

Her words kept me awake: I can't have both of them. It was true, but I couldn't stand the idea of Brittany dating Erik while I still had feelings for him. But what could I do about it? I had Colin. That meant Erik was free to date Brittany or any other girl.

It was hard to imagine Erik even wanting to date Brittany. She didn't seem like his type. But then again, she *was* my identical twin. If he was attracted to me, he would be at least somewhat attracted to her, too.

I finally fell asleep, but not for long. The phone rang at 4 a.m. "Sam, get up." It was Erik, sounding frantic. "We're leaving."

"I thought Jack said 5," I mumbled.

"There's a police car out in the parking lot. My dad's freaking out. Just throw on some clothes and meet us outside by the van. Hurry up!"

I got Brittany up and we both dressed and tossed everything in our duffle bags. When we got outside, Colin and Jack were already in the van. Erik was waiting to load our stuff. I could see the police car in the parking lot, but nobody was in it.

"How long has it been here?" I asked Jack as I got in the van.

"Not long. I couldn't sleep, so I was awake when it arrived. I saw the officer go into the front desk area. Haven't seen him since. Could be nothing, but we can't risk it."

"Everything's packed. Let's go." Erik climbed in and Jack took off down the road.

"Do you really think the cops are looking for us?" I asked Jack.

"I *know* they're looking for us. I'm sure GlobalLife put out an alert right after they found out what happened to Worthings. But there's a better chance that GlobalLife will find us before the police do."

"How would they even know where to look?"

"GlobalLife has very sophisticated monitoring programs, Sam. And they're one of the few corporations allowed to tap into the government's surveillance programs. It's one of those 'you help us, we'll help you' deals. That's why we need to try to avoid any places that are monitored with cameras or at least stay out of the camera's sight."

Jack turned the light on in the van. "Erik, check the map. We need to have some alternate routes planned, just in case."

Erik got the map out. Brittany had claimed the seat next to him and was making herself comfortable, leaning against his shoulder.

I sat in the third-row seat, next to Colin, who was well enough to sit up. The only clothes he had were dirty and torn so he had to wear some of Erik's clothes. It worked out because Colin and Erik were almost the same size.

"I missed you last night," Colin whispered in my ear, kissing me. I kissed him back.

Erik glanced back and caught us but quickly looked away.

"Are you feeling better?" I asked. "Did Jack run more tests?"

"Yeah. He said the drugs they gave me are finally out of my system. And my blood work showed that everything's almost back to normal. I still feel a little weak, but Jack said I'll feel stronger in a day or so."

"You should get some sleep now that we're on the road."

"No. I'm wide awake. And I feel like I can actually think with those drugs out of me. So now can you tell me what happened to you, Sam? Where did you go all those weeks? How did you end up in Texas? And why is GlobalLife after you?"

"There's a lot I need to tell you, but I'm really kind of tired. Could I sleep a little before we talk?"

"Sure. Here, you can lie on me." Colin put his arm up.

"I would, but I don't want to hurt your ribs." I leaned against the seat instead, positioning a pillow under my head.

I closed my eyes and tried contacting Erik's mind. *Erik, I need to talk. Are you listening?*

Erik didn't respond so I assumed he hadn't heard me.

Erik. Please listen. I need to talk.

Silence. Then finally he answered. *I have to read the map. What do you want?* His thoughts were cold. He kept his eyes on the map.

"*It's Colin. He's asking what happened. I don't know what to tell him.*"

"*Tell him the truth. You had no problem telling Brittany all of our secrets.*" His tone turned argumentative.

"*Yeah, I probably shouldn't have told Brittany everything, but I learned my lesson, okay? So given that, maybe I should be more careful with what I tell Colin.*"

"*He's your boyfriend. You have to tell him.*"

"*Yeah, but maybe I shouldn't tell him everything. Like maybe I shouldn't tell him about the timer. Or my abilities. It might freak him out.*"

"*He loves you, Sam. He's made that perfectly clear. He's not gonna freak out.*"

"*Well I would freak out if I found out he was some type of genetic mutant.*"

"*So now we're 'mutants'? Gee, thanks.*"

"*You know what I mean. We're different. There's nobody like us.*"

"*Brittany seemed to be okay with it.*" He looked down from his map to see her resting on him.

"*Yeah, I guess you're right. I need to tell him.*"

His tone turned caustic. "*Or you could just lie to him. Not tell him how you're feeling. Not tell him anything. Even though he needs to know. Make it easier on yourself.*"

His comments hit me hard. He was calling me a coward and a selfish one at that. I cut my thoughts off from him and went to sleep.

We stopped around noon at an old gas station in the middle of the Arizona desert. There were no restaurants around so we ate beef jerky, nuts, crackers, and other nonperishables that Jack had packed. We sat at a picnic table that was next to the parking lot. It was nice to be outside and get a break from the van. The air was dry and the desert sun was toasty warm.

"Pretty nice for January," I commented, rolling up my sleeves to soak in the sun.

"I guess for you two," Erik said, looking at Colin and me. "The rest of us are used to warm winters."

Jack got up. "I'm going to use the restroom and then we'll head out."

"I'm gonna go, too." Colin said, getting up.

"Again?" I asked. "You just went."

"Geez, Sam. What are you, the bathroom police? Leave him alone," Brittany scolded, embarrassing me.

Jack and Colin headed to the small building next to the gas pumps. The building was made to look like an adobe hut. A display of cactus souvenirs was set up outside near the entrance. The place clearly catered to tourists needing a break from the road.

Minutes later, Jack came out carrying some bags, followed by Colin, who also had a bag.

"What did you guys buy in there?" Brittany asked.

Jack put the bags in the back of the van. "Oh, just some supplies."

"What kind? Did you get any soda?" I got up to check.

Colin pulled me back to my seat. "Hey, buckle up. We're leaving." He fastened the seat belt around me and smiled. "And stay out of those bags."

I gave him a confused look as I tried to figure out what he was up to.

"Since we left so early, we should be at Dana Point by evening," Jack said as we drove away. "But it's such a highly populated area that I want to stop before we get there and find a place to stay for the night. I told that guy I'd stop by his house around 8 to pick up Luke's stuff. So we'll have to leave early in the morning."

Luke was the twin brother that Erik never knew. Or at least that's what we thought based on a dream I'd had back in Texas. We assumed that Luke was like Brittany, with no special abilities and no enhanced genes. Jack had various theories about why GlobalLife created these twins. One theory was that the twins were made to serve as a control in the genetic manipulation experiments. Another theory, and one I refused to consider, was that they were created to be human organ donors in case something happened to Erik or me.

Luke had been working at an equipment rental place on a beach in Dana Point. The old guy who owned the place let Luke stay at his house temporarily until he could get out on his own. But just recently, Luke had died in a surfing accident. We needed a sample of his DNA, so we were heading to the old man's house to collect Luke's belongings. The DNA sample would confirm that Luke was Erik's twin but also might help slow the timer that was set to go off in Erik in just a few short months.

"Are you going to that guy's house alone, Dad?" Erik asked. "Because I was thinking I could go with."

"You can't go with me, Erik." Jack laughed, assuming he was kidding. "You look identical to Luke. The guy would think he was seeing a ghost."

But Erik wasn't kidding. He wanted to see the room where his one and only brother had lived. It was the only connection he had to him. I could see the disappointment in Erik. He turned to stare out the window and kept quiet for the next few hours.

We reached California early that afternoon. Jack stopped at another roadside motel. It was much more welcoming than the one the night before. A giant neon cactus sat on the roof along with a flashing vacancy sign. The window of the lobby was lined in festive lights that looked like chile peppers.

The rooms were nothing special, but Brittany was excited to see the giant TV. The last motel had a tiny TV that only got three stations. As soon as we walked in our room, she grabbed the remote, searching for her celebrity gossip shows.

"I'm gonna go see what Colin's up to," I said. Brittany didn't respond. She was too busy checking out all the channels.

As I walked out, I bumped right into Colin. "Where are you going?" he asked.

"I was coming to see you. What are you guys doing over there?"

He blocked my path to their door. "You know, guy stuff."

I laughed. "Guy stuff? What does that mean? Why are you acting so weird?"

"I'm not. Why don't you go hang out with Brittany for a while?"

"She's watching TV. I'm not supposed to 'bother her' while she's watching her shows."

"Maybe you could read a magazine." Colin continued to block me from his room.

I laughed again. "What are you talking about? I don't have anything to read. I was just gonna hang out with you in your room. See what Jack and Erik are up to."

"No!" Colin exclaimed. "I mean, why would you want to do that? You've seen us all day. You're probably sick of us." He smiled. He was definitely up to something.

"I'm not sick of you. I'm not sick of any of you. Now let me by, please."

As I tried to push past him, he leaned down and kissed me. He kept kissing me until I finally pulled away. "Colin, that was nice but it's kind of awkward standing outside the motel like this."

Colin looked defeated but he was determined to keep me out of his room. "Then let's watch TV with Brittany."

"You really wanna watch celebrity gossip shows? Because, I'm telling you, she won't let us change the channel. And she won't let us talk."

"That's okay." He opened the door and we went inside. Brittany didn't even notice.

After a couple hours, we were up to date on which celebrities had recent nose jobs, which were getting divorced, and who had better hair at the latest award show.

Colin looked at his watch, then got up to leave. "Wait here. I'll be right back."

"Um, okay," I said, giving up on trying to figure out his odd behavior.

A few minutes later, Jack, Erik, and Colin all showed up at our door. "Ladies," Jack said in a formal tone, "we request your presence in the room next door."

Brittany and I looked at each other, then back at them. "Is something wrong?" I asked suspiciously.

"Nope, nothing's wrong." Colin came over and took my arm like he was escorting me down the aisle.

Erik did the same to Brittany. They walked us over to their room. Jack opened the door. Inside a string of cactus-shaped lights hung from the ceiling. Under it sat a table with a small white cake topped with candles. Next to the cake were some pizza boxes and bottles of soda along with a small pile of presents. As Brittany and I stood there perplexed, Colin, Erik, and Jack said in unison, "Happy birthday!"

5. DANA POINT

It *is* my birthday, I thought. I had completely forgotten about it. I didn't even know what day it was.

"How did you—"

"I told them," Colin interrupted. "Last night." He put his arm around me and walked me to the table.

I glanced over to see Erik with his arm around Brittany. "I know it's technically not your birthday, but since your birthday already passed and it's so close to Sam's, we thought we'd celebrate them together."

Although Brittany was my twin, our lab-created embryos were placed in different mothers and the surrogate had Brittany a week before I was born. She loved reminding me that she was a week older than me.

"That's so sweet," Brittany gushed, kissing Erik on the cheek. "And you guys even got us presents?"

"It's not much," Colin admitted. "We were limited to what they had at that gas station."

"So that's why you two were so secretive," I said. "I couldn't figure out why you wouldn't let us look in those bags."

"And pizza? How'd ya get that?" Brittany asked.

"The guy at the front desk said there was a pizza place down the road a few miles. I just got back from picking them up," Jack explained. "On the way there, I passed a small grocery store and picked up a cake and some soda."

I grabbed a paper plate and some pizza. "I can't believe you guys did all this. I wondered why you wouldn't let me in your room, Colin."

"Yeah, you really fought me on that. And then I had to sit and watch all those hours of Brittany's TV shows." Colin smiled at Brittany.

"Hey! Those shows are considered news," Brittany insisted.

"I'm not sure that knowing the real hair color of some actress is news, but okay," Colin kidded.

"Time to open your presents," Erik said after we finished the pizza. He grabbed one of the packages from the table. "Who's first?"

"Oooh, me!" Brittany raised her hand like she was in class.

"Here, catch." Erik tossed her a package.

Brittany opened it to find some fruit-flavored lip gloss packaged in a small cactus-shaped tin. "I love it! I had some like this when I was a kid!"

Jack laughed. "Keep in mind that the gas station didn't have much. Sam, you're next."

He handed me a small paper sack. Inside was a pair of little green alien earrings made of plastic. "These are hilarious!" I said, trying them on.

"They were in the sale bin," Jack confessed. "The guy said they were left over from his store in Roswell. I got Erik a matching keychain. He's always been fascinated with aliens."

Erik smiled, pulling out his new key chain and dangling the plastic alien so we could all see.

Brittany opened another present, which was a pink t-shirt that said 'Arizona' and had palm trees printed on it. She raced into the bathroom to try it on.

Then it was my turn again. I opened up another bag to find a plastic snow globe that had a cactus scene inside.

"I thought it would remind you of home," Colin said. "The snow part, not the cactus."

I laughed. "Yeah, I got that."

Jack stood up to take the pizza boxes to the trash. "Well, that's it. Sorry we couldn't do a better job."

"You guys did a perfect job! Check these out." I turned my head side to side to show off the aliens dangling from my ears.

Brittany came out wearing her new shirt. "Yeah, thanks! This was awesome!"

"I'll cut the cake," Colin said, getting up.

"I have one more thing for Sam." Erik headed to the door. "It's in the van. Go ahead and cut the cake."

When Erik came back, he had one hand behind his back. "It's kind of dumb, but I got these for you, Sam. Here. Happy birthday."

Erik handed me a jar with tiny holes in the lid. Inside were some bugs flying around. And then I saw a light. Fireflies! It was a jar of fireflies. But it was so much more than that. The fireflies were a memory that Erik and I shared. A memory of the few but meaningful nights we spent sitting and talking on his porch swing, looking out at the fireflies lighting up the field behind his house.

"Thanks, Erik." I glanced up at him, but he looked away.

Colin set a piece of cake on the table next to me. "Sam, I didn't know you liked fireflies."

I held up the jar. "Yeah. I like how they look like little sparkly lights in the grass. They make me happy."

"Then I'll have to get you lots more." Colin kissed my cheek, then went back to the cake table to serve everyone else.

Erik was sitting across from me. I caught his eye and thought to him. *Thanks for the gift. It means a lot. Really.*

He looked away again. *It's just some fireflies.*

After that, Erik cut off his thoughts so I couldn't hear them. It left me wondering what the gesture meant. Did he still have hope for us? Or were the fireflies his way of ending whatever it was that we had together?

After the party, Jack did some work on his computer and Erik accepted Brittany's invite to watch TV in our room. Colin and I went outside and sat on some metal lawn chairs that were sitting off to the side of the motel next to a rusted-out grill.

"Nice night," Colin commented. "Must be weird having your birthday without snow."

"I hadn't thought about it, but yeah, that is weird."

I knew that this was my chance to tell Colin everything. I couldn't put it off anymore.

"Colin, I know I've been avoiding talking about what happened to me." I kept my eyes on the ground. "And I guess the reason is because I'm kind of nervous about it."

"Why?" Colin scooted his chair closer to mine and held my hand. "You can tell me anything."

"I'm worried about what you'll think of me after I tell you."

"Sam, why you would you say that? You know I'll love you no matter what."

"Yeah, but this is . . . well, okay. It all started back at Dave's cabin." I told Colin how I was captured right before Christmas and held at GlobalLife, where they did a procedure on me that gave me special abilities. I explained what GlobalLife had done to my genes all those years ago. And then I told him how I escaped from GlobalLife, found my way to Texas, and met Erik and Brittany. I stopped before continuing, waiting for his response.

"I don't know what to say, Sam. Other than that I hate GlobalLife even more now. I wish I could have helped you get away from them. If you could have got a message to me somehow I would have done something, Sam. I would have found a way to help. I would have got—"

"Wait. Don't you think I'm some kind of freak? After what I said? GlobalLife changed my DNA. I have these powers, these abilities. Doesn't that make you think differently of me?"

"Why? You're still the same person." He paused. "Listen, Sam, I admit that the whole genetic manipulation thing is kind of freaking me out but it's not because of you. I'm freaked out by the fact that some corporation can do something like that and get away with it."

"But, Colin, I'll never be normal. I'll always be like this."

He turned his chair to face me. "Yeah, and I hate that they messed with your genes like that. But I don't see you any differently. So you have better hearing than me. I already knew that. And you used to tell me about those dreams you had, so I knew about that, too. You said you have enhanced vision and strength? I'm jealous but that's cool. And now you can read minds." He hesitated. "Okay, that's a little strange. Well, maybe more than a little strange. But I can get used to it, as long as you let me have some private thoughts." He smiled.

"I won't read your thoughts, Colin. Erik said it's intrusive and I agree."

"Erik? Does he know about you?" Colin looked confused. I hadn't yet told him about Erik or why we were even going to California.

"Um, there's more I haven't told you." I paused. "Erik is like me. He was part of the same project except he was held at the GlobalLife lab in California. They actually kept him there for years, until Jack took him. As far as we know, Erik and I are the only people who have this genetic enhancement."

"So GlobalLife is after both of you?"

"Yes. And there's more." I told Colin about how Erik and I could communicate telepathically. He accepted that better than I thought he would, so I continued. I told him about the timer that was running inside Erik and me and how it was programmed to kill us. I explained how Jack hoped our twins' DNA would disrupt the timer, slowing it.

"Hold on. So you're telling me that you're gonna die?" Colin stood up. "Sam, why didn't you tell me this right away? You need to go to the hospital! See some specialist. Get this timer thing out of you!"

"Calm down. None of that will work. This isn't something that can be fixed in a hospital or at a doctor's office."

"Why aren't all of you freaking out about this?"

"Because it doesn't help, Colin. And getting angry about it doesn't help either. So we've decided to take action. We have a plan for how to fix this. Brittany's DNA will help me and the DNA from Erik's twin will hopefully help him."

"But that just buys you time! That's not good enough! There's gotta be someone who can stop the timer before it goes off!"

"GlobalLife can, but we can't go there."

"Then I'll go there. I'll get whatever you need." Colin was determined.

"No, Colin. It doesn't work like that. We don't even know what we're looking for." I explained Jack's theory about why GlobalLife put the timer in us and told him about the missing base pairs in our DNA.

By the time I was done explaining everything, Colin was furious, but not at me. He was mad because he felt so helpless. We went back to my room, where Brittany and Erik were still watching TV. Brittany was wearing Erik's sweatshirt again.

Erik noticed there was something wrong the second we walked in. *"You told him,"* he thought to me.

"Yes. Everything," I thought back.

"He doesn't look too good."

"No, he didn't take it too well. But finding out your girlfriend might be dead in a couple years is a lot to handle."

"Yeah, I haven't quite accepted that either. About myself, I mean. Well, and you, too, but not in the girlfriend way." I could hear Erik's mind fumbling. *"You know what I mean."*

"We should probably get some sleep, Brittany," I said, signaling the guys to go.

Erik got up. "Yeah. We'll see you tomorrow. Hope you enjoyed your birthdays!"

"Can I sleep in your shirt, Erik?" Brittany asked.

"Sure, I don't care," he said, thinking nothing of it. But Brittany took it as a sign that he liked her. Her face was beaming with joy.

Colin stood there in a daze. "See you in the morning, Colin." I gave him a quick kiss. Rather than leave, he hugged me and wouldn't let go.

"Um, okay, Colin. Goodnight." I wiggled out of his arms.

Colin and Erik left.

"What's wrong with Colin?" Brittany asked.

"I told him everything that's been going on. He didn't take the news about the timer too well."

"I thought Jack was fixing that." Brittany didn't fully understand the seriousness of the timer but I figured that was a good thing.

"Well, he's working on it. But it's not fixed yet." It will never be fixed, I thought. Slowing the timer wouldn't fix it. Erik's days were numbered and so were mine. My birthday was just another reminder of how little time I had left.

The next morning, we packed up and headed to Dana Point. Traffic was a nightmare, making us late getting to the house where we were supposed to pick up Luke's stuff.

"I'll go park the van at the beach parking lot," Erik said as he pulled over to let Jack out. "Is 20 minutes enough time?"

"It better be. While I'm gone I want all of you to stay in the van," Jack ordered. "Don't go walking on the beach. We can't be too careful."

"Jack, wait," I said, as he stepped outside. "I think I should go with. I'm the one who had the dream about this. I should make sure this guy is the same guy I saw in the dream."

Jack considered it. "Well, I guess that's not a bad idea, although I told him it would just be me."

"You said you told the guy that you were Luke's uncle, right? Then tell him I'm your daughter. Luke's cousin."

"Fine. Let's go. But don't say anything. I'll do the talking."

We walked up to a small blue house that was right on the beach. The house didn't look like much, but given the location, it was probably worth several million dollars. Jack rang the doorbell, but nobody answered. We rang again. No answer.

"He probably took off," Jack mumbled, annoyed with himself. "I knew we should have left earlier. I forgot how bad the traffic is. Even worse than when I lived here."

"Maybe we should go around back. Maybe he's outside."

We walked around to the back of the house and saw a man sitting on the deck reading a newspaper. It was the same man from the dream I'd had days earlier. "That's him," I whispered to Jack.

"Excuse me, but are you Mr. Blackstone?" Jack yelled up at the man.

The man looked around, confused.

"Mr. Blackstone? Harold Blackstone? We're down here," Jack yelled again.

The old man walked to the side of the deck. "You Mr. Reid? You're late!"

"Yes, I'm terribly sorry about that. I wasn't prepared for the traffic."

"It's California. We're known for traffic. You should have left earlier."

The old man seemed very cranky. He hadn't seemed that way in my dream.

"Should we go to the front door?" Jack asked.

"Yes. Hurry up." The old man took his paper and went inside. He met us at the front door.

"Again, I apologize for being late. I'm sure you're a very busy man," Jack said.

"Who's this?" The old man pointed at me.

"Oh, this is my daughter. Agnes." I shot Jack a look. Agnes? I thought. That's the best fake name he could come up with?

The old man smiled. "That's a nice name. That was my mother's name. Come inside."

Jack smiled at me. I had no idea how he knew that little fact. But hearing his mother's name seemed to brighten the old guy's mood a bit.

"Shame about your nephew. He was a good kid. Just a little lost. Needed some help getting back on track." The old man sat down, so we did as well.

The house was all white inside except for the furnishings, which were dark leather and wood. Very masculine. The back of the house was all windows, providing a jaw-dropping view of the ocean. I could see massive waves off in the distance. Jack said the beach was known for surfing, which is probably what had drawn Luke there.

"Did Luke stay here long?" Jack asked.

"Oh, I'd say he was here for maybe five or six weeks. Not long. I barely noticed him living here. He was real quiet."

Jack glanced at his watch. "Well, Agnes and I are in a bit of a hurry. I'm taking her on a tour of colleges, and we have an appointment at USC soon. So if we could just get Luke's things."

"All right. They're in his room. This way." The old man led us to a side bedroom. It was very small. There was just enough room for a twin bed, a tiny desk, and a bookshelf. "His stuff's all there in that box. He didn't have much. Just some surfing trophies and some books."

Jack took the box, scanning the room for any other clues about the boy. "What about his clothes?"

"Clothes? Why would you want those?" The old man gave Jack a strange look.

"My son. Agnes' brother. He wanted them. You know, something to remember his cousin by. My son's the same age as Luke."

The man didn't seem to buy the story. "There's a bag of clothes in the closet. I was planning to donate them, but go ahead and take them if you want."

"Great. Thanks." Jack handed me the box, then went to the closet to retrieve the bag of clothes. "Well, we should be going. Thank you again for saving his things for us."

"No problem." The man looked at Jack suspiciously. "So tell me again what happened to his parents? His mother was your sister, right?"

Jack tried to stay calm, but I could tell his mind was scrambling to come up with a story to tell the guy. We knew nothing about Luke or the family who raised him.

"Um, yes. She died in a car accident a while back. Along with Luke's dad." Jack started walking toward the door. I followed, deciding that now was an appropriate time to read the old man's mind. I had to know what he was thinking.

"Luke said he never knew his dad." The old man wouldn't let it go. He knew Jack was lying.

Jack opened the door and the old man grabbed it from him. "Are you sure you're Luke's uncle? Because he never mentioned an uncle. Or a cousin." The old man glanced over at me.

"We weren't that close, but yes, I'm his uncle." Jack hurried through the door.

As we left, I focused on hearing the old man's thoughts. *"These people aren't related to Luke. They look nothing like him. I gotta call Bill down at the station. Have him check this guy's story out."*

In trying to listen to him, I tripped going through the doorway, spilling the contents of the box all over the ground. Jack set his bag down to help me pick up the mess. The old man shook his head and shut the door.

"Jack!" I whispered. "The old man. He's on to us. He's calling some guy at the police station. We gotta get out of here."

Jack stood up and looked down the street. "It's been almost 20 minutes and I don't see our van yet. Let's get down there. Hurry."

We walked fast toward the meeting spot. With my superior vision, I spotted our van off in the distance. "I see it, Jack. But it's at least a mile away, and there's all these people blocking the road, trying to walk over to the beach. It may take a few minutes for the van to get here."

Suddenly we heard sirens in the distance. Then the sirens got louder. Jack grabbed my sleeve and yanked me behind a large flowery bush.

He kept his eyes on the street. "I can see the van, now. I hope Erik knows to turn around."

"This would be a good time to have a cell phone," I mumbled.

"Cell phones are nothing more than human tracking machines and listening devices, Sam. They're the fastest way to get caught."

I sighed. "Yeah, I know."

The van kept driving toward us despite the sirens. "Why does Erik keep going this way?" Jack asked. "He's going to run right into the police!"

"The police have no reason to stop him. They'll just drive past."

"It's a work van with out-of-state plates in a neighborhood full of multimillion-dollar houses. Of course they'll stop him." Jack seemed annoyed with my naiveness.

The sirens stopped and we noticed a police car was now on our street. The car pulled into the driveway of the old man's house.

"Talk to him," Jack blurted out, nudging me as he kept watch on the van.

"Talk to who?"

"Erik. Talk to him with your mind."

"I can't do that. He's like a mile away."

"You can do it. You two share a very strong connection."

"Okay, I'll try. But I'm not making any promises."

We watched as a police officer went into the old man's house. The other officer waited outside in the car.

"Erik? Can you hear me? Let me know if you can. It's an emergency. The cops are at the house we were just at. They're looking for us. You can't bring the van down here. Jack and I are hiding in the bushes. Don't come down here." I put all my energy into connecting with Erik's mind. I imagined him being next to me rather than way down the street. *"Erik. I need you to listen. Can you hear me? Don't bring the van down here."*

I got no response from Erik's mind. "He can't hear me, Jack. It's no use."

"And now I've lost sight of the van. A truck turned out in front of it at the intersection." Jack pointed behind me. "Look, he's leaving."

The police officer left the old man's house and got into the squad car. He backed the car out and started driving down the street. Then suddenly, he stopped the car right in front of the bushes where we were hiding. Jack looked at me and I looked at him. I felt my heart racing. What were they doing there? Why did they stop?

The officers stayed in the car. I could hear their police scanner. "Officer Daniels. We need you to file a report down by the entrance to Salt Creek Beach. A teen girl has been hit by a car. First name Brittany. Last name unknown. Emergency personnel is on the way."

6. SILENT TREATMENT

I grabbed Jack's sleeve. "Did you hear that?"

"Hear what? What happened?" Jack didn't have my enhanced hearing so hadn't heard the scanner inside the police car.

"It's Brittany! The police radio said she'd been hit by a car down by the beach!"

"What? I told them not to get out of the van! What are her injuries?"

"They didn't say. Oh my God! Jack, what if she's really hurt?"

"Calm down. The car could have just grazed her. Traffic is barely moving on that road."

"We've gotta get down there!"

The police car was now working its way down the crowded street. I ran out from the bushes, still holding Luke's box of possessions. Jack followed behind with the bag of clothes. As I ran, I could see our white van coming out of a side parking lot between two buildings.

"Sam, come meet us. You should be able to see us now. Hurry up." It was Erik, talking in my head.

"Jack, this way. Hurry!" I yelled. Sirens blared as the ambulance made its way down the crowded street.

I pointed in the direction of the van as Jack followed. When we got to the van, Colin opened the door for us. Erik was driving, but Brittany was nowhere to be found.

"What happened to her?" I asked frantically. "They said she was hit by a car! Where is she? Why did you leave her?"

"It's okay, Sam," Colin assured me. "It's an act. Just a distraction so we could get the cops away from you and Jack."

"And us," Erik added. "There's cops everywhere around here, especially down by the beach."

Jack crawled up to the front seat. "Where is she now?"

"She's meeting us behind this store." Erik parked in a loading dock behind a t-shirt shop. "There she is."

Colin opened the van door again and Brittany hopped in. Erik sped off down the street.

"Wow, that was close," Brittany said, trying to catch her breath.

"So a car didn't hit you?" I scanned her face and body for injuries.

"No. I'm okay. I didn't get hit. It just looked like I did. My mom's friend used to have this scam where she pretended to be hit by a car so she could sue the driver. She actually made a good living doing it. Anyway, a few years ago I had her show me how. And it works. People really believed it."

"But how did you get away?"

"I got up and told people I was okay. Then I ran off before the ambulance and cops got there."

"Why did you tell people your real name?"

"Yeah, I guess I should have used a fake name. But lots of girls have the name Brittany so it's not like they'll know it's me. I didn't give them my last name."

Erik was driving fast and making Jack nervous. "Erik, slow down. We're going to get stopped for speeding. When we get to a more secure area, pull over and I'll drive. And then I need you to find us a different road to take. Freeway traffic is too heavy around LA."

"Yeah, all right." Erik slowed the van.

"I can't believe you did that, Brittany." I looked at Colin. "And I can't believe you guys let her."

"Yes. That was irresponsible," Jack scolded.

"Well, what were we supposed to do?" Erik asked. "We had to get the cops away from you guys."

I leaned toward the front seat. "How did you even you know the police were coming after us?"

"You told me," Erik said nonchalantly.

"You heard me in your thoughts? Why didn't you respond back?" I was beyond annoyed.

"I tried, but you must not have been listening. You were probably too distracted. I told you to focus, remember? Even when you're under stress, you can't lose focus. It's like that time back at the farm when you lifted the truck and those dogs came by."

Colin glanced at me wondering what Erik meant. In telling Colin "everything," I left out a lot of the details about Erik and me.

"Pull over right up there," Jack pointed to a small roadside farm stand. Erik parked and Jack took his place in the driver's seat.

"So what happened back there with the old man?" Colin asked me when we were on the road again.

"The guy knew Jack was lying. His mind was filled with all this talk about calling the police."

"I thought you didn't listen in on people."

"Yeah, but this was an emergency. I could tell the guy wasn't believing our story, so I had to know what he was thinking. And good thing I did or we'd be in police custody right now. And I'm on their most-wanted list."

"I think it's more like the missing person list," Colin corrected. "At least that's the list you were on back home."

"Speaking of home, I never asked you, what did the local news say about that explosion at the GlobalLife building?"

"They said there was a chemical explosion in one of the labs. It took almost the whole building down."

"And you're sure that Dave got out of there?"

"The news named all the people who died. He wasn't on the list. But I never heard from him again. I went to your house every day, but nobody was home. I stopped by Dave's house, too. I even drove up to Dave's cabin, but he wasn't there either."

"And what did the news say about me?"

"The day of the explosion someone reported you missing. I totally freaked out because I hadn't heard from you since before Christmas. Well, other than the fake message GlobalLife left me. Then when I couldn't find Dave to ask him about you, I didn't know what to do. It's like you both just disappeared. About a week later, the police got an anonymous tip saying you weren't missing after all. The news said that you'd run away and were no longer considered missing. My dad told me to accept it and move on, but I wouldn't do it. I knew you wouldn't just run away."

"And what about Allie?"

"She looked for you, too. She even asked her mom to help. She mentioned something about hiring a private investigator. Her parents have the money to do it. They've probably already hired someone to find you."

"That's not good, Colin. I don't need any more people looking for me."

"I wouldn't worry about it. If the police can't find you, I doubt some small-town Minnesota P.I. can."

Colin glanced out the side window. "This is my first time in California. This part almost looks like home. All farmland. Of course, the weather's a lot better."

"Yeah. The weather was part of the reason I picked Stanford."

"So I guess you're not going there now."

"Nope. The college plans are on hold indefinitely. I worked my whole life to get accepted there, and it was all for nothing."

"You never know. Maybe this will get worked out somehow." Colin tried to sound optimistic.

"That's not gonna happen, Colin. This is my life now. Always running. At least until the—" I didn't want to mention the timer again in front of him.

It was too late. He knew what I meant. I could tell by the worried look on his face.

"Just forget I mentioned it," I said before he got worked up again. "Getting upset doesn't help."

Colin got quiet and looked out the window. After a while, he turned to me again. "So is it weird for you that we're going to Stanford?"

"No. Not really. It's more weird imagining my dad there. I can never picture him or my mom at my age. But you should have seen him on the college tour last fall. It was like he was a teenager again."

"I guess I didn't tell you, but I got an acceptance letter for college. I got it right before all this happened."

"Colin, that's great! Which college?"

"U of M, Mankato. They offered me a football scholarship."

"That's awesome, Colin!" I gave him a hug, but he didn't seem too enthusiastic.

"It doesn't really matter now. I'm not going. I won't even be graduating from high school."

I'd been so focused on getting Colin healthy that I hadn't considered all that he was missing back home. I'd graduated early and wasn't even thinking about school.

"Colin, you can still graduate. You can catch up on what you missed when we get back."

He seemed confused. "Back? Who's going back?"

I explained my most recent dream to Colin and how we were planning to go back to Minnesota.

"I'll have to leave as soon as we get the flash drive, but you can stay and finish school. And then you can go to college. And med school. Just like you planned."

"Wait. What are you saying, Sam? You want me to stay behind? I thought we were together on this. I don't care about college. I can do that later. Right now I need to do whatever I can to help you get that timer shut off. And I need to make sure you're safe. I'm not staying in Minnesota. I'm going with you."

"No, Colin. I can't have your whole life being ruined. Think about all that you're missing back home. School. Sports. Your family. And you're in danger when you're with me. It's not safe. I can't let you go with us."

"Are you serious? You really don't want me to come with you? I can't even believe you're saying this."

"It's just for little while. Once Erik and I get this timer thing stopped and find a place that's safe, you and I can be together again."

He turned his back toward me.

"Hey, don't be mad."

"I'm tired, Sam. I'm gonna sleep." He moved farther away and rested his head on the back of the seat.

I instantly regretted what I'd said. I had given it no thought. The words just came out. Like Colin said, I assumed he would continue on this journey with me, but then, when he talked about college, it was like a brick hit me over the head. I couldn't let him destroy his life. GlobalLife had already ruined enough lives. Colin deserved a normal life. He needed to finish high school and go to college.

Later that day, Erik took over driving and I went up and sat next to him. Brittany sat behind us with her headphones on. Jack and Colin sat in the back row.

"Why aren't you sitting back with Colin?" Erik mind-talked to keep our conversation private.

"He's mad at me. He's not even speaking to me."

"What happened?

"He told me that he got into a school in Minnesota. They offered him a football scholarship. I was so excited for him. And then it hit me that being here with us, he was missing high school. And if he stays with us, he won't graduate. And he'll miss going to college and playing football. His whole life will be ruined."

"So he decided to stay behind and finish school?"

"No. He doesn't care about that. He wants to stay with me and make sure I get the timer turned off. And whatever happens after that."

"And you told him he couldn't?"

"Well, no. Not really. I mean, I guess I kind of did. I told him to stay in Minnesota and that I'd find him later, once we were safe."

"Well no wonder he's mad!"

"What's that supposed to mean?

"It's not your decision, Sam. If he wants to go with you, that's his decision, not yours. How would you feel if it were the other way around?"

I paused to think about it. *"Okay, I would want to go with him. But it's different for me. I don't have anyone left. He still has his parents. His sisters. His friends. He has a future back home, not with me."*

"If he felt that way, he wouldn't be mad at you right now. Don't you get it? He wants to be there for you, Sam. He wants to protect you. That's what guys do. They want to protect their girl. And you're telling him that he can't. I'd be pissed, too, if I were him."

"But I don't need him to protect me. If anything, I'd be protecting him. I'm the one with special powers."

"That's not how guys think. We think it's our job to keep you safe. Yeah, we know you girls can take care of yourselves, but you have to at least pretend that you need us."

"I was just trying to keep Colin out of this." I glanced back to see Colin leaned against the side of the van, asleep.

"So what are you gonna do?" Erik asked.

"I have to think about it. I mean, maybe he'd be safer going with us than staying at home. If he's at home, GlobalLife could take him again and use him to get to me."

"That's probably true, but don't tell him that. You have to tell him that you NEED him to go with us."

"But that's a lie. I don't need—"

"Then maybe you should think about your relationship, Sam. Because if I only had one person left in the world that I loved, I would want that person to be right here with me through all of this."

"What are you trying to say? That I don't love him?" My thoughts got defensive. *"If I didn't love him, I wouldn't be trying to protect him by making him stay home."*

"Just think about it, Sam. That's all I'm saying."

"Well, what would you do if your genetically-enhanced girlfriend was being chased by powerful people who would kill anyone who stood in their way?"

"If I loved her, I would risk everything for her. If she told me to stay home, I'd go anyway. I mean, I barely know you and I would do anything—" Erik stopped.

"What did you say?"

"Nothing. Never mind. I'm done with my relationships 101 lecture for today. Want to play a road game?"

"Sure."

We spent the next few hours spotting license plates and making words from the letters. "CCA," I said, reading the plate of the car in front of us. "Let's see, that stands for the Calico Cat Alliance."

Erik shook his head. "Nope. Not good enough. Try again. Here's one. HLA."

"Hairy Lions Anonymous," I said in a serious tone.

Erik laughed. "That was a little better."

"Hey, let me try," Brittany said from behind us. "That red truck over there. HAS. Hmm, that stands for Hot And Sexy. I should have that license plate. Or actually, Erik should." Brittany leaned up and started rubbing Erik's shoulders. I rolled my eyes then glanced at Erik, who seemed to be enjoying it way too much.

"That feels good, Brittany. My back is killing me after sitting in this van for hours. I'm used to working on the farm all day."

"That's why you have these huge muscles." Brittany moved her hands up and down his biceps.

The scene was making me ill. I turned to look out the window. I was no longer interested in the road game.

"Erik, get off at the next exit," Jack instructed from the back of the van. "We'll get some gas and see if they have a pay phone. We're getting close to San Francisco. I need to call Paul and get directions to his place."

"Do they even *have* pay phones anymore?" I heard Colin ask Jack.

"Of course they do." Jack sounded annoyed. "You kids and your dependence on cell phones." We all started to laugh. "It's not funny. You're all too dependent on technology."

"Calm down there, old man," Erik yelled back at him. "Remember, you've got two technologically-advanced people up here. We could take offense to that."

"What do I always say about technology, Erik?" Jack yelled back.

"Just because you CAN do something doesn't mean you SHOULD," Erik answered as if he'd heard it a thousand times.

Erik drove into a gas station that looked like it was built in the fifties. And sure enough, right in front of the station was a public telephone.

"Look at that! It has a cord and everything," Erik kidded. "It should be in a museum. Wish I had the camera."

"Pump the gas, son," Jack said, shaking his head.

Everyone got out of the van while Jack went to use the phone. It was almost sunset. Fields of grapes surrounded us on both sides. It was quiet and peaceful. Much better than the chaos of Southern California.

Colin walked toward the grape fields, looking out at the setting sun. I followed him.

"Hey," I said, trying to see if he would acknowledge me.

"Yeah." It was an acknowledgment but not a warm one.

"You've been quiet for hours."

"I've been sleeping. And thinking."

"What about?" I knew the answer but figured I'd ask anyway.

"Doesn't matter."

"Listen. I'm sorry about what I said earlier. Can we please just talk about this?"

Colin remained quiet as he gazed at the sunset.

"I was just trying to protect you, Colin. I was trying to give you a normal life. I didn't want you to give everything up for this stupid life that I'm stuck with now." I paused. "But I realize that I can't make that decision for you."

I waited. He wouldn't respond.

"Look at me, Colin." I turned him toward me. "I want us to be together, okay? I do. But being with me is dangerous. So that's why I told you to stay behind. I didn't want you involved in this. I can't deal with you getting hurt again. Or worse. GlobalLife almost beat you to death. They almost killed you with those drugs. And I can't stand to think of that happening again."

"And how do you think I feel, Sam, knowing that they implanted this . . . this thing in you that's programmed to kill you? Do you really think I can just go back to school? Back to basketball practice? Hang out with the guys, knowing that you're gonna die soon? How could you even think I'm that type of person? After all these years? After all I've done for you?"

I was sure my speech would end with hugs and forgiveness. Instead, it ended with silence and no resolution. Colin walked back to the van. I was left alone, afraid that nothing I could say would ever fix this. I'd pushed him away in the past but this was too far. I'd said too much. I'd described a future without him in it. And Colin had had enough.

7. PAUL'S HOUSE

"Sam, we're leaving. Come on." Erik was calling me from the van. I got inside to find Jack in the driver's seat and Erik beside him. Brittany was in the second-row seat with her headphones on. I crawled to the seat behind her and sat next to Colin. He had his back to me, staring out at the now dark sky.

Erik glanced back, noticing Colin. *"Still fighting?"* he thought to me.

"No. I think we're done fighting," I thought back. *"I think we're done period."*

"I want all of you to listen up." Jack's voice filled the van as if on loudspeaker. "Erik, tell Brittany to get those headphones off."

Erik jabbed Brittany's leg. "What?" Brittany removed one side of her headphones.

"The commander has instructions for us," Erik joked. "Listen up."

Jack ignored his comment. "This friend of mine that we'll be staying with. His name is Paul. Paul Jacobs. He worked with me at GlobalLife years ago. But unlike me, he actually resigned and took a new job."

"Instead of just disappearing one day and taking a lab subject with you?" Erik kidded.

"Anyway, when Paul was at GlobalLife he had access to highly secret technology. Because of that, he was convinced that they were monitoring him after he left. Bugging his phone. Following him. He was so paranoid he went into hiding for a while. He's better now, but still, he's kind of a nervous guy."

Jack turned on a light in the van to check a piece of paper that he had scribbled directions on. "He lives outside of the city. He tries to live off the grid, like Erik and I did, but not to the same extent. He does have a cell phone but uses it just for work. Same with Internet access. As I told you, he's now a professor of genetics at Stanford. His research area is cancer prevention. But he knows about the genetic manipulation done at GlobalLife all those years ago. That's why he left."

"So then he knows about me," Erik added.

"Well, no, not exactly," Jack replied. "I sort of left that part out."

"You've been in contact with him all these years and he doesn't know about me?"

"Well, at first I wasn't sure if I could trust him. He was still working at GlobalLife after I took you, Erik. I couldn't be certain that he was really on my side. As the years went by, I was confident he was one of the good guys, but I didn't want to risk talking about you over the phone. You can't be sure who's listening, even on those *ancient* landline phones."

"Isn't he gonna be freaked out seeing me? And finding out about Sam?"

"No. Nothing surprises this guy now. He's seen too much over the years. And because of that, he tends to believe a lot of conspiracy theories. He might mention a few while we're there."

"Like what?" Erik asked.

"Things like the existence of robotic soldiers trained to kill without human oversight. Government mind control. Rigged elections. Stuff like that. But he's a good guy. And he's doing us a huge favor, so I need all of you to be sure and thank him. He could get fired if the university found out we were using their lab."

Jack pulled off the interstate onto a side road. It was very dark and the road wound back through thick trees. We finally arrived at a small brick house lit only by a single outdoor light. Jack searched for a number on the house. "Yes, this is it. Everyone out."

The man must have heard the van outside because he was waiting for us at the front door. "Jack, so good to see you again."

Jack shook his hand. "Paul. It's been too long. Good to see you, too."

Paul was short and thin with long, wavy gray hair and black-rimmed glasses. He had on jeans and a light blue dress shirt with the sleeves rolled up. His look was part hippy, part professor.

"Come in. All of you." He motioned us inside. "So, Jack, tell me who these young people are."

"Well, this is Samantha and her boyfriend, Colin," Jack said pointing to us, "and over there is Sam's twin sister, Brittany." Jack walked over to Erik. "And this young man is my son, Erik."

Paul looked puzzled. "Your son? You don't have a son. Who is he really? Your nephew?"

"No, he's my son. Well, not my biological son." Jack waited for Paul's response. The rest of us stood awkwardly around the room.

"And how long have you had this son?" Paul asked slowly.

"Fourteen years. Well, he's been with me longer than that, but—"

Paul went over to Erik, then looked back at Jack. "You're not telling me that this boy is the same boy who—"

"Yes, that's what I'm telling you," Jack interrupted.

Paul didn't seem that surprised. "How did you manage that, Jack? And how did you keep him from being found all these years?"

"It's a long story. We can discuss it later."

"So, Erik, you're okay?" Paul asked. "No side effects?"

"Um, not that I know of." Erik looked at his dad.

"He was fine once I got him out of there. He does have abilities, if that's what you're wondering."

"Fascinating." Paul studied Erik again, like he was an experimental breakthrough.

"Well, should we get our things from the van?" Jack asked, eager to change the subject.

"Yes. Certainly. Get what you need. Are you hungry at all? Because I made some dinner. I wasn't sure if you'd already eaten."

"Oh, that's very kind, Paul. You didn't need to do that."

"Nonsense. I never have guests. This is a special treat for me."

We gathered our things from the van and brought them into the living room. Paul was clearing off a table for dinner. The table was covered in stacks of files, which Paul neatly set aside on the floor.

The home was older, probably built in the forties, with dark wood floors and thick wood trim. Built-in cabinets filled with books lined one wall. From the living room, I could see two bedrooms down the hall and a bathroom. The house was very clean and orderly. Brittany scanned the room for a TV, but there was none.

During dinner, Paul told us about his work at Stanford. Being a science enthusiast, I loved hearing about his research. "My dad was also a genetics professor," I told Paul. "He was doing research on cystic fibrosis."

Paul's interest piqued. "How interesting. Where does he teach? Maybe I've heard of him."

I didn't know what to say. I still had a hard time telling people that my parents were dead. I looked over at Jack for help.

"Sam's father passed away a few months ago," Jack explained. "Her father used to work at a university in Minnesota."

Paul became flustered. "Oh, I'm so sorry, Samantha."

"I should probably tell you about Sam and explain why we're here."

Jack described the whole story about me, leaving no details out. I worried that he was telling Paul too much, but Jack seemed confident that we could trust him. When Jack got to the part about why we needed the lab, Paul's mood seemed to darken.

"You can try slowing the timer like that, Jack, but I don't think it's going to help much."

"I'm sure it will work. I built a model, a very sophisticated computer model, and adding Brittany's DNA to Sam's DNA slowed the timer. It disrupted it. It should work the same way for Erik."

"That may be true for your model, but I'm not confident that it will work in real life. I know you have knowledge of genetics, Jack, but you're really more of a software expert, wouldn't you say?"

Jack seemed offended. "Well, yes. But I do know a great deal about genetics. I have a degree in it."

"I'm not discrediting that at all, Jack. And I mean no offense. But your job at GlobalLife was on the software side. And, well, I work in genetics every day." Paul could sense he was hurting Jack's ego. "None of that matters. The point is that we can try what you're saying, but you need to be aware that there's little chance that it will work the way you want."

I suddenly felt sick. If what Paul was saying was true, I had less than two years to live and Erik had mere months. Jack had been sure the procedure would buy us several more months, maybe even years. And with that extra time, we would find a way to shut off the timer for good. I'd convinced myself of it.

"Well, let's not talk about what-ifs just yet, Paul," Jack said. "We won't know until we try. So when do you think we can get in and use the lab?"

"Unfortunately, not until Friday. Some grad students are working in the labs 24/7 this week trying to finish up a project. They have to be done by Friday morning. After that, it's all yours."

"Oh, that's quite a delay. Could we at least test some DNA samples from that boy we believe to be Erik's twin?"

"Certainly. In fact, I can do that for you tomorrow. Just give me the sample."

"Would you mind if I came with and did it myself?"

"No, I don't mind at all. I understand." I could tell that Paul trusted few, if any, people, so Jack's request wasn't at all unreasonable to him.

"So what are the rest of us gonna do for three days?" Brittany asked.

Jack shot her a look. She was not acting grateful as he requested but sounded more like a child, upset that she wasn't being entertained.

"You're going to prepare yourselves for whatever we might encounter after this," Jack said sternly. "Do scenario planning. For example, what happens if we have another incident like we had at Dana Point? That was a close call and we weren't prepared for it."

"We can do that," I said before Brittany could protest.

"And Erik, I want you to keep helping Sam practice her abilities."

"Okay," Erik said.

Jack got up. "Well, it's been a long day. We should get to sleep."

"Yes, of course," Paul said. "I was thinking the girls could sleep in the side bedroom. I set a couple cots up for them. You men will have to take the sofa out here and put some sleeping bags on the floor. Sorry, but it's all I have."

Everyone went to bed. In the morning, after Jack and Paul left, the rest of us took turns getting ready in the one and only bathroom. Brittany went first and then sat outside on the back porch listening to music. Colin went next, which left Erik and me alone in the living room.

"So what do you think after hearing what Paul said last night?" I asked Erik. "Do you think your dad's idea to slow the timer won't work?"

"I don't know what to think. I mean, Paul seems smart but he also seems a little crazy. Did you check out his books? Half of them are about conspiracies. I think he really believes that stuff. And he lives out here alone in the woods."

"Excuse me, but now you sound like me when I first met you. I thought you and Jack were lunatics, remember? The way you lived off the grid. No city services. No Internet. No cable TV."

"Okay, maybe I shouldn't judge. But I trust my dad more than Paul, and if he says it will work, then that's what I believe. What do you think?"

"I think Paul has a point. Having something work in a computer model doesn't mean it will work in real life."

"Well, I'm not gonna worry about it. We'll find out soon enough."

Erik got up and glanced down the hall, checking to see if the bathroom door was still closed.

"So I talked to Colin last night," he said, sitting down again.

"About what?"

"About you. Geez, Sam, what the hell else would we talk about?"

"I don't know. Sports, maybe."

He laughed. "Okay, just so we're straight. If Colin and I talk sports, I'm not gonna report back to you."

"Yeah, whatever. So what did you say?"

"I asked him what was going on with you guys. I said that he seemed pissed off at you."

"And what did he say?"

"That he's pissed off at you." Erik smiled, knowing that I hated it when he didn't provide details.

"Come on, Erik."

"Okay, okay. He said that you asked him to move on with his life. That you don't need him."

"No! That's not at all what I said. I told him—"

"He said you want to be there for him when he needs it, like when he was so sick the other day. But then you don't let him be there for you, like now with this whole timer thing."

"And those were his words?"

"I paraphrased, but basically, yes. Listen, Sam, Colin's still mad at you. But after hearing my dad tell our whole story again last night, Colin wants to be there for you more than ever. So let him." Erik paused. "Unless that's not what you want. And if it's not, then you need to be honest with him about where you see this thing going between the two of you. I would want to know that."

I sat there trying to take in what Erik had said. He was right about being honest with Colin. But I was confused and wasn't sure what to tell him. Even though I loved Colin, I was starting to become less confident in our future together. And Erik was the reason for that. When Colin came back into my life, I thought my feelings for Erik would go away. But they didn't. And how could I commit to Colin when I was still so hung up on Erik? When I still got so jealous seeing Brittany flirt with him? If I'd never met Erik, I'd have no problem committing to Colin.

I looked up to see Erik staring at me. Had he been listening in on my thoughts? From his expression, I knew that he'd heard everything.

8. DECRYPTION

The bathroom door opened and Colin came out. "Whoever wants to go next, go ahead. I'm done in there."

Erik quickly got up. "I'll go, unless you wanna go, Sam."

"Um, no. Go ahead." I was completed mortified. I couldn't believe Erik had listened in on my thoughts! And I hadn't stopped him! I wasn't very good at blocking him from hearing me. Actually, I was terrible at it. And because of that, now Erik knew that I still had feelings for him. Feelings that were keeping me from moving forward with Colin.

Once Erik left, Colin came into the living room and sat down next to me.

"Hey. Can we end this? I don't like not talking to you."

I wrapped my arms around him, giving him a hug. "I don't like it either. And I don't know what I was thinking telling you to stay home. I don't want you to stay behind, Colin. I need you."

Colin pulled away and smiled at me. "Of course you do. You always have. You just need to be reminded every now and then."

I hugged him again. "Then the decision's made. You're coming with us."

"So what's on the agenda for today?"

"Like Jack said, I need to practice my abilities more. Erik didn't have much time to teach me stuff back in Texas."

Colin sat back and looked at me. "I know that you and Erik just met, but you guys seem really close."

I didn't respond. I wasn't sure what he meant. I felt like he was testing me but I was not at all prepared.

"Erik really cares about you, Sam. You know that, right?" He waited for my reaction.

"Um, no. I don't think that's true. I mean, he just met me." I tried to act natural but I could feel my heart beating faster. I didn't know where this was coming from. It's not like I'd been flirting with Erik in front of Colin.

"Yeah, well, I know guys and I can tell that Erik has feelings for you." Colin paused. "So I confronted him on it."

"You did what? When was this?"

"Last night. I told Erik to back off. Leave you alone."

"And what did he say?"

"Well, it wasn't what I was expecting. He told me that he doesn't think of you that way. He said you're like a little sister to him."

I wondered if Erik really did see me that way. After all, he'd been paying more attention to Brittany the past few days. And he'd been giving me advice about Colin. Maybe he'd moved on and thought of me differently now, in which case, his hearing my thoughts was even more embarrassing.

"He said I was like his little sister?"

"Yeah, which is good, right? Because when I'm not around, you'll have him watching out for you. We actually talked a lot last night. He seems like a good guy."

"Sure. He's great," I said half-heartedly. "Like the brother I never had."

After about 10 minutes, Erik appeared in the hallway. "Sam, you're next." I quickly tried to make my mind blank in case Erik was listening in again.

After I got ready, I met everyone outside on the back porch. Erik was already giving directions to Colin and Brittany.

"I need to work with Sam on her abilities. Maybe you two can work on those scenario plans my dad talked about."

"That is so dumb," Brittany whined. "Plans never work. You have to react in the moment. That's always worked for me."

"Come on, Brittany," Colin said, "let's try to come up with some ideas. At least it's something to do." Colin had always been good at persuading people. Maybe it was his good looks or his easygoing nature. Whatever it was, he was a natural-born leader.

Brittany got up. "All right. But let's go inside. There's too many bugs out here."

"What do you want to start with?" Erik asked once Colin and Brittany were gone.

"Telepathy. I need to know how to block someone from reading my thoughts." I figured Erik would know why I was asking to practice this skill, but I didn't care. "You showed me once, but I can't do it. I need to practice."

"Sam, that's not a survival skill. I'm the only one who can read your thoughts. And I'm not a threat. Why don't we focus on something more useful, like being able to use your abilities when you're distracted or stressed?"

"Later. I really need to learn this mind-blocking thing."

"But, Sam, it's a waste of—"

"Erik, just teach me."

"Fine. But we're not spending more than an hour on it."

Erik went over thought-blocking again, just as we'd done back in Texas. I practiced it over and over. But no matter how much I tried, he could still hear my thoughts.

I sighed, frustrated. "Maybe it's you. You're listening too hard."

Erik laughed. "There's no such thing as listening too hard. I wasn't even trying to listen and I could still hear your thoughts. I have to consciously tune them out to keep from hearing them."

"Well, that's just great. I'll never have another private thought around you."

"That's not true. I always make an effort to block out your thoughts."

"And then you selectively choose when to listen in."

"I do not. Why are you saying that?"

"No reason. Never mind." His comment had me questioning my earlier assumption. Maybe he hadn't heard my thoughts about him.

We continued training the rest of the morning, then spent the afternoon with Brittany and Colin discussing the scenario planning. By six, Jack and Paul were back with sacks full of groceries.

"Well, Erik, the test showed that Luke was indeed your twin." Jack took the groceries to the kitchen and set them on the counter. "I took a closer look at his DNA and he didn't appear to have any enhanced genes, just like Brittany."

"You say that like it's a bad thing," Brittany said, peeking into the grocery sacks.

"I guess I should go through his stuff," Erik said.

"Yes. See if you can learn any more about him." Jack glanced back at the living room. "Hey, I need to talk to Paul about some things, so I'd like all of you to help with dinner. Paul shouldn't be expected to make our meals. I got burgers for tonight. There's a grill out back. Can one of you get it going?"

"I will." Colin hopped up from his chair and headed outside.

Brittany started to leave. "Sorry, but I don't know how to cook."

"Then pretend you do," I whispered to her as I yanked her back into the kitchen.

As we got dinner ready, Jack and Paul talked in the other room. I used my enhanced hearing to listen in on part of their conversation.

"When you work on it, you should only use this computer," Paul said. "It's never been connected to the Internet. It's no frills but it will get the job done. I had this built special."

"You have to. These days, you can't find a basic computer. All of them have webcams and microphones. They can see and hear everything. Not to mention the built-in location trackers. Heck, just using the keyboard sends them the fingerprints of whoever's using the thing."

"And as soon as you plug in a computer these days, it automatically connects to the Internet. That's why I made this one, Jack. There's no way to connect it to the Web."

Listening to Jack and Paul was like listening to a couple of kids talking about their toys. They had such excitement for technology, especially for their homemade tech toys such as Paul's specially designed computer. But at the same time they didn't trust technology. And that distrust led them to avoid the very technology that they found so interesting.

"So what do you think is on this?" I glanced into the other room to see Jack holding up a CD.

"I used to have all kinds of theories, but now I don't know. I'm guessing it's some old research files Dan stole from GlobalLife. I really should've talked to Dan more before he was killed."

"Come on, Paul. It was an accident. He shouldn't have been out on the boat that day in those rough waters."

"Dan had been boating his whole life, Jack. He was safer in the water than on dry land."

Jack changed the subject and I tuned them out.

At dinner that night, Jack explained what he and Paul were talking about. "This morning, Paul showed me a package he got from Dan Barnes, a mutual friend of ours. The guy worked in IT security back at GlobalLife. Paul kept in touch with him over the years. Unfortunately, a few months ago, Dan had a boating accident and drowned." Jack looked over at Paul, who was shaking his head, showing his disagreement with the word "accident."

"I got the package after Dan died," Paul explained. "His wife called and said that Dan left me something in his safety deposit box at the bank. She didn't even know what it was. I drove all the way down to LA to get it. I couldn't risk having it get lost in the mail. I figured it had to be important if he'd been keeping it in a safety deposit box."

"What was it?" Erik asked.

"It was an envelope with some type of code handwritten on the front," Paul replied. "And inside was a CD."

"I can't decipher that handwritten code, but you might be able to, Erik," Jack said.

Paul turned to Erik. "Jack tells me that you're a math genius. He said he used to give you complex codes to crack simply for fun."

"He's exaggerating about the genius part but yeah, I love figuring out codes."

I knew Erik was smart but not code-cracking smart. Knowing that made me even more attracted to him. I tried not to think about it.

"It's over there on the desk," Paul said. "Feel free to work on it tomorrow, or tonight if you want."

"What was on the CD?" I asked.

"I don't know," Paul answered. "It's encrypted so I couldn't get it open. The package has been sitting in my closet ever since I got it."

"I'm going to spend some time working on it and see if I can get the file open," Jack said.

"Why are you so interested in this file, Dad?" Erik asked. "Do you think it has something to do with Sam and me?"

"Probably not. But we're almost certain it has to do with GlobalLife and something they don't want anyone to know. And that information could be very valuable."

"Then I should get going on that code. Maybe it will tell us what's on the file." Erik got up to clear the plates. "Code-cracking. Man, I haven't done that for years."

That night, while the rest of us were in bed, Erik stayed up to work on the code. From my bedroom, I could see a glimmer of light from the back porch, where he was sitting.

"Hey, Sam. Are you up?" Brittany whispered from the cot next to me.

"Yeah, why?"

"I wanted to tell you that I talked to Colin today while you were out doing your crazy magic tricks."

"They're not magic tricks, Brittany. They're genetically enhanced abilities," I corrected.

"Yeah, whatever. Anyway, did you know he got a football scholarship?"

"Yeah, he told me."

"You know, my old boyfriend back home got a football scholarship. I was gonna go with him when he went to college. It was gonna be my way out of that town."

"Your old boyfriend was a total jerk, Brittany. Why would you wanna go anywhere with that guy?"

"Because I didn't have any other options. And he wasn't so bad when his friends weren't around. He just liked showing off around people."

"By screaming at you? Hitting you? Humiliating you? That's showing off?"

"So he has a temper. Most guys do."

"No, not like that, Brittany. Your boyfriend's temper was out of control. He was abusive. That wasn't normal."

"Every guy I've ever dated acts like that, so it *is* normal."

"Then you've been dating the wrong guys."

I flipped on my side to go to sleep, but Brittany wouldn't let me.

"How does someone like me get a guy like Erik or Colin?"

I turned back to face her. "You don't use short skirts and cleavage, Brittany. You show them that you're more than a body. That you have a brain, and a personality, and a sense of humor. Guys like Colin and Erik are attracted to that."

"But I don't have those things."

"Of course you do."

"No. My mom always said I was nothing more than a pretty face and that I had to use that to get what I needed out of life."

"No offense to your mom, but that wasn't good advice. She was wrong. You're way more than a pretty face. You just need to let people see that."

"By doing what?"

"Well, for one, by showing interest in things. Reading. Learning about stuff. What are you interested in besides clothes and celebrities?"

"I don't know. Travel, I guess. Learning about different countries."

The answer surprised me. "That's good. So start learning about different countries. Learn a language."

"I tried that. I flunked Spanish. I'm not smart like you."

"You probably flunked Spanish because you didn't even try. Did you sleep through the class?"

"No. I texted Blake during that class. Sometimes naughty texts." She giggled. "He loved those!"

"That's why you flunked, Brittany. You didn't put any effort in."

"But guys are annoyed by smart girls."

"Guys like Blake are. Because when you act like you're stupid, it makes jerks like Blake feel smart. And it makes him feel like he can control you. That's why he treated you like he did."

Brittany got quiet for a moment. "Do you think I could ever get Erik to like me the way he likes you?"

"Erik and I are just friends. I've told you that."

"But he looks at you differently than he looks at me. He treats you differently."

"I don't know why you're saying that. He treats us both the same." It was little white lie but it seemed warranted, given Brittany's fragile self-esteem.

"Then how do I get him to see me as more than a friend?"

"I don't know. I'm the last person you should ask for dating advice. I'm just lucky I found Colin. And I already told you what to do. Stop trying so hard. Stop using your body as your only tool for attraction. And don't pretend to be dumb. Because I know you're not. Now can we go to sleep?"

"I guess. But one more thing."

"What?"

"I think Colin wants to marry you."

I sat up, resting back on my elbows. "When did he say that?"

"He didn't actually say those exact words, but I know he wants to."

I lay back down. "He doesn't wanna marry me, Brittany."

"I asked him if he loves you and he said that he does and always has."

"Yeah, well, that doesn't mean he wants to get married. And why are you asking him stuff like that?"

"Because I'm your sister. I'm trying to figure out what the guy's intentions are." Brittany laughed, which made me laugh.

"So what exactly *are* his intentions?"

"I didn't ask him that specifically. But you're all he talks about. And it's obvious that he doesn't want anyone else but you. It's kind of weird, really. I mean, he's kind of young to be deciding that, right? You'd think he'd wanna date other people."

"Sometimes the right person comes along at the wrong time."

"Hey, is that a country song?"

I laughed. "I don't know. Probably."

"So if he asked you, would you say yes?"

"If who asked what?"

"Sam, just answer the question."

"Would I marry Colin? Like, right now? No. I'm too young."

"Hmmm, okay. Good to know."

"What does that mean? Are you not telling me something?"

"I'm tired. I'm going to sleep."

"Brittany? What did you mean by that? Did Colin say—"

"Goodnight, Sam." Brittany rolled on her side and covered her head with the blanket.

He's not thinking of proposing, I thought. Brittany's just trying to stir up trouble. Make me think things that aren't true. But then again, it wasn't out of the realm of possibility. Knowing that I could be dead in two years could prompt Colin to act. The idea of it made me anxious. I wasn't ready to be a bride.

The next morning, Erik was back on the porch working on his code. Jack was sitting at the dining room table typing on the laptop and talking to himself. Brittany slept in, not seeing a need to get up. Colin was in the kitchen making breakfast.

"Hey, Sam. I'm making eggs. You want some?"

"Yeah, sounds good. Did everyone else eat?"

"No. Jack and Erik are too busy to eat. They've been working since dawn. Erik probably slept for three hours. He's obsessed with cracking that code. Where's Brittany?"

"She's sleeping in. Hey, what did you talk about with Brittany yesterday?"

Colin stopped scrambling the eggs. "Not much. Why? Did she say something?"

"Um, a few things, but she tends to exaggerate. Never mind."

Colin divided the eggs onto two plates and we went to sit at the table with Jack. Suddenly the porch door swung open and Erik raced inside.

"I've got it! I know what the code says!"

9. ORIGIN

"So what does it say?" Jack moved his computer aside.

Erik put a sheet of paper on the table so everyone could see. It read, "Superior Genetics Project: Origin of Foreign Nucleobases."

Jack grabbed the piece of paper. "Origin of foreign nucleobases? Erik, are you sure you decoded this correctly?"

"Yes, I went back and checked it and rechecked it. It was a really complex code. After I figured out which numbers stood for which letters, I had to figure out the right sequence. And then the sequence had to be reordered."

Jack kept staring at the paper as if doing so would change what it said. "It can't be. This is too easy. How could it be that the very thing we're looking for is right here on this disk? Of all the places this could have ended up, it ends up here? At Paul's house?"

He got quiet and a worried look came across his face. "What's wrong, Dad," Erik asked. "What are you thinking?"

"GlobalLife would never want the information on this file to get out. And if it did get out, they'd want to know where it was and who had it. So I'm wondering if this file has some type of hidden locator device built into it that goes off when you open it."

"But the file came from that Dan guy. I thought you and Paul knew him," I said.

"Yes, and he was a good guy. I'm probably being overly cautious." Jack thought for a moment. "Well, if there's even a chance that the disk has the answers we're looking for, then I have to risk opening it. I just can't believe that the information about those base pairs is what's on this thing. Maybe luck is finally coming our way."

"I wouldn't say that just yet, Dad," Erik said. "Why don't you open the file first and then we'll see."

"I'm hoping I can. I've been working on this for hours, and everything I thought would work hasn't. So now I need to get creative."

"Then we'll leave you alone so you can get back to work." Erik got up. "Sam, let's go out back and work on some more stuff. Maybe we should practice getting those scenarios running in your head again."

"That's my least favorite ability. Let's practice something else," I suggested, thinking of how that ability hadn't helped me much in the past. Also, in order to get the scenarios running, my body had to release a high level of stress hormones and I really didn't want to feel stressed today.

"What are Colin and I supposed to do all day?" Brittany was finally up and dressed. She came over to the table.

"I've got an idea." Jack glanced up from the computer. "Erik, you and Sam work on listening to Brittany's and Colin's thoughts from different places and different distances. It will be good practice for both of you."

Erik headed for the door. "That's a good idea. Colin? Brittany? You up for that?"

"I guess," Brittany muttered. "But I still don't like that whole mind-reading thing you guys do."

We all went outside and Erik gave instructions to Colin and Brittany. "Okay, now just think about whatever you want. Once you get to your spot, yell back at us to let us know you're there. After two minutes, come back and we'll try something else."

Colin went down the hill and into the woods. Brittany followed him, stopping halfway down the hill.

"Ready," I heard Colin call out.

"Me, too," Brittany yelled.

Erik nodded for us to begin. At first I tried to hear Brittany's thoughts. I got nothing until about 30 seconds in. *"How could Paul not have a TV? Who doesn't have a TV? We were dirt poor and Mom still got us a TV. And cable."*

I stopped listening to Brittany and changed my focus to Colin, imagining him in front of me. I could hear his thoughts right away. *"I've gotta get some alone time with you, Sam. Maybe we could sneak away for an hour out here in the woods. It would be just like that time we drove out to Baxter Park and you and I—"*

"Stop! We're done!" I yelled, startling Erik. "Time's up!"

"Are you sure? I think that was only a minute." Erik checked his watch.

"Nope. Two minutes. Your watch must be slow." I could feel my face blushing. "Colin. Brittany. We're done," I called out to them.

When they were back up the hill, I yanked Colin off to the side. "Why were you thinking those things? You know that Erik could hear you!"

"Oh, I thought you were listening to me and Erik was listening to Brittany."

"No! We were listening to both of you!"

Colin shrugged. "I don't care. You're my girlfriend. Erik knows that. It's no big deal."

"Yeah, it *is* a big deal," I whispered. "Those were private memories. I don't want him hearing that stuff. I mean Baxter Park? You had to bring that up?"

"We had a good time there." He smiled, wrapping his arms around my waist. "A *really* good time."

"Yeah, I remember. But that's between us. I don't want other people to know. It's embarrassing." I tried to pull away but he wouldn't let me.

"Okay. I won't think that stuff anymore. Well, at least not when *he's* listening in." Colin leaned down and whispered to me. "So what about my offer? Do you want to get some alone time later?"

"I don't know. We'll see how the day goes." I couldn't believe Colin could think about making out with everything going on. That was the last thing on my mind.

"You guys ready to try something else?" Erik asked. He didn't act weird, so maybe he hadn't heard Colin's thoughts, or at least not all of them.

"I want to try this mind-reading thing." Brittany went up to Erik. "I want to see for myself what it's like communicating but not talking."

"You know that's not possible, Brittany," I said. "Only Erik and I can do that."

"But we could pretend, just for fun. Come on," Brittany urged. "It won't take long. I'm tired of everything being so serious. Can't we have a break?"

"Okay. What are you suggesting?" Erik asked.

"Well, it could be like when we were kids. You know that telephone game where you whisper stuff to people? Except instead of doing that, you'll listen to our thoughts and write down what we say, giving it to the other person."

It was juvenile and silly, but Erik agreed to it. After all, it would only take a few minutes. Erik would play the role of "mind messenger," listening to their thoughts and delivering the written messages back and forth.

Erik asked Brittany to pick the topic that she and Colin would discuss. "Let's see. I would like to talk about the latest spring fash—"

She stopped, glancing over at me. "On second thought, I would like to discuss travel, a topic I am interested in."

Her attempt to impress Erik sounded completely forced. She blushed and looked down at the ground.

"That's a good topic," I said, trying to save her. "So, Brittany, what about travel would you like to discuss?"

She looked up, surprised that nobody was laughing at her. "Um, well, I would like to talk about Paris. I've always wanted to go there."

"Okay," Erik said. "Then let's pretend Colin is a Parisian and you're asking him about his culture."

"And, Sam, don't listen in," Brittany ordered. "Only Erik can."

"Why?" She ignored me, so I went and got a pen and some paper for Erik to write the messages. Then I sat off to the side and watched.

The conversation began. Erik listened to Brittany's questions about Paris, then wrote them down and gave them to Colin. Then Erik listened to Colin and wrote his responses down, giving them to Brittany. It continued back and forth. After a few minutes, Erik was doubled over in laughter. Soon Brittany was laughing, too.

"You guys are done. Now what's so funny?" I asked.

"Colin. He was hilarious," Erik said. "At first, he tried to think with a French accent. That was funny enough. And then you should have heard his answers to Brittany. Well, they're all written down so you can read them, but they're even funnier with the accent. Colin, you should be a comedian, man."

"And that part when you said—" Brittany was laughing so hard she couldn't finish.

Colin's sense of humor and quick wit were one of the many reasons people liked him. It had obviously won over Erik and Brittany.

"Well, I guess we should get serious again. See that shed over there?" Erik pointed to a small wooden structure at the far end of the backyard. "You guys go in there and start thinking really fast, like you're in danger. Jump from one thought to another. The thoughts don't even need to relate to each other."

Brittany made a face. "I'm not going in that shed. There's probably snakes and rats in there."

"I'll keep them away from you," Colin assured her as he led her to the shed.

"Sam, you go inside the house and see if you can hear their thoughts," Erik instructed. "That way, we'll see if you can hear through several walls. I'll stay out here."

"Oh, sure. Give me the hard stuff."

"I'm being easy on you today," he said as I walked back to the house. "I didn't even ask you about Baxter Park."

I could feel him smiling. I went in the kitchen, ignoring Erik's comment.

"Okay, start now," I heard Erik yell from outside.

I listened for any thoughts from Brittany or Erik. Thirty seconds passed. Then a minute. Still nothing. After another minute, I heard a few words from Colin, but then he cut out again.

I went outside to find Erik. "I hardly got anything. I guess it doesn't work with all the walls in the way."

Colin and Brittany came back over by Erik and me.

"It didn't work for me either," Erik said. "I only got a few words. That's really weird. You two think about something right now. Sam and I will try again with you next to us."

Erik and I listened but again only heard a few words here and there and no complete sentences.

"This happened to me once before," I said. "It was when I was on that bus to Texas. I met that girl, Ruby, and I tried to read her thoughts but I could only get a few words. She had her cell phone in her hand so, maybe this is dumb, but I was thinking that the phone was interfering with her brain waves, making it so I couldn't read and interpret her thoughts."

"That's not dumb. That makes total sense," Erik said. "Except that nobody has a cell phone, right?"

We all shook our heads. Erik glared at Brittany.

"What are you looking at me for?" Brittany asked. "I don't have a cell phone. If I did, I'd be using it."

"Something's not right." Erik looked up and around. "We heard everything when you guys were down in the woods. So what's different? It's like there's some type of interference."

I noticed a sound off in the distance. "Erik, do you hear something?"

Erik listened. "Yeah. It kind of sounds like a helicopter."

Brittany yawned, stretching her arms out. "So you hear a helicopter. Who cares?"

Erik listened closer. "Helicopters fly low. They survey what or who is on the ground."

I looked at Erik. "GlobalLife has helicopters."

"Everyone inside!" Erik yelled.

We sprinted back to the house. When we got inside, Jack was looking out a back window. "When did you notice it, Erik?"

"Just now. It came out of nowhere."

"It's not close enough for me to see any detail on it. Tell me what it looks like."

Erik joined him at the window, using his enhanced vision to get a better look at the helicopter. "It's all black. No markings."

"Go check out front," Jack said. "See if anyone's there. Be discreet. Don't open the drapes."

Erik ran to the front window. "Nothing. There's nobody there."

Jack went to the kitchen. "I want all of you to get over here. Hurry up!"

We joined Jack in the kitchen. "It's still off in the distance, so listen up. We're going to run to Paul's underground shelter. It's hidden in that shed." He pointed to the shed Colin and Brittany had been in earlier. "Got it?"

We nodded.

Jack motioned Erik to move in front of us. "I want you to go first, Erik, and open the door to the shelter. It's right in the middle of the floor. Everyone else follow him. Go as fast as you can. I'll be the last one in. Ready?"

The sound of the helicopter got significantly louder. "Erik, now!" Jack shouted. Erik bolted out the door and the rest of us followed him into the shed. We got into the shelter and Jack shut the door behind us.

We moved to the far end of the shelter and waited. The helicopter sounded like it was circling the house. As we listened, we stood there in total disbelief. It didn't make sense. We'd come all this way only to have GlobalLife swoop down and get us now? Out of nowhere? For that to happen, someone would have had to tip them off. And the only person who knew we were there was Paul.

Jack was thinking the same thing. "I can't believe he would tell them we were here. He wouldn't. I know he wouldn't. But if it wasn't Paul, then how the hell did they find us?"

Erik went up to Jack. "Maybe it's not GlobalLife, Dad. Maybe it's a military helicopter, like the kind that used to go over our farm. Maybe they're just doing some type of training exercises."

The helicopter continued to circle above us.

Jack nervously rubbed his beard. "We can only hope that's what it is."

"What is this place?" Brittany whispered.

"It's an old bomb shelter," Jack said. "Paul made it into an underground bunker because he's so paranoid about things. Good thing he did. It's the only place we can hide. If that's GlobalLife, their equipment won't be able to detect us out down here."

He stopped to listen. The helicopter was still circling. "If they truly suspect that we're here, they could have people all around us. Around the house. In the woods. They'll eventually find—"

"Dad, listen," Erik pointed up. "Do you hear that? It sounds like it might be leaving."

We all listened. It did seem to be heading away from us.

"It may not be above us anymore, but I still hear it," Jack said. "We're staying here until we're sure it's gone."

After an hour of waiting, Jack slowly opened the shelter door. He went up and looked around, then came back. "Okay, I don't see anything. Let's go."

"I want you to keep watching for it, Erik," Jack said when we were back in the house. "I need to keep working on that file. If you hear or see anything at all, let me know."

"So now we're stuck in here?" Brittany plopped down on the sofa.

I sat down next to her. "You could read one of Paul's books. He's got plenty to choose from."

"Yeah, right, Sam. Like I really wanna read a book about," Brittany glanced at the books on the shelves behind her, "alien encounters, war profiteering, or artificial intelligence. Yeah, that's fun. Let's look for a TV instead. Maybe he has one hidden in a closet somewhere."

"He doesn't own a TV," Jack called out from behind his laptop. "He's never had one the whole time I've known him. Doesn't see the need for one."

Brittany rolled her eyes as she got up and picked out a book. "Here's one. *The Pyramids and Other Ancient Mysteries.* Do you want that one, Sam?"

I grabbed the book. "Yeah. I love reading about the pyramids. Because really, how did people build those back then? I don't understand how they did it without big equipment."

"Aliens," Colin said. "Whenever you can't explain something, blame the aliens. Works every time."

"I can't explain women," Erik mumbled from the chair next to me.

Colin laughed. "Because they're aliens. Mystery solved."

"Ha, ha," I said.

"Do you think aliens look like humans?" Brittany asked.

"No," Erik replied, "but I don't think they look like the movie aliens with the massive heads and big black eyes."

We continued discussing the crazy topics in Paul's books for the rest of the afternoon. Erik kept checking outside but the helicopter never returned.

"I don't think it was GlobalLife, Dad." Erik went to sit at the table with Jack. "If it was, like you said, they would have sent someone up to the house."

Jack didn't respond. He was concentrating on whatever was on his laptop screen. His face looked both worried and confused.

"Dad, are you listening?"

"What? No. What did you need, Erik?" Jack was very distracted by something.

"Never mind. Doesn't matter."

Jack looked up from his laptop. "Since it's safe out there now, why don't you guys go outside before dinner? Get some fresh air."

Erik laughed. "What are we, 5? You're sending us outside?"

"Just for a little while. Paul will be home soon and I need to talk to him about something."

"All right. Everyone out," Erik ordered.

We all went out back. Erik and Colin searched the shed for some sports equipment while Brittany and I sat on the porch. After a while, I went inside to get a drink of water and heard Jack and Paul talking intently in the other room. It sounded like they'd been discussing the helicopter incident.

"Yeah, I should have told you about those training exercises they do," Paul said. "There's a military base just north of here. But you usually don't see them at that time of day. And the training is often on the weekends, so it is suspicious. Good thing you thought to use the shelter."

Jack moved on. "So going back to what I told you earlier about what I found in this file. You don't really believe that, do you, Paul? Because if you do, then I think you've read too many of those conspiracy theory books. I know the file is very detailed but this is obviously a hoax. And here I spent all night and all day getting this file open. For some silly hoax."

"Dan wouldn't go to all this trouble for a hoax." Paul lowered his voice. "Listen, Jack. I'm now certain that Dan was killed. And I know it was GlobalLife. They did it because of what was on this disk. It finally makes sense."

"Come on, Paul. He wasn't killed. It was an accident."

"It wasn't an accident. I didn't tell you the whole story, Jack."

"Okay. So what's the story?"

"I talked to the medical examiner who did Dan's autopsy. He said there was a drug in Dan's body that's not even on the market yet. It's in clinical trials at GlobalLife Pharmaceuticals. If administered in very high doses, it burns the skin from the inside out. You feel like your body is on fire. And then paralysis follows. So Dan must have jumped in the water trying to relieve the burning and then the paralysis hit and he drowned."

"Are you sure about that?" Jack kept his voice down.

"I talked to the medical examiner myself. I tried contacting him later to ask him more about it, but it's like he disappeared. I don't know if he went into hiding or if GlobalLife got him, too."

"How would GlobalLife know that Dan had this file?"

"I don't know, Jack. Maybe they could see that the file was copied from their server. Dan's house was burglarized soon after he died.

Nothing was taken, but they tore the place apart. They had to have been looking for that CD."

"So the information in that file is worth killing for." Jack said it slowly, as if something had just occurred to him.

"Yes. And I can't believe I'm still alive with that in my possession all these years. I'm guessing GlobalLife figured it didn't exist after all. Either that, or they didn't know where to look next."

There was silence for a minute. Then Jack finally spoke. "Paul, what you're saying is that—"

"I'm saying that what you found on that disk is the real deal. That's the answer you've been looking for, Jack. Although I know it's the last answer you expected. Or wanted."

Jack lowered his voice. "If this is true, then I don't know what to do now. This changes everything."

"Are you going to tell Sam and Erik?"

"Yes, I have to. They need to know."

Jack stood up and I snuck back outside. Erik, Colin, and Brittany were laughing and kicking a soccer ball around in the back yard.

"Hey, come inside," Jack called from the kitchen. "We need to talk."

"Aww, do we have to, Dad?" Erik called back, using a child's voice. "But you told us to play outside."

Colin laughed. "Yeah, come on. Just a few more minutes."

"This is serious," Jack said. "Get inside."

Everyone filed into the house and sat at the table, where Paul was already seated.

"I got the file open," Jack announced.

"Yeah, so what did it say?" Erik asked.

Jack sighed. "I don't know how to tell you this. I can't even find the right words."

"We've heard just about everything by now, Dad. I don't think you can shock us anymore."

"That code you figured out, Erik, was right. This file identifies the source of those unique nucleobases in your genes. The ones that we need in order to repair that section of your DNA and stop the timer."

I was getting impatient. "Yeah, we know all that. So what are they? Where did they come from?"

Jack hesitated. "Well, they're uh, they're not from Earth." He paused for a moment. "What I'm trying to say is that they're not human. The base pairs came from alien DNA."

OPTIONS

Erik laughed. "That's real funny, Dad. So what does it really say?"

Jack's tone darkened. "I'm not kidding, Erik."

"I get it, Jack," I said. "You heard us talking about aliens earlier, so now you're making a joke about it." I turned to Paul. "We were looking at some of your books, Paul. Hope that's okay."

Paul didn't answer. He kept his eyes on Jack.

"I wouldn't joke about something like this," Jack said. "I can't believe it myself. In a million years I wouldn't consider this to be a possibility. I never even believed in aliens. Well, I believe other life forms exist in some far off galaxy but not—"

"Wait a minute," Erik stopped him. "So this isn't some stupid joke you're playing on us? Because now I'm almost starting to think that you're serious."

Jack sighed. "I don't know how else to say this to make you believe me. According to this file, those nucleobases in your DNA—the ones that I've never been able to identify—are from an alien life form."

"Then the file is fake," I insisted. "You can't trust anything it says."

"She's right," Erik agreed. "This is a hoax, probably to get us to go on some off-beat path looking for something that doesn't exist."

"But nobody knew we would open it," Jack pointed out. "Anyone could have opened that file."

"Well, it found us. So is that just a coincidence?" I asked.

"It was given to Paul, not us," Jack corrected.

Erik and I shot a suspicious glance at Paul.

"Don't start making accusations that aren't true," Jack warned. "I knew Dan, the guy who made this file. And like Paul was saying earlier, Dan wouldn't steal this information from GlobalLife and preserve it on a disk if it wasn't of utmost importance. And he wouldn't have given it to just anyone."

"If this shit were true, then he would have emailed the file to the news media," Erik said. "You don't hide something like that in some bank deposit box."

"GlobalLife owns stakes in the major news outlets, Erik. This would never get out. And if it ended up at some reporter's desk, do you think they would even believe this? Only a handful of people would take this seriously."

"I had no idea that's what was on the disk," Paul admitted. "I thought it was just backup files from some old GlobalLife research. As you can tell from my books, I love a good conspiracy, but even I never would have guessed this could be true."

Colin leaned over to see the laptop screen. "What else is on the disk? Is there information on how they got these base pairs?"

"Yes," Jack said. "I was getting to that. The file describes an archeological site in northern Greece. The site was discovered in the 1980s. I remember hearing news stories about that. When they began uncovering the site, they found tombs filled with ancient artifacts. It was really amazing how well things had been preserved."

"So what does that have to do with the base pairs?" I demanded. I didn't mean to yell at Jack, but I needed him to get to the point.

"In one of the tombs, there were drawings on the wall. Some of them showed stick figures coming down from a circular shape in the sky. Here's a photo of one of the drawings." Jack turned the laptop so we could all see. The drawing did look like a man coming from a spaceship.

Jack continued. "The tomb had all kinds of pottery, gold, a few jewels. But they also found a stone box that contained remains of something that didn't appear to come from an animal or a human. When it was analyzed, they found the remains were made of elements not found on Earth. According to this file, further analysis revealed that the remains contained an alien form of DNA."

"So who's 'they' that you keep talking about? Who discovered this?" Erik asked.

"GlobalLife. Their agricultural division was trying to buy up land in Greece for years because of its moderate climate. The country has excellent growing conditions, making it perfect for their seed testing. Some of the land they wanted to buy was in and around a rural village. The Greek people would only approve the land purchase if GlobalLife Ag agreed to build some basic infrastructure in the area. In the process of doing that, they had to dig up and level the ground in some spots. One day, they dug right into the top of this buried tomb."

Jack brought up some photos of the excavation site and showed them to us.

"The Greek people were outraged because they said the excavation work should be done by local archeologists," Paul added.

"But GlobalLife used their power to get that shot down," Jack explained. "So nobody really knew what they found in the tomb, other than what they gave to a local museum, which wasn't much."

Erik and I didn't respond, so Jack kept talking. "Going back to the file, it says that GlobalLife Genetics isolated the alien genes and began experiments in which they inserted the genes into lab mice. But it didn't work so well. The mouse DNA wasn't sure what to do with foreign material. So GlobalLife told it what to do, using microscopic computers and software. And it worked. That led them to the idea to use software to control what the genetic material did once it was in the cells. And that's how we ended up here."

I still refused to believe it. The scientist in me wanted more proof. "How detailed is that file? Does it include a breakdown of the base pairs' composition? Does it show sequencing?"

Jack pointed to the laptop. "Yes, that's all in here; the history of the base pairs and the science behind them. Honestly, I don't know how Dan even got this information out of the building. He was in IT security, but they watch those guys like you wouldn't believe."

"Does it say if this alien thing had special abilities?" Erik asked.

"Some of the drawings from the tomb did show what appeared to be superhuman abilities. One showed a man lifting a huge rock over his head to indicate great strength. Another showed a line between the minds of two stick figures, probably to show telepathy. These are all in here." Jack scrolled down the file, showing us the images.

I ignored the drawings. "What about the software that controls it. Is that described, Jack?"

"No, not the type that was used in the human experiments. This file doesn't even mention the human trials."

Jack closed the laptop, then sat back in his chair. "I have to admit that I thought this was a hoax at first, too." Jack hesitated. "But Paul has reason to believe that Dan was killed because of what was in this file. And I'm starting to think that he's right. GlobalLife wouldn't want anyone to know about this."

The room got silent. "Also, there's so much detail in this file that I have to believe this is real," Jack said. "And just to verify that this originally came from GlobalLife, I did check for the GlobalLife seal that's built into every file. I had to hunt for it, but it was there."

"I need to get some fresh air." I raced outside, feeling like I might throw up.

It was dark out now and I could hear the sounds of an owl close by in a tree. I sat down and focused on its call, trying to calm myself.

"It's crazy," I said aloud to myself. "There's no way. It's gotta be some type of joke."

I heard the screen door squeak open. It was Colin. He came and sat down next to me. "Do you want to talk about it?"

Tears began running down my face. "This can't be true, Colin. And if it is, then I can't deal with it. I can't. I don't want to."

Colin put his arm around me but didn't say anything. He didn't get upset about the news because he knew I was upset enough for the both of us. We made a good couple that way. Whenever one of us was stressed, the other person remained calm. It had always been that way and I loved that about us.

"Why is this happening to me? It's too much. I still haven't gotten over what they did to my parents." The tears flowed even more when I thought of my parents. I had tried so hard to get over their deaths. I had come to accept that I would never see them again, but my grief for them still lingered.

Colin held me closer. He kissed my forehead as I rested my head on his shoulder.

"I'm barely keeping it together, Colin. I mean, I keep telling myself that I've moved on, that I'm okay now, but the truth is, I'm not at all. I miss them so much, especially now, when I need them more than ever."

"Then tell me that, Sam. You don't have to hide that stuff from me. I don't ask you about it because you always act like you're fine."

"Well, I'm not fine. I feel so alone without them."

"You're not alone. I'll always be here for you."

I pushed him away. "Why? Why would you want to be with me, Colin? Didn't you hear what Jack said? I'm not even human! Part of me is alien! Like little green men alien!" I couldn't believe what I was saying.

"Sam, I don't care what's in your cells." Colin laced his hand in mine. "I love you. You know that."

"Then you're crazy. Or you must have a thing for aliens." I said it seriously, but the silliness of the words helped put a stop to my tears. "This whole alien thing. It can't be real, right? Do you think it's true?"

"I don't know. That was the last thing I expected Jack to say. But he seems pretty confident that it's true and that the file is legit."

"I can't believe that a company like GlobalLife would be able to just take the remains of an alien as their own property. That's assuming the story is true, which I'm not convinced that it is. But still, how could the world's leaders or the world's top scientists allow something like that to go to a corporation?"

"It just shows you how powerful GlobalLife is. And how connected they are."

"Come on, Colin. An alien? Found in a tomb? That would be the biggest discovery of all time. Even if nobody knew what to do with it, a discovery like that belongs to everyone, not to some corporation. It should be in a museum."

"Maybe the world leaders, scientists, or whoever thought the remains were useless. And then GlobalLife found out that they weren't. Or maybe they allowed GlobalLife to have the alien remains hoping for an even bigger discovery like—" Colin stopped.

"What bigger discovery? What were you gonna say?"

"Nothing. I was just thinking out loud."

"No. What's the bigger discovery that everyone is waiting for?"

But before he could answer, it hit me. "Erik and me. That's what you mean, right? We're an even bigger discovery than the alien?"

"I don't know. I guess. I mean, finding the alien would be huge news. But then what? People would lose interest. The real story would be finding out how we could use the alien remains to improve life on Earth, right? Something like that would get attention. And could change life as we know it."

"You're right. The people who know about this would want to keep it a secret. Because if it did turn out to be some life-changing discovery, GlobalLife and whoever else is involved in this would make billions." I paused to think about it. "Erik and I are proof that the alien genes can live in humans. We're proof that the genes can give people these powers. That's why GlobalLife will do anything to get us back."

"Sam, can I talk to you?" Erik was standing at the screen door behind us.

Colin got up. "I'll leave you two alone."

"Thanks, Colin."

Erik came outside and stared into the dark woods. "Look. No fireflies. Makes me miss home. Before all this happened."

"Yeah. That seems so long ago." It was hard to believe how much had changed in just a week. "So how are you feeling? Because I'm a total mess."

Erik sighed as he sat down next to me. "I'm right there with you."

"What have they been talking about inside?"

"My dad was showing me the file. Paul was talking about the gene sequences a little. He thinks that GlobalLife is trying to create different gene sequences using these base pairs so they can patent and sell them along with the software that goes with them."

"Great. Just what the world needs." I said sarcastically. "And these are the same sequences that are in us?"

"Yeah. Well, Paul says that you probably have more of them since you're younger than me. He said that GlobalLife probably tried some new sequences in you that they didn't put in me in order to give you even more abilities."

"So what are you saying, Erik? That you believe this now?"

"If you see what's in that file, Sam, it's pretty convincing."

"I still don't believe it."

"If it *is* true, what do you think?"

"It makes me hate GlobalLife even more! I just want to annihilate them. And everyone involved with this project. And I'm not a violent person."

"I know you're not. I feel the same way."

"I already hated GlobalLife for messing with our DNA. But this is so much worse. Putting nonhuman substances into our cells? Making us into, I don't know what we are—alien-human hybrids? It makes me sick just saying it."

"I guess my dad shouldn't have got you those alien earrings," Erik joked.

I jabbed his arm. "Erik, this isn't funny."

"I know. Sorry. When I can't deal with shit, I turn to humor."

"It's okay. I can't deal with it either. I had enough to worry about. This alien thing was the last straw. It's more than I could handle. And now you're saying that GlobalLife put some proprietary genetic cocktail inside of us that they hope to mass produce some day?"

"It's just Paul's theory, Sam. We don't know if he's right."

"Why else would GlobalLife be doing this? They want power and profits. Selling superhuman genes to the highest bidder seems pretty profitable to me."

"Well, as long as they never catch us, then they'll never be able to test what the genes can do."

"But as long as it's in us, they'll be hunting us down for the rest of our lives." I realized after I said it that the rest of our lives wasn't really that long.

"Erik, you know what it means if these base pairs really did come from alien genes?"

He stared at the ground. "It means that my dad won't be able to shut the timer off."

"So we have two options. We either go back to GlobalLife or—" I stopped, not wanting to say it.

Erik looked up at me. "Or we die."

11. WAITING

"Sam? Erik?" Jack called from the door behind us. "I need you two to come inside. We have to talk next steps. Plans have changed a little."

Erik and I got up and went to the living room. Colin, Brittany, and Paul were sitting there waiting for us. Erik sat in a chair next to his dad. I took a seat next to Colin.

"This latest, um, discovery," Jack began, "does not change the fact that we need to slow the timer function in the two of you."

Erik rolled his eyes. "Dad, you *do* realize that now it's pointless to—"

"Nothing has changed." Jack's voice was stern. He refused to accept that his son's death, or mine, was now inevitable. "We're going to slow the timer as previously planned. After that we'll address the next course of action needed to get it turned off for good."

"But, Dad, there's no way to—"

"Erik. Enough!" Jack interrupted, raising his voice.

We waited in silence for Jack to continue. "As I was saying, we're going forward with the procedure. We can have access to the lab tomorrow, which is a day sooner than we planned. I want to get there early. We'll be leaving here at 5."

"So what exactly happens during this procedure?" Erik asked. Unlike me, he'd had little to no medical care during his life.

"It's simple, Erik. You're basically getting a shot. The DNA from Luke is placed into a vector, which carries the DNA into the nucleus of your cells. And that vector is injected like a vaccine. The same is true for Sam but we used Brittany's DNA. Paul and I already prepared the shots when I was at Stanford with him the other day."

"And then what?" I asked.

"Then I'll monitor your cells for changes. Hopefully, they'll respond just as they did in my computer model. I'll take blood samples midmorning and midafternoon and see how things are going."

"Are Colin and I going to Stanford, too?" It was the first time Brittany had spoken since Jack revealed what was in the file.

"Yes, we're all going," Jack replied.

Brittany seemed pleased. Going anywhere was better than sitting in Paul's house with nothing to do.

"Since you'll be hanging around campus all day, you should come up with a story explaining why you're there," Paul advised. "I would suggest saying that you're all touring the university. You'll need to come up with fake names and histories for yourselves. The professors and other staff are very curious by nature, so expect a lot of questions."

"That's good to know. Thanks, Paul," Jack said. "Oh, and since we're doing this earlier than expected, we're leaving here on Friday."

For the rest of the evening, we went over the story that we would tell people if they approached us at Stanford. Jack made dinner, but hardly anyone ate. The revelations from the file left all of us feeling a little sick. Jack tried to act like everything was fine, but I knew he was feeling as hopeless as the rest of us.

The next morning, I woke up at 2 a.m. feeling anxious, wishing we could leave California that very minute and head to Minnesota. The dream I'd had about that note from Dave was now my only glimmer of hope. There had to be something on that flash drive he sent the professor that could help Erik and me. It was a long shot. But it was all I had left to keep me going.

"Sam? Are you up?" Brittany's voice startled me.

"Yeah. Why?"

She turned to face me. "What Jack said tonight. Does that mean you and Erik are like, aliens?"

I could tell that Brittany wasn't trying to be mean with her question. She just didn't understand.

"No. It's not like that. There's just a tiny piece of our cells that has this, um, genetic material that's from an alien life form."

From her silence, I knew that Brittany was imagining little green men with big heads and black eyes living inside my cells.

"But that doesn't mean it's from aliens like you see in the movies," I said, trying to erase the image from her head. "Nobody knows what aliens really look like. Those remains they found in that tomb were too decomposed to re-create whatever they came from. For all we know, the aliens looked like us."

"And you've had this stuff in you all this time? Since you were born?"

"Technically, before I was born."

"Do you think they could get it out of you?"

"No. It doesn't work that way. It's part of me. And Erik. It's built into our DNA."

"So you'll never be, like, normal?" Brittany's voice turned sad.

"Normal can be defined different ways. I think I'm normal now. I feel normal, well, except for the abilities I have."

"But, I mean that you can't do normal things, like have a kid someday?"

I hadn't given the idea any thought. But Brittany brought up a good point. If I somehow survived this timer thing and found a way to hide from GlobalLife, I would still have these altered genes in me. Although I could probably have kids, would I want to, knowing that they, too, would have this alien-human DNA? It wouldn't be fair to pass that on to them. And it would put them in danger. Not to mention it would create a whole new generation of people with alien-human DNA.

"Sam, did you hear me?" Brittany was still waiting for my response.

"Having kids is the last thing I'm worried about. I'm not even gonna make it past—"

"Stop," Brittany interrupted. "You're not gonna die, Sam. Neither is Erik. Jack will fix this. Everything will work out." Brittany voice was shaky. She cleared her throat before continuing. "I waited my whole life to get a sister. And even though you really annoy me sometimes and you have no fashion sense," she paused, "I still want you around."

"Well, if, or when, everything turns out okay, maybe I'll let you help me with that fashion thing."

"Really?" Brittany's mood lightened. "Why wait? I could help you now."

I laughed. "Go to sleep, Brittany."

I finally fell asleep but not for long. "Hey, Sam." Colin was sitting at the edge of my cot. "Jack told me to get you guys up."

"But I went to sleep like an hour ago," I mumbled.

"You stayed up all night?"

"I couldn't really sleep."

"Because you're worried about today."

"No, not really. I'm more worried about what happens *after* today."

"Let's take one day at a time." Colin kissed my cheek. "Now get up. We're leaving soon."

"Okay. You guys hit the showers first. It will give us girls a few more minutes of sleep." I rolled over and pulled the covers over my head.

"Come on. You'll never get out of bed if you do that." Colin yanked my blanket off.

"Hey!" I yelled, waking Brittany up.

"Too loud," she muttered, putting the pillow over her head.

The overhead light turned on above us. "Get up, you two." It was Erik, but I only knew that from his voice. The bright light blinded me in my half-asleep state. "Paul is already at the lab, so the sooner we get there, the sooner we can do this."

"All right," I said, finally adjusting to the light. "But just so you know, you guys are horrible at waking people up."

"Horrible, but effective," Erik responded, nudging at Brittany as he pulled her blanket away.

We were out of the house by 5, just as Jack planned. When we got to the university, it was so dark that we couldn't even get a view of the campus. The lab was in the school of medicine. Paul had everything out and ready for us.

Erik went first. "It wasn't that bad, Sam," he said when it was done. "Just a sting. But you kept the needle in there long enough, Dad." Erik rubbed his arm.

Jack shook his head. "You're fine, Erik. Sam, you're next."

As Erik described, I felt the prick of the needle, but that was about it.

"So it's that easy to put DNA into someone?" Erik asked.

"Well, it's not quite that easy," Paul said. "Getting the DNA fragment into the cells is tricky. I won't go into how that's done. But as for the actual injection? Yes, that's all there is to it."

"That's kind of scary," I said. "I mean, think about it. You could put DNA into a shot, like a flu vaccine. You could alter the DNA of a whole population and they wouldn't even know it."

"I like how you think, Sam," Paul said, complimenting my attempt at a conspiracy theory. "And what you're saying isn't that far off from reality. In fact, what we just used is actually called a genetic vaccine. Different types of genetic vaccines are already being developed to prevent illness. But that's not to say they can't be used for something more sinister."

Jack smiled. "Okay, I think that's enough of that, Paul. Do you have the software ready to test the blood samples?"

"Yes. It's already on my computer on the desk over there." Paul pointed to the laptop he built that had no Internet connection, no webcam, and no microphone. He had loaded it with the latest gene analysis software from the university, a move that could get him fired if anyone found out. "Jack, that laptop is yours to take when you leave here."

"No, Paul. I can't take your computer. You had it specially built."

"That software on there is the latest and greatest. You'll need it to keep monitoring for changes in their DNA. Take it. It's yours."

"Well, thank you. You've done so much for us, Paul. I really can't thank you enough."

"I wish I could do more, but I just don't know enough to help them. That's all new territory." Paul kept his references to our enhanced DNA generic in case the university was listening in. He truly trusted no one.

"Is there a cafeteria around here? Or a vending machine?" Brittany asked Paul.

"Oh, yes. You can eat in any of the dining halls. Most of them are open now. Or you'll find vending machines just down the hall."

"We have some time to kill," Jack said. "We'll go have breakfast. Where's the nearest dining hall?"

"Right this way. I'll show you." Paul led us out of the lab and to the outside.

"Why don't you join us, Paul," Jack offered. "It's on me."

"No, I should really catch up on some work." Paul pointed straight ahead. "See that building over there? There's a dining hall on the main floor, off to the right. You'll see it as soon as you walk in."

"Thanks. We'll catch up with you later this morning," Jack said.

The dining hall was on the main level of one of the residence halls. Students were racing about, some already heading out of the building with their backpacks.

"You have to get up this early in college?" Brittany asked. "I thought in college you stayed up late partying and slept until noon."

"*Some* college students do that, but not the ones who are serious about their education," Jack lectured.

"I don't know, Jack," I kidded. "Uncle Dave told me some interesting stories from his years at MIT, and I'm guessing you had a part in at least some of those."

Jack blushed. "Well, that was a long time ago. I don't remember."

Erik smiled and rolled his eyes, knowing his dad was lying.

The dining hall greeted us with the smell of pancakes and maple syrup. "That food smells awesome," Colin commented as we entered. "I didn't think I was hungry. But now I'm starving."

We got in line with the students. Some came in their pajamas. Others were dressed for class. They all looked close to my age, probably freshmen or sophomores. As we waited in line, a pretty blond girl wearing a tight white t-shirt and dark jeans came up to Erik.

"Aren't you in my biology class?" she asked him.

The encounter took Erik by surprise. He'd been checking out the food, which we could see from our place in line.

"Um, no. I'm just visiting." Erik moved his eyes from the food to the girl. Standing taller than her, he could see right down the plunging v-neck of her shirt.

"I could have sworn you were in my class." The girl moved closer to him and started twirling her hair around her finger, a classic "notice-me" move that I never understood—or tried. "So do you think you'll go here?"

"I'm considering it. Along with some other colleges." Erik was playing it cool. For a guy who grew up home-schooled out in the middle of a farm field, he was very good with women. Sometimes too good.

"Well, I hope you end up here," she said, smiling up at him. She put her hand on his arm. "You know, I'd be happy to show you around campus later. And tonight some friends and I are going to a party if you wanna come along."

Jack motioned us to go through the food line. "Okay, we're all paid for."

I looked back at the girl, who was now scribbling on some paper. "Here's my number. Give me a call later. I'd love to give you that tour." She gave him a look that implied the tour would be of much more than just the campus.

Erik took the piece of paper and smiled as he watched her walk away. Colin came up and punched him in the shoulder. "Damn, man! We're here like two minutes and you've already got a girl's number? And she is hot! Too bad you can't call her."

"What a slut," Brittany muttered as she brushed past Erik, who was still staring at the pretty blond.

"Um, Erik, you're holding up the line." I yanked on his sleeve.

"Oh, yeah." He finally woke from his daze and moved forward.

During breakfast, Brittany couldn't stop talking about the food. "There's so much to choose from. I can't believe people eat this way every day." Coming from a home where food was scarce, the massive buffet was shocking to her.

"Get some more if you want," Jack said. "We're in no rush."

Colin got up from the table. "Then I'm getting back in line."

"Yeah, me, too," Erik said.

The dining hall was getting busier and the noise level was rising. Brittany sat there staring at every guy who walked by.

"Sam, you gotta see this guy who just came in. He's so hot." She stood up. "I'm gonna get back in the food line so I can get a better look at him." She started to leave then stopped. "Hey, Sam. Now Colin's getting hit on."

"What?" I quickly stood up to see past the crowd. Sure enough, some tall, pretty girl with dark hair was hitting on Colin. She had the flirtatious head tilt going and kept swinging her hair around. Then she got close to him and started whispering in his ear. Or maybe she was talking close so he could hear her above the noise. Whatever she was doing, I didn't like it. But Colin seemed to enjoy the attention. He was standing there laughing at whatever stupid things she was saying.

"What is it with these girls?" I asked Jack, who was now the only person left at the table. "First your son gets hit on. And now Colin!"

Jack didn't respond. He was completely engrossed in reading a newspaper that had been left on our table. He had no clue what was going on.

"I'll be right back." I walked over to Colin.

"Colin, we should go." I stood close to him and wrapped my arm around his.

The brunette ignored me. She backed away slightly but kept staring up at Colin.

"Anyone ever tell you that you look like that actor?" she asked. "What's his name? I can't think of it. But you totally look like him."

"Colin, come on. Your food's getting cold." I tugged on his arm.

"Yeah, okay. Nice meeting you, Katy."

"You're leaving?" She gave him the pouty lip expression. "Well, we should hook up later. My classes end at 2 today."

"Um, sorry I can't." He kept his eyes on her.

I yanked him away before either one of them could say anything else. When we got back to the table, Colin dug into his food as if nothing had happened.

"What was *that* all about?" I asked.

"What was *what* all about?"

"That girl! The one hanging all over you."

"You mean Katy? She wasn't hanging on me. She was really nice. She's studying biochemistry. You would've liked her."

"No, I don't think so. She told you she wanted to hook up later. Don't you think that's a little slutty?"

"She didn't mean that type of hook up. She just meant get together. Hang out."

"Sure she did," I muttered.

Brittany came back with another plate of food.

I looked around the dining hall. "Did you see Erik when you were up there? He's been gone forever."

She pointed behind me. "He's back there with some girl."

"That same girl?"

"No, someone else."

"Are you serious?" I got up to look for him.

"What do you care?" Brittany asked.

I sat back down again. "I don't. I just think these girls are a little aggressive."

"It's the same as back home," Jack said from behind his newspaper. "Girls are always flocking to Erik."

We sat at the dining hall for a couple hours waiting to do the first blood test. Students came and went and eventually the place quieted down. During that time, Erik had been approached by two more girls.

"Meet anyone you liked?" I asked Erik.

"Yeah, sure," he answered casually.

Colin smiled. "Bet you wish you went to school here, Erik."

"Hey, about that. Dad, I think I need to go to college. I think I could learn a lot." Erik laughed and gave Colin a look.

"I wish you could, son," Jack said, not getting their joke. "College would be good for you."

"It would be *really* good for you," Colin said, laughing.

"All right. So is it time or what?" I asked, not wanting to discuss Erik's love life anymore.

Jack looked at his watch. "Oh, yes, let's go."

We headed back to the lab. Paul was there waiting for us. Jack drew some blood from Erik and me, then went to work analyzing it. After a half hour of waiting, we were getting anxious.

"Well, any news yet?" Erik asked.

Jack sighed. "Yes, but it's not good."

12. COLLEGE TOUR

"What do you mean?" Erik stood over his dad, staring at the laptop screen.

Jack sat back, folding his arms across his chest. "Nothing is happening. There's no change. Not even a little."

"Isn't it too soon?" I asked. "We only did this a few hours ago."

"If I had only inserted the new genetic material into your cells, then yes. But the vector had the software in it as well. That software tells the cells what to do with the new genetic material. In my model, the timer slowed right away. I figured it would work a little slower in real life but not this slow. It's been several hours now. It should have at least started to work."

Paul was listening from across the room. "Jack, I wouldn't get too fixated on that model. The body reacts slowly. Just give it time."

"Yes, I know. I'm just anxious because I need this to work."

"We *all* need this to work," Erik corrected.

As we sat there waiting, a short, round man in a white lab coat walked in. "Paul, I need to schedule this lab for next week. I've got some grad students that need it on Monday and Tuesday."

Paul seemed flustered by the man's presence. "Yes, that's no problem. I'll put it on the schedule. I'll block off both days."

"Good. Thanks." The man glanced over at us. "Do you have visitors, Paul?"

"Oh, uh, yes. These are some prospective students visiting the university."

"I see. Welcome, prospective students." He smiled as he came over to shake my hand. "I'm Professor Wilkins. I work here in the genetics department with Paul."

I returned the smile. "Nice to meet you."

"And your name?" he asked.

"Oh, it's uh, Sara." I almost forgot the fake name I'd picked out.

Jack stepped in to save me. "I'm Archie Miller. I'm taking them around campus today. Sara is friends with my son, Matthew. He's over there." Erik did a quick wave. "And this is Jessica, Sara's sister. And the young man over there is Alex, my nephew."

"Very good. Are all of you from California?"

"Yes," Jack answered. "San Diego."

"Great city. So what brings you to Stanford? Are you interested in a certain program? I'm guessing someone here is considering genetics."

"Yes, Sara is," Jack replied.

The man turned back to me. "Excellent. Well, Sara, I teach mostly graduate level courses, but I can tell you about the undergraduate program."

"Paul has already given me a ton of information. But thank you for offering," I said.

"Paul does mostly cancer research. He focuses on a very specific type of gene therapy. Is that what you're interested in?"

"Yes," I answered, getting more nervous with each question.

"Well, that's one option. But just so you know, my area of research is really an up-and-coming field of study. It might change your mind."

"Um, okay. What is it?"

"It's called epigenetics. Do you know what that is?"

"I've heard of it, but I'm not really sure what it is." I knew exactly what it was but figured I should let the guy explain it to me.

"It's the study of how and when genes are expressed. You see, genes aren't always turned on. Chemical reactions controlled by genetic switches actually turn genes on and off at strategic times. For instance, how does a cell know that it should be a liver cell and not a skin cell? Genetic switches! The genetic switch tells the body to make a liver cell instead of a skin cell. But only when the switch for that section of the gene is turned on."

"That's very interesting." His explanation was so basic I felt like a child. Growing up with a father who taught genetics, I had learned about these switches years ago. And I'd experienced their effects firsthand when I was held prisoner at GlobalLife. If only he knew.

"I'm working on a big project right now. If you end up in our program here, there's a good chance that you could help a grad student work on it."

"What's the project?" Jack asked.

"I can't go into all of the details, but it has to do with these genetic switches and their effect on health. It's funded by a grant from GlobalLife Genetics. Have you heard of them?"

Jack tried not to react. "Yes, I believe I have. They're an international company, right?"

"Yes. Their headquarters are in Sweden. I've actually been there. Beautiful facilities. And their technology is simply amazing. At least what I was allowed to see."

Paul walked over to us. "I'm sorry to interrupt, but they're scheduled for a tour soon."

"Oh, certainly. Go ahead. I didn't mean to take up all your time. My office is just down the hall if you have any questions for me, Sara." Professor Wilkins left.

Paul closed the door, then raced over to Jack. "Remember when I said I had some suspicions about my colleagues? He's the one I was most worried about. He's been working on GlobalLife research for years."

"We should get out of here in case he comes back," Erik said.

"Yes. And Jack, you need to be at the Student Health Center at 11," Paul reminded him.

Jack checked his watch. "Oh, right. I didn't realize it was so late."

"Student Health Center? Why are we going there?" I asked.

"Paul has a friend who works there. A medical doctor. I'm having him check Colin over."

"What?" Colin stood up. "When were you gonna tell me this?"

"I wasn't thinking about it until just now."

"I'm not sick! I feel fine."

"You almost died a few days ago, Colin." Jack sounded like a concerned father. "And we're not getting on the road tomorrow until you're checked out. I don't want another incident like last time. I want the doctor to look at your injuries. Make sure you're healing okay."

"But I told you. I feel fine. I don't need to go—"

"Colin, please just do it," I urged. "It would make me feel tons better if you did. It's one less thing I have to worry about."

Colin sighed. "So how long is this gonna take?"

"Not long." Jack shook his head. "I swear, you and Erik are like little kids. He's afraid of shots. You're afraid of the doctor."

Brittany laughed. "Colin has to go to the doctor," she sang in a kid voice.

Colin's checkup took about a half hour. When it was over, Jack talked to the doctor briefly, then we went out for lunch.

"See, that wasn't so bad, Colin," Jack kidded.

"I didn't need to go. The doctor said I was fine."

"You got stitches because the cut on your forehead's not healing," Jack pointed out. "I hardly call that fine."

"You got stitches? Let me see." I brushed Colin's hair aside to see a row of fresh stitches.

"And his other cuts were starting to get infected," Jack added. "Which reminds me, I have to stop at the drugstore later."

Colin was getting annoyed. "Can we talk about something else now?"

After lunch, we headed back to the lab for more blood work. Then we waited as Jack analyzed the results. Paul was off teaching his afternoon class.

Around 2 we heard the door open. It was Professor Wilkins again. "Hey, you're back. How was the tour?"

Jack slowly closed the laptop. "It was very informative. You have a lovely campus here. They were all very impressed."

Wilkins sat down in Paul's chair. "It's the largest contiguous campus in America. Did they tell you that on the tour?"

"Yes, they did," Jack lied.

"Good. So what brings you back to the genetics department?"

"I'm actually friends with Paul, so we're just killing some time here. We have an appointment at the college of business later this afternoon."

"Oh? Who with?"

Jack froze. "Um, I don't remember. I'd have to look it up."

"I know several professors over there. Was it Professor Jamison? Or Kendoff? Myerson?"

"No, those names don't sound right."

It was my turn to save Jack. "Hey, Archie. I wanted to go see some of the artwork she talked about on the tour. Can we do that now?"

Jack looked relieved. "Yes. That's right. We should go see that artwork."

"Okay. Well, nice seeing you all again." The professor finally got up and headed down the hall.

I watched to make sure he was really gone. "That was weird. Why would he come in here again?"

Jack opened his laptop. "Okay. I have some good news. There is a tiny amount of change in the timer. It's beginning to feel the effects of the new DNA and the software. It's still not reacting the same as my computer model, but at least it appears to be disrupting the timer sequence."

"That's great, right?" Colin, the most optimistic of any of us, was smiling from ear to ear. The rest of us sat there, unimpressed. It would take more than a "tiny change" in the timer to get us excited.

Brittany got up. "We should get out of here in case that guy comes back."

"Yes, but I need to do one more round of testing later on, before we head back to Paul's house."

"Why don't we just go back there now?" Erik suggested. "You can do the test at his house."

Jack thought about it. "I guess I could. I was doing the tests here in case this new software fails and I need to reload it. But it seems to be working without any problems. So we can go. Let me leave a note for Paul."

"Before we leave, could we do a quick walk around the campus?" I asked Jack. "I did the tour last fall but, well, I was supposed to go here in a few months, and since I can't now—"

"You don't have to explain." Jack put his arm around me. "Of course we can see the campus, Sam. You can take as long as you need."

We spent an hour walking around, seeing the giant sculptures outside, and checking out some of the buildings. I felt a lump in my throat as I remembered being there with Mom and Dad. I was so excited when I got that acceptance letter. As soon as I read it, I saw myself living in the dorms, sitting in the lecture halls, and combing through all the great books in the library.

"You fit right in here, Sam," Colin said as we strolled through the middle of campus on our way back to the van. Erik, Brittany, and Jack were ahead of us. "I can see why you were so excited to go here."

I noticed all the students scattered around the lawn reading books. "Yeah, I would've really liked it. But it's not gonna happen now."

"I bet you'll go here someday, Sam."

"I bet I won't."

"Hey, wait." Colin stopped. "That's a good idea. Let's make a bet."

"There's nothing to bet because I know I'm not going here."

"Just give me a minute to think."

"Come on, Colin. We have to get to the van."

"Okay, I got it. I know what we can bet."

"All right. I'm all ears."

"If you end up going here, which I admit is a HUGE long shot, then," he paused, "you have to marry me."

"What?!" I said it so loud that Erik and Brittany both glanced back at us. I waved them on. "What did you just say?" I asked, much quieter this time.

He smiled. "You heard me."

"Um, okay. And if I don't go to Stanford—the chances of which are about 99.99%—then what happens?"

"You get to *choose* to marry me. You can say yes or no."

I laughed. "Great, thanks for giving me the option."

"You're welcome. So is it a deal?"

"Colin, that's crazy! Plus you know I'm not going here."

"Then it works in your favor. You get a choice."

"Wait a minute. So are you asking me to—"

Colin interrupted. "Do you see a ring anywhere?"

I felt myself blushing. "No."

"Then for now, it's just a bet. Shake on it." He put his hand out.

"This is insane. But okay. It's a bet." I shook his hand and the deal was done.

On the way back to Paul's house I went over the whole bet thing in my head. Had Colin planned that? It seemed so out of the blue. He couldn't have. But Brittany made those comments about him wanting to marry me. So maybe he was tossing the idea out there to see how I'd respond. Maybe he was now certain I was going to die soon and decided to propose. Just thinking about it was making me stressed. I was too young to die *or* get married.

An hour later, it was time to run more tests on Erik and me. Jack worked on analyzing the results while the rest of us made dinner. Although we'd made dinner together all week, we still weren't very good at it. In fact, watching the four of us try to cook a meal was completely comical. The kitchen was only big enough for one or two people, so we were constantly bumping into each other.

"What's going on in there?" Jack yelled after hearing us drop yet another pan.

"Nothing, Dad," Erik called back.

Brittany started laughing, which made everyone laugh.

Jack came into the kitchen holding his laptop. "Well, I've got some results back. And it looks like the timer is finally slowing the way I predicted it would."

I went up to see the laptop screen. "That's great! How much is it slowing? Can you tell?"

"I haven't measured it yet. It's better to wait and give it more time. I'm guessing it will slow even more."

Colin walked in from outside with a platter of chicken. He was stuck on grill-duty again.

"Colin, the timer is slowing just like Jack predicted," I told him.

He set his platter down and gave me a hug. "Sam, that's awesome!"

As we celebrated, Paul walked in. Jack gave him the good news.

"Jack, I'm so happy it worked," Paul said. "I didn't mean to be a downer, but you never know about those computer models. And I didn't want you to get your hopes too high."

"No worries," Jack assured him. "You were just being a good scientist. Well, it looks like dinner's ready so I'll go put the laptop away."

Paul smiled. "Wow. Dinner's ready when I get home? I hate to see you guys leave tomorrow. I'm going to miss all of you."

"Believe me. A few more days with four teenagers, you wouldn't be saying that," Jack kidded as he left the kitchen.

"Hey!" Brittany protested.

After dinner, we all played a trivia game that Paul had stashed away in a closet. Jack didn't want us talking or thinking about the alien DNA or the timer. And playing the game did just that. At least for those couple of hours.

Since Paul would be at work by the time we left on Friday, we thanked him and said our goodbyes before heading to bed.

The next morning, Jack ran another round of tests on Erik and me. The analysis showed that the timer was still slowing at the same pace as the night before.

We packed up the van, then left Paul's house and headed into town. We had to get some supplies for the road, including the things Jack needed to take care of Colin's stitched-up forehead. Jack spotted a bookstore and decided to buy a few newly released conspiracy theory books for Paul.

"We're so close to campus, I'm going to drop them off rather than try to mail them later," Jack decided. "He doesn't have class until 10. It'll be a nice surprise for him."

When we got to the genetics department, Paul wasn't in the lab. We checked his classroom; it was dark.

"He probably just stepped out," Jack surmised. "Let's go back to the lab and wait a few minutes."

We waited but Paul didn't show.

Jack checked his watch. "It's almost 10. Erik, go down and see if he's in the classroom. He's gotta be there by now."

Erik went to the classroom but was back right away. "It's still dark in there. Maybe they moved the class. Or canceled it."

Jack got up and searched for a pen. "I'll just leave the books here and attach a note. We can't keep waiting. We need to get on the road."

As Jack was writing the note, Professor Wilkins came racing in, flustered. "What are you doing here?"

Jack looked up from his note. "Oh, hello. We're heading out of town and wanted to say goodbye to Paul."

Wilkins gave us a strange look. "Haven't you heard the news?"

13. SIDE EFFECTS

"What news?" Erik asked.

"The news about Paul," Wilkins answered. "I can't believe you didn't—"

"What happened?" Jack interrupted.

"When Paul came in this morning, he wasn't feeling well." Wilkins' speech was fast and a little shaky. "I was talking to him and he seemed disoriented. He didn't look good. But he insisted that he was fine. I came back later to check on him and I found him here on the floor." Wilkins pointed to an area about a foot from where he was standing. "He wasn't responding so I called the ambulance right away. They were here within minutes and took him to the hospital."

"What hospital? Give me the number," Jack demanded. "I need to find out what—"

"No," Wilkins said. "That's not necessary. The hospital already called here. About an hour ago."

"And?" Jack asked anxiously.

"They said Paul had a brain aneurysm." Wilkins hesitated. "And I'm sorry to have to tell you this but . . . well, he didn't make it."

Jack slumped into a chair, too shocked to stand.

"I'm sorry. I thought you knew." Wilkins seemed on edge. I was getting a weird vibe from him.

I glanced over at Erik. *"Erik, do you feel that?"* I thought to him.

"Yes, there's something he's not saying. Let's see what he's thinking."

Erik and I focused on Wilkins' mind. He was standing right in front of me so his thoughts were loud and clear.

"I've gotta get out of here! I'm a horrible liar. These people will see the guilt on my face! I can't believe I did this! I do their research. I keep quiet. Isn't that enough? How could they force me to kill a man? A friend! Just because they found out he had some file? What the hell was in that file that was worth killing a man for?"

My heart began to race as I realized what Wilkins had done to Paul. I listened for more, but Wilkins turned to leave.

"Well, thank you for telling us," Jack said, still in shock.

Wilkins nodded at Jack, then quickly walked out. As he raced down the hall, I continued to hear his thoughts. *"The police will never believe who was really behind this. I'll be the one they come after! My career is over! Why did I have to keep working with GlobalLife? I knew all that money would only get me into trouble."*

I watched as Wilkins sprinted out of the building. I could no longer hear his thoughts.

Erik searched the room for hidden cameras. Hidden microphones were also a possibility. "Dad, get up."

Jack didn't move. He was white as a ghost. Erik grabbed a piece of paper from Paul's desk and scribbled something on it. He handed it to Jack.

Jack read it, then bolted from his chair. "We should go." Brittany and Erik gave him a strange look. He shot them a look back that made it clear they were not to speak. We all left the building in silence and didn't speak again until we were in the van.

Once we were on the road, Jack started asking questions. "Now what exactly did you hear, Erik?"

"That Professor Wilkins somehow did this to Paul. He didn't say how he did it. Could have been an injection of something. I don't know."

"So that's why we raced out of there?" Colin asked. "You're saying that the professor guy killed Paul?"

Brittany gasped. "Seriously? That's awful. I liked Paul. He was so nice."

"And Wilkins said GlobalLife made him do it," Jack confirmed. "Are you sure about that, Erik?"

"Yes. Well, he said something about GlobalLife. I can't remember exactly how he said it."

"He said that he had done all this research for them and kept quiet," I explained, filling in the story. "And he said they made him do it because they found out Paul had a file. It has to be that file we just opened. But how did they know?"

Jack sped down an on-ramp to the interstate. "We have to get away from here. This is proof that GlobalLife is watching that whole place. The lab. Paul's office. Who knows? They could have been watching his house. Those helicopters the other day? They probably *were* from GlobalLife."

"Dad, slow down. I see cops ahead." The police were over a mile away but Erik could see them with his enhanced vision.

Jack slowed down. "Keep a lookout for more of them."

"If GlobalLife knew we were there, they would've come and got us," I pointed out.

Jack shook his head. "We don't know who was watching. It's a huge corporation. If there were people from GlobalLife watching Paul or Professor Wilkins, those people may not even know about you and Erik. I told you, GlobalLife only lets a small group of employees in on these high-level projects."

"So that's good, right?" Erik asked. "If they don't know about us then it's not a big deal if they saw us."

"I'm worried that GlobalLife had a camera planted in Paul's lab. If so, the main security offices at GlobalLife will review the video. Someone there will recognize us."

"But Paul would have known about a camera," I said. "He told us he checked that room for cameras all the time."

"Yes. But they could have placed the cameras there last night, knowing this was going to happen to Paul. I'm sure that GlobalLife is monitoring Paul's lab today to see who shows up looking for him. And since we were the first ones there after his death, I know they'll be trying to identity us. We should have never gone back there this morning."

"Why would they wanna kill him?" Brittany asked.

Jack sighed. "Sounds like they found out he had that file. But the fact that this happened at the same time we were there has me very concerned. It could be a coincidence, but I just don't know."

We drove for several more hours, heading east through California. Eventually Jack stopped for gas. "I need one of you to drive for a while."

Erik tried to read Jack's face. "Are you all right, Dad?"

Jack seemed to be in a fog. "I need some time to think this through. Paul's death. Or murder is more like it. I just don't know what it means. Is it a message for us? Do they know where we are? Are they following us right now?"

Colin volunteered to drive. Jack went back to the third-row seat. Erik stayed in the passenger seat and Brittany and I sat behind him.

We got back on the interstate and I tried connecting with Erik's mind. *Erik? Are you listening? You should probably talk to your dad. He seems really upset about losing his friend.*

"It's more than that. I think . . . worried that . . . next."

"What did you say? Your thoughts were cut off."

"He's worried . . . next."

"Erik, I'm only getting part of what you're thinking."

"That's . . . because . . . part . . . saying."

I tapped Erik on the shoulder. "I can't hear what you're thinking."

"Yeah, same here. You keep cutting out. It's like when we were trying to hear Brittany and Colin the other day and that helicopter went by."

"It could be cell tower interference," I suggested.

"We always have cell towers around us. That's never affected us before. Let's try again."

"Can you . . . me . . . now?" Erik smiled at me as he imitated an old cell phone commercial.

"No. I only heard a few of the words." I thought back to him. "Did you hear any of that?" I asked him out loud.

"I heard 'no', 'few,' and 'words,'" Erik said.

"And I only heard part of what *you* said."

Erik turned back around as we both thought of possible explanations.

I nudged his shoulder again. "Erik. Is there something in the van that could cause some type of interference?"

"What are you thinking?"

"Well, maybe I'm being overly cautious after what happened, but what about that laptop Paul gave us? What if it's bugged? Sending out a signal? Or what if someone put something on or in the van?"

Erik bolted out of his seat and crawled back to where his dad was sitting. "Erik?" I looked behind me. "What are you doing?"

He was talking quietly to his dad, likely telling him my theory. Jack got the laptop from behind his seat and starting taking it apart. After a few minutes, he put the laptop back together. Erik shook his head at me, indicating there was nothing in it.

"Colin, pull off at the next exit," Jack said. "I need to check something."

When we stopped, Jack checked under the van, under the hood, and anywhere else a locator or listening device could be hidden. Then he got back in the van. "Well, it's all clean. But that was a good idea, Sam. It was worth checking. Colin, do you want to keep driving?"

"Sure, no problem." Colin stayed in the driver's seat and Erik sat next to him.

Jack took the back seat again. "We're driving till we get to Minnesota. No stops, except for meal and restroom breaks. So everyone will have to take a turn at the wheel."

I looked over at Brittany, who wasn't listening. She'd put her headphones back on and was staring out window.

"I've got a road game if you guys are interested," I said to Erik and Colin.

"Sure," Colin answered.

"Okay, I'm in," Erik said.

"Well, it's kind of stupid but we've got nothing else to do. It's like a scavenger hunt. We each make a list of things for the other person to look for. So for example, if I'm making Colin's list, I could say that he has to find a purple convertible, a black minivan, a car that has beads hanging from the rear view mirror, and so on. First one to check off all the items wins. Got it?"

"Yeah," they both said.

"Okay. I'll make the lists. Let me get some paper."

"Wait a minute," Colin said. "You both have like, superhero vision and can see miles ahead. That's not fair."

"Then you can make the lists for Sam and me," Erik suggested. "Make them extra hard."

Colin agreed, coming up with items for both Erik and me to find. I made the list for Colin. We started the game and Colin found two items right away, which irritated Erik.

"Sam, you made his list too easy," Erik complained.

Colin smiled. "Because she wants me to win, don't you, sweetie?"

Erik looked back at me. "Sam, did you rig the game in his favor?"

"No. He's just lucky."

"There! Right there! A car without a hubcap!" Colin exclaimed. "Now I got three!"

Erik shook his head. "That's it. No more Mr. Nice Guy. I haven't been using my distance vision to look ahead, but that's over now."

"Bring it on, my friend," Colin kidded. "Bring it on."

I rolled my eyes at their competitiveness. "It's just a game, you guys."

Erik sat up straight. "So I need a car with Alaska plates." He leaned forward toward the front window, then sat back and rubbed his eyes.

Colin laughed. "What's wrong there, partner? That superhero vision not working for you today?"

Erik leaned forward again. "Huh, I guess it's not." He rubbed his eyes, then opened them again. "I can only read the plates on the cars right ahead of us. Usually I can read them from at least a mile away. Hey, Sam, how far can you see?"

"I don't know. I wasn't trying to look that far. I was just looking in the area around the van to make it fair for Colin."

"I told you she wants me to win," Colin said to further annoy Erik.

"I'll try looking farther out." I hadn't practiced using my vision skills much. In order to see really far, I had to imagine my eyes and mind connecting. I focused on a car about a mile away. But after multiple attempts, it still looked blurry. I focused on another car. Still blurry.

Erik was getting impatient. "Sam, how far can you see?"

"I can only see what a person with regular vision would see."

"Yeah. Me, too."

"Does it come and go?" Colin asked. "Or do you have to do something to make it work?"

"You have to focus, but that's it," I responded.

"Kid with a balloon in the car!" Colin yelled. "Got another one!"

"Okay. You win," Erik declared. "Game over. Maybe I'm just tired. I'm gonna sleep for a few hours." He went to the back of the van next to Jack.

I went to sleep, too. I woke up four hours later. It was dark out and Colin was still driving. I decided to test my vision again, this time my night vision. I looked out at the dark road. Normally I could see perfectly in the dark. This time everything remained pitch-black. I closed my eyes and tried again. Still nothing but darkness. I didn't want to worry anyone so I kept quiet about it.

"Colin, let's stop at the next food exit." Jack's voice startled me. He leaned up behind my seat. "We'll get something to eat and switch drivers."

It was another half hour before we reached an exit. Our only option was a truck stop restaurant, but we didn't care. Everyone just wanted a break from the van.

During dinner, I tried mind-talking to Erik again, but it didn't work. Our telepathy problems seemed to be getting worse.

Erik was sitting next to me. He leaned over and talked quietly. "I told my dad we were having problems with it. He's gonna run some tests after dinner."

"Where? In the van?" I asked.

"He just needs to draw some blood." The waitress was back at our table with the check. "Let's talk later."

Before getting back on the road, Jack took some blood samples from Erik and me. Then Erik drove while Jack analyzed the results. Brittany went to sleep on the second-row seat, leaving Colin and I in the seat behind her.

"So what does he think is wrong?" Colin asked.

"I don't know but I'm not gonna worry about it. We've had enough bad news today with Paul. I don't need any more."

"Here, why don't you go to sleep." Colin put his arm up so I could lean against his chest.

"No, it'll hurt you. You're still too bruised up."

"It's okay. This is my good side. Come on." As I rested on him, he kissed my head and gently rubbed my arm. The van was getting cold and his warm chest felt good. It put me right to sleep.

Hours later I was still in the same spot. Colin was tapping my arm. "Sam, wake up. Jack needs to talk to you."

"What time is it?"

"It's 9:30."

I sat up next to Colin. Jack was in the seat in front of me.

"What is it? Is something wrong?"

Jack turned back. He had the laptop open in front of him. "Yes. Putting that DNA in you and Erik has slowed the timer, but it came with a few side effects."

14. LUKE'S JOURNAL

"I probably don't want to hear this, do I?" I leaned over the seat. "What it is now?"

"Well, the DNA continues to disrupt the timer. You can see that right here." Jack pointed to the screen, which showed a bunch of coding. He scrolled down. "But then if you look here, you can see that it's also affected the switches in your DNA that give you your abilities. It's trying to turn them off."

"So my abilities will go away?"

"If it continues like this, then yes. Erik said you already noticed them weakening."

"Yeah. I'm having trouble hearing his thoughts. Both of us have lost the ability to see far away. And I've lost my night vision."

"If it's happening that fast, then in a few days, you may no abilities left. Same for Erik."

"Are there other side effects?" Colin asked.

"Not that I can tell," Jack replied. "Just the loss of abilities."

I noticed Erik was still up front driving. "How did Erik react to the news? He's had these abilities his whole life. It's gotta be strange for him to not have them anymore."

"Yes but he'd rather have more time than have his abilities. Still, it'll be an adjustment for him. You two should talk later." Jack turned back toward the front of the van and continued working on the laptop.

Colin slipped his hand in mine and rested it on the seat. "How do you feel about this?"

"Okay. I only had my abilities for a few weeks. So I guess now I'll just go back to being normal."

"You were starting to like them, weren't you?"

"Kind of. They made me feel a little safer. Like I might be able to protect myself."

"I can tell you're gonna miss the telepathy the most."

"Why do you say that?"

Colin lowered his voice so Jack wouldn't hear. "Because you can talk to Erik without people listening."

It was true that the telepathy was my favorite ability. And it *was* because I could talk to Erik. But how did Colin know that? Was it that obvious?

"I really don't talk to Erik that much. I mean, with my mind."

"Yeah, you do. I can tell when you and Erik are doing the mind-talk thing. I knew you two were doing it today, before it stopped working."

"Does it bother you?"

"Yeah, actually it does," he admitted. "It's like you guys have this secret language or something. And I don't want Erik taking advantage of that. I mean, seriously, did you think I believed Erik when he said that crap about seeing you as his little sister? But I trust you, Sam. So I don't make a big deal about it."

The van was coming to a stop. Erik had pulled off the interstate and parked at a gas station.

I leaned up and tapped Jack on the shoulder. "Hey, Jack, I can drive. I've been sleeping for hours. I'm wide awake."

"All right. But I need to get some gas before we take off again."

Everyone piled out of the van. Erik and I stood outside while the rest of them went in the gas station to use the restroom.

"So what do you think?" I asked Erik.

"About our abilities? I'm kinda bummed to tell ya the truth."

"Yeah. Me, too."

"I've had them for so long that it's weird to think they're going away. I always thought having them made me some kind of freak. But then I met you and I started to think it was cool that I could do this stuff. Plus, I finally had someone to talk to, telepathically I mean."

"Yeah, I'm gonna miss that," I confessed.

"I know. I'm gonna miss that one the most." He paused. "We could get them back someday."

"How would that happen?"

"You know the part of our DNA that has the missing base codes? My dad was saying that if those were filled in, the timer would stop and our abilities would be restored."

"But we'll never get those base codes," I reminded him. "You can't exactly buy alien genes at your local drugstore."

"Yeah, I know." Erik's voice trailed off and I immediately knew that I'd said the wrong thing.

I nudged Erik's arm. "Hey, I don't know why I said that. There's always a chance that—"

"I should use the restroom before we go."

"But wait—"

Erik left before I could say anything more.

We got back on the interstate. I was driving and Colin sat next to me. "Do you need me to keep you awake? Pick a topic. I can talk about anything."

"That's all right, Colin. I'm not tired. You can sleep if you want."

"Okay, maybe just a couple hours. But wake me up if you want me to drive."

Within an hour, everyone was asleep. There were hardly any cars on the road. Occasionally a semi would startle me as it roared past on its way downhill. The silent van gave me time to think. My thoughts kept going over all the sad things that had happened that day. Losing Paul. Losing my abilities. Losing my communication with Erik. It was a day of losses.

The past few months had been such a roller coaster of good and bad. The good was finding Brittany. And Erik. And seeing Colin again. But there were also so many bad things that had happened. My parents' deaths being the worst. I found it ironic that some of the best moments in my life had occurred during the absolute worst time of my life.

I kept driving into the morning. As the sun began to rise everyone started to wake up. I heard Jack's voice from the back of the van. "Sam, have you been driving all night? We need to stop. Get off at the next exit."

Colin was waking up beside me. "Where are we, Sam?"

"Wyoming. We're almost in Nebraska."

Colin checked the view from the window. "I've been asleep that long?"

I stopped at a large travel center. Jack got out of the van and came over to the driver's side. "Why didn't you wake someone, Sam? I didn't want you driving all night. That's a dangerous stretch of road."

"I felt good so I kept going. Besides, I practically had the road to myself. And we haven't hit any weather problems."

We were extremely fortunate that it had been the driest and mildest winter on record for the middle of the country. Normally, that stretch of road would be nearly impossible to drive on during that time of the year.

Jack opened the door, motioning me to get out. "I'll take over driving now. Everyone up. Take a restroom break. And we might as well get some food while we're here."

After our brief stop, we hit the road again. I went to the back of the van to sleep. When I got up, we were almost through Nebraska. I heard Erik digging through some boxes behind my seat.

"What are you doing back there?" I asked him.

"Going through Luke's stuff. Can you move over?"

I sat up, giving Erik a place to sit. He set the box down between us.

"Luke didn't have much," Erik said, sifting through the box.

"Well, it sounded like he moved around a lot."

Erik picked up one of Luke's surfing trophies, then tossed it back in the box. "I wonder how long he lived like that. He was basically homeless."

"We don't know that. All we know is that he was living with that guy. Before that, he could have been living with someone else."

"If he had a home, he wouldn't have asked the old man if he could stay there. And he would have had more stuff than this."

Erik took a book from the box. "It's a surfer's guide. Lists all the best beaches for waves. He's got stars by some of them, like he was rating them."

As Erik flipped through the book, a photo fell out. He didn't notice so I picked it up. There was a nice-looking young couple in the photo. They were smiling and the man and woman each held a baby. It was an old photo and had yellowed a little. It'd been folded and the crease had distorted part of the image. I looked closer at the faces of the man and woman. They looked familiar. Very familiar. The man looked just like Erik, but about 10 years older. The woman had Erik's eyes and smile.

"Look at this photo, Erik. It fell out of that surfer's guide."

Erik put the book aside. "Yeah, it's an old photo. So what?"

"Look at the man in the photo. Don't you think he looks familiar?"

Erik looked but didn't react.

"Erik, he looks just like you. Well, like you in 10 years. And the woman. She has your eyes. Don't you see the resemblance?"

He held the photo up to the window. "No, not really."

"And they have two babies. Twins. Do you get what I'm saying?"

"Yeah. And they're not my parents, Sam. Why would Luke have a photo of our parents?"

"But they look just like you."

Erik checked the photo again. "Okay, so they look a little like me. But it doesn't matter. Even if it is them, what do I care? They were part of the GlobalLife project. They gave their kids to a corporation. Like I really want to think about them, Sam." He tossed the photo back in the box.

"But Erik, don't you want to keep that somewhere?"

"Hey, check this out." Erik picked up a small leather-bound book with a string tied around it.

"It looks like some type of journal. Open it up, Erik."

He undid the string and looked inside. "There's a bunch of equations in here. Math equations."

I scooted over to see what he was looking at. "That's not basic math, Erik. That's like really advanced math."

"I know. I used to work on stuff like this back in Texas. It was kind of a hobby. Some people do crossword puzzles. I figure out math problems. I know, it's nerdy."

"It's not nerdy." His genius math skills only made me more attracted to him.

"Hey, you know what this looks like?" Erik reached behind the seat for his dad's computer bag. He pulled out the envelope that Paul had given us. "This code I solved." Erik turned over the envelope to look at the handwritten code on the front. "I think the same code is here in Luke's journal. Yeah, look. It's the same."

I compared the two codes and sure enough, they were an exact match. "Why would Luke have that same code? That's impossible."

Erik took a minute to think. "That IT security guy who left this envelope for Paul. What was his name? Dan something? He must have somehow known Luke. But how?"

"I don't know, Erik, but this is freaking me out. Why would they know each other?"

"Dan probably saw something about Luke in the files at GlobalLife. And if they had been in contact with each other and if Paul was right about GlobalLife following Dan, or I guess, killing Dan, then—"

"GlobalLife was also tracking Luke. Which means your brother's death may not have been an accident."

We sat there, trying to think of any other possibilities.

"Paul said that Dan died months ago," Erik said. "If GlobalLife really did kill Luke, why did they wait so long to do it?"

"Maybe Dan told Luke about you and Luke tried finding you. If that were true, GlobalLife would want to follow him to see if you really were alive. After a few months, Luke probably gave up looking and that's when the accident happened. He knew too much for GlobalLife to leave him alone."

Erik searched the box for other clues. "There's nothing else in here. Just his surfing trophies."

I flipped through the leather journal. "How could he be so smart in math? With his lifestyle, he must've missed a lot of school and probably didn't even graduate."

"Some people have a talent for math. I always have. It comes natural to me. I guess he was the same way."

"Erik, did you see the other codes in here?" I showed him a page in the journal that had several more codes.

"No. I didn't see those. Let me work on them and I'll see what they say."

While Erik did that, I went up and sat with Brittany, who was complaining to Jack. "This van is starting to stink, Jack. Can't we stop and spend the night somewhere so we can shower?"

"We're almost in Iowa. We're not that far, now. We'll be in Minnesota by evening, then we'll get a motel where everyone can clean up."

Brittany folded her arms. "Then we need an air freshener. Or make Colin and Erik change clothes."

Colin shot a look back at her. "Me? I don't stink. Why are you blaming the guys? Maybe you girls stink."

"Hey, there." Their argument was making Jack laugh. "Nobody stinks. I'll get one of those scented pine trees at the next gas station."

Brittany made a face. "No. I hate those things. They stink even worse. I'd open a window but it's freezing out."

"That reminds me. We need to get winter coats," Jack said. "The weather forecast for Minnesota is for highs in the forties."

Colin laughed. "The forties? Sam and I would wear shorts in that weather!"

"No, you wouldn't," Brittany insisted. "Nobody would. That's freezing."

Colin turned to her. "Just wait. If it's that warm in February, you'll see Minnesota people wearing shorts."

"Well, we're still getting coats," Jack said. "At least us Texans are. I'm guessing there's a store or two off this exit. Might as well stop here."

Jack took us to a thrift store that was right off the interstate exit. Everyone picked out coats, hats, and gloves. Brittany protested about wearing "used" clothes, although I knew that she'd probably worn thrift store clothes her whole life.

We got on the road again and were now only 6 hours away from my old hometown. I was getting excited even though I knew going back would be dangerous. I'd been all over the country the past week and seen some beautiful places, but I still missed Minnesota, the only place I knew as home.

"Jack, where are we going to stay when we get there?" I asked.

"I was going to ask you and Colin for suggestions. We need to be outside of town, someplace small, no chain hotels."

Colin looked back at me. "There's that motel off county road 10. That one with the big wooden sign? Remember that, Sam? I don't even know if it's in a town."

"Yeah, I know which one you're talking about. That would be a good place. And it even has a pay phone out front for Jack," I kidded.

"That's right, it does." Colin crawled back to where I was sitting. "Are you getting nervous about going back?"

"No. Well, yes, because of GlobalLife. But I miss home. I wish we could go to my house or go see Allie."

Jack overheard us talking. "Listen, Sam. We can't risk driving by your old house or anywhere near where your friends hang out. Same for you, Colin. Your parents will be looking for you."

"Probably not," Colin said. "Before I was drugged, that guy from GlobalLife said he left a fake message with them using my voice. They, or the fake me, told my parents that I took off to go search for Sam."

"Well, we can't be sure they believed that," Jack said.

"I'm pretty sure they did. Right before GlobalLife took me, I had this huge fight with my dad because I wanted to go look for Sam and he wouldn't let me. I'm sure he thinks I just took off. I'm 18. When he was 18, he ran off with my mom. He probably thinks like father, like son."

"You didn't tell me you had a fight with your dad about me," I whispered to Colin.

"Don't worry about it," he whispered back.

Jack glanced back at us in the rear view mirror. "Sam, that professor we're going to see. Do you have any idea where he lives?"

"No. I only met him that one time after the memorial service."

"Then hopefully he'll be listed in the phone book so we can find his house."

Colin smiled. "Phone book? What's a phone book?"

Jack didn't answer, just shook his head.

"I figured out one of these codes." Erik crawled over the seats, landing up front next to Jack. He had a piece of paper with him. "You're not gonna believe what this says."

15. DIRECTIONS

Jack looked confused. "What code? What are you talking about?"

Erik briefly explained what we had found in Luke's journal.

"This is very concerning," Jack said. "How could they be connected? How would Dan know Luke?"

"I don't know, Dad. But listen. There's this other code in Luke's journal that's like the one I figured out at Paul's house."

"Yeah, so what does it say?" I asked.

He held up the paper he'd used to work out the code. "'Erik Reid. Comfort, Texas.'"

Jack snatched the piece of paper from Erik. "It even has the correct spelling of your name! So Luke knew about you?"

"Yeah. It's almost like he wanted to find me. But he wrote my name in code so nobody would know."

Jack tossed the paper on the floor of the van. "But who would have told him about you? It had to be Dan. But how would Dan know that you're alive? And how did he know the name I gave you? That information wasn't in the GlobalLife files. Dan found out some other way. Someone else told him about you. And then Dan must have told Luke. Either that or Luke found out some other way. This is very bad, Erik. There's someone else out there who knows you exist and knows your real name."

"Maybe GlobalLife told Luke my name. Maybe they were trying to get Luke to find me so they could capture us both. GlobalLife knows about me because of what happened at the trailer. You said those guards were wearing recording devices that link up to GlobalLife security. So they knew my name from the recording."

"But Luke died before any of that happened," Jack said. "So someone knew about you before the trailer incident. Luke made that code weeks or maybe months ago. Were there other codes in there?"

"Yeah, and I started figuring out another one. But I must have done something wrong. The numbers should stand for letters, like in the other code, but instead I got a mix of numbers and letters."

"The numbers could be the message," I suggested. "They could be an address."

Erik looked at the piece of paper again. "It doesn't sound like an address. What I ended up with was 64D09N."

"Sounds like a locker combination," Brittany said, "or the combination to a safe."

"There's another code in the journal," Erik said. "Let me see what that one says." Erik got to work while the rest of us tried to come up with possible meanings for the strange sequence of numbers and letters. Within the hour, Erik had finished the other code. "This one is also a mix of numbers and letters. It's 21D57W."

"Oooh, I got it. It's a license plate number." Brittany suggested.

"Hmm, maybe," Jack said, "but I feel like it's something else."

Colin leaned up front. "Hey, Jack, your exit is coming up. I-35 North. That's what you need for Minnesota."

"Oh, yes, thank you. I would have missed that."

We were in Des Moines now, the city where I'd ditched that truck driver and met up with Ruby and the bus to Texas. That whole event seemed so long ago even though it had only been a few weeks.

For the rest of the drive, Erik and Jack sat up front discussing their theories about Luke. They ended up with no conclusions, but I could tell Jack was getting even more concerned. Someone knew about his son, and it didn't seem to be someone from GlobalLife. It was someone else. And the fact that he didn't know who they were or why they had an interest in Erik was making Jack a nervous wreck.

We finally reached the outskirts of the Minnesota town where Colin and I grew up. Colin showed Jack the way to the motel. It was kind of a dump, but the only other options were either too close to town or too far away. And we were so desperate to get out of the van that we didn't care about the condition of the motel. We just wanted a hot shower and some dinner.

After we cleaned up and ate, everyone met in the "boys'" room to discuss next steps. Luckily, the professor that I'd seen in my dream, Michael Fisher, was listed in the phone book.

"So we have an address, but now what? We just show up at his house tomorrow?" I asked Jack.

"We'll drive around first and see if we notice anyone watching his house. We'll go in the morning. If he's not there, we'll have to try again later. But I really hope he's there. We need to know if that flash drive can help us. Because if it can't, we have to make another plan fast."

There is no other plan, I thought. If this doesn't work, we're screwed. Erik's timer would go off in a few months, then he'd be gone. I'd be next. Since having that dream about the professor, I'd put all my trust in Dave. There had to be something useful on that flash drive.

Jack continued. "When we get to his house tomorrow, I want you to go to the door, Sam, since he knows you. Tell him you need to talk and then ask him if we can come in. If he says no, don't go inside the house by yourself. You never know who could be waiting in there."

"So if that happens, you just want me to leave?"

"Make a plan to meet him somewhere public, like a park."

I agreed to the plan but I wasn't confident in it. I'd only met this guy one time and wasn't sure if we could trust him.

"We'll plan to leave around 9," Jack said. "We're not coming back here, so be sure to pack everything up. Any questions?" Nobody answered. "All right then. See you in the morning, girls."

Brittany and I left and Colin followed us out.

"Hey, Sam, wait." Colin tugged at my coat. Brittany went inside our room and shut the door.

"Yeah, what it is?"

He laughed. "Don't I even get a kiss? We've been stuck in that van forever. You can't go running off yet. We're finally alone."

I kissed him, then stayed close for a hug. "Colin, I'm really freaking out about meeting this guy tomorrow."

"It's gonna be easy, Sam. The guy knows you. He said he owed your dad a huge favor. Now it's time to pay up. He's not gonna turn you away."

"I guess. But what if I was wrong about that dream? Or what if the dream was real but there's nothing on that flash drive that can help us?"

"Don't think that way. The dream was real. And there's something on that flash drive. Otherwise Dave wouldn't have sent it to the guy."

"I hope you're right." I shivered. "It's cold out here. I'm going inside. I'll see you tomorrow."

Colin smiled. "Maybe Brittany wouldn't care if I stayed over there with you tonight. I'd keep you warm."

I smiled back. "Goodnight, Colin." We kissed once more before I went inside.

I couldn't explain why, but that night I felt like Colin and I were getting on track again. Maybe it was being back home in Minnesota that made me feel closer to him. I wasn't sure, but things just seemed right again.

Morning came too soon. As I got ready, I began to feel nervous, not just about meeting with the professor but also finding out what was on that flash drive. What if it was bad news, like the file we'd opened at Paul's house? The last thing I needed was more bad news.

When we got to Professor Fisher's house, we noticed the lights were on inside. Jack circled the house looking for any suspicious cars or trucks. There were only a few cars parked on the street. It was Sunday morning and most people would be at church services. Jack parked on the street a few houses house down, so Fisher wouldn't be alarmed by the sight of a big white van when he opened the door.

I went up to the house by myself, as planned, and rang the bell. No answer. I rang again. I could see a shadow through the curtain. I rang once more. It seemed like he was looking outside to see who it was. Finally he opened the door, but just barely. He seemed agitated.

"Samantha? Is that you?" Fisher spoke softly but very rushed.

"Yes. Remember me? Stephen and Ellie's daughter?"

"Yes, of course. I can't believe you're here. Come in." He opened the door just a little bit more.

"Um, no I can't. I mean, I can but I have some people with me." I pointed back to the van. "Can they come in, too?"

Fisher poked his head outside and turned it right and left, surveying the street. "Who are these people? Who's with you?"

"Well, Colin, my boyfriend. You met him at my house."

"Yes, that's fine. He can come in."

"And I have some other people with me. There's a man and his son. The man is a friend of Dave's."

Fisher grabbed my coat sleeve. "Dave? You mean your Uncle Dave? Where is he? I've been trying desperately to find him. Is he with you?"

"No. His *friend* is with me. His friend has a son. And then there's a girl. She's my sister."

"You don't have a sister!" Fisher snapped. He began scanning the neighborhood for whoever he thought was after him. "What is this? Is this some setup? Where are they?"

"Who? I don't know what you're talking about."

"Those bastards from GlobalLife. I know they're coming for me. And they used you to get to me, huh?"

"What? No!" I was getting impatient. "Listen. We just need to ask you some questions. That's it. Now can they come in or not?"

He hesitated but could see my desperation. "All right. But tell them to hurry up."

I ran back to the van, making sure to warn everyone about Fisher's highly paranoid state. Everyone raced to the house.

Fisher was waiting at the door. "Get inside. Quickly now." Once we were inside, he slammed the door and locked the deadbolt. He turned to Jack. "So you're a friend of Dave's?"

"Yes," Jack replied. "We went to MIT together many years ago. And this is my son."

Erik put his hand out, but Fisher ignored him. He'd noticed Brittany standing behind Jack and couldn't stop staring at her. "Samantha, this girl. She looks just like you. How can this be?"

"She's my sister. My twin sister," I clarified.

"Tell me how this is possible," Fisher's eyes remained focused on Brittany. "How could your parents not know about her? Or did they know and they kept her a secret? But that doesn't make sense."

I moved in front of her. "It's a long story. And we don't have much time."

Fisher glanced over at Jack and Erik, still suspicious of them. "What is this about, Samantha? Why did you show up on my doorstep? And why are these people with you?"

I figured it was best to get right to the point. "I think you have a message for me. A message from Dave."

Fisher listened but didn't agree or disagree.

"I think you have a flash drive. A strange looking flash drive that can only be accessed with your fingerprint."

Fisher got up close to me. "Have you been spying on me? Why would you do that? Did you hide cameras somewhere?"

I backed away from him. "No. I have dreams sometimes. Premonitions. And I had one that showed you getting a flash drive. Along with a piece of paper. I think it was a note from Dave."

"You have premonitions? How?"

"I don't know," I lied. "I've just always had them. But sometimes they're not accurate. And sometimes they're just dreams. So was I right? Did you get a flash drive?"

Fisher hesitated. "You're sure you can trust these people?"

I nodded. "Yes. One hundred percent."

"Okay. Then yes." Fisher sat down. "I have the flash drive. And I *had* the note from Dave, just like you said, but I burned it. I didn't want the evidence around. But the note didn't say much. It was written to me. It just said to make sure you get the flash drive."

"So what was on the flash drive?" I asked, still fearing the answer.

He shrugged. "A file with some type of directions. That's it. You're supposed to go somewhere on a plane."

"A plane? I can't get on a plane. GlobalLife has people working in airport security."

"It's not a commercial plane. It's a private jet," he explained.

"Dave couldn't get a private jet. There's no way. He doesn't have that kind of money."

Fisher gave me a strange look. "Of course he does. Dave must have millions stashed away. You've known him all these years. You know he has money to rent a private plane. Heck, he could probably buy one."

"Well, I knew he made a lot of money when he sold his company but not—"

"He made a LOT of money, Samantha. Millions. From the way he lives, I don't think he ever spends it. I guess I shouldn't say that. I don't know him that well."

Dave did live frugally. He'd probably invested those millions and doubled or even tripled his fortune over the years. So it was possible that he rented a private plane.

"Where is this plane taking me?"

"I'm not sure. I'd have to open the file again. I opened it at my office the other day and I haven't looked at it since. Only GlobalLife has those fingerprint flash drives. So I knew this involved them. And now I'm afraid to go anywhere. Just opening that flash drive, I found out stuff I shouldn't know."

"Dr. Fisher, we really need to see what's on the file," I insisted.

He stood up suddenly. "Oh, before we do that, I have something else for you." He took an envelope from a bookshelf behind Jack. "When I heard you'd gone missing, Sam, I didn't think I'd ever see you again to give you these, but here. These are for you."

He handed me the envelope. Inside was a stack of photos. The photos were pictures of Mom and Dad and me from various years.

I flipped through a few of them. "Where did you get these?"

"Your dad's office. They were in his desk drawer. One of my students was using the desk and found them."

Fisher had no idea how much those photos meant to me. They were the only photos I had of my parents. "Thank you. Really, I can't tell you how much—"

"Can I see?" Brittany came and sat beside me. I gave her the stack of photos and watched as she looked at each one. It was the first time she had seen her real parents. I felt my eyes tearing up.

She held up one of the more recent photos. "Your mom was so pretty."

"She's your mom, too, Brittany," I reminded her.

"I know. I'm just not used to that, yet. And look at your, I mean, our dad. Since I never had a dad, it's kind of weird just saying that." She paused to look closer at the photo. "He looks really nice, Sam."

"He *was* nice. To everyone. So was Mom." I could feel a tear running down my cheek. I couldn't get into this with her now or soon I'd be a crying mess. I glanced up, trying to focus again.

Jack noticed me struggling. "So, Dr. Fisher, do you think we could see that file now?"

Fisher ignored him and looked at me. "Samantha, I'd really like you to explain why these people are here with you."

I wasn't sure what to say. Jack stepped in again. "Dr. Fisher. As you stated earlier, knowing too much can put you in danger. And you already know more than you wanted to know. If we tell you everything, that's just more information that could put you in harm's way. Now do you really want to know about us, given the risk?"

Fisher considered it. "No. I guess I don't. All right. I'll go get the flash drive and the computer."

Fisher disappeared down the hall then came back with his laptop, setting it on his dining room table. We all gathered around him except for Brittany, who was still immersing herself in the photos of our parents.

The flash drive was just as I'd seen in my dream. An ultrathin, oval-shaped device as wide as a fingertip. Fisher inserted the drive into the computer and then pressed his index finger on one side. It immediately opened a document, which was nothing more than a single-page letter from Dave.

The letter was written to me. It read, *"Sam, After you get this, I want you to leave right away. A private jet has been reserved and is waiting for you. When you arrive at the small airport, tell nobody your name. Just use the reservation number below. You don't need ID or anything else. The plane will take you to another small airport, where a car will be waiting. The driver will say a code word to you. The code word is what I called you when you were a child. If he doesn't say that word, don't get in the car. The car will take you to a safe house. I know you have questions, but you just need to trust me.—Uncle Dave"*

Below the letter was the name of the small airport where the private plane was waiting, along with the phone number and address. Under that was the reservation number; 64D09N21D57W.

"Well, that's it," Fisher said. "That's all that was in the file."

I felt hopeless again. Dave's note said nothing about alien genes. Nothing about missing base codes. How would getting on a plane help me? It didn't even say where the plane was going.

Erik pointed to the laptop. "Hey, Dad. Check out that confirmation number."

Jack bent down to see the screen. "What about it?"

"Doesn't that remind you of something? Where did I see that?" Erik closed his eyes to think. Then he opened his eyes and nudged Jack with his elbow. "Luke." He said it quietly so Fisher wouldn't hear.

Jack knew instantly what he meant. The plane reservation number was all jammed together, but it exactly matched the number and letters that Erik had deciphered from the codes in Luke's journal; 64D09N 21D57W.

16. REUNION

Jack looked closer at the combination of letters and numbers. "Dr. Fisher, do you have a world atlas or other type of world map?"

Fisher was taken aback by the odd request. "Well, yes. I have an atlas."

"Would you mind if I took a look at it?"

"It's in my office. I'll go get it." Fisher went down the hall and to a side room.

"Those numbers and letters are the exact same, Dad," Erik said.

Fisher came back with the atlas. "What do you need this for?"

"Oh, just a silly trivia game." Jack laughed. "My son and I were having a debate in the van over a geography question. I had to settle it or we'd never stop arguing."

Jack opened up the atlas and used his finger to pinpoint a spot on the map. Then he closed the atlas and handed it back to Fisher. "That's all I needed. Thank you."

Fisher gave him an odd look and set the atlas aside.

"Would you mind giving us a few minutes alone?" Jack asked Fisher. "I really don't want to get you more involved in this than you already are."

Fisher looked over at me. "Samantha?"

"I agree. It's best if you don't know too much."

Fisher went down the hall into a side bedroom.

Jack lowered his voice. "That wasn't at all what I expected to see on that flash drive. It explains nothing."

"Wait. What were you and Erik just talking about?" Colin asked. "Something about Luke's journal?"

Erik explained. "Remember how I was decoding that stuff in his journal and those two codes I worked on ended up being a mix of letters and numbers?" Erik quickly checked to make sure Fisher wasn't listening. "The letters and numbers were the exact same as the reservation number for the private plane."

"And seeing them again, I finally figured out what that those numbers and letters were," Jack said. "They're latitude, longitude. 64 degrees, 9 minutes north and 21 degrees, 57 minutes west."

"So is that where the plane is taking us?" I asked.

"That's what I'm guessing," Jack said. "The thing I can't figure out is why Luke had the exact same location written in his book, in code form no less."

"What's the location?" Colin asked. "Where is the plane going?"

"Iceland." Jack paused, unable to believe it himself. "Reykjavik, Iceland."

"Where's Iceland?" Brittany whispered to Colin.

"It's an island in the Atlantic Ocean."

"It actually crosses into the Arctic Ocean as well," Jack added. "It's closer to Europe than North America. It's a small country. Not highly populated."

"Iceland?" I felt like we were being tricked again. "Why would Dave send us to Iceland? Jack, I'm starting to think this isn't real. GlobalLife fakes messages all the time."

"How did you feel when you had the dream about this? Did you feel like it was really a message from Dave?"

"I used to think so, but now I'm not so sure," I admitted.

I thought back to the dream. At the time it seemed so real. I could almost feel Dave's presence through that note he wrote to Fisher. If I went by feeling alone, I would believe it one hundred percent. But now my logical side was telling me not to get on that plane.

Erik came over to me. "Sam, after you had that dream, did you have any doubts about the note or the flash drive?"

"No. I felt like Dave was trying to help me somehow."

"Then that's your answer. You can't go by how you feel now. When you had that dream, or premonition, your abilities were strong. You could sense that the dream was real. Now your abilities are fading and fear is clouding your judgment. You can't base your decision on that."

"He's right," Jack added. "Your premonitions have been on target every time. If this was a GlobalLife hoax, you would have felt it back when you had the dream."

"Then I guess we're going to Iceland," I said.

Jack looked at Erik then back at me. "You're going, Sam. I'm not so sure Erik and I should go."

"What? Dad, of course we're going!"

"The letter was meant for Sam. Not us. We need to keep looking for a way to stop the timer. And I'm pretty sure it's not in Iceland."

"But Jack, we don't know that," I said. "Maybe Dave found what we need. Maybe he has the base codes."

"Or maybe he's just trying to keep you safe, Sam. Iceland is a good place to hide out. This could all be a way to keep you far away from GlobalLife so you can live a halfway normal life. How would Dave even know about the base codes?"

Jack was right. If Dave had somehow escaped from GlobalLife, then his main goal would be to find me and hide me far away from GlobalLife so I could live my life in peace. And it's true that Dave wouldn't know about the base codes or the timer. How could he? It was top-secret information. Dave didn't have access to those files.

Colin put his arm around me. "I don't know about you guys, but I'm going with her. I'm not letting her do this alone."

"Same here," Erik said. "Sorry, Dad. But you can't forbid me from going. I'm 19. I can make my own decisions. Staying here does nothing. We have no leads on finding those base codes. At least this is something. A chance that maybe there's another answer or another clue that might help us turn the timer off."

Jack considered it. "Well, I'm not so sure about that. But I'm not sending the three of you up there not knowing what this is about. So we're all going. That includes you, Brittany."

"What if they won't let us on the plane?" Brittany asked. "What if it's only for Sam?"

"We'll just have to try," Jack said. "And I think we should leave today. The sooner we get out of this area, the better. But I need a place for the van. It has all my equipment. I can't just leave it sitting on the street."

Fisher overheard us as he walked into the room. "What about the van?"

I went over to him. "They're all coming with me, so we need a safe place to store the van while we're gone. Any ideas?"

Fisher went to the front window. "Hmm, it's quite a bit larger than a normal van, but it might fit." He turned back to us. "I know of a storage facility. It's a short drive outside of town. A friend of mine owns the place. He has a lot of open spaces. I'm sure you could have one. And if you paid him for several months in cash, he wouldn't even make you fill out any paperwork. That way your name wouldn't be attached to it."

Jack looked relieved. "That would be perfect. It's exactly what we need. Oh, and one more thing. I hate to involve you like this, Dr. Fisher, but since we're dropping off the van, would you mind giving us a ride to the airport? I know you don't want to leave the house, but—"

"I can take you there. Actually I feel better about things now that I'm not holding on to this anymore." Fisher gave Jack the flash drive. "Destroy it. I don't want it anywhere near here."

Jack smiled. "I understand. And thank you for being so helpful. We appreciate it. So I guess we'll unload what we need from the van and then we can go."

As we walked down the street to the van, I looked around at the old historic houses. They reminded me of *my* old house and I suddenly felt sad, knowing that I would never come back to this town again. I would never have a chance to say goodbye to the places and people I missed, like— "Allie!" I accidentally yelled it out.

Colin raced over to me. "Sam, why are you yelling? We're trying not to attract attention."

I lowered my voice. "I know. Sorry. But I forgot about Allie! We have to go see her!"

"What? We can't do that. We can't let anyone know we're here."

"Colin, you told me her mom hired a private investigator to find me. We can't have someone like that looking for me. GlobalLife could find out. They probably already have. They'll either kill the investigator or follow him until he finds me."

"Some local investigator is not gonna find you, Sam. I'm sure he's not very good."

"But Allie's parents wouldn't hire some local guy. They can afford someone better. Someone with a lot of experience."

"I guess. But still, I don't think this person would ever find you."

"But what if GlobalLife figures out who hired the investigator? GlobalLife will think they know something about me. They'll come after Allie and her parents!"

Colin stopped. "Shit! You're right!"

We got in the van and sat behind Jack, who was cleaning out the glove compartment. Colin told him about the private investigator and our theory about how Allie and her family were at risk of being harmed.

"No. You can't go talk to her. It's too dangerous." He continued to clean out the front of the van.

"What's dangerous about it? We go to her house, we talk to her, and then we leave," I explained. "You can drop us off on your way to drop off the van. Then come pick us up. That way nobody will see the van sitting out front. Her house is on the way to that storage place."

Jack still wouldn't agree to it, so Colin tried. "Think about how many people they've already killed, Jack. We can't let them kill three more innocent people. All we're asking is to have a few minutes with her."

He paused to think about it, then let out a long sigh. "Fine," he reluctantly agreed. "But once you get in her house, you stay there. No going outside. No walking down the street. Just stay put. And you'll only talk to her, right?"

"I don't think anyone else will be home," I said. "Her dad usually goes into work on Sunday and her mom is always traveling."

Jack shook his head. "I don't know how you two talked me into this."

Colin and I quickly gathered our things from the van and put them in Fisher's SUV.

"So I'll lead the way and you follow," Fisher told Jack.

"We have to make a quick stop." Jack glanced over at Colin and me.

"What? Why?" Erik asked.

"I don't have time to explain it now, Erik," Jack said. "You can ask Sam about it later."

Erik and Brittany both looked at me to explain, but I refused to tell them anything. I knew they would only argue with me about it. Erik

160

tried to contact me privately through my mind, but our telepathy skills were almost nonexistent now.

Jack dropped Colin and me off at Allie's house around noon. Her house was on a big corner lot. It was a huge old Victorian-style house. It looked more like a mansion. When we got to the door, we could hear the TV on inside. We rang the bell several times.

"I'm coming," Allie yelled as she came to the door. When she finally opened it, she looked like she'd seen a ghost. "Oh my God! Sam?! Colin?!"

I looked back at our van, parked a few houses down. Jack wouldn't leave until we were safely in the house. "Allie, you need to let us inside."

The sound of my voice woke her from her shock. "Yeah. Come in." She pulled me into a hug. "Where have you been, Sam? I've been looking for you for weeks! And Colin was helping me, but then he was gone, too."

She released me and went to hug Colin. "Where did you go, you big idiot? I thought you were gonna help me and then you just disappeared."

As she let him go, tears started running down her face. Allie hated people seeing her cry. She quickly wiped the tears away, but they kept coming. "I can't believe you guys are here. I thought I'd never see you again."

"Come on. Let's sit down." I guided her to the sofa. Colin locked the door behind us then sat down next to me.

Allie stared at Colin. "What happened to you? Why are you all bruised?"

The remnants of GlobalLife's attack on Colin still showed on his face. "It's a long story, Al, but I'm okay."

"Tell me everything," Allie ordered. "Where have you guys been?"

Colin signaled for me to do the talking. "We can't tell you everything, Allie. We're only here because we need you to stop that investigation. Colin said your mom hired a guy to look for me. We need you to tell the guy that I'm fine and that he needs to stop looking."

"Yeah, okay. Although I asked my mom about it the other day and she said he'd found nothing. Like you just disappeared into thin air."

"Good. Now you just need to make sure he doesn't keep looking. Will you do that?"

"Yeah, but you have to tell me more. Like where you've been. The news said you were missing and then they said you ran away. What really happened, Sam?"

I hated lying to Allie but it was my only choice. It was for her own good. "Okay, I'll tell you." I paused, trying to quickly come up with a story. "What you heard on the news was right. I ran away. I couldn't deal with being here anymore. Memories of my parents were everywhere. And Dave was trying to take over my life. I hated it. So I left."

Allie looked confused. "But that's so unlike you, Sam. Leaving town? Without telling anyone? Not even me?"

"I know. And I'm sorry about that. I should have told you. But I knew you'd try to talk me out of it."

"I don't understand. I mean, I get that maybe you needed to get away for a few weeks, but why didn't you come back? Why didn't you tell someone where you were going?" Allie wasn't buying it. I had to come up with something else.

"Okay, here's what's really going on. I did run away but there's more to the story. Colin and I are, um, we're um, getting married. In a couple weeks."

I glanced over at Colin. He looked at me like I was insane, but Allie didn't notice. She was too distracted by the news.

Allie burst from her seat. "Oh my God! Really? You're really getting married?"

I grabbed Colin's hand and kissed him. "Yes. We figured, why wait until we're older? We love each other and we want to get married now. But you can't tell anyone this, Allie. They would only try to stop us. Dave. Colin's parents. They would ruin it for us. So we're just in town to get some of my things and then we're leaving. And we can't come back here again, at least not for a long time."

Allie lived for a good love story and she ate this one up. "My two best friends are getting married! I'm so happy for you guys! Sam, let me see the ring!"

"Oh, we don't have rings yet. But we'll get them."

Allie gave Colin a strange look. "Do you want—"

"No." Colin abruptly cut her off.

"What was that about?" I asked.

"Nothing," Colin answered, keeping his eyes on Allie.

Allie took a seat again, sitting at the edge of the sofa. "So Colin, how did you propose?"

Colin gave her an awkward smile. "Um, I think that should stay between Sam and me."

"No, come on, tell me," Allie pleaded.

I knew Colin wouldn't come up with a story so I stepped in. "After I ran away, I missed Colin so much that I had to call him, just to say goodbye."

"Why would you say goodbye? Why not just ask him to come be with you?"

"Because I didn't want him to miss school. And graduation. It was too much of a sacrifice for him. So anyway, he pretended to go along with it, pretended to say goodbye, but of course, he ended up coming to see me. And no, I can't tell you where that was, Allie. But it was somewhere warm and sunny. So I was sitting at this cafe one day thinking about how much I loved and missed him when the waiter comes over and gives me a postcard. It had a picture of that old movie theater downtown. You know, the one where Colin and I had our first date?"

Allie was getting more and more excited. "Yeah, I know it. Go on."

"I turned over the postcard and Colin had written a note, but it was written like a movie theater listing. It said, 'The Wonderful Life of Samantha and Colin, Showing today, and every day, for the rest of our lives. Please join me for this invitation-only event. A ticket has been reserved in your name.'"

Colin stared at me like I had now completely lost my mind. I smiled at him, then back at Allie.

"Oh, that's sooo romantic," Allie gushed.

"It's really kind of lame," Colin muttered. I squeezed his hand, urging him to go along with it.

"So I turn around and Colin's standing there with a bucket of popcorn and a dozen roses. And then he got on one knee and proposed."

"Awww, Sam, that is so perfect for you! Because it's not too sappy, which you hate. But it's clever, which you like. And then the movie theme because you love movies! Colin, that was sooo perfect!"

"Uh, yeah, thanks," he said, after I squeezed his hand another time.

"So the wedding's in a few weeks?" she asked.

"Yes, so we need to—"

Before I could finish, we heard someone at the door. Colin had locked it, but someone was trying to get in. And from the struggle this person was having with the door, it had to be a break in. GlobalLife! I thought. They must have been watching Allie's house and seen Colin and me. Now they were trying to break in! Colin and I froze, not sure what to do. Then suddenly, the door burst open.

17. REYKJAVIK

A tall, thin woman entered the room, placing her purse on the floor. I felt my heartbeat return to normal when I realized it was Allie's mom. At first, I didn't recognize her. She was covered head to toe in a long black coat with a red scarf wrapped around her dark, wavy hair.

Allie got up and went to the door. "Mom, what are you doing here?"

Allie's mom hung her coat and scarf on a hook near the door. Like her daughter, she was always well dressed. She had on a dark gray tailored suit with a crisp white blouse unbuttoned enough to show off a large diamond necklace that matched her diamond earrings.

"I took an earlier flight home. I couldn't get my key to work in that door. Remind me to ask your father to fix that." She leaned down to kiss Allie on the cheek. "Hello, sweetheart. How are you?"

Allie's mom hadn't even noticed us sitting in the living room.

"Mom. We have company. Now don't freak out." Allie walked her mom over to us.

"Oh my goodness. Samantha? Colin? What are you doing here? I thought you were missing. I hired a—" Allie's mom talked fast, just like her daughter.

"Mom. You need to call off that investigator. They don't wanna be found. They're getting—um, never mind."

"Hi, Mrs. Taylor," I said as her and Allie sat down. "Nice to see you again. What Allie was saying is that Colin and I have decided to, um, live together. Away from here. Out of state. His parents don't approve, so we need to keep this quiet. Please don't tell anyone."

Mrs. Taylor looked at Colin, then back at me. "Well, you're both of age. Eighteen, right? I think you're old enough to make that decision."

Allie jumped up from her chair. "Sam! Your birthday! I almost forgot! I have a gift for you. I'll go get it." Allie headed for the stairs, then stopped. "You don't have to leave right away, do you? Please say no."

I checked the clock on the wall. "I'm sorry, Allie, but we do have to get going soon."

Allie's face turned sad. "Oh, then let me get your gift. Stay right there."

Mrs. Taylor smiled at Colin and me. "My daughter is going to miss you both terribly. She talks about you all the time."

"We'll miss her, too." Awkward silence filled the room as I struggled to find more to say. "So, where were you traveling back from?"

"California. I had some business out there."

Silence again. "You work in banking. Is that right, Mrs. Taylor?"

"Call me Eve. And actually, I work in investment banking."

"Allie said you travel overseas a lot."

"Yes, my company has offices around the world. Because of that, I'm often stuck traveling to different countries. I get very little time at home. I wish it weren't that way. I rarely see Allie and soon she'll be off at college."

We heard Allie running down the stairs. "Okay, here you go." She handed me two boxes, neatly wrapped. Allie loved giving presents. "I got these before you left. This one is a graduation gift. The other one is for your birthday."

I unwrapped the graduation gift, which was in a wide, flat box. Inside was a laptop bag made from soft brown leather. It looked very expensive.

"Allie, this is way too much. I can't accept this."

"You're taking it. I searched forever to find one you'd like. So what do you think?"

"I love it! But it's still more than you should've spent."

Allie rolled her eyes at me. "Open the other one!"

Inside the smaller box was a silver necklace that had a pendant on it. The pendant looked like the capital letter I with an open circle around the middle.

I held it up to see it better. "Thanks, Allie! This is really cool. Is this a Greek letter?"

"Yeah. It's the letter phi, the twenty-first letter in the Greek alphabet. I learned all about when I was going to school there. It's got like all these different meanings in math, science, art. I can't remember them all."

"It represents the golden ratio," Mrs. Taylor explained. "The ratio is found in nature, and it's been used to create some of the world's most beautiful architecture and paintings. In fact, you can see it in the works of Da Vinci and Dali. The ratio is even employed in the financial markets."

"See? It's really cool," Allie said. "You can look up all the other meanings on the Internet. I know you don't like sparkly stuff, so I thought you might like this. I got it at a store in Athens. But it's all silver! I didn't get it at one of those tacky tourist shops."

I put the necklace on. "I love it, Al. Thanks!"

Colin got up. "Well, we should really get going, Sam."

"Yeah, okay." It was time to go but I didn't want to. I wasn't ready to say goodbye.

As we walked to the door, Allie ran ahead of us. "Do you really have to leave? When will I see you guys again?"

I looked at Colin. "We don't know, Allie."

"Take lots of pictures at the wedding, even if it's at the courthouse." She said it quietly so her mom wouldn't hear. "And next time I see you, I'll give you guys your wedding present." Allie grabbed me for another hug. "I'll miss you so much." Her voice was shaky and almost made me cry.

Allie cleared her throat and let me go. Then she hugged Colin. "I'll kill you if you don't take care of her. You know that, right?" She spoke just loud enough for me to hear. "And make sure she still goes to Stanford."

Colin smiled. "Got it. We'll see you later, Allie."

Mrs. Taylor came over to the door. "I know you two are adults, but the mother in me can't help worrying. Do you need anything? Food? Money?"

"No," I said. "We'll be okay. But thank you."

She smiled. "Well, please call us if you do."

"I guess this is it." Tears were now running down Allie's face as she spoke. "Now promise me that we'll see each other again."

"We promise," Colin and I said in unison.

"Oh, Sam, your bag." Mrs. Taylor went to grab the laptop bag I'd left on the sofa.

"Thanks," I said, taking it from her. "I got so caught up in the goodbyes that I almost forgot it."

Colin tugged on me to leave. "We really need to go. We'll see ya, Allie. Bye, Mrs. Taylor."

Allie and I had a final hug, then Colin and I left. As soon as the door closed behind us, I started crying.

Colin held my hand as we walked. "Sam, we'll see her again someday."

"No, we won't. That was the last time I'll ever see her."

He knew it was more true than not, so we continued in silence until we got to Fisher's SUV.

"What's wrong? What happened?" Erik asked when he saw me crying.

Colin answered for me. "She's upset about saying goodbye to Allie."

"Because I know I'll never see her again," I said, wiping my tears.

"Was she the only one home?" Jack asked Colin.

"No, her mom was there. But we didn't tell either of them the truth. Sam made up this story about her and me running off to get married."

"Oh really." Erik smiled at me. "And when is this happening, Sam?"

"I had to tell her something. And that's the only thing she'd believe. I told her we didn't want anyone else to know. Oh, and she promised to call off the investigator."

"Where did you get this?" Erik picked up the leather laptop bag.

"Allie gave it to me as a graduation gift. And she gave me this for my birthday." I held out the necklace for them to see.

Jack turned back. "Is that phi? The Greek letter?"

"Yeah. Allie went to school in Greece last semester. She got this when she was there."

"That's the symbol for the golden ratio," Jack said.

"Yeah, that's what her mom was saying."

"Did you have any trouble with the van?" Colin asked Jack.

"No. It fit right into the storage locker. There were plenty of empty ones. I paid the guy enough to cover the next six months, just in case we're gone for a while. And if we don't come back, I guess the guy gets a van and some very sophisticated equipment."

"I can always go and pick it up for you," Fisher offered. He seemed to be in a better mood than when he'd dropped us off. And more trusting of Jack.

About an hour later, we arrived at the small airport. As everyone unloaded the SUV, I went inside to present the reservation number.

Two pilots were waiting at a front desk area. When I read off the numbers and letters, they nodded and one went outside to prepare the plane.

The other one stayed behind. "I can get your things. Go ahead and board. If you need a restroom, it's right down the hall."

"Wait. Some other people will be coming with me."

"Older man and his son?" the pilot asked.

"Yeah, how did you know—"

"Is there a girl, too?'

"Yes. And one more guy," I said.

He nodded. "I was told they might be coming with us. Tell them they can board. I'll get their things loaded on."

The pilot went out to the plane as Jack and the others came into the small building. "Did you tell the pilot about us?" Jack asked.

"Yes. But he seemed to already know about everyone. Doesn't that worry you?"

Jack glanced out at the plane. "Everything worries me, Sam. But at this point, we don't have any options. We have to trust your instincts that the letter was really from Dave." He went back outside to let Fisher know it was okay to leave.

As we boarded the private jet, Brittany couldn't contain her excitement. "Look how big these seats are! Ooooh and they're leather," she said, running her hand along the first seat.

The jet had three rows with two seats on each side of the aisle. Brittany took a seat in the second row. "Just a few weeks ago, I was dirt poor living in a trailer and now I'm riding on a private jet! This is so amazing!"

I hadn't heard Brittany mention the trailer since leaving Texas. She hadn't said a word about it, at least not to me.

I took the seat in front of Brittany, and Colin sat across the aisle from me. Erik and Jack sat in the last row.

Before we left, the pilot went over safety procedures. He ended his speech by pointing out a metal cabinet that was next to his leg. "If you need any drinks, they're in this cooler. And you'll find some nuts, chips, and other food in this drawer here. Enjoy the flight."

He returned to the cockpit, where the other pilot was waiting. "Sam, did you hear that?" Brittany whispered from behind my seat. "We even get snacks! This is so awesome!"

When we got into the air, a screen unfolded from the ceiling. Brittany's excitement continued. "No way! Are we getting movies, too?" The beginning of a movie started to play, answering Brittany's question. "This is like the best thing ever!" she squealed, grabbing a blanket from a storage area above her seat and making herself comfortable.

"Well, she'll be entertained for the next six hours," I said to Colin.

I watched the movie for a while, then quit because it was so bad. It was a botched attempt at a romantic comedy. But Brittany seemed to like it.

Colin was reading a newspaper. When he was done, he came over and sat next to me. "Hey, how are you doin' over here?" He kissed my cheek. "Still sad about Allie?"

I put my head on his shoulder. "Yeah. I hate thinking that I'll never see her again. It's like when I thought I'd never see you again."

"But you did," he said, taking my hand. "I showed up right in front of you."

"Yeah, with a gun to your head."

He laughed. "Okay, the circumstances could have been better, but we did find each other again. And someday, we'll find Allie again."

"I hope so."

"So how did you come up with that story? Because I hope you know, I would never propose that way."

I turned to face him. "Hey, I thought it was cute. The movie theater postcard. The title with our names in it."

"Ugh, no way. That's not my style at all. I can't believe Allie even bought that story."

"She loves that over-the-top romance stuff. I knew she'd be so distracted trying to imagine the scene in her mind that she'd forget all about whether it was something you would or wouldn't do."

"I guess it's a girl thing then. I wasn't imagining anything. I couldn't get past the whole postcard idea. I've never even bought a postcard, Sam. Not even on vacation."

"Okay, okay. I get it. You didn't like my story."

He started laughing. "And why would I give you a bucket of popcorn with a dozen roses? The smell alone would make you sick. Butter mixed with flowers? And where would I get a bucket of popcorn?"

When he put it that way, it was kind of funny. I laughed, too. "Okay, I get it! It was stupid."

"I'm just giving you a hard time. And just so you know, if I ever do propose, you'll have a much better story to tell." He kissed me again, then headed back to his seat.

"Hey, where are you going?" I asked, wanting his shoulder back.

"I'm going to sleep." He smiled at me. "Maybe I'll dream of popcorn and roses."

I threw a pillow at him. "I hope you do! It's very romantic!"

I watched the last few minutes of the movie. Afterward, Erik came over and sat with me. "So what's new?"

"Well, let's see. I recently found out that I'm part alien, I'm losing my superhero abilities, and I'm heading to Iceland." I paused. "That's about it."

He smiled. "Wow. Sounds just like me."

"I shouldn't joke about it."

"Why the hell not? Worrying hasn't helped us. Might as well try to laugh about it."

"Seriously, though. Maybe Jack was right. Maybe you two should've stayed behind. This trip might be a total waste of time. And you don't have time to waste, Erik."

"I wasn't gonna let you go without me." He lowered his voice. "We may not be as, uh, close as before, but I still care what happens to you, Sam. And I wasn't ready to say goodbye." He leaned over to whisper in my ear. "I'd kind of miss you if you weren't around."

I backed away, glancing over at Colin, who was now asleep. "I just don't want this trip to take us off track. We have to get this timer fixed soon or—"

"If this trip doesn't lead anywhere, we'll keep going till we find the answer."

Another movie began on the screen above us. We heard Brittany's voice behind us. "Oh, I love this one!"

Erik looked up at the screen. "*Doggone Love?* Seriously?" He leaned over to whisper. "Twins don't share the same taste in movies, do they?"

"No, we're definitely different that way," I whispered back.

"Did you watch that last one?"

"Part of it. I lost interest when that girl lured the guy back with her voodoo spell or whatever it was."

Erik laughed. "Yeah, that was so stupid. I mean, do you girls really want to be with a guy who is only with you because he's under some magic spell? Some fake attraction?"

"No. At least I don't."

"I'm gonna go talk to my dad. Enjoy the movie, Sam. I'm sure this one will be way better than the last one."

The movie was so boring that I fell asleep, waking up right before we landed. When I looked out the window, all I could see was the ocean. As we got closer, I started to see land and little houses. I knew nothing about Iceland, other than that it was an island. And not a warm one.

We arrived at the airport at 11 p.m. Iceland time. The tiny airport was empty except for a lady working at the desk.

We got our bags and waited by the door for the car that would be picking us up. Five minutes passed. No car showed up. Then another five minutes. I started to get nervous and went over to talk to Jack. "Someone should be here by now. What should we do?"

"Just keep waiting. I'll go see if the woman at the desk knows anything." Jack came back right away. "Well that didn't work. She doesn't speak English."

As we waited, a man wearing a maintenance uniform came out of a room behind the desk. He went up to Jack. "Sir? Could you help me with something? It won't take long." He said it in perfect English.

Jack turned to him. "What is it? I'm waiting for a car."

"I'm trying to fix a leak in the ceiling back there." The man pointed to the room he'd just left. "I can't reach this one spot. If it's not fixed soon, that leak could do some real damage. They'll fire me for sure. I need this job. Please. It'll only take a minute."

Jack walked behind the desk and stood outside the room. "You mean where you've got that ladder? I can't reach that either. It's too high."

"Well, maybe he can help." The man pointed to Colin. "He's very tall. Please. It will only take a minute." The man seemed desperate.

Jack sighed. "Colin, come here." Colin went over to Jack and listened while the maintenance man explained the situation. Colin followed the man into the room. Jack went over to Erik. "We'll be right back there."

"All right, but hurry up," Erik said.

A few minutes later, a black limo pulled up. "A limo!" Brittany yelled. "Oh my God! I've never been in a limo! I've gotta see this!" She ran outside and into the limo.

"Brittany! Wait!" I ran after her, followed by Erik. We poked our heads into the limo and found her already seated at the far end. Erik and I stepped in to grab her. "Brittany, get out," I yelled at her. "You don't even know—"

The door slammed shut behind us. "Erik, open the door," I said, pulling on Brittany. "The wind must've slammed it shut."

Erik went to open the door, but it was locked. He pressed the unlock button but it didn't work. I tried the door closest to me. It was locked, too. We both tried the remaining doors. All locked. Then just outside the limo we saw a man in a dark coat and hat who appeared to be the driver.

I banged on the side window to get his attention. "Hey, we need to get out! There's two other people back there!" I pointed to the airport building.

The driver saw us but didn't react. We watched as he walked to the front of the limo and got inside. Erik pounded on the piece of dark glass that divided us from the driver. "Wait! We need to wait for two more people!"

The driver ignored him and started driving away from the airport with the three of us trapped in the back.

18. ROOM 402

"Erik, make him stop!" I screamed. "This is the wrong car! They didn't even ask for the code word."

Erik banged even harder against the glass divider. "Hey! Stop! Let us out!"

Brittany and I kept trying to open the doors and windows but they were all locked. We heard a loud bang and looked back to see a bright, fiery light in the dark night sky. It was coming from the airport building. Part of the building had exploded, leaving fire and plumes of smoke in the air.

I moved closer to the back window. "Oh my God! Erik, look!"

"What the hell? This can't be happening!" Erik beat on the glass again, trying to get the driver's attention. "Who are you? Let us out! I swear I'll break this thing!" But the glass wouldn't break. It didn't even crack. If we still had our abilities, Erik would have broken the glass without a problem. But now both he and I had normal strength, which wasn't enough to help us.

"They're in that building!" I screamed. "Colin and Jack are in there! We have to go back!" Brittany and I pounded on the back and side windows.

Erik sat back. "You can't break it, Sam. It's reinforced glass."

I stopped, frozen in disbelief as I watched the airport get farther and farther away. "It was a set up. The whole thing was a trap. That

176

guy asking for help at the airport? They wanted Colin and Jack separated from us."

Erik stared out the window at the now distant flames. "I don't know how this happened. It was so fast. We were only in here a second."

"It was my fault." Brittany was crying now. "I'm sorry! I'd never been in a limo before. I thought this was the right car."

We looked at her but neither one of us was in the mood to comfort her or tell her it wasn't her fault. Because it *was* her fault. And now we were trapped in a limo, not knowing who was up front or where we were being taken.

"How did they know we were coming here?" Erik asked.

"I don't know. But I don't think we should talk anymore. You know they're listening to us right now." I checked the inside of the limo for hidden microphones. "Yeah, we know you're listening!" I yelled into the air.

We didn't speak the rest of the way, except for Brittany who continued to cry and say how sorry she was. The limo finally came to a halt at a gated entrance. The driver rolled his window down and mumbled something to a man at the gate.

We drove into a parking garage. The limo stopped again and the door next to Erik unlocked. He bolted for the door but a large man opened it and pulled Erik from the car, cuffing his wrists with zipties. Another huge man stood next to the first man. He pulled me out, cuffing my wrists as well.

Brittany refused to move from her seat at the back of the limo. "This one won't come out," the first man said.

"Then go around. Get her from the other side," the other man ordered.

The guy went to the back of the limo and yanked Brittany from her seat.

I scanned the parking garage for any markings that might indicate our location. I couldn't see anything other than rows of luxury vehicles. Whoever parked there had money.

The men led us into an elevator. It went up just one floor before stopping. When the elevator doors opened, we were greeted by two men wearing black uniforms. They yanked us out of the elevator, then stood close behind us, pushing us forward.

We entered into a vast and opulent room that appeared to be the main floor of an office building. It had marble floors and pillars and an intricately carved, circular marble desk sat in the center of the large space. Huge tapestries hung on the walls, the type you might see in a European castle. The room was so long that it seemed to go on forever.

As I took it all in, trying to figure out what this place could be, I turned around and realized that Brittany wasn't behind us.

"Brittany!" I called out. "Brittany? Where did you go?" I scanned all directions looking for her but she wasn't there. "Erik where is she?"

His eyes searched the room. "I don't know. I thought she got off the elevator with us."

"What did you do with her?!" I screamed, whipping around to face the man behind me.

He grabbed my shoulders and turned me forward again. "She's going to a different floor," he said calmly.

"A different floor?! Then I'm going to a different floor!" I tried to run but the man grabbed my coat and yanked me back.

"Sam, stop," Erik said, motioning me to look behind. The guard that had Erik was holding a needle that would soon be in my neck if I didn't behave.

Not wanting to be drugged, I moved along, keeping pace with Erik. "If you do anything to Brittany, I swear—"

"Quiet!" the man behind me said. His voice was so loud it echoed in the room.

We continued to walk forward through the lobby, past several large marble statues. The first one was of a beautiful woman and the next one was a perfectly sculpted man. They were like ancient Greek statues you would see in a museum. Off in the distance I could see a third statue, which looked like a globe. And after that was a wall of windows, likely the entrance.

The men steered us left down a long hallway. It was lined on both sides with large black doors that had giant chrome numbers on them. We stopped at a door numbered 402. Within seconds, an old, slender man with white hair opened the door. He was wearing a tuxedo with tails. "Welcome," he said, smiling at Erik and me. "Come in."

The two men pushed us into the room, then left, closing the door behind them. The old man kept smiling, as if the situation was completely normal.

The room was spacious with very tall ceilings. Large, deep red velvet drapes hung on the walls. Dark wood panels covered the floor. There was a large fireplace on one wall, next to a four-poster king size bed covered in a velvet, cream-colored comforter and layers of crimson-colored pillows. A couple black leather chairs and a velvet-covered crimson sofa sat against the other wall. Behind them were floor to ceiling bookcases filled with leather-bound books.

The old man approached us, his face still grinning from ear to ear. "I'm Walter, by the way. I've been longing to meet you both." He stepped back and stared at us, putting his hands together as if he might start clapping. "Ahhh, such a lovely couple. You will certainly make them proud."

"Make who proud? Where are we?" I demanded. With the other men gone, I felt it was time to release my anger again.

My reaction removed the smile from the old man's face. "Yes, well, I'm sure you have many questions, my dear. The answers will come in time. Be patient."

Erik butted his face up against the old man's. "Answer her questions. Now!"

Walter stood still, unnerved by Erik's outburst. "Young man. You do not frighten me. Please step away."

Erik backed off, keeping his eyes on the man.

"This room, you see, is very secure so there's no need to expend any energy trying to leave." The man pointed up. "The ceiling is infused with a chemical that will render you powerless if activated. Should you decide to act in an uncivilized manner, the minuscule holes lining the ceiling will open and release the toxin. And we don't want that, now do we?"

His smile returned. "Now that we have that out of the way, let me release you." He pulled a scissor-like tool from his pocket. "And just so you know, the guards are still outside the door. And cameras are placed throughout the room." He cut my zipties then went to remove Erik's.

"Are you gonna tell us anything?" I asked him. "Anything about where we are? Or why we're here?"

"That's not my role. I don't deal with those types of questions. I am in charge of hospitality, a much more pleasant topic. Now, let me show you around."

Walter went over by the bed. Erik and I remained by the front door. "Well, don't just stand there," he scolded. "Come over here."

He waited for us to join him, then continued. "The fireplace turns on and off on its own so don't try using it yourselves. As you can see, next to it is this beautiful bed. This bed was hand-carved in Italy centuries ago by artisan craftsmen. Isn't it majestic? The linens are a finely woven silk blend, soft and sumptuous. An excellent choice, I must say." He ran his hand along the turned down sheet.

He walked over to the other side of the room. "If you have some reading time, there are some marvelous books on these walls. Classics, of course. Not the rubbish they publish now."

We followed him across the room again. "The bathroom facilities are right through here." He pushed on a door which opened into a huge bathroom with white marble floors and counters. There was a walk-in shower and soaking tub at the far end of the room. Stacks of thick, white towels filled a tall open cabinet. It was by far the largest and most lavish bathroom I'd ever seen. "All your toiletries are in the side cabinets. His and hers."

He paused as if running through a checklist in his head. "Oh yes, your clothing. It's all in the armoire and the closet." He walked briskly to the closet and opened the doors. "Everything is the proper size for you both. I think that's it. Any questions?" He paused. "Let me clarify. Any hospitality-related questions?"

"How long are you keeping us here?" Erik asked.

"Perhaps you didn't hear me, young man. I said hospitality questions only. Your length of stay is not my decision. But with a room like this, who would ever want to leave?"

"Where's my sister?" I knew he wouldn't tell me but I had to ask. "Why isn't she staying with us?"

Walter glared at me. "People like her have separate quarters. They don't allow her kind on this floor."

Rage overtook me and I lunged at the old man but Erik held me back as Walter pointed at the ceiling again.

"It's quite toxic," he said with a sickly grin. "I'll let you two get settled. Why don't you freshen up before heading to bed? I know it's late but I took the liberty of ordering you a light snack. I wasn't sure if you would have eaten already."

There was a knock on the door. "Oh, there it is now." Walter opened the door, then rolled in a cart that had a tray of fresh fruit and a carafe of water on it. "Just a light snack. One shouldn't have a heavy meal before bed, you know. Goodnight, then. Pleasant dreams."

Walter left, closing the door behind him. Erik immediately ran up to it, trying to make it open. Then he ran to the drapes, desperate to find a window. But the drapes hid a solid wall.

"Erik, you heard him. It's a waste of time. The place is built like a prison. I guess that confirms where we are."

Erik collapsed on the bed. "GlobalLife. Must be another one of their genetic research facilities."

"Why does it look like an office out there and a hotel in here?" I scanned the room again. "This is so freaky, Erik. I feel like I'm in some alternate universe. This is nothing like the facility in Minnesota. There, they locked me up in an all white concrete room and strapped me to a metal bed. This doesn't make any sense."

"It's probably just one of their psychotic mind games. Put us in some fancy room tonight and then tomorrow they'll lock us up in a room like you described and torture us."

"Great, now I'll be worrying about that all night. Thanks, Erik." I sat on the bed with him. "But why would they put us together in the same room?"

"I don't know. But I'm sure they're listening to everything we're saying!" He yelled it at the ceiling. "Go to hell! All of you!"

I leaned over to Erik and whispered. "We have to get out of here. They have Colin and Jack. We have to try and save them."

Erik didn't believe it. He was convinced Colin and Jack had met a far worse fate. I could see it on his face.

"I'm sure they weren't in there when it happened, Erik," I said, trying to reassure him as well as me. "The explosion didn't even take out the whole building. Just part of it. GlobalLife probably used it as a distraction to get to us. That was probably their original plan. Brittany running into the limo just changed the plan."

"Sam, the explosion was meant to kill Colin and my dad. To get them out of the way." Erik tried to keep his voice down but couldn't. He was too angry. "They don't need them. They need us. They killed them, Sam!"

"No! I won't believe it! I refuse to! They can't take anyone else from me. I won't let them."

"It's too late. There's no way my dad and Colin got out of there."

"Why are you saying that? I don't know why you're acting like this."

"Because it's over, Sam!" he shouted at the ceiling. "Those bastards have us locked up in some foreign country in the middle of the freakin' ocean! Well, GlobalLife? You win!"

"Stop it!" I lowered my voice. "Do you really wanna just give up like that, Erik? Because I refuse to. I got out of that prison they held me in before and I'll get out of this one, too."

Erik finally quieted down. "Don't you get it, Sam? They had this whole thing planned. That letter from Dave. The private plane. The guy at the airport. And we fell for it! All of it! How could we be so stupid?!"

"You mean how could *I* be so stupid! That's what you meant to say, isn't it Erik?" My temper flared and I struggled not to scream at him. "You're blaming me for this, aren't you? Sam and her stupid dreams, right? I know that's what you're thinking. I brought everyone up here and now we're all gonna die. Just say it!"

"I'm just trying to understand this, Sam. Let's say your instincts were right and that letter *was* from Dave. Why would Dave lure us up here to get caught?" He paused. "Are you sure you can trust Dave? Maybe he's not as—"

"Stop! Don't you dare say anything bad about him! He's the closest thing to family I have left. I've grown up with him. He treats me like a daughter. He would never betray me like this!"

"Dammit, Sam! He's not even your real uncle! And the guy works for GlobalLife! He's worked there for years. You don't even think it's a possibility? Why the hell else would he send us to Iceland?"

I shoved Erik hard. "Dave did NOT do this! And he only works at GlobalLife because they threaten him whenever he tries to leave."

"So if you're not blaming Dave for this, then are you saying that someone else wrote that letter? So you're saying you were wrong about your dream?"

I got off the bed. "Yeah, I guess I was! Are you happy now?"

"No. Because we're still stuck here and we're never getting out."

I stormed into the bathroom, slamming the door shut. Once inside, I wanted to cry but I wouldn't let myself do it. I had to be strong. And I couldn't let Erik give up so easily. I needed him to believe that we could escape. Erik hadn't been in this situation before. I had. When I was held prisoner in Minnesota, I, too, thought I'd never get out. But I did. And I had to help Erik see that it was possible.

I needed time alone so I took a long shower. Afterward, I put on a robe that I found in the bathroom. It wasn't a comfy, thick robe like you get at hotels. Instead, it was short, silky lingerie-type robe that offered no warmth at all. To kill more time, I went through all the drawers on my side of the sink. They were full of expensive brands of makeup, perfume, and lotion. As I brushed out my hair, I realized that I didn't have any clothes to change into. I went back out into the room. Erik was sitting in one of the leather chairs.

"I forgot to get clothes," I mumbled as I opened the armoire searching for underwear. In the bottom drawer I found silk and lace bikinis and bras, not at all what I would normally wear. I searched the other drawers looking for pajamas but the only thing I could find was more lingerie. No shorts, no t-shirts, no pajama pants. Just lingerie like you would pack for a honeymoon. Hanging from the top of the armoire were some women's skirts and silk blouses. Erik's side had men's dress shirts and ties.

I went over to the closet. Again, there was nothing I would normally wear. Just dresses and an assortment of high heeled shoes. On Erik's side, there were dark suits, more dress shirts, and more ties. Not even a pair of jeans. For either of us.

"Can't find anything to wear?" Erik asked from across the room. He seemed to have calmed down.

"It's a very limited selection." I went back to the armoire and looked on Erik's side. He had men's pajama pants but no pajama tops. I held up the pants but they were way too big for me to wear. In his other drawer, there were socks and boxer briefs. "Do you care if I wear some of your stuff?"

"Why? They didn't give you pajamas?"

I held up a short, black, slip-like dress, one of my only "pajama" options. "They gave me this. I think it's called a chemise. My mom had some of these."

He eyed the lingerie. "What's wrong with that?"

I rolled my eyes at him. "Are you kidding? There's nothing to this thing! And they're all like that." I pulled a few more of them out. "Some are even worse."

"So what do you wanna wear?"

"Maybe one of your shirts?" I held up a men's button up shirt that was so long it covered my knees. "And look what they gave me for underwear. I don't wear stuff like this!" I dangled the silk bikinis in the air.

"Those are nice," he said, smiling.

I shook my head, taking his shirt and a pair of bikinis into the bathroom. I came out looking and feeling ridiculous in the oversized shirt.

"Okay. Bathroom's yours. You've got pajama pants in the drawer over there. For some reason they only gave you the pants. No shirts. Not even a t-shirt."

He shrugged. "I usually don't wear anything."

I glared at him. "Well, you're wearing something tonight!"

"I didn't say I wasn't. I was just saying that—never mind. I'm gonna take a shower."

The bed was so high that there was a step stool next to it. I pushed it aside and crawled into the huge bed. The sheets were luxurious. The softest I'd ever felt. I stared up at the ceiling and around the room looking for the cameras Walter talked about. I couldn't find them anywhere.

While Erik was gone I wondered where he was going to sleep. I looked over at the velvet sofa. It was super small. A guy Erik's size would never be able to sleep on it. *I* couldn't even sleep on it.

Erik came out of the bathroom in his pajama pants and no shirt. "So, I guess I'll take the floor." He looked around for a blanket.

"Here, take one of these blankets." I lifted the comforter but there were no blankets. Just the sheets and the comforter. "Sorry, they don't have one."

"Great. So I guess I'll just take a pillow."

The thought of Erik sleeping blanket-less on the cold, hard floor didn't seem right. "Just sleep in here. It's a king size bed. There's plenty of room for both of us."

"Are you sure?"

"Yes. Come on."

Erik got into bed, turning his back to me. I shut off the light but the fireplace remained on. Since we couldn't turn it off, the light of the fire lit the room.

"Hey," Erik said from the other side of the bed. "Sorry about what I said earlier. I shouldn't have said that stuff about Dave. And I don't blame you for this. I was just really pissed off. Still am. Because I don't know how to get us out of this."

"I'm sorry, too. Let's just forget about it. Goodnight, Erik."

An hour later, the fire went out and the room got very cold. I buried myself under the comforter but was still chilled. I wanted to huddle next to Erik for warmth but didn't want to give him the wrong idea.

Another hour passed and I started shivering. The movement must have woke Erik up. "Sam, are you cold or what's going on over there? The whole bed is moving."

"Um, yeah, I'm a little cold," I whispered back.

"Come here." Erik turned onto his back and laid his arm out.

"No, I don't think so."

"I'm not gonna try anything, Sam. I'm just trying to get you to stop shivering and shaking the whole bed so I can sleep."

I moved over and nestled in his arm, resting my head on his chest. Even shirtless, he was warmer than me. Getting warm again made me sleepy. I fell asleep and didn't awake until morning.

"Sam." Erik nudged me. "I think someone's at the door."

I sat up and pulled the covers over me. We waited as the door unlocked. I could hear a woman's voice saying something to the guard.

And then the woman entered the room. She had beautiful shiny black hair. A tailored tweed suit. Crisp white dress shirt. And diamond earrings. I instantly recognized her. Mrs. Taylor. Allie's mom.

19. INTERVIEWS

"Well, don't you two look cozy." Mrs. Taylor walked toward us as the door closed behind her. "Samantha, it's nice to see you again."

I was so shocked I couldn't speak. I was convinced the whole scene wasn't real. But it was. Allie's mom was standing right there in front of me. In the room that was now my prison. In Iceland!

"Do you know her?" Erik asked me, keeping his eyes on Mrs. Taylor.

"Yes, she knows me quite well," Mrs. Taylor answered. "She's friends with my daughter. They grew up together."

"Is that true, Sam?" Erik looked at me. "Sam?" He elbowed me to wake me from my shock.

"She's just surprised to see me, aren't you, Samantha?"

I didn't answer.

She came closer to the bed. "So tell me, are you enjoying your stay so far?"

"What are you doing here, Mrs. Taylor?" I asked, finally able to speak.

"There's no need to be so formal, Samantha. You've known me forever. Just call me Eve. And to answer your question, I'm here on business. I work for GBL Capital Management."

Erik sat up straighter and crossed his arms. "And what is that?"

"It's a worldwide investment firm. A division of GlobalLife International. GBL is short for GlobalLife. We tend not to promote that, so the connection isn't widely known. Surprisingly, not everyone appreciates all the wonderful advancements GlobalLife brings to the world."

"So why would an investment firm hold us prisoner?" he asked.

"The building you're in actually belongs to GlobalLife Genetics. It was built about a year ago. It's a beautiful building. And the labs are incredible. You'll see them later. Anyway, I'm here to meet with some people about financing the project you're involved in. Thanks to the two of you, we have people lining up to invest. Or at least they will be after the big event we're holding this weekend. And to address your earlier wording, Erik, you are *not* a prisoner here. Look at this place. Does it look like a prison?" Eve turned around, showing off the room.

I glared at her. "You're holding us captive. You won't let us leave. It's no different than what GlobalLife did to me in Minnesota."

"It's completely different, Samantha. That old, run-down lab in Minnesota was deplorable. And I'm sorry you had to suffer there. Worthings was incompetent. To think that he would put someone like you in those conditions. It's horrid! We're all glad to be rid of him. This time around, we want you to be comfortable. You'll receive the very best care. And your every need will be attended to."

I pointed to the ceiling. "Comfortable? You have toxins ready to be released on us! You have cameras watching us! You're listening to our every word."

Eve laughed. "What? No, no. None of that is true. Who told you that? Walter? Oh, he's always telling tales like that. Silly old man. Just look around. Do you see any cameras? Listening devices?"

"I know they're hidden in here," I snapped.

"Who are you going to believe, Samantha? A senile old man you just met? Or me, the mother of your closest friend?"

Her question made me wonder about Allie. "Does Allie know where you are? Does she know about any of this?"

"She's my daughter, Samantha. Of course she knows."

"You're lying. If she knew she would have told me. "

"I'm afraid not, Samantha. The truth is that Allie has known about you since she was a young girl. You see, my daughter has never been your friend. She was simply playing the role all those years so we could keep an eye on you. In fact, the whole reason we live in Minnesota is because of you. I would never choose to live there. It's a flyover state. An agricultural wasteland. Now that you're here, my husband and I can finally pack up and leave."

As she spoke, I tried to imagine Allie faking our friendship all those years. I couldn't. It wasn't possible. We'd been friends since kindergarten.

"Allie would never pretend to be my friend," I fumed.

"Think about it, Samantha. My daughter has nothing in common with you. She has no interest in science. She's a writer. She wants to be a journalist. And she's obsessed with fashion, just like me. If she could have chosen her friend, she would have picked someone with similar interests who was popular and beautiful, like her."

She looked at me for a response, but I had none. "She betrayed you, Samantha. Isn't that proof that she was never your friend?"

"What are you talking about? She didn't betray me."

"How do you think you ended up here? How did we know where you were going?" She smiled. "We were so fortunate to have you land on our doorstep yesterday. Not the smartest move on your part coming back to Minnesota like that, but—"

"I don't understand. Are you saying Allie put some type of tracking device on me? No. She wouldn't do that."

"That was a beautiful leather bag my daughter gave you, wasn't it?" She sneered.

I ignored her smug response. "If you wanted me, why didn't you just take me when I was at your house?"

"We have a protocol to follow, Samantha. Anyway, that's all in the past. You're here now. That's all that matters."

I could feel Erik's temper rising. "Just get to the point. What are they gonna do to us here?"

"Mr. Chamberlin, the man who has replaced Dr. Worthings as head of GlobalLife Genetics, will answer your questions later." She smiled. "For now, enjoy the facility. Relax. Have some breakfast."

We heard the door unlocking again. A man rolled in a cart filled with pastries, juices, and fresh fruit. Dome covers seemed to hide plates of hot food.

"I'll let you be. So good to see you again, Samantha." Eve walked to the door.

"Wait," I called after her. "What about Brittany? My sister. When can I see her?"

She turned around, a sick grin on her face. "It's sweet that you're still so naive, Samantha." She left, locking the door behind her.

"What's that supposed to mean?" I slumped back on the pillows. "I can't believe this, Erik. Allie's mom?"

"Did you ever suspect anything? Did her mom ever act weird around you?"

"No. Like she said, I just saw her. Yesterday, when I went to see Allie. And she seemed perfectly normal. She even offered to help Colin and me if we needed it." I paused to replay the scene in my head. "And Allie. She was so upset about Colin and me leaving. She went on and on about how much she'd miss us and how we were all best friends. At least that's what she said. But I guess it was all a lie."

"Sam, you can't believe her mom. Allie probably doesn't know about any of this."

"But what if Allie *did* put a tracking device on me? She could have easily put it on that leather bag, just like her mom said. Erik, why did

I go to her house? That was so stupid! I should have never gone over there."

"There's no way you would have known, Sam."

"I always wondered why she was my friend. It never made sense."

"What do you mean?"

"It doesn't matter. Just forget about it." I pulled the comforter over me. "Are they ever gonna turn that fire back on? It's freezing in here." Right after I said it, the fireplace turned on again.

"Yeah, they're not listening," Erik said sarcastically.

"You want something to eat?" I went over to the cart of food and wheeled it next to the bed.

"Anything. I'm starving."

I gave Erik the plate of hot food and took some fruit and a muffin for myself. "So what do you think they're gonna do to us?"

He shrugged. "Treat us like lab rats. Drug us. Hook us up to machines and monitors."

"Then why are we in a place like this?" I moved closer to Erik so I could whisper. "Why not just put us in a room like I was in before?"

"I told you, Sam. They're playing mind games with us," he whispered back. "Hoping to win us over. They probably think it will make us go along with whatever they have planned for us."

"I still don't get why they're keeping us together, Erik. Aren't they worried we'll come up with an escape plan?"

"Guess not. And what's with the fancy clothes? They gave me suits and ties. That's it! What's that about? And what happened to the clothes that we were wearing when we got here? They were right over there and now they're gone."

I didn't answer. The clothes were the least of my concerns. "Erik, what do think happened to Brittany?"

"I don't know. And I don't think they'll tell us."

"Did you hear how everyone talks about her? It's like she's some second-class citizen, not even allowed on the same floor as us."

Erik set his fork down. "Sam, do you smell something?"

"I smell the food," I said, looking down at his plate of eggs.

"No, something else. Like flowers or perfume."

I sniffed the air. "Yeah, I smell it now. It's flowery, like gardenias. My mom used to have perfume that smelled like that."

"Where is it coming from?"

The smell was getting stronger, filling the entire room. "I can't tell. It's almost like it's pouring out of the air vents."

We each took another deep whiff, trying to figure out the source. I suddenly felt so sleepy that I had to lie back down on the bed. Erik did the same. Soon we were out cold.

When I started to wake up, I could hear conversations around me.

"She's much more advanced than the other one," I heard a voice say. "Now that we've removed that fragment of DNA, we'll be able to observe and test how her abilities are advancing."

"Why aren't we adding the missing base pairs to complete the sequence?" another voice asked. "We've got both of them now. We don't need the timer as a safeguard anymore. Chamberlin didn't even have us enable their internal locators. He's convinced they're never leaving here."

"Chamberlin's not ready to add the base pairs yet. Hell, I don't even know where they are. I can't imagine they'd keep the genes here. I'm thinking they're in Sweden, locked down in some vault. Chamberlin probably has to go get them himself."

"Well, he better hurry because the boy's time is running out."

"Hey, I think she's waking up. Give her more of the drug."

I felt myself getting sleepy again. The voices faded as my mind filled with images of the airport from the previous night. I was inside the building as smoke from the explosion filled the room. I heard a whole new set of voices as the scene came to life.

"Colin, stay close to the ground where the air is clearer!" The voice sounded like Jack's. "Crawl forward and to the right!"

"Jack, where are you? I can't see anything." I heard Colin say.

"Something fell on my leg," Jack said. "I'm stuck. Just go!"

"No, I'm not leaving you here! Tell me where you are."

"The smoke is getting worse, Colin. Just get out of here!"

In the light of the flames I could see someone moving along the floor. "Hold on, Jack. I can get this off you. Don't move."

A loud thud sounded as Colin pushed what appeared to be a heavy desk off of Jack's leg. "Okay, let's go."

Jack coughed from the smoke. "I don't think I can walk on it."

"Then I'll drag you. Grab my arms."

The room was black with smoke now. The windows had been blown out, sending smoke billowing into the night sky. Suddenly I saw bright headlights coming toward the building. A car approached, stopping suddenly. A shadowy figure jumped out of the car and ran into the smoke-filled building.

"Who are you?" I heard Colin yell between coughs.

"Don't talk. Try to hold your breath till we're out," a voice said. I couldn't identify the voice, but it sounded like it belonged to a man.

I could see Colin crawling out of the building, dragging Jack with the help of the unknown man. Soon Colin and Jack were both in the back seat of the vehicle. The car sped away from the burning building.

"Tell me who you are," Colin said, still coughing.

"I'll tell you everything when we get there."

I slowly woke up. I opened my eyes to find that I was still in bed, wearing the same men's dress shirt. The breakfast cart sat next to me, right where I had put it. I rolled over and bumped into Erik, who was starting to wake up as well.

"Sam, what happened?" Erik had on the same pajama pants as before. It was like nothing had changed, except that the gardenia smell was gone.

"Did you fall asleep?" I asked Erik.

"I guess I did. But for how long?"

"I don't know. The breakfast tray looks new. Like it hasn't been touched. When we fell asleep, we'd eaten part of it."

"Sam, I think it's a whole different—"

"Shhh," I hushed Erik, not wanting GlobalLife to hear our theory about what had happened. The less they heard, the better. "So you want some breakfast, Erik?"

"Why is she talking about breakfast? We just woke up from being drugged and—"

"What did you—" I quickly shut up, realizing that I'd just heard Erik's thoughts for the first time in days.

"Erik, listen. Do you hear me? In your head?" I picked up a plate on the breakfast tray, trying to act normal for the cameras that I assumed were somewhere around us.

He smiled. *"Loud and clear, Sam."*

"Yes! Now we can talk without them hearing. Listen Erik, I think they took us and did stuff to us in the lab."

"Yeah. I think so, too. The flowery smell must have been some type of drug they put in the air to knock us out."

"Whatever they did to us restored our abilities. But we can't tell them we can do this. They'll have to find out on their own. For now just act normal."

"I'm really hungry," I said aloud. "I think I'll have some eggs."

"Me, too," Erik said. "I'm starving."

We took our food over to the sitting area on the other side of the room. I used our newly restored telepathy to tell Erik about the conversation I heard when I was knocked out. But I didn't tell him anything about my dream of Colin and Jack being alive. I didn't want to get his hopes up if it wasn't true.

Erik tried to remain outwardly calm after hearing the news that the timer was still going but his thoughts were angry. *"So they're gonna wait until the last minute to turn it off? And nobody even knows where this alien DNA shit is?"*

"That Chamberlin guy knows where it is. At least that's what it sounded like."

"Did they say when he was gonna go get it?"

"No. But maybe we could listen to their minds and find out."

"Be real, Sam. They know we have the telepathy back again. They'll find a way to make sure we can't hear their thoughts."

"Yeah, I guess. Hey, before we passed out, I was thinking about how we should play this thing out."

Erik got up to refill his plate. *"What do you mean?"*

"I mean, I think we should try to go along with whatever it is they're doing here."

"What? No way!" He practically shouted it in my head as he came back to sit down.

"Listen. We need to learn things. Figure out how this place works. We need people to tell us stuff. And they won't do that if we fight them. We need to act like this is normal. Maybe even pretend that we like it here."

"Are you crazy, Sam? No. I'm not doing that."

"Do you wanna escape or not? If we go along with them, we might get answers. But if we fight them, they'll punish us. So which do you want?"

Before we could finish, the door opened. It was Allie's mom again, along with a young woman. The woman was tall, thin, and exotic looking with long black hair.

"Good morning. I'm glad you're both up." Eve walked toward me as the other woman followed behind. "This is Natalie. She'll be helping you get ready, Samantha. I know you're not good with basic grooming, like proper makeup application or hair styling, so Natalie is here to teach you. She'll get you ready today. Tomorrow you can attempt it yourself. You need to make yourself presentable each day. That means hair done and makeup on."

Natalie came over and extended her hand to me. "Hello, Samantha. Follow me, please."

"But I'm still eating—"

"Samantha, listen," Eve interrupted. "You, too, Erik. We have a very important man here today. He's our largest investor and has been with the project since the beginning. He's crucial in helping us attract new investors to the project. But he won't do so unless he continues to see proof of its potential. And you two are part of that proof. So he will be meeting with each of you today. Separately."

"What happens at this meeting?" Erik asked suspiciously.

"He has a series of questions for both of you. He has seen your files and knows what you're capable of. He'd love for you to show him your abilities, but since you've just had the procedure done, I doubt you'll be able to just yet."

"What procedure?" I asked, as Natalie pushed me toward the bathroom. "What did you do to us?"

"Can't you tell? You should notice some of your abilities returning by now. You've been asleep for a day. It's Tuesday morning. We had our team remove that inferior DNA from that one section of your genes."

Erik and I didn't respond because it was what we assumed had happened.

"And yes, we know about your telepathy. That's why we all wear these devices." She held up a small, circular piece of metal with a green light in the center. "It scrambles the brain waves in the air so you can't read them." Eve went back to the door. "I'll be by later to retrieve you for your interviews."

After she left, Natalie ordered me to shower. While she waited outside, I tried talking to Erik. But my telepathy wasn't strong enough yet to reach him in the other room.

"Are you ready?" Natalie called.

"Yes. Come in." I waited by the sink in my skimpy robe.

Natalie started going over how to apply all the makeup that was stashed in the bathroom drawers.

"You see, the eyelid is your canvas and this is your palette." She held up a tray of eyeshadow, then applied some to my left eyelid. "This darker color goes in the crease. You try."

I took the eyeshadow and started putting the color on the eyelid that wasn't yet done.

"No, no. Like this." She grabbed the eyeshadow brush and redid it.

"I'm not really into makeup," I said, thinking how ridiculous it was to be worrying about makeup at a time like this. "I usually just wear a little blush and mascara."

"That's child's makeup, Samantha. You need to look like a woman. A woman of status and culture."

Natalie continued with the makeup lesson. An hour later we were finally done. I knew that by tomorrow, I would forget everything she'd taught me. And I didn't care. Why did I need to look good to sit in a GlobalLife prison all day?

Next Natalie worked on my hair, showing me what to do with all the bottles and sprays under the sink. It appeared that they were specially chosen for my naturally wavy, and sometimes frizzy, hair. The hair lesson took another hour.

When it was over, Natalie stood back to look at me. "Now the clothes. I'll be right back." She left, then returned holding a deep blue dress and some black heels. The dress was a perfect fit, almost like it had been specially made using my exact measurements. I walked out of the bathroom to find Erik still sitting in the chair, looking completely bored.

"What took you so—" Erik stopped when he saw me. My form-fitting dress, makeup, and flawless hair took him by surprise.

Natalie smiled. "She looks lovely, doesn't she? I'll be leaving now, Samantha, but Jonathan will be here soon to coach you on what to say."

She left and I went over to Erik. He was still staring at me. "You look really good, Sam."

"As opposed to what? How I normally look?"

Before he could answer, the door opened again and two well-dressed men walked in. The first one greeted us. "Hello, I'm Jonathan and this is Kendall." The men looked nearly identical. Both were young with short blond hair and dark suits.

"Erik, you'll be coming with me," Kendall said. "I'll show you how to do a proper shave, then we'll clean up that mop of hair on your head."

"I already know how to shave. And what's wrong with my hair?"

Kendall gave Erik a look that implied he had no choice in the matter. The two of them left for the bathroom and Jonathan sat down next to me.

"So you'll be meeting with Mr. Owens today." Jonathan sounded as if I'd won a prize. "He's our biggest investor. Very powerful man. And an excellent dresser. Has all his clothing handmade using the finest of fabrics."

"When am I meeting him?"

"In an hour. But before that, we need to go over some things. For instance, just look how you're sitting. All hunched over, legs twisted up like a pretzel. Sit like this."

He sat sideways on the small velvet sofa, his shoulders and head upright. His legs were together but not crossed and his hands rested on his knees. "This is how a lady sits. Now try it."

Jonathan spent the next 50 minutes lecturing me on proper body language and how to answer questions. He gave me words and phrases to use that seemed to come from the GlobalLife employee handbook. "As you know, GlobalLife is a leader in tomorrow's technology. And I'm honored to have such an important role in shaping the future." Jonathan spoke like he was recording a commercial. "Now repeat that back to me."

"I can't even remember what you said. Why can't I just answer his questions?"

"Just repeat it back to me. Hurry up."

I sighed. "GlobalLife is a leader in—" I stopped when I saw Erik.

He came out of the bathroom wearing a dark suit, white dress shirt, and tie. He was cleanly shaven and his hair had been trimmed.

Jonathan stood up. "Excellent job, Kendall. Much improved. Samantha, I hope you memorized what I said because it's time for you to leave for the interview. Erik, come over here so I can go over what I just told her."

Erik walked past me and I got a whiff of his cologne. He smelled as good as he looked. I felt an indescribable attraction to him once again. Just like I had when we first met back in Texas. Even more so.

"Just look at them together," Kendall swooned. "Aren't they a wonderful couple? A perfect match."

"Yes, they certainly are," Jonathan agreed.

The door opened and Eve walked in. "Samantha, you look so much better. And Kendall, you've done a splendid job with the boy."

Kendall smiled, reviewing his work again.

"Samantha, let's go. Mr. Owens is in the conference room." She took my arm and led me out. The office was buzzing with people, a much different scene than when Erik and I had arrived there. It felt strange to not be cuffed or secured in any way. But it's not like I could like make a run for it. Armed guards stood at the building entrance and a few more were scattered around the lobby.

Eve took me to a hallway in the back of the building. We entered a room with the longest table I'd ever seen. Tall leather office chairs surrounded it. At the end of the room was a wall of windows that displayed a stunning view of snow-covered mountains.

A man in a black suit was standing with his back to us, looking out at the wintery scene. He turned when he heard us enter.

"Mr. Owens. Sorry to keep you waiting. This is Samantha." Eve pushed me toward the man. "Samantha, this is Mr. Preston Owens."

The man appeared to be in his mid-seventies. He was taller than average and had a full head of gray hair that was held in place with some kind of hair product. He had a very distinguished look. I could tell that he was used to holding the power in the room. In fact, Allie's mom seemed almost fearful of him. She tried to cover it up by standing straight and smiling a lot.

"Well, I'll let you two talk," Eve said. "I'll be just down the hall. Call me when you're done."

Eve left and Owens motioned me to sit down. "Very nice to meet you Samantha. You're a beautiful girl. And I hear that you're very intelligent." Owens' mannerisms and the way he spoke reminded me of how rich people are portrayed in old movies.

"Thank you, Mr. Owens. What is it you would like to know?"

He turned and looked out at the mountains again. "Such a majestic country, don't you think? Practically untouched by man. Nature in all its beauty. I love it so much that I built a home here. Just one of many. I have homes all over the world."

He continued talking about Iceland, causing my mind to wander. *When is this interview going to start?* I thought. *Does he just like listening to himself talk?*

"Samantha, do you hear me? If you do, clear your throat."

Owens was still staring out the window and had started talking about the weather. I looked around to see if someone else had entered the room.

"Do you hear me? If so, tell me. Cough. Or do something."

I realized that his voice was in my head. I was hearing Owens' thoughts, even though the brain wave scrambling device was clearly displayed on his suit jacket. It was the same circular piece of metal that Eve wore.

I coughed, then cleared my throat.

"Good. Now you need to listen to every word I say."

20. DINNER DATE

I tried hard not to react. I was sure we were being monitored. "What did you say was the average temperature here in Iceland?"

Owens turned away from the window. "I believe the average yearly temperature is 46 degrees. That's Fahrenheit. Chilly for most people, but I don't mind it. I'm originally from upstate New York, so I'm used to the cold."

He sat down and began asking me basic questions about where I grew up and what subjects I liked in school. As I answered, I listened to what he was telling me through his thoughts.

"Now remember that I can't hear your thoughts, so don't try to think back to me with your mind. You'll just have to listen to what I'm thinking while you continue to talk out loud for the cameras. Got it?" I gave him a quick smile to let him know I understood. *"I've been involved with GlobalLife for many years. I'm one of the Founders. It's a very powerful group. You'll learn more about them later. I'll be here all week preparing for the event on Saturday."*

As he talked, I kept wondering how I was able to hear him. I moved my hand along the neckline of my v-neck dress, pretending to adjust it but stopping right where the brain wave scrambling device was on his jacket.

Owens picked up on my question. *"I have a device on that disables it. Don't try to ask me any more questions. It's too obvious. Now I'm working on a way to get you and Erik out of here. But you both need to help. I can't do this alone."*

I couldn't believe what I was hearing. Why would this guy want Erik and me to escape? And why would he help us? I desperately wanted to ask him but couldn't.

"I know you need those base codes and I know for a fact that they are in this building. There are two small vials of the alien genes hidden somewhere on this floor. I don't know exactly where. You and Erik will need to find that out. When you do, you'll need a password to access them. The vials will also be protected with some type of biometric. I'm not certain what that is. I know it's not a fingerprint or retinal scan. That technology is too old and too easy to copy. You need to find out what else it could be."

"And so I've always been interested in science," I said, continuing to talk about myself while also trying to hear Owens' thoughts.

"I'm going to try to show you maps of the building and the surrounding area. I don't know if you've ever received an image instead of words via your thoughts but you need to try. You'll need these maps for your escape. I will imagine one section of the building at a time, showing key points of entry and exit. Memorize them. I will then show you the outside, including a route to the place you'll need to go when you escape."

I put all my energy into interpreting his thoughts as he imagined each section of the building. I built my own map in my head, starring sections of importance. We finished just as Eve walked through the door.

"I wanted to check in and see how things are going." Eve turned on an exaggerated smile for Owens.

"I think we're done here," Owens said, getting up. "Samantha is a remarkable girl. Just as you described. I'm very impressed."

"Oh, I'm so glad to hear that." Eve put her arm around me, making me cringe. "Well, should I get Erik?"

"Yes, let's move this thing along. I've got a lunch meeting I need to run to."

I heard Owens again in my head as I left. *"One last thing. Colin and Jack are safe."*

The words were unexpected. I tried to hide any emotion, but inside I was jumping for joy. I hadn't yet told Erik about my dream of Colin and Jack escaping the airport because I didn't think it was true. But now it was confirmed and that, along with Owens' plan to help us, filled me with happiness and hope.

"Well, you must have taught her something," Eve said to Jonathan when we were back in the room. "She somehow managed to win him over. Erik, let's go."

"Listen to Mr. Owens. Listen to his every word," I thought to Erik as he met Eve at the door.

Erik didn't respond, but I knew he heard me. A half hour later, Erik returned. We were finally alone in the room.

"Did he tell you?" I thought to Erik, making sure to hide my excitement from the cameras.

"Yeah. But who is that guy? And why is he helping us?"

"Maybe he doesn't like this genetic manipulation thing. Who cares why? With his help, we might actually get out of this place! And now we know that Colin and Jack are okay!"

"How do you know that?"

"Owens told me. He didn't tell you?"

"No. But I could barely hear his thoughts. Eve stayed in the room during the interview and kept talking to him. I guess she didn't trust me to answer his questions the right way. So my dad and Colin are okay?"

I told Erik what Owens said, then explained the dream I'd had that showed Colin and Jack surviving the airport explosion. *"I didn't say anything to you because I wasn't sure if it was true,"* I thought to Erik. *"But now we know it is! They're safe, Erik!"*

I hugged Erik, then realized the cameras were watching. I quickly pulled away.

"What's wrong?" he asked.

"It looks suspicious. Us hugging without talking. They'll know we're using telepathy."

"They already know. You heard what Eve said."

"Yeah, but still, we shouldn't make it so obvious. If they think we're using it all the time, they'll think we're planning something. We need to make them trust us. Make them think that we have nothing to hide."

"Yeah, like they're gonna believe that, Sam."

"I'm just saying that it wouldn't hurt to try to hide it more, okay?"

The door opened and two men entered carrying a table and chairs. They set the table with white linens and china and put a bouquet of flowers in the center. Then they placed two silver-domed plates on the table. The men motioned us to sit down, then left.

"Everything is so formal here." I lifted the dome off my plate. "Salmon and roasted asparagus? For lunch?" Off to the side was a tossed salad and a roll.

"I hate fish. And asparagus," Erik mumbled. "Next time, make it a burger and fries!" he shouted at the ceiling. We still hadn't found the listening devices, but the ceiling seemed like an appropriate hiding spot for them.

I felt old sitting there eating a fancy lunch while wearing a designer dress and heels. Erik looked like a rich businessman in his expensive suit and tie. He took his tie off and undid the first few buttons of his shirt. He stared at the ceiling again. "And along with that burger, give me some jeans and t-shirts!"

"Yeah, I'll take the same!" I called out. "And sneakers!" I slipped off my heels. My aching feet instantly felt better.

As we ate, Erik told me, telepathically, what Owens had said during his interview. Apparently the password we needed to access the alien genes was encrypted as some type of code, or cipher as Owens called it. He imagined the cipher in his mind so Erik could see it. It was the same type of code that Erik had cracked before. The same type that his brother, Luke, had left in his journal.

Owens explained that GlobalLife used this type of mathematical cipher to secure top-secret files. Over the years, Owens had lost trust in GlobalLife and had been trying to access their files in order to learn more about what was really going on with the enhanced genetics project, also known as The Samantha Project. But Owens couldn't get the files open because he couldn't find anyone who could figure out the ciphers. So he created a temporary Internet game site to see if someone out in cyberspace could do it. The first one to crack the code would get $1,000. The game attracted lots of people but only one who could crack the sample code that was posted. And that person was Luke.

Erik went on to say that Owens contacted Luke and hired him to figure out the actual ciphers. But before Owens hired him, he did some background checks on Luke. And that's how he learned of Luke's connection to GlobalLife and Erik. Before Luke died, Owens was trying to help Luke find Erik and get him up to Iceland, where the missing base codes were.

"Well, that explains why your name was in his journal," I thought to Erik as we ate dessert. *"And it explains why he had the longitude and latitude for Reykjavik. But why didn't Owens just go get you himself? Why involve Luke?"*

"He said it was too risky, given his connections to GlobalLife," Erik thought back.

"So how did Owens know about the alien genes? Did he know Dan, the guy who made the file we got from Paul?"

"I don't think so. Owens didn't mention Dan or the file. It sounds like Owens has been involved with this project since the alien genes were discovered. He said he used to know a lot more about it until he started objecting to GlobalLife's plan for the genes. The past few years, he's been getting less and less information from them. That's why he's been breaking into their files."

"Then I guess he's always known about me. He said he was a Founder. That was the same group of people who were supposed to be at that meeting in Minnesota. But the meeting never happened, so I never met any of them."

"What's a Founder?" Erik asked.

"I'm not sure. I think it's one of those secret societies. Invitation only."

The door opened again and the men who had brought us lunch were back to clean it up and take the table and chairs away.

"I wonder what's next," I said, out loud this time.

"We just hang out in these uncomfortable clothes and wait."

I walked to the shelves of books. "We could read. They've got plenty of books here."

"We need to start planning," Erik thought to me. *"And I need to work on that cipher. Not being able to write it down makes it harder to work on. It'll take me days."*

"When you work on it, you need to look like you're doing something else. Grab a book and pretend to be reading." I scanned the books on the shelves. *Hey, here's a book on the golden ratio. Remember that necklace I got from Allie with the Greek letter, phi? That symbol is supposed to represent the golden ratio."* I felt my neck, noticing that the necklace had been taken.

I picked out another book and we both sat down to read. The books provided a good cover because we could easily mind-talk without having a fake conversation.

"What kind of biometric would they use to protect the alien genes if they're not using fingerprints or retinal scans?" I thought to Erik.

"I have no idea. But before we even think about that, we have to find out where they put this stuff. Where do you hide a vial of alien DNA? One of the labs? Does it have to be stored some special way?"

"Human DNA is usually stored in a solution and frozen. But I remember my dad saying that newer methods allowed it to be stored dehydrated at room temperature. So I guess it could be either way."

We continued mind-talking until early evening, when Walter showed up in our room. "Mr. Chamberlin has invited you to join him for dinner this evening in the dining room. Perhaps you'd like to freshen up first?"

Erik and I looked at each other, then looked at ourselves. "No, we're ready to go." Erik said, getting up.

Walter let out a dramatic sigh. Apparently we weren't aware of the proper protocol for dinner preparation. "You should at least wash your hands," he said in a disgusted tone.

He got up closer to me. "And perhaps you could brush your hair, miss." My hair had so much product in it that it hadn't moved all day. I was sure it was fine, but I went to the bathroom anyway to appease him.

"Young man, a tie is required at dinner. Do you need me to pick one out for you?" I heard Walter ask Erik.

"No," Erik answered, sounding annoyed.

Once we met his approval, Walter took us down the hallway at the back of the building. We passed a series of conference rooms like I'd seen earlier. At the end was a door that opened to a formal dining room. A man in a tuxedo was waiting for us.

"Mr. Chamberlin." Walter bowed to him like he was a king. "Your guests have arrived. Shall I show them to their seats?"

"No. That's not necessary. I can show them." Chamberlin waited for Walter to leave, then came up closer to greet us. "So you're the Samantha I've heard so much about." His smile seemed forced. "I was looking forward to meeting you in Minnesota, but, well, we all know how that turned out."

He turned his focus to Erik. "And how fortunate we were to find you, Erik, alive and well after all these years. Come and sit down. Both of you."

Chamberlin looked to be around 45. He had dark brown hair and eyes and was of average build, shorter and smaller than Erik. He led us to a table that had been set for the three of us. Plates of food were waiting, along with glasses of wine. "Please, go ahead and eat. I don't like talking on an empty stomach."

"So you manage this office?" I tried to sound relaxed, but being around the guy was making me edgy. Knowing Worthings and the horrible things he was capable of, I figured his replacement had to be just as evil. Maybe even worse. Who else would take the job? Nobody with any sense of right and wrong.

"I manage the whole GlobalLife Genetics division. I took over when Worthings was, shall we say, dismissed." I was certain that Chamberlin knew I'd killed Worthings, but the topic was not pleasant dinner conversation so he moved on. "I've been working out of this office the past year, getting it up and running. The building is brand new. It has the latest technology, the latest equipment, and the most exquisite design. It's very pleasing to the eye, don't you think, Erik?"

Erik hadn't been paying attention, which I could tell was irritating Chamberlin. He looked up when he heard his name. "The building? Yeah, I guess it's okay."

"Okay? Are you blind, young man? This is one of the most magnificent buildings ever built. It's a work of art. It was designed using the golden ratio, a mathematical equation that represents perfection. It's been proven that designing buildings, or artwork, or even people using this golden ratio results in—"

"People?" Erik finally became interested.

"Don't EVER interrupt me!" Chamberlin glared at Erik, pausing to make sure he understood. "As I was saying, it results in objects that people find appealing. And alluring. Like they are looking at perfection. Just look at the room we're in now. The columns, the ceiling, the artwork. Sheer perfection!"

Erik and I continued to eat, wondering how long we'd be stuck there listening to the guy.

"Did you know that the golden ratio even shows itself in our DNA?" It seemed like a rhetorical question but Chamberlin stared at me, waiting for an answer.

"Um, no. I didn't know that," I replied, growing more and more uncomfortable around this strange man.

Chamberlin talked about architecture and paintings throughout the rest of the meal. During dessert, I couldn't take his rambling anymore and decided to get to the point. "Why is it that you asked us to dinner tonight, Mr. Chamberlin? Did you have something to tell us?"

He seemed annoyed. "Yes. But that's business. This is dinner. And during dinner, one talks about topics such as art or music. Clearly, you both need some etiquette training."

Erik and I quickly finished our desserts, then sat quietly and waited while Chamberlin ate his dessert slowly, bite by bite. When he was finally done, he put his silverware down and smiled at us.

"All right, then. Dinner is over so I will address your questions now." He took a sip of wine. "As Eve might have told you, we were not pleased with the way Worthings dealt with you, Samantha. I hope you've noticed, and appreciated, the more civilized approach we've taken in regards to your care."

I gave him a half smile to acknowledge the better conditions.

He turned to Erik. "We were also perturbed to find out that your caretaker, and our long-lost employee, Jack Reid, took it upon himself to insert that inferior DNA into your cells."

I could feel Erik's anger. "He's my *father*, not my *caretaker*!" Erik got up from the table. "And he did it to save me from that timer! You know, the one that's gonna kill me soon?!"

"Sit down, son," Chamberlin ordered. "That timer will be fixed soon enough. As long as you're here, safe in our care, you'll be just fine. Now, please, sit, so we can continue our conversation."

Erik sat down again.

"So you can fix the timer? You have the antidote here?" I knew it wasn't an antidote but wanted to see what he'd say.

"Yes. And it's safely locked away. So no need to worry about that."

I tried reading his mind, attempting to get past his brain wave scrambler but couldn't.

"How long are you keeping us here?" Erik asked.

"That's not your concern. The timeline depends on many factors. For now just enjoy your surroundings." Chamberlin paused to gaze at the elegant dining room. "Enjoy the fabulous cuisine. The designer clothing. Given where you came from, Erik, I don't see why you'd ever want to leave this place."

Erik ignored the comment. "What do you have planned for us?"

Chamberlin grinned. "We have many wonderful things planned. For both of you. But let's talk in the short term. This week, we'll be getting you groomed for your coming-out party, which is Saturday night. We'll be presenting you both at our first-ever Black and White Gala. It's an event put on for the Founders. One of the most influential members, Preston Owens, whom you have already met, is helping us plan the event. At the gala, you two will be introduced, then will spend time mingling and meeting with our prospective investors. We're hoping to raise hundreds of millions of dollars to keep this project on track."

"Who are the Founders again?" I asked.

"They're a group of highly educated, well-bred, innovative members of society. High-level judges. Heads of state. Military leaders. Captains of industry. It's a diverse group. We have members from all over the world."

"And how do you join this group?"

Chamberlin laughed. "You don't join, Samantha. You are born into it, although a select few have been offered an invitation. But that is very rare. Actually Eve and her husband were invited many years ago, which was a huge honor for them. But they're both brilliant in fields of study that the Founders needed. And they fit the profile well."

"So what do these Founders do? What's their purpose?" Erik asked.

"They are futurists. They plan. They lead. They make the hard decisions that have to be made in order to achieve their goal."

"What exactly is their goal?" I asked.

"To take the human race to a higher plane of being."

I looked at Erik, who seemed just as confused as me. "I don't understand. What does that mean?"

"To take humanity to a new level. A level that strives for perfection. You see, humanity is filled with imperfection. But it doesn't have to be that way. These flaws hold us back. Make us weak and vulnerable. Just consider the human body. It's constantly in disrepair. And eventually it's so broken down that it dies."

"That's the way life works. You live. You die," Erik said.

Chamberlin got excited. "But it doesn't have to be that way! The Founders have known this for centuries. They just haven't been able to find a way to evolve us from the point we're currently at. We here at GlobalLife have. The time has finally arrived! It's time to finally move forward!"

When he saw that we didn't share his excitement, he stood up from the table. "Well, I guess that's enough stories for one evening. You both seem to be losing interest."

"No. Not at all," I said, hoping to get more out of him. His explanation thus far had been more cryptic than helpful. "What do you mean when you say the time has arrived? Have they made some discovery?"

Chamberlin leaned over the table and smiled at us both. "Yes. You are the discovery. Both of you. You two are going to change the course of humanity from this point forward."

21. WALTZ LESSON

I felt sick. GlobalLife and the Founders were using Erik and me for something I didn't yet understand, but I knew that the plan was far bigger than I'd ever imagined. And I knew that it wasn't good.

Chamberlin motioned us to get up. "I think it's time to say goodnight. You both need your rest. It was a pleasure dining with you. And I do hope you enjoy your classes this week." He walked to the door. "Come this way. Walter will take you back to your room."

Erik and I went out in the hallway, where Walter was waiting. Before leaving, I had to ask him one more thing. "Mr. Chamberlin, when can I see my sister? I haven't seen her since we arrived and I really need to talk to her. Could I see her tomorrow or—"

"Sister? You mean that girl from the trailer? No you can't see her. We don't allow her kind on this floor."

"Her kind?" I scowled at him. "What is that supposed to mean?"

"We have a motto here, Samantha. It's one you should become familiar with. And the motto is this: 'We are only as strong as our weakest link.'" He paused. "Think about that, Samantha, in regards to the girl from the trailer."

Chamberlin closed the door of the dining room and Walter escorted us down the hallway. When we got back to our room, I heard the motto in my head again and tried to figure out what

Chamberlin meant. So Brittany is a weak link? In what? His master plan?

"Erik, did you get what he was saying about Brittany?"

"That she's weak? Inferior? Who knows? I don't understand half of the things that guy says."

"I'm really worried about her, Erik."

"Maybe Owens could help. If he's willing to help us, maybe he'll help her, too." Erik was trying to be optimistic, but it wasn't making me feel any better. Brittany wasn't even allowed on our floor. What did that mean? What kind of conditions was she living in?

Erik went to the bathroom to get ready for bed. While he was in there, I tried listening for Brittany's thoughts. I was sure they had one of those brain wave scrambling devices on her, but I had to at least try. After a few minutes of hearing nothing, I gave up. It was no use. I would have to find a different way to connect with Brittany.

"Are you okay with me sleeping in the bed again?" Erik came out of the bathroom in his pajama pants. My eyes fixated on his bare upper body. Erik was naturally muscular from his work on the farm, but the genetic enhancements had made him even more sculpted.

"Um, yeah, whatever," I said, trying hard not to focus on his body. "I'll be right back."

I went in the bathroom and came out wearing one of the silk chemises from my drawer. Erik was sitting up on the bed. He did a double take when he saw me.

I suddenly felt embarrassed. "Yeah, I know. I'm gonna freeze in this, right? But those shirts of yours are so big that I thought I'd just wear one of these stupid—"

"You know, maybe I should try sleeping on the sofa."

I laughed. "You can't sleep on that. It's too small. I could barely sleep on that sofa."

He hesitated, then got into bed. When I climbed in, he scooted far away from me. He was acting very strange. I knew I shouldn't, but I listened to hear what Erik was thinking. I couldn't hear anything, but I did see flashes of images. I focused harder, trying to see them better. As the images slowed, I could see they were of Erik and me in bed. He was slipping my silk chemise off and his hands were moving over my bare skin. Then I saw us kissing and getting more intimate. I quickly got out of his head.

"Erik!" I shouted, sitting up.

I startled him and he bolted upright. "What?! What is it?! Is something wrong?"

I didn't dare tell him I'd been tuning into his mind without permission. "Um, no. Nothing's wrong. I was having a nightmare. Sorry to wake you up."

"That's okay. Here." He snuggled next to me, putting his arm around me. "Go to sleep."

"Oh, you don't need to—" I stopped. Because truthfully, I liked him there next to me. I was growing close to Erik again and my attraction to him was getting stronger by the minute. It was wrong and it wasn't fair to Colin, but I couldn't help how I felt. I went to sleep, telling myself the feelings were simply a side effect from being held captive. A way for me to deal with the stress of the situation.

The next day began like the previous one, except this time Erik and I had to get ourselves ready while Natalie and Kendall watched. "You're not using enough eyeliner," Natalie scolded me. "You can't be afraid of it. You won't poke your eye."

After my hair and makeup were done, I put on another dress, this time a red one that was snug on top but flared out at the waist. Erik donned another designer suit and tie. He looked even better than the day before.

Eve came in midmorning to update us on our schedule. "Mr. Owens was so impressed with you both at the interviews yesterday that he's asked to meet with you again next week."

I smiled, knowing that the meeting would provide us with more information about our escape.

"As you know," Eve continued, "we've restored your abilities, but they won't be fully functional for a few more days. For that reason, you won't be undergoing any tests in our lab until next Monday."

"So what are we doing this week?" I asked.

"You'll be attending classes to prepare you for Saturday night's event. Today you have instruction in ballroom dance and conversation skills."

Erik laughed. "Conversation skills?"

Eve seemed annoyed by Erik's laughter. "After last night, Mr. Chamberlin suggested we teach you what things are appropriate to talk about and when. You'll also learn the proper wording for topics that arise that might be considered controversial by some."

"And the dancing?" I asked.

"It's for the gala this weekend. You two have the honor of the first dance. We can't have you stumbling around like clumsy, awkward teenagers. Anyway, the rest of the week will be filled with more dance lessons as well as etiquette lessons. You'll also attend foreign language classes, where you'll learn some basic phrases that will help you communicate with the non-English speaking guests who will be attending the event. Oh, and tomorrow you'll have a tour of the facilities led by our PR department."

I was elated to hear news of a tour. It was just what we needed to help us better use the maps in our heads. "Sounds great, Mrs. Taylor. We look forward to it."

My willingness to participate surprised her. "Well, I'm glad to hear some enthusiasm from you, Samantha. Now I have some appointments to get to. Enjoy your day."

Eve left and I could hear Erik yelling in my head. *"A tour! Can you believe they're giving us a tour? Are they crazy?"*

"They must be so convinced that we could never escape that they're almost challenging us to try so they can see us fail," I thought back. *"Hey, with our days so packed with activities, when are you gonna work on the cipher?"*

"I'll have to do it at night. I worked on it a little last night. I was having trouble sleeping."

I remembered the images I'd seen in his head of the two of us. I wondered if that was the reason he wasn't sleeping.

We heard a knock on the door and a tall, thin man with jet black hair walked in. He wore a tuxedo, which seemed to be the outfit of choice for the men who worked there.

"Hello, hello! I'm Terrance and you must be Samantha." He took my hand and kissed it. "And you are Erik, I presume?" He shook Erik's hand. "I'll be teaching you both the art of ballroom dancing. And we don't have a minute to waste! Let's go!"

Terrance spoke so fast it was hard to keep up. He walked fast, too, racing back to the door. "Come on, come on. Less standing, more dancing. We have a lot of work to do."

We followed him out to the lobby. As before, it was buzzing with people. Guards remained at the building's entrance. We stopped at a large set of double doors that were just to the right of the entrance. Terrance opened the door and we entered a huge ballroom. It had big marble pillars around the outside edges holding up a balcony where people could stand and watch from above. A giant crystal chandelier hung from the center of the room.

"Now, what do you know about dance?" he asked Erik and me.

"Um, I've been to a few dances at school," I said, thinking of the winter formal Colin and I had attended before I was captured by GlobalLife.

"A school dance? That's it?" Terrance turned to Erik. "And you, young man?"

"I've never been to a dance."

Terrance gasped and threw his hands up in the air. "Oh, how will I ever get you two ready in time?" He thought for a minute, then clapped his hands together as if he had committed to the challenge. "Okay, then. First and foremost, you must know that dance is simply a connection shared by two people. The footwork? The movement? It's all an expression of the two people involved. When the couple is in sync, the dance is in sync. It's a fact. I've seen professional dancers perform horribly when they are not in sync. To dance well, the couple must be completely focused on each other. They must share a connection. They must long for each other. And then everything will click."

"Erik!" Terrance shouted at Erik, who hadn't been paying attention. "Come over here by Samantha."

Erik walked over and stood next to me. Terrance rolled his eyes and positioned Erik in front of me.

"Now hold her." Terrance's tone turned dreamy. "Show me how you feel about the girl."

Erik looked confused. "I don't know what that means."

Terrance sighed. "Pretend that you have no words. Pretend that your body is your only tool of expression. Hold her in a way that expresses your feelings for her."

I stood there feeling awkward as Terrance waited for Erik to move. After what seemed like forever, Erik put his arms around my waist, keeping a safe distance between us, like kids at a junior high dance.

"That's how you feel about this girl?" Terrance asked. "Come on, you can do better than that. Remember, you can't express yourself through words, only actions. How do you feel about her at this very moment? Show me."

Erik paused, then pulled me into a hug. I blushed, not sure what he was doing.

"Hmmm, so you're protective of her," Terrance observed. "Well, I suppose that makes sense, given your situation. But you need to show more. Express more of your feelings for her."

"Are we gonna dance or what?" Erik was getting uncomfortable and so was I. The last thing we wanted to do was put our feelings on display for Terrance and the people he worked for.

"If that's all you'll give me today, then yes, I'll move on. But you must think about what I said. When you're dancing, let your feelings for the girl guide you. Now, let's begin with the traditional slow waltz. It's very easy. Let me show you."

Terrance tapped the floor twice and waltzing music filled the room. He danced across the floor with an invisible partner, showing us the steps. Then Erik and I tried, stepping on each other as we kept moving the wrong way. We practiced for the next two hours but seemed to be getting worse at it.

"No, no, no!" Terrance yelled at us. "Are you even thinking about each other as you dance?"

"I was thinking more about lunch," Erik answered. "Can we eat soon?"

"You're thinking about food?! As you're dancing?! I can't deal with this!" Terrance marched to the back of the room and disappeared out a side door. The music continued to play, filling the ballroom.

"Good. He's finally gone," Erik said. "Think we can leave?"

"Just walk out the door? No." I went over and checked the door just in case. "See? It's locked. Thanks a lot, Erik. Now we'll be stuck in here the rest of the day. He probably isn't coming back."

"He'll come back. He just needs to cool off. We're too much of a challenge for him."

"So you've really never danced before?"

"I was home-schooled, remember?"

"I know, but you said you had girlfriends. I figured you might have taken one of them to a dance."

"They weren't girlfriends," Erik corrected. "They were just girls I dated. It was nothing serious."

"Well your dad made it sound like—" I stopped, not meaning to bring up the conversation I'd had privately with Jack.

"Why was my dad talking to you about my dating life?"

"How should I know? Never mind. I barely remember what he said."

"Well, I didn't go to any dances, Sam. Ever. You're the first person I've ever danced with. That's why I'm so bad at it."

"I'm not very good either. I've only gone to four dances my whole life and I only danced at a couple of them. The rest I kind of just stood around and drank punch."

"You want to try again? While he's not staring at us?"

"Sure," I said, getting in position.

Erik went slower this time, gently gliding me across the floor. He looked up, focusing on me instead of his feet. I did the same, locking my eyes on him. And it was like something clicked. Suddenly we were actually dancing. Smoothly and effortlessly. Like on air. We were perfectly in sync.

"Bravo! Bravo!" Terrance's voice echoed above the music as his shoes click-clacked across the floor.

We stopped dancing. Erik looked annoyed at being caught.

The music suddenly ended when Terrance reached us. "See what I mean? THAT is dancing! Total connection with each other. Did you feel it? How could you not? I could feel it from across the room."

Terrance walked up to Erik. A huge smile came across his face. "You love this girl, don't you? It's clear that you do. It shows in your dancing."

Then Terrance came over to me, putting his face right next to mine. "But you, Samantha. You hesitate when you dance with him. You're still not sure of your feelings for him, correct?"

I backed away. "Can we just go now? Erik is starving."

"Interesting," Terrance mused, observing the tension he had created. "Yes, you may go. We'll work on the Viennese waltz tomorrow."

Lunch was waiting for us when we got back to our room. Erik was quiet throughout the whole meal. I didn't want to talk about what Terrance had said about us, and I figured Erik didn't either. So I was surprised when he brought it up later that afternoon while we were waiting for our etiquette coach.

"That stuff Terrance said today. You know he was just messin' with us, right? Trying to get in our heads? Make us dance better?"

"Oh, yeah. Of course," I assured him.

"Well, I just wanted to make sure. I didn't like him putting words in my mouth, not that you believed any of that."

"I knew what he was doing. But I wonder how we were able to dance so well at the end of the lesson."

"Because we didn't have Terrance staring at us. Telling us what to do."

"You were really good, Erik."

He shrugged. "Just beginner's luck."

But it wasn't just luck. Something had happened when we were dancing after Terrance left. I felt it and I knew Erik did, too. And Terrance wasn't just messing with us. It was like he could read us, or at least me.

What Terrance had said about me was exactly right. I wasn't sure about my feelings for Erik. Because I didn't understand them. As much as I loved Colin, there was something about Erik that drew me to him with an intensity I couldn't explain. And the more time we spent together, the stronger it got. I couldn't stop looking at him. Wanting to be near him. And his touch was so intoxicating that I tried to avoid it, knowing where it could lead.

I kept telling myself that I was drawn to Erik because our relationship was new and fresh and exciting. But it was more than that. Something sparked between us the day we met and had never gone away.

That afternoon, we had our etiquette class, which focused on table manners. We were given an overview of all the different types of silverware, plates, bowls, and glasses used in formal dining. I knew some of it already, but Erik had no clue people actually ate that way. He didn't even know so many types of silverware existed.

After the class, we were shuffled off to the formal dining room to practice our new skills. Erik and I sat at a small table lit by candles and were served multiple courses as our instructor watched from afar. The food was delicious but we were too on edge to enjoy it. The instructor kept criticizing us every time we did something wrong.

When we got back to the room, Erik worked on the cipher. I went right to bed. I wanted to get a full night's rest so I would be alert for our tour the next day. I was sure it would give us information about the building that we could use for our escape. And maybe even information that would help me find Brittany. But I should have known better.

22. THE TOUR

The tour was scheduled for the morning. Erik and I were allowed to get ready without the oversight of Natalie and Kendall, but they did come by to inspect us before we left.

I had on a skirt and a blouse. Natalie didn't like how they looked and made me wear yet another dress with heels. My feet were killing me from wearing heels every day. I longed to have my jeans and sneakers back. Erik felt the same. The suits and ties were driving him crazy.

We sat on the tiny sofa, waiting for our tour guide. "I bet it's an old guy in a tuxedo," I joked.

Erik closed his eyes as if making a prediction. "I'm gonna guess a middle-aged guy. In a suit, not a tux. With a foreign accent."

"I like it. Let's go with that." I heard the door unlocking. "Here he comes. Get ready."

We were both surprised to see no man at all. Instead it was a young woman in her twenties with blond, flowing hair and bright blue eyes, wearing a fitted v-neck red cashmere sweater, tight black skirt, large diamond earrings, and very high heels. For her tall, thin frame, she had an exceptionally large chest that couldn't possibly be natural. She looked like a swimsuit model. Erik couldn't stop staring at her.

I stood up as the woman walked toward us. "Hi, I'm Rachel." She shook my hand. "I'm here to take you on the tour. You must be

Samantha." She looked down at Erik, who was still sitting. "And you're Erik, right?"

Erik was too mesmerized by her looks to speak.

"Yes, that's Erik," I said, answering for him. Idiot guys, I thought. It's like their brain shuts down around a beautiful woman. "Erik, get up, we're leaving." I patted his shoulder.

"I love the suit, Erik." Rachel smiled at him. She seemed like the type of woman who enjoyed the effect she had on men and used it to her advantage whenever possible.

He smiled back at her, finally getting up. "Oh, thanks. They *are* really nice suits."

I rolled my eyes, remember how just minutes ago he was complaining about them.

"Have you worked here long?" I asked Rachel as we walked out.

"About a year. Since the place opened actually. Drew invited me to come up here with him. He actually got me this job."

"Drew? I don't think we've met him yet."

She gave me an odd look. "Drew Chamberlin. He said you had dinner with him the other night."

"Oh, yes. I didn't know his first name."

"He's kind of formal that way. I don't know if he mentioned me at dinner, but we used to date. Well, I guess we kind of still do, but I've pretty much moved on. I'm hoping to leave here in a few months and go back to Los Angeles. That's where I'm from. I used to be a model, but now I really want to be an actress. And I can't exactly do that here in Iceland."

I tried to guess how old she was. Maybe 25? Chamberlin was at least 20 years older. Rachel led us toward the entrance of the building, where guards stood blocking each door.

"So we'll start the tour over here. These statues are—"

"Rachel, sorry to interrupt, but I was wondering, why do they have so many guards around here?" I figured that playing stupid was the best way to get information from her.

"Drew says there's something really valuable in here that needs a lot of protection. He wouldn't say what it is. It could be one of the paintings. Or one of the artifacts over there." She pointed to a glass case near the side wall. "The GlobalLife execs are really into that ancient artifact stuff. Last year they bought some piece of pottery for like five million dollars."

"But the guards kind of make it feel like a prison." I said it quietly so the guards wouldn't hear. "They distract from the beautiful artwork. And are they really necessary? I would think that a company like GlobalLife would have the latest security technology."

"They do. In fact Drew just installed this new thing where you have to use your brain as the password."

"What do you mean?" I asked innocently.

"Like instead of using a security badge, you say or think something and that gets you in the building or lab or whatever. I guess the device is supposed to read your brain waves as you say or think the words. Drew says that everyone's brain waves are different and that's why it works. He called it a brain wave fingerprint. He said it's way better than other types of security because nobody can copy a brain wave."

"So they're using that here?"

"They only use it in some sections of the building. And I think we're the only office that uses it right now. Hey, Erik, you're awfully quiet. Do you have any questions?"

Erik stood there staring at her. "No. No questions."

"Okay, well, I have this whole speech I'm supposed to go through, so we better get started. As I was saying, this globe statue was made in Italy." She lowered her voice. "This next part is all scripted. I don't really talk this way."

She raised her voice back to normal. "The globe represents GlobalLife's commitment to ending world hunger, curing disease, promoting peace, and making the world a better place for every person on the planet. It represents their never-ending efforts to make continuous improvements in areas such as agriculture, human health, clean water, renewable energy, and economic stability."

As Rachel talked, I stared at an engraving on the base of the marble globe. It read, "We are only as strong as our weakest link." It was the exact same phrase Chamberlin had used when I'd asked him about Brittany.

Rachel noticed me reading it. "Weird, isn't it? Drew says that phrase all the time. I don't even know what it means."

We went to the next statue and the one after that, with Rachel explaining their history and design. Then she moved to the tapestries along the wall. Below each one was a gold plate with an inscription. When we got to a tapestry featuring a large tree, she went off script again. "GlobalLife is obsessed with this golden ratio thing. So are the Founders. This is the symbol for it." She pointed to a symbol on the gold plate. "It's phi, a Greek letter. When Drew first talked about it, I thought he was talking about a fraternity. Isn't that funny? He didn't think it was funny. But hey, a lot of fraternities use it. And sororities."

"Why are they so obsessed with it?"

"It's supposed to equate with perfection. And these people like stuff to be perfect. Drew always says, 'Perfection above all else' and 'Errors are nothing more than a side effect of weakness and stupidity.'" Rachel mimicked Drew's voice as she repeated his words. "He likes to make these phrases up and then say them over and over again. Drives me crazy."

"What does the golden ratio have to do with this tapestry?"

"Drew said the golden ratio is found in nature, like branches and leaves. I guess it's shown in this tree." She pointed to the tapestry.

"You'll learn more about it later, when I talk about the building. It was also designed according to the golden ratio."

The tour continued as she described each painting on the wall. I soon figured out that the tour was nothing more than a lesson in art history and design. We were able to see the layout of the building but weren't able to find out anything about what went on inside the various rooms. The tour was simply meant to give us something to talk about with the investors on Saturday night.

The tour script included a few facts about the company but nothing we didn't already know. Rachel raced through those parts; they seemed to bore her. She didn't appear at all interested in GlobalLife or anything they were doing. Clearly, Chamberlin had only brought her up there to show her off at gatherings. And to accommodate his other, more personal needs. She didn't seem too bright but she was very nice and I actually felt comfortable around her.

"Say something, Erik," I thought to him. *"The tour's almost over. She's gonna think something's up with you."* He'd been quiet almost the whole two hours.

Erik finally spoke up. "Rachel, what's down all of these hallways?"

"Well, the hall where your room is has employee residences. When our employees have to be here for weeks or months for a special project, they stay here instead of a hotel." She pointed behind us. "The hallway we were just in has offices. And that one along the back wall? All conference rooms. Pretty boring. That's why those areas aren't on the tour."

"And what about the labs? Do we see those next?" I asked her.

"No. Those aren't on the tour either. But there's nothing to see. Just a bunch of equipment."

"What's on the second floor?" Erik asked nonchalantly. "More labs?"

"Um, I don't know. Nobody's allowed up there. I mean, the people who work there are, but the rest of us aren't." Rachel's evasive answer had me even more worried about Brittany.

"Do people ever stay up there?" I asked her. "Are there rooms up there like they have down here?"

She became flustered. "I don't really know. So anyway, that's the tour."

Rachel walked us quickly back to our room, trying to avoid any more questions. "Nice to meet you both. I'll see you at the party on Saturday."

"Did you hear all the stuff she told us?" I thought to Erik once Rachel had left.

"What stuff?"

"Weren't you even listening? The stuff about the brain wave fingerprint? That's what they're using as a biometric to protect the alien DNA. It has to be! That's the other level of security we need to get past in order to access the genes."

I felt no excitement in Erik's thoughts. *"So what? You don't know whose brain waves they're using. And even if you did, how are you gonna get someone's brain waves?"*

My enthusiasm faded because he was right. Both of us could read brain waves but not capture them in the air and store them for later use. To do that, we'd have to somehow replicate them in our own minds.

"Erik, do you think you could copy my brain waves?"

"What are you talking about?"

"Like if you listened carefully, picking up on the changes in the pattern and electrical impulses in my brain, could you replicate those same things in your brain?"

"Why would I do that?" Before I could answer, he realized what I meant. *"Sam, that's not gonna work. Like I said, you don't even know whose brain waves to replicate."*

"It might work. And I'm thinking it's gotta be Chamberlin. He wouldn't let anyone else have access to those alien genes."

"Okay. I'd agree with that. But that doesn't get us very far."

"Rachel said the person would have to say or think something while standing in front of whatever they're trying to open. Like a word or a phrase."

"And how will we ever find out what word or phrase to use? That's impossible."

"Just forget it, Erik. I'll figure it out myself. Work on your cipher."

"So now you're mad at me for being realistic?"

"Yeah, I am. I think you could be more positive. And you could have paid more attention on the tour and asked more questions. Rachel told us a lot today. She's a good source of information. You would've known that if you're weren't staring at her boobs all morning."

"Hey! I wasn't staring!"

"You were totally staring. But I get it. She was hot."

"Very hot." He stared dreamily into the air as if she were in front of him again. *"Very, very hot."*

"Oh, please, so you're in love with her now?"

"No, she's not my type," he said, waking from his fantasyland.

"Not your type? She's gorgeous! She's every guy's type."

"Yeah, but a girl's gotta have more than looks. I like a girl with brains. And someone's who's not all about money. And Rachel's well, she didn't seem too bright. And she's obviously after guys with money or she wouldn't be dating Chamberlin."

"I'm sure if she let you, you'd go out with her."

He smiled. *"If she let me, I'd do more than that."*

I punched his arm. *"Erik, you just met her!"*

He shrugged. *"I'm a guy. What can I say?"*

I walked away in disgust.

"Hey, it's not like it's gonna happen, Sam. And I don't know why you even care."

I ignored him and went into the bathroom, leaving him alone to dream about Rachel.

Our dance lesson was after lunch. Terrance taught us the Viennese waltz. It was faster than the other waltz we'd learned, and we both found it more difficult.

"You're not connecting with each other!" Terrance scolded. "Do like you did yesterday. It was magic. Pure magic. Do that again!"

All I could think about was Erik imagining he was dancing with Rachel and not me. It was silly for me to feel jealous. After all, he had no chance with Rachel. And I had a boyfriend. Still, Erik's infatuation with Rachel was distracting me from learning the steps. In fact, Erik was actually doing better than me.

"Samantha, focus!" Terrance shouted at me. "Focus on the feeling of his arms around you. Focus on the way he leads you across the dance floor."

I snapped to, noticing that Erik was doing his best to lead us across the floor while I continued to mess up, always stepping in the wrong direction.

"Let him lead, Samantha," Terrance ordered. "We'll be here all day if you don't get this right!"

Erik caught my eye. *"What's wrong with you? Let's get this over with."* We turned and stepped to the right. *"I'm not even thinking about her, if that's what's bothering you."*

"I wasn't thinking that." I stepped on his foot. *"Oops, sorry!"* I kept my eyes on my feet to avoid another misstep.

"Then what's the problem? Just relax. And don't look at your feet. It makes it harder. Just keep your eyes up here. Look at me."

I did as he said. He was right. It was easier when I kept my eyes on his. I took a deep breath and focused on the feeling of his hand around my waist, guiding us across the floor.

Suddenly we were getting in sync again. Soon we were dancing without thinking about the steps. And it was actually fun. I think even Erik liked it.

Terrance applauded. "That's excellent! Wonderful form! Bravo!" He stopped the music. "I would love to let you continue, but apparently you have other plans. I must dismiss you for today. But I commend you for putting forth so much effort. You truly let your feelings shine through, especially you, Erik. Excellent job!"

Back in our room, Erik seemed pleased with himself. "Guess I'm not so bad at this dancing thing."

"Maybe Rachel inspired you. You're probably hoping to get a dance with her on Saturday."

"That's a good idea," he said, knowing it would irritate me. "Sam, I'm just kidding. I told you, I wasn't thinking about her."

"Then what were you thinking about? The footwork? Because I'm still having trouble with that."

"I was thinking about my partner. Which is what *you're* supposed to be thinking about. Or maybe you weren't listening," Erik kidded, getting back at me for my comments about his behavior on the tour.

"I *was* listening. But I don't understand Terrance's advice. If I think about you, then I can't concentrate on the dance."

"I didn't think it would work either. But then I tried it and it actually worked."

"What did you think about?"

"I don't know. Just stuff from when we first met. Like the look on your face when you found out I could read your mind. And that time on my porch when you finally told me your real name." He laughed. "Oh, and when you came in my room to wake me up that one time."

The time he was practically naked and I walked right in, I thought. I'd been trying to forget that embarrassing moment. "So that's all you did? And you didn't even think about your feet?"

"I did at first. But then I got lost in my thoughts and somehow we were dancing. I guess crazy Terrance is right. You just need that connection with your partner."

Although I *had* felt a connection with Erik during our dance lesson, I had trouble keeping the connection. My mind would wander to Brittany and then I'd get worried. Or I'd think about Colin and start feeling guilty. Or I'd have Terrance yelling at me.

I wouldn't have even cared about mastering the stupid dance, but Erik and I had decided that we had to impress people at Saturday's gala. Putting on a good performance on Saturday night might win us privileges, like the ability to walk the halls without an escort.

Soon after we got back from our dance lesson, Walter came by to take us to the dining room for another dinner. He explained that our etiquette coach would be observing us as he did the previous night and would also be awarding us a grade. Anything other than an A would mean additional hours of training.

"Erik, take my cue on which fork to use," I thought to him as we walked to the dining room. *"You keep using the wrong one. So just watch me, okay? I don't wanna be stuck in that class again. We have better things to do."*

"This is so dumb. Who cares what fork or spoon you use? Or what glass goes with what—"

Erik's thoughts ended abruptly. I looked over to see that he'd spotted Owens and Rachel in the hallway outside the dining room.

"Hey, guys!" Rachel said when she saw us approaching. Walter rolled his eyes and muttered something under his breath. He didn't approve of Rachel and didn't think she belonged at GlobalLife.

"Samantha. Erik. How nice to run into you," Owens said. "I was just going over some last-minute details with Rachel regarding the gala on Saturday. Are you prepared for your unveiling?"

"Yes. Absolutely." I heard Walter muttering again in the background—this time something about my statement being an exaggeration.

"Glad to hear it," Owens said. "So your week has been going well?"

"Yes, very well." I smiled as I contacted Erik's mind. *Erik, talk about something so I can hear Owens' thoughts.*

Erik rambled on about how much we had learned on the tour, likely hoping to impress Rachel. Then he described our success with the waltz. While he talked, I listened to Owens.

"Did you locate the DNA yet? Smile if you did."

I kept a straight face to indicate that I hadn't.

"Then I've got a plan. On Saturday night, all the attendees are required to wear the brain wave scrambling device so that you and Erik can't hear their thoughts. But I'll be wearing the device that disables it. The same one I have on now. The device also works for people I'm next to. So I'll strategically place myself around people who might know where the genes are. You and Erik will need to stay close and listen to what they're thinking. Have you had any luck figuring out the biometric? Smile for yes."

I smiled to indicate my answer. Erik was starting to run out of things to say, so Owens sped up his thoughts.

"Good. Very good. One more thing. Your sister. Brittany. I know what they did with her."

23. CHAMPAGNE TOAST

I was sure Owens would say that GlobalLife had killed Brittany.

"Is something wrong, Samantha?" Rachel asked. "You look like you might be sick."

"No. I'm just tired from all the dancing. Erik, tell them about the Viennese waltz we did today."

Erik gave me a funny look because he'd already described it. Then he picked up on my clue. "Oh, you mean about the history of it? Okay, yeah, so anyway . . ."

As Erik talked, Owens continued. *They moved Brittany to a different GlobalLife facility but she's still in Iceland. Chamberlin knows your telepathy is back to normal and he didn't want you trying to connect with Brittany. Given that you're her sister, he was worried that you might be able to hear her thoughts despite the brain wave scrambling device. But I have people working on getting Brittany free. So I need you and Erik to stop worrying about rescuing her. You need to focus on getting yourselves out.*

" . . . and that's pretty much it." Erik ended his story, smiling nervously over at me because he had no clue what else to say.

"Well, it sounds like you've been very busy these past few days," Owens said. "Rachel and I need to get back to work but I'll see you both on Saturday. Enjoy your dinner."

Erik and I endured the formal dinner. We definitely didn't enjoy it. During the meal, I was so distracted I almost used the wrong utensil twice.

"What are you doing?" Erik yelled at me in this thoughts. *"You said you knew this stuff!"*

"Okay, okay. I won't screw up again."

We ended up getting a B plus, which was bad enough to earn us an hour more of class. Erik couldn't complain because without my help, he would have flunked, getting us stuck with at least five or six more hours of class.

When we were back in our room, I went through everything Owens had told me. Erik was as concerned as I was about Brittany's safety. *"Where would they take her? Why not just let her go?"* he thought to me.

"Exactly. What do they need her for now? They have us. You don't think it's because of what your dad said about—"

Erik had the same thought. *"Organ donation? It could be. Who knows what they'll do to us next week in the lab. Maybe something they haven't tried before. Something that could damage us. And they need Brittany, in case, well, in case something happens."*

"So if my heart stops for whatever reason, they'll just give her heart to me and let her die? No! They can't do that! She's a person. A human being! Not some device that stores organs. We've gotta save her, Erik!"

"I don't know how we can help her, Sam. If Owens said he has a plan to get her free, then we have to count on him to do that. And if he screws it up, then we need to put all our effort into getting out of here so we can go find her."

"We need to work harder, Erik. We can't be stuck in here for weeks or months. We've gotta get out faster than that. And we can't leave without getting the alien genes."

"I'm working on it. I've got the first part of that cipher figured out. I think I can finish it by next week. You should start studying that map of the building

Owens gave us. Look for any weak spots. Memorize how the cameras move. When the guards change."

Finally, Erik was getting on board. Up until then, Erik was convinced we had no chance of escaping. I wasn't sure what changed his mind, but knowing he was all in boosted my confidence that we could get out.

The next couple days, Erik and I continued going to classes. We spent several hours learning greetings in different languages in order to welcome our foreign visitors. We also had more dance and conversation lessons.

In between classes, we used every spare moment to brainstorm where the alien genes might be stored and who, besides Chamberlin, might have access to them. When Erik took breaks to work on the cipher, I studied the building maps in my head. Every time I walked the halls, I paid attention to see which guards seemed least attentive. Unfortunately, they were all attentive, constantly watching our every move.

On Friday, we tried copying each other's brain waves. It was a skill we were now convinced we would need to access the genes. With Chamberlin in charge, the brain wave fingerprint technology had to be the biometric being used to secure the genetic material. Our first attempts at this skill went nowhere, so we decided to try again after the gala.

By Saturday, we were both exhausted. Our captors must have realized they'd overworked us because breakfast didn't arrive until late morning. But right after breakfast, the day of preparation began.

First there was a review of acceptable topics of conversation. Next was a last-minute quiz on table etiquette. Then came one final practice of every type of waltz we had learned. And last, was the actual getting-ready phase, which meant Natalie and Kendall were back.

Natalie began with my hair, straightening it, then pinning it up so it was off my neck. She wove in tiny strands of sparkly beads so that when she was done, you couldn't even see the strands. You just saw the sparkle from the beads.

My dress for the evening was delivered early in the day. It was all-white satin that was covered in tiny crystal beads that shimmered from every angle. The dress was sleeveless, held up by delicate, almost invisible straps. It was fitted except for the bottom third, which flared out a little. It was just long enough to lightly sweep the floor when I walked. The neckline dipped to a V in front without being too revealing. Once I was dressed, Natalie added the finishing touch. Diamond earrings and a matching diamond necklace.

By 6:30 that evening, I was finally ready. I came out of the bathroom to find Erik standing around looking bored and restless.

"Okay, she's ready," Natalie announced as she gathered her things to leave.

Erik looked up. "Sam, is that you?"

"Funny, Erik."

"No, really. You look like a model or something."

I spun around to give him the full effect. "Well, it better look good because it took long enough to get ready."

Erik smiled. "Yeah. You definitely look—Wow! I don't even know what to say."

I checked out Erik as well. He was wearing a tuxedo with a white shirt and black bow tie. The tuxedo didn't look like the old man tuxedo that Walter wore. It had a modern, clean cut that fit Erik well.

"Wow to you, too, Erik. You look really nice. I love the tuxedo."

"Thanks, but I feel like I'm going to a wedding or something."

"I know. Same here. This is almost like a wedding dress. I guess we'll all look like we're getting married with this black and white theme."

There was a knock on the door. Walter entered followed by Rachel. She was wearing a long, fitted white strapless gown. She also had her hair up, showing off huge diamond earrings.

Rachel ran up to me. "Oh my goodness," she gushed. "You're so pretty, Samantha! They're going to love the dress. I picked it out, but it looks even better on you than I thought it would. Don't you love how it sparkles like that?"

Before I could answer she ran over to Erik. "You're so handsome, Erik!" He blushed as she turned back to me. "But I love most any guy in a tux. I think it's so sexy!" Erik looked disappointed; her compliment was now meaningless.

"Well, now that I know you two are ready, I'll head back to the dining room. There's a cocktail hour going on now. Dinner will start shortly. Walter will bring you to the dining room, but you'll wait outside. Drew will make a short speech and then announce you. And that's when I'll come out and get you, okay? And then after dinner, when we get to the ballroom, he'll announce you again and you'll do the first dance. I told you this a hundred times, I know, but I just wanted to go over it once more."

I smiled at her. "Yes. We've got it, Rachel. We won't screw it up."

"Oh, I know you won't. Ignore me. I'm just nervous. This is a big event. Drew's counting on me to make sure everything goes perfectly. See you soon!" She raced back out the door, leaving us with Walter.

"You both look," he paused, "appropriately dressed this evening." It was the one and only compliment we would ever get from Walter. "Shall we go?"

We walked down the hall past the front entrance. The guards were still there, but even they wore tuxedos rather than their usual dark suits. The entire entrance area was decorated with large white trees covered in sparkly white lights. The regular lights were dimmed to allow the soft glow coming from the trees to fill the room.

We got to the dining room and waited outside as Rachel instructed. I could hear Drew's speech. Most of it was stuff about how great GlobalLife was, curing illness, feeding the hungry, and other lies. Finally, he paused to introduced us.

Rachel came out the door. "Ready?" she whispered to us.

"And now, the moment you've all been waiting for," Drew announced. "The arrival of our stars for the evening. Prototypes of the future. May I introduce for the very first time, Samantha and Erik. The golden couple."

The golden couple? I glanced at Erik, who seemed just as confused. Rachel pushed Erik toward me, reminding him to take my arm as we walked out onto a small stage that had been set up. Bright lights shined down on us and people stood up and clapped. I peered through the light to see the room of onlookers. There were people of all nationalities. I could hear different languages and accents in the crowd.

"They are simply amazing," I heard one woman say.

"What a gorgeous couple," another woman said.

I noticed two ladies near the stage staring up at us. "Oh, can you imagine?" the one lady said to her friend.

"They'll be even more gorgeous. And perfect in every way," her friend responded.

I looked back to see a large banner hanging behind us. On it were the words "Celebrate The Golden Couple" along with the Greek letter phi. Just like the one on the necklace Allie gave me.

"Samantha, turn around," Drew scolded as he smiled at the crowd.

The clapping got louder as everyone stood up. The room gradually quieted. Drew went to the microphone again. "Thank you. I can see you're all as excited as I am about these two. And I encourage you to express your enthusiasm for the project by continuing to invest in the research that will bring this technology to life in all of us." He gave them a huge salesman grin. Then he came over next to us and said loudly and forcefully, "This is the future, my friends! Let us celebrate it!"

Everyone clapped again. Drew made us stand there for a minute, then led us off the stage. Rachel was waiting to take us to the head table that was set up in the front of the room. We were stuck sitting next to Drew and some foreign investors. Owens sat at the far end of the table. His device didn't work from a distance, so we couldn't listen to anyone's thoughts.

People stared at Erik and me as we ate. Apparently, they weren't allowed to talk to us until later at the dance. And even then, they were only allowed a few minutes of our time.

With the bright lights off us, I could see better. I scanned the room to get a look at everyone. There was a sea of sparkle from the diamonds and other jewels the women were wearing. All the ladies wore white gowns and the men wore tuxedos, like a room full of brides and grooms. I spotted Allie's mom flittering from table to table, trying to gauge how much money she would get out of the night.

When we got to the ballroom, Erik and I had to wait outside while everyone filed in. I could see inside as people entered. The ballroom was filled with huge floral arrangements made out of black and white flowers. There were also trees adorned in white lights like the ones in the lobby. An orchestra was set up somewhere near the back of the ballroom. I could hear the music but couldn't see the musicians.

After everyone was in the ballroom, Rachel came out with Terrance.

"You must make this your very best waltz," Terrance instructed. "The best one yet! Remember, you must feel the connection between you. Feel the passion! The love!"

Erik and I tried not to laugh as we watched him almost act out each word.

Sensing we weren't quite feeling the connection, Terrance nudged Erik toward me. "Give her a kiss for luck," Terrance ordered. Erik hesitated. "What's wrong with you? She's beautiful. Kiss her!"

I gave Erik a look to let him know it was okay. Anything to get Terrance to shut up.

Erik leaned in and softly kissed me on the lips. It was only the second time we'd kissed. The first time, back in Texas, was incredible. But this kiss topped even that! It ignited that intense chemistry between us that I'd been trying so hard to ignore.

"Okay, there's the music," I heard Rachel say.

Erik pulled away. I could see from his face that the kiss was just as intense for him.

"Good luck!" Rachel said as she guided us to the doors.

"You'll do wonderful! I know you will!" Terrance called out from behind us.

We walked into the ballroom. People were hovering above us watching from the balcony. Others were lined up along the outside of the dance floor. Erik got in position, putting his hand firmly around my waist. We stood tall and kept our eyes locked on each other. And then we began. I could feel it after our first step. We were completely in sync. Even more than during practice. Erik guided us across the floor, turning and stepping as if he'd been doing this his whole life. I followed his lead, not even thinking about my footwork.

The music eventually stopped and the room was silent. Did we screw something up? I thought. It seemed like we did everything right. And then the applause began. Louder than it had been in the dining room. I could hear words coming from the crowd. "Absolutely magnificent!" "Such talent for people so young!" "The future indeed!"

The music began again and people joined us on the dance floor. "Great job, Erik," I said, as we continued to dance, "especially since that was your first real dance in public."

"Thanks. I'm just glad it's over. I hate having people stare at me."

"So are you gonna ask Rachel to dance?"

"Maybe later. But I don't know. You look even hotter than she does tonight. I might just stick with you."

"Was that supposed to be a compliment? Because that last part kind of—"

Erik smiled. "It's a compliment."

When the next waltz started, we took a break and stood off to the side of the dance floor. People stopped by to say hello and tell us how much they enjoyed watching our dance. I attempted to use some of the greetings I'd learned for the foreign guests, but I kept getting strange looks followed by polite smiles. I'm sure my pronunciation was off.

The night continued with more smiling, meeting, shaking of hands, and dancing. Occasionally, Rachel or Drew would make Erik or me dance with someone. Rachel later explained that these people had made a large investment in the project, earning them a dance.

Midway through the evening, Owens approached me, asking me to dance. I agreed, of course, and he updated me on the plan.

"Act natural and pretend we're talking," he thought. *"Did Erik figure out the cipher yet? Does he have the password?"*

"Almost," I whispered, still smiling.

"Good. So tonight I'm hoping to find out where the genes are stored. I'm now certain that Drew is the one who has the vials or at least has access to them. I'm going out in the hallway soon to introduce Drew to a friend of mine. A potential investor. I want you to accompany me. As we're talking, I'll ask Drew some questions. He may or may not think of the vials. But listen closely in case he gives you any clues. Did you get all of that?"

"Yes," I said as the music changed. "It was nice dancing with you as well."

Owens left and Erik took his place. *"What was that about?"*

"I'm going in the lobby soon to meet with Drew, Owens, and some other guy. As they talk, I'll listen to Drew's thoughts. Owens has the device on and will be right next to Drew, so I should be able to hear what he's thinking."

"Should I go with?"

"He said just me. I'll fill you in when I get back."

A few minutes later, Owens came back and we went out into the lobby. We walked over to an old man wearing a tuxedo and black cowboy boots. I remembered seeing the man earlier when I'd overheard Drew at dinner saying how the boots were inappropriate for a formal ball. Drew was mingling with some other people. He quickly ended his other conversation and came over to Owens.

"Preston, I see you've brought a friend with you tonight." Drew gave a quick nod to acknowledge me, then focused on the man I didn't know.

"Yes," Owens said. "This is Orton Wolcott, owner of Wolcott Oil. They're based in Houston. Orton, this is Drew Chamberlin. He's the head of GlobalLife Genetics. He's currently based here in Iceland."

"Pleasure to meet you, Mr. Wolcott." Drew shook his hand. "And I assume you've met Samantha already?"

"No. That's why I asked Preston to bring her out here. I wanted to see the girl up close." Wolcott turned to shake my hand. "Hello, Samantha. It's good to finally meet you. It must be a real privilege for you to be part of such a historic project."

"Yes, it is," I lied. A privilege to be part of a project that's experimenting on me and keeping me prisoner? I thought. Did he even know about the project?

Owens quickly turned the conversation back to business. "As you can see, Samantha and that boy, Erik, are truly a success. It's time we get this project moving forward."

"Yes, and now is an excellent time to get in on this opportunity," Drew added, preparing to go into his sales speech.

Owens stopped him. "Drew, before you continue, Orton had some concerns he wanted you to address."

"Of course. Ask me anything." I could tell Drew was annoyed by the interruption but tried to hide it by smiling.

"Preston says these genetic sequences that GlobalLife has come up with are top secret. And he's assured me that nobody can replicate them. Is that correct?"

Genetic sequences? So that's what the investors think? That GlobalLife just developed some unique genetic sequences? Then they haven't told them about the alien DNA. The investors think it's just a change to human DNA. I wondered how many people actually knew the truth.

Drew nodded. "Yes, that is correct. The genetic sequences and the software that goes with them are proprietary to us."

"So you've got these secrets in a vault somewhere? How can I be sure they won't be stolen and copied by some other company?"

Drew seemed offended by the question. "We here at GlobalLife use the latest security technology. I, myself, am the guardian of the genetic material. So you can rest assured that the material is safe."

"Yes, well, I've heard that before," Wolcott said. "Then I invest millions only to find some competitor comes out with a similar product, making my investment worthless."

Owens sensed Drew's blood boiling at the man's comment. He stepped in to address Wolcott's concerns. As he did that, I listened to Drew's thoughts.

"How dare he question the security of the genes! As if I'm incompetent! If he only knew that they were right here behind me. If anyone tried to find them, do you think they'd look in the lobby? Of course not! Putting them here was brilliant! And all my idea!" Drew struggled to maintain his fake smile as Owens talked.

I glanced behind Drew to see what he was talking about. What was behind him? Nothing, really. Except a statue. Was that what he meant? The marble globe? But how? There was no way to open it.

Drew's thoughts were active again. *"I'm the one who suggested using the brain wave fingerprint. And I never get credit for it! I wish I could think those words right now and watch that damn thing open. Just to see the look on this idiot's face!"*

"Drew, do you want to explain the next steps for investors?" Owens looked at Drew, who heard the word "investors" and got his sales face on again.

Drew turned to me. "Samantha, now that you've met Mr. Wolcott, you can return to the ballroom."

Mr. Wolcott shook my hand again. "It was a pleasure meeting you, Samantha. I look forward to seeing you at future events."

"I'll escort her back to the ballroom," Owens said. "Please continue. I'll return shortly."

"Did you get anything?" Owens thought to me as we walked away. *"Do you know where the genes are?"*

I looked back at the globe. Drew was still standing right in front of it in full sales mode, his hands gesturing as he talked. Mr. Wolcott stood across from him looking bored.

Owens glanced back. *"What? The statue?"*

He waited for me to answer, then remembered that I couldn't. *"Okay, well, it must open somehow. So we know it's in the globe. And Erik's working on the cipher and you know the biometric. So all you need is access to the globe without anyone around?"*

I smiled at him. Truthfully, we needed more than that, but access was the only thing Owens could help with.

"Let me work on that. I'll figure out a way to get you time alone with it."

We were back in the ballroom. "Enjoy the party, Samantha."

As Owens left, I tried to contain my excitement from what I'd just heard. Erik's and my chances for getting the genes had just improved.

And it was all because Drew got his ego bruised over a simple question. Owens didn't even have to try to get Drew to spill the secret. Wolcott did it for him without even knowing.

I scanned the room to find Erik. He was talking to Rachel and some other woman on the left side of the dance floor. By the time I reached him, Rachel had taken the woman to meet someone else.

"How'd it go?" Erik thought to me.

"I got it! I know where the genes are and I know for sure that we need Drew's brain waves to access them!"

"So where are the genes?"

"In the globe. That big marble globe in the lobby."

"They can't be in there. You can't open a marble statue."

"Apparently you can because that's where they are. You must have to say the phrase and then it opens and you put the password in."

"So what's the word or phrase he uses to open it?"

"I don't know yet."

"Sam! We have to know that in order to open it. And you have to hear him say it or think it so you can copy his brain waves."

"I know. But we'll have to figure that out later. Hey, this was a real score! Be more excited!"

"Okay, okay. I'm excited." He smiled.

As we stood there, one of the waiters walked up and offered us some champagne.

"Why not?" I said to Erik. "I've never had champagne."

"Me either. We'll each have a glass." He took two crystal champagne flutes from the tray and handed me one. *"To getting the genes and getting the hell out of here,"* he thought. We clicked glasses and sipped our champagne.

I immediately felt the effects of the alcohol. "This stuff is really strong. I've only had wine before, and that was only when my parents let me, like at holiday meals."

"I'm more of beer drinker myself." Erik finished his glass. The waiter came by again and offered him more champagne. "Sure, I'll have another. Sam?"

"No, I don't think—"

"She'll have another one, too." Erik took two more champagne flutes.

I finished the first glass and set it down on a nearby table. I took a sip of the second glass. "I don't think I should drink all of this, Erik. I'll be completely drunk."

"You won't get drunk from two glasses of champagne. Look how tiny these are." He held his glass up. "Besides, this stuff probably costs a fortune. You won't get good champagne like this again."

The dance was winding down and people were beginning to leave. A few people remained on the dance floor, but it seemed like they'd had too much to drink. They were laughing loudly as they stumbled around.

"I was told to escort you back to your room." Walter had appeared out of nowhere.

"Um, okay," I said, feeling a little light-headed.

"You need some help there?" Erik asked, noticing my condition. "Here, hold my arm." He laughed as I reached for his arm and missed. "It was only a couple glasses, Sam. And you didn't even finish the second one."

"I just got dizzy for a second," I said as the feeling passed. On the walk back, I felt some dizziness again, but it ended when I got back to the room and had some water.

"Feeling any better?" Erik took off his suit jacket and laid it on the chair.

"Well, I don't feel sick. But I do feel kind of weird. And completely relaxed." I rested against the wall of pillows on the bed.

Erik sat down next to me. "I feel a little weird, too. Must be the champagne kicking in."

He took off his bow tie and unbuttoned his shirt a little. "Feels good to finally get that tie off."

My eyes focused on him. I had an overwhelming urge to kiss him. "Erik, come here."

"I *am* here. Wow, you *must* be drunk. Do you need more water?"

I reached up and unbuttoned more of his shirt. "I mean, come closer." I smiled at him.

He glanced down at my hand on his shirt and smiled back. "Um, okay." He leaned over and I grabbed his shirt, pulling him in for a kiss. But unlike our other kisses, this time I didn't hold back. I kissed him like I'd wanted to for so long.

Erik was surprised but quickly got past it. As we kissed, I could feel us connecting, our energy flowing back and forth between each other. I didn't understand the feeling, but I didn't want it to stop.

I continued to unbutton his shirt. Before I could finish, Erik tore it off and threw it on the floor. I ran my hands along his ripped abs as he slid the straps of my dress off.

"You don't know how long I've wanted to do this," I whispered to him.

"I've wanted to do this since the day I met you," he whispered back, unzipping the back of my dress.

We got off the bed and my dress fell to the floor. I slid his pants off, taking a moment to notice how perfect he was. His body was almost like a statue. Like he'd been sculpted to look that way.

Erik drew me closer to him. As we kissed, his hand moved down my back, stopping at my lace bikinis. "I love these on you. And I'll like 'em even more when they're—"

I grabbed his hand. "Wait. Maybe we shouldn't."

He took his hand back and continued. "We should. We definitely should."

"I want to, but I think—"

"Don't think, Sam. You think too much. Just go with it," He lifted me back on the bed, then lightly kissed my chest, weakening me again.

I brought his lips up to mine and felt his hand back flirting with my bikinis.

"Maybe now . . . isn't a . . . good time," I said between kisses.

"Now is a very good time, Sam." He moved his lips softly and slowly down my neck.

"No. I can't."

Erik stopped and looked up at me. "Are you serious?"

"Yeah." I slid out from under him.

"Why? What's wrong?" He paused, giving me a strange look. "Wait, this isn't the first time you—"

"No. It's just that this isn't like me. I don't know why I'm doing this. Maybe it's the champagne. It's making me, well, I just have this intense need to, you know—"

"Exactly. Me, too. So let's do this." He continued his kisses, this time faster and more aggressive.

I pushed him away. "It's not like I don't want to. I definitely want to. But I know that I shouldn't." My mind was thinking of Colin, but there was no need to bring him into the conversation. Erik was well aware of Colin. "You know, I really haven't even known you for that long."

"So let's get to know each other better." He reached for me but I held him back.

"Erik, it's not happening." I paused, and for a moment I almost changed my mind. He was so incredibly hot and our connection was stronger than ever. Knowing how intense our kiss was, I couldn't even imagine what going further would be like.

He smiled as he moved his hand along the curve of my hip. "Well, if you don't want to do *that*, we could do plenty of other things."

I smiled back. "Don't tempt me, Erik. I'm weak."

"Then let me try harder," he teased, kissing me again.

"Come on. Let's just go to bed."

He looked at me, still smiling, but didn't move.

"I meant go to sleep," I clarified. "Could you get me something to sleep in?"

"What you're wearing is fine with me."

"Erik. Please."

He got up and brought over one of my silk chemises. "These things are so damn hot. Do you know how hard it is to control myself with you lying next to me wearing this every night?"

I took it from him and slipped it on. "Probably as hard as it is for me to sleep next to *you* every night with that perfect, half-naked body."

He crawled up next to me. "Then let's make it easy on ourselves," he whispered in my ear, "and give in to our urges."

"Nice try. Goodnight, Erik."

The next morning, I woke up feeling chilled. I pulled the covers up and snuggled next to Erik. I felt my skin next to his and it felt good. And then I realized that there was nothing else between us. Nothing! We were lying there completely naked!

24. ABOUT LAST NIGHT

"Erik, wake up!" I moved away from him, yanking the comforter over me.

Erik rolled over. "What? Is it morning already?"

"Yes! Wake up!"

"Why? I'm tired. What's wrong?"

"I need to know what happened last night."

"What are you talking about? At the party?"

"No. Here. Last night. In our room."

He smiled. "Oh, yeah. That."

"What do you mean by 'that'? What did we do?"

"You know what we did. You were here, Sam."

"I can't remember. I passed out. Or fell asleep. Last I remember we were almost—"

"Doing it?"

"Yeah. But we didn't, right?"

"No. You made us stop. And I gotta tell ya, Sam, that was just mean. Go all that way and then—"

"If we didn't do anything, then where did our clothes go?"

Erik lifted the covers.

"Don't look! I'm naked under here!"

"So we're naked. Big deal. We didn't do anything."

"Then how did we get like this? Last night, I asked you to get me something to sleep in. Then I put it on and I don't remember anything after that. Did you wear anything to bed last night?"

"Yeah. Don't you remember? You made me. You even told me to wear one of my dress shirts to bed." He smiled and kissed my cheek. "You said you couldn't resist me otherwise."

I pushed him away. "Erik! This is serious. So you're saying that we were fully clothed when we went to bed?" I crawled over him to see clothes piled on the floor next to his side of the bed. My silk chemise was lying right next to his pajama pants and dress shirt.

"Maybe we got hot in the night." He smiled. "I mean, temperature hot."

"This room is always freezing at night. That can't be it. So you don't remember us going any farther?"

"No. At least not in real life."

"As opposed to what?"

"Well, I had a dream, but I've had those all week so—"

"What dream? A dream of us doing it? Last night? Are you sure it wasn't real?"

"I think I'd know if it was real, Sam."

"Maybe not. We were kind of out of it. We drank that champagne. What if it was spiked with something?"

"Like what? It was just champagne, Sam. And everyone was drinking it."

"This is GlobalLife, remember? They could have spiked it with something that would make us—"

Erik laughed. "Have sex? And why would they do that?"

"I don't know. But think about it. Why are we stuck in the same room together? They have rooms all down this hallway. And why won't they give us more clothes to sleep in? And everyone keeps saying we make a great couple. And then Terrance tells us to kiss. Says you're in love with me."

"I think you're reading too much into it, Sam. I don't think GlobalLife is that interested in us doing it."

Erik got out of bed, not caring that he was naked, and went into the bathroom.

"Wait, I'm not done talking about this," I called after him.

He came back out with a towel around his waist. "There's nothing to talk about. Relax. We didn't do anything. I'm gonna take a shower. Care to join me?"

"Erik!" I protested.

"What? I've already seen you naked."

I shook my head. "Just go."

As Erik showered, I grabbed his shirt from the floor and put it on. It still smelled like him. I breathed it in, closing my eyes and trying to remember last night. I could replay the entire scene in my head up until the point I fell asleep. I had no memories of me telling Erik to get dressed. Or watching him get dressed. And if I couldn't remember that, what else was I not remembering? Was I really that drunk last night? From a glass and a half of champagne?

Erik came out of the bathroom still wet and toweling off.

"Could you cover up, please?" I turned the other way to give him privacy. "You can't just walk around naked."

He laughed. "Why not? Does it bother you?"

"Yeah." I glanced back to see that he'd wrapped the towel around his waist. "It's distracting. I can't think straight."

I went to the armoire to find him something to wear. Erik came up behind me and began kissing the side of my neck. "Let's finish what we started last night. Maybe it'll help with that distraction problem."

"Here's some clothes." As I turned to give them to him, he leaned down and kissed me, taking the clothes and tossing them on the floor. My heart raced as our kiss, once again, sparked that intense connection that I still couldn't describe or explain.

I felt myself giving in, wanting to be with him even more than last night. I looked up at his piercing blue eyes. Then down at his perfect body. I couldn't get enough of him. His towel dropped to the floor and before I knew it, we were back on the bed.

Stop fighting it, I told myself. You like him. He's insanely hot. He's an awesome kisser. I had nearly convinced myself to give in when I noticed a flicker of light in the corner of the ceiling. I thought it was just my eyes. Then I saw it flicker again, so fast that I wouldn't have even noticed it if I hadn't been staring right at it.

"Erik! The cameras! Get off. The cameras are watching us!"

Erik didn't move. "What?" He considered the cameras for a moment, but it didn't seem to bother him. "Just ignore them. Now where were we?"

"Erik, stop. I can't do this with an audience. That's disgusting!"

"Then pull the covers over us," he muttered, continuing to kiss me.

"No. Now get up."

He groaned. "I am. That's why we need to—never mind."

"I'm not kidding around. Go get dressed."

He rolled onto his back. "I can't believe this is happening. Again! You're killing me, Sam!"

"I'm sure you'll survive."

I grabbed some clothes and went to shower while Erik got dressed. While I was in there, I kept trying to explain what had happened. Why was I acting that way with Erik? Sure, Erik was hot and we shared some crazy connection. But how could I cheat on Colin? He was the guy I loved. The guy who'd always been there for me, no matter what. I barely knew Erik. Although we'd become close friends, I'd never meant to take things any farther than that.

I started coming up with reasons for my behavior. I figured a part of me was convinced that Erik and I would never leave that place. That we would be stuck there forever and I would never see Colin again. So I was simply trying to find comfort in Erik. Even with my reasoning, I felt a tidal wave of guilt wash over me because as hard as I tried, I couldn't stop my craving for Erik. And I knew he felt the same way about me. I could feel it whenever we were together.

I put on a skirt and blouse and came out of the bathroom. Breakfast had arrived and Erik was already eating, wearing dress pants and a shirt.

"So are you mad at me?" I asked, taking the seat next to him.

"No." He smiled. "I'll wear you down eventually. Maybe tonight."

"I don't think, so, Erik. Besides, the cameras will still be there."

"Then I'll have to make you forget about them," he teased.

I changed the subject. "So what do you think they'll make us do today? We don't need those lessons anymore, now that the gala is over."

"Maybe they'll give us a day off."

"I doubt it."

But it seemed that we did have the day off. After breakfast, nobody came by to get us. Nobody showed up in the afternoon either. So Erik spent the day working on the cipher while I made a list of all the possible phrases that Drew might use to unlock the globe.

"I bet Rachel knows what it is," I thought to Erik later that afternoon.

"He wouldn't tell her that, Sam."

"Well, maybe it's one of those phrases he uses all the time."

"No. I think it's just a bunch of words. Like a bunch of passwords put together."

"That would be hard to remember. It's gotta be a phrase that has meaning to him."

"Well, good luck trying to figure that out. I'm almost done with this cipher. Just one more piece to figure out and it's done."

"Erik, that's great!"

"Yeah, but it doesn't do us any good if we can't open that thing. And how are we supposed to get access to it with security guards everywhere?"

"Owens is working on that. He told me last night at the party. Hey, we should try mimicking each other's brain waves again. Let's practice tonight after dinner."

"Tonight? We've been working all day. We should at least take a break and—" His eyes wandered over to the bed.

"Erik, we're not doing that. So don't even start thinking about it."

He smiled. *"You know I had to try."*

As we were mind-talking, dinner arrived along with Eve.

"Good evening, Samantha. Erik."

"Mrs. Taylor," I responded back.

"I hope you both had a restful day. I wanted to stop by and tell you what a success you were at the gala. We raised more money than I ever imagined we would. You really impressed everyone. Of course, they've all seen the recordings of you, Samantha, from back at the Minnesota facility. So they knew about your abilities. But to see you live and in person, it really sold them. And we let Erik be a surprise. They didn't even know there was a male version until last night. They were thrilled! The money just came rolling in after they learned of Erik."

"So Mrs. Taylor, how much do these people know about the project?"

"They know it's the way of the future. They know it will make them part of a very select group."

Eve, like everyone at GlobalLife, talked in vague terms. She sounded like she was reading off a brochure.

"I mean, do they know about the base codes? Do they know that's why we have these abilities?"

"They know about the unique sequencing of your DNA. And how GlobalLife is patenting those sequences so they can sell them and use them to improve humanity," she said, once again in brochure-speak.

"But do they know where GlobalLife got those base codes? Do they know about the alien genes?"

"It doesn't matter where the genetic material came from. They don't need to know that. Besides, the type of DNA we offer for sale will be much different than what's in those genes. It will be more of a hybrid mix, like what's formed in the two of you. Your regular genes have incorporated the foreign genes so successfully that we're hoping to replicate those sequences rather than those from the original foreign genes."

The term "foreign genes" was more acceptable to Eve than "alien" genes. Knowing the term bugged her, I kept using it.

"So GlobalLife won't need the alien genes anymore?"

"Well, we need to keep them as a backup, just in case, but for the purposes of replication, no. Which is fortunate because, obviously, there's a finite supply. Just what we have here and then the remainder in—" Eve stopped, knowing she'd said too much.

"What were you saying?" Erik asked.

Eve ignored the question. "Starting tomorrow you'll be spending time in the lab. They'll be doing some testing on you. But don't worry, Samantha. It's nothing like they did before. That was simply barbaric," she said, trying to sound sympathetic. "Anyway, you'll spend a few hours in the lab each day, some days longer than others. Any questions?"

"No," Erik answered.

"Then enjoy your week. And again, thank you both for a wonderful performance last night."

As she left I called after her. "Mrs. Taylor?"

Eve turned back. "Yes, Samantha, what is it?"

"I was wondering how Allie was doing. Have you talked to her?"

Eve seemed surprised that I would even ask. "Allie? Oh, she's doing wonderful. Achieving at school. Enjoying time with her friends before we move. I did tell you we're moving, didn't I?"

"Has she said anything about me?"

Eve looked as though she felt sorry for me. "Samantha, you know she wasn't really your friend. I already explained that to you. My daughter was just doing as I told her to do."

"That's a lie. Allie's been my friend for as long as I can remember. And she'll always be my friend."

"That's sweet. Live in your little delusional world if it makes you feel better. Now goodnight."

We watched her leave. Erik reached over and grabbed my hand. "Hey, don't listen to her. She's a total bitch. You know she's making it up."

I felt a lump in my throat. "That's what I keep telling myself, but what if it's true? What if Allie was just pretending to be my friend all these years?"

"When did you become friends?"

"In kindergarten. We were five."

"You can't force a 5-year-old to be someone's friend, Sam. A kid that young wouldn't understand. She was your friend because she chose to be your friend. Why are you letting that bitch get into your head?"

"Because maybe she's right. Allie is completely different than me. She's super pretty. Super outgoing. Super fun to be around. When we got older, I wondered why she even stayed friends with me."

"What are you talking about? You're pretty and outgoing and fun."

"I'm not any of those things. And you didn't know me in high school, Erik. I was quiet. I didn't go out much. I didn't wear the right clothes."

Erik nudged my chin up. "Look at me. That girl was your friend." He talked softly to avoid being overheard. "Eve is trying to mess with your head. Make you think they've controlled everything about you. Don't believe her. You're only doing what she wants."

I whispered back. "But the last time I saw Allie, she gave me that leather bag and I'm sure it had a location tracker on it. That explains what happened at the airport. That's how we ended up here. So why would she do that if—"

Erik put his finger to my lips and started mind-talking. *"Stop. That was all Eve. She did that. Not Allie. Now stop letting that bitch get to you."*

We had dinner and then pretended to read while we got to work attempting the brain wave mimicking. *"I don't even know how to start,"* Erik thought. *"When we tried this on Friday, nothing worked. Do you have any new suggestions?"*

"I don't know. I guess I was thinking that I'll say something out loud and then you listen to my brain waves as I say the words. You need to pay close attention to how the waves change when I use different tones and inflections. Then try to replicate that when you think those same words back to me. When I hear your thoughts in my head, it should sound like me, not you."

"Okay. I'll try it. Go ahead."

I paused, trying to think what to say. *"I'll say it slow. 'I wish we could go outside.' That's the phrase you should replicate. I'll say it again the same way. 'I wish we could go outside.' Now you think it back to me the same way."*

Erik closed his eyes. *"I wish we could go outside."*

"No. It didn't work. It sounded like you *saying it. It has to sound like* me. *"*

"How am I supposed to make my thoughts sound like a girl?"

"You have to concentrate, Erik. Focus on how I sound. The tones and inflections."

"I can't do it. I can't sound like a girl. Not even in my thoughts."

"Don't think of it that way. Just imagine that I'm in your head, thinking those words. And then just let them come out. You have to stop your own thoughts from getting in the way."

"Why don't you try it. I'll say something to you and then you mimic it back."

"Okay. But this time just think it instead of saying it. Go ahead."

He smiled. *"I'd really like to unbutton your shirt and—"*

"Erik. Come on. Say something else."

"Fine. Ready? I really want a cheeseburger and fries."

He thought it again. And then I thought it back to him.

Erik shook his head. *"No, it just sounds like you repeating what I said."*

We did this over and over, trying different phrases.

After a few hours, we gave up. *"Let's try it again tomorrow,"* I thought to him. *"It has to work. Otherwise we'll never get that globe open."*

"We'll never get it open because we don't even know what phrase or word will open it. You know, Sam, maybe we'll have to forget about the alien genes and just focus on getting out of here."

"Then we'll never get the timer turned off. We have to get the genes."

"I guess, but another option is that maybe we let GlobalLife turn the timer off and then try to escape."

"No. We can't wait. Who knows what they'll do to us once they fix it. They might move us to a new location. Then we'll never escape. At least here we have Owens helping us."

"We may not have a choice if we can't get the globe open, Sam."

"I don't want to consider that yet. Let's just see what happens tomorrow. Maybe we can get someone at the lab to tell us how brain waves work. You never know. We might get something useful out of them."

I got up and put the book I was pretending to read back on the shelf. "I'm going to bed. They'll probably make us get up early tomorrow. Maybe we won't have to dress up. That'd be nice for a change."

"Yeah, the suits are getting old. But I like those dresses you wear." He came over and tried to kiss me but I backed away.

"It's not gonna happen, Erik, so don't even start."

"It was just a kiss. Geez. I can't even do that now?"

When I got into bed and closed my eyes, I began seeing flashbacks of the GlobalLife facility in Minnesota. I saw myself being poked and prodded and hooked up to machines that gave me such excruciating headaches that I passed out.

I feared this time would be no different, despite what Eve said. Maybe the lab experiments would be even more painful. My stomach was in knots, not allowing me to sleep. Erik knew I was worrying. When either of us had intense feelings, the other person could sense it without even entering the person's mind. He moved closer and wrapped his arms around me.

"Erik, we're not—"

"Shhhhh. I'm not doing that. I'm just helping you sleep. Just relax. Everything will be okay tomorrow. It's not gonna be like last time."

I could feel his calmness transferring to me. Being so close to him helped stop my thoughts from racing. I finally fell asleep.

We were awoken early the next morning. Breakfast arrived along with two sets of clothing. Two pairs of baggy white cotton pants with a drawstring waist and two short sleeve pullover cotton shirts. They looked like hospital scrubs but in white instead of hospital green.

"I don't feel good, Erik," I said, looking down at myself in the all white outfit. The flashbacks starting running through my head again. I could see myself strapped to the bed, unable to move. I could hear Worthings' voice in my head. I ran in the bathroom and splashed cold water on my face.

"Sam, what's wrong?" Erik called from outside the door.

"Nothing. I'm okay," I said, even though I wasn't. I wondered if I was having a panic attack, although I'd never had one before. I became short of breath and starting sweating. I splashed more cold water on my face.

"Sam, I'm coming in." Erik opened the door and stood near the sink. "What's going on? You're shaking."

I was shaking. And I couldn't stop.

Erik took my arm. "Come sit down. Maybe I should try to get someone. They must have doctors around here."

"No. I'm not sick. I'm just freaking out."

"It's gonna be okay, Sam. We'll be together." He led me to the bedroom and sat me down on the bed.

"You don't understand, Erik. It was horrible. Last time was horrible. The pain was unlike anything I can describe. I can't go through that again." I continued to shake.

He put his arm around me. "Sam, I didn't know. You never told me what happened to you in Minnesota. Why didn't you tell me about it before?"

"Because I didn't want to think about it. When I do, look what happens." I held up my shaking hands.

"Listen to me, Sam. I won't let them hurt you. If they try to, I'll attack them. I'll get us out of there."

"You can't! They paralyze you with drugs. And when the drugs wear off, you still can't move. They keep you held down with these big metal clamps." Saying it was making my hands shake even more. "Now I feel like I can't breathe."

Erik cupped his hands around mine, trying to stop the shaking. "You sure you don't want me to get someone?"

"Why? So they can give me something to knock me out? No. They'll be here any minute now." I took a deep breath. "I don't know why this feeling just hit me. I put on these clothes and it's like every memory, every detail of what happened in Minnesota came flooding into my head."

"Hey, I'll be right there with you today, okay? And I'm not letting them hurt you. They'll have to go through me to get to you. Understand?"

I nodded, still shaking.

"Just look at these biceps." He flexed his muscles, smiling. "Nobody's getting past these."

We heard knocking on the door and a man walked in, a middle-aged man with glasses and graying hair wearing a white lab coat. I took a deep breath, putting all my trust in Erik's words that this time, it would be different.

25. REVELATION

"Hello, I'm Dr. Siefert," the man said. "I'm in charge of the lab you'll be working in today. How are you two this morning?"

"We're okay." Erik spoke for both of us as we got up from the bed.

The man looked at me to say something but I remained silent.

Erik wrapped his hand around mine. "She's a little nervous."

"There's no need to be," Siefert said. "These are very simple tests. In fact, today we're mostly just talking. Gathering information from you both."

"Are you strapping us down with those clamps?" I asked him.

"No. Of course not. Why would you think that?"

I wouldn't answer, so Erik did. "She had a bad experience, you know, before."

"I see. Yes, you mean in the Minnesota lab. Well, we do things differently here. So there's no need to be worried. Shall we go?"

Siefert led us to the back of the building, then down a hall to one of the labs. The room wasn't at all like the white, prisonlike bunker I was held in at the GlobalLife facility in Minnesota. It wasn't like the stark, cold labs you see in movies either. Instead, it was homelike with dark brown wood cabinets, granite countertops, and a seating area off to one side with a bright orange sofa and brown leather chairs. The lighting was warm and soft, not the harsh fluorescents typically used in labs. There were no steel carts with scary equipment and no hospital beds with metal clamps.

Seeing the place made me relax enough that I could finally release the firm grip I had on Erik's hand. *"You okay?"* he thought to me.

"So far," I thought back.

"This is Alison Kiewitz and this is Haden Gates," Siefert said as two people approached us. "They'll be working with you today. I have a meeting now but I'll be by later to see how things are going."

Alison was an attractive woman in her thirties with short, black hair and glasses. Haden was an average-size guy with brown, wavy hair. He was probably in his early forties, but the blue bowtie he was wearing made him seem older. Neither one of them appeared to be as frightening as the scientists in the Minnesota lab, but I knew looks could be deceiving.

Alison and Haden introduced themselves, then invited us to sit down on the orange sofa. As we walked over there, we passed several lab workers seated in high stools along one side of the wall. Some of them were looking at screens that were built into the granite countertops; others were working with 3-D models that hung as digital images in the air in front of them.

Erik and I sat next to each other. Alison and Haden took the chairs across from us. Alison started. "Well, today we'll give you a download of what we've learned so far. Then we'll go through a series of questions to see how your abilities are developing."

"Before we get started, can I get you anything?" Haden asked. "We have coffee, soda, water."

I shook my head.

"No, thanks," Erik said. "We just had breakfast."

Sitting there, I got a chill and shivered.

"Are you cold, Samantha?" Alison tapped the table in front of us. The top suddenly collapsed inward and out popped what looked like a fire pit with fake coals and an orange glow. The surrounding area instantly became warm.

"It's new from the GlobalLife Home Technologies Division," Haden explained. "Pretty nice, right?"

I didn't answer. I wasn't impressed with anything GlobalLife created. I hated them too much.

"So you mentioned that you were gonna tell us what you've learned," Erik said. "What do mean by that?"

"Oh, I meant that we'll go over our observations," Alison clarified. "Things we've noticed since you arrived."

"Can we start with that?" I tried to sound positive, as if it was a good thing they were observing us, even though I couldn't stand the idea of it. The building may have been nicer than the one in Minnesota, but they were still treating us like lab rats.

"Sure." Alison looked over at Haden for his agreement. He nodded for her to continue. "Well, first I'll say that you both performed very well on the coursework we put you through last week. It was a lot to learn in a short amount of time and you did you an excellent job. So we're happy to see that."

"And you really impressed Mr. Owens," Haden added. "As you probably already know, Preston Owens is very important to this project and always has been. He's very difficult to impress. And he can be a bit intimidating so it's remarkable how poised you remained at the interview and how well you were able to answer his questions."

"We've also noticed how well you two communicate with your minds," Alison said.

I started to panic. What did she mean? Were they able to hear Erik and me talking through our thoughts? If so, had they heard us talking about stealing the genes?!

Erik was thinking the same thing. "So you're able to see us communicating?"

"Well, we can't exactly *see* it in terms of understanding what you're saying. It's not like thought bubbles in a cartoon," Haden explained. "But what we *can* do is measure the electric current, or energy, going between you. You see, brain waves are really just electrical impulses. So when you use your brain, there's energy being given off. That's true for everyone. But with your enhanced genes, you two are able to capture those waves of energy and interpret them. Does that make sense?"

"I think so, but could you explain it a little more?" Erik asked, hoping to get more information from him.

"Think of it like this," Alison chimed in. "Sam has a thought in her mind that creates all these electrical sparks, which then creates energy that's released into the atmosphere. Normally, the brain wave energy just hangs out there in the air and nothing happens. But you're able to identify that energy and interpret it in your own mind. And it's not just words you're interpreting but also the feelings that go with them."

Haden pointed to something on his belt. "This device I'm wearing, that all of us are wearing, disrupts that energy as soon as it leaves our minds. So the brain wave is essentially too scrambled for you to interpret, like a radio station that won't come in."

"So I still don't get how you've been seeing us communicate," I said.

"This building is constantly detecting energy fields." Alison went up to the monitor on the wall behind her. "For instance, if you look at our fitness center, here," she tapped in the air and a map of the building appeared with a large red spot in one area, "you can see all the energy being given off." She tapped on the screen again. "Here's the conference room next door, which is currently empty. It's blue, indicating a low energy spot."

Alison came back and sat down. "The detection system has shown a lot of energy coming off you two, especially when you're in your room. Obviously it shows the normal energy given off by your body. But we see big spikes when you two are talking telepathically, which you seem to do quite often."

"But we can't hear what you're saying," Haden explained. "Keep in mind that even if we didn't have this technology, we'd still know you were talking telepathically. I mean, why wouldn't you? If I had that power, I would use it."

"What was interesting to watch this past week was how the telepathy affects you both," Alison said.

Erik and I looked at each other, unsure what she meant.

"Think about learning that waltz, Erik. You'd never done anything like that before, correct?"

Erik nodded.

"Then how you were you able to perform it so well at the gala? To lead Samantha across the dance floor like that?"

He shrugged. "I don't know. Practice?"

"A few hours of practice wasn't enough to be that good. What we found is that when you really focused on Samantha, connecting with her mind, your brain learned that dance significantly faster. The energy coming from you during those lessons and again at the gala was incredible. It's as if your brain was on overdrive, firing at a rapid pace to learn this new skill. And it's all because you connected with Sam, harnessing the energy from her brain."

"Just imagine if we could all do this someday," Haden said. "And don't just think about the energy being given off. Think about what's in that energy. Think about the knowledge in those brain waves. Imagine if we could all share in that knowledge. Some people are better at math. Some people are better at science. Some people are geniuses, like Einstein. Now think if we could combine all those brain waves, pooling them together so we all had access to them. It would be like having one superpowerful brain rather than a single, inferior brain."

"That doesn't sound like a good thing," I muttered. "I'd rather have my own brain."

Erik gave me a look. *"Just go along with it, Sam. Say it's a good idea. We have to gain their trust."*

"But I suppose it wouldn't hurt to have access to some extra brainpower now and then," I added, smiling.

"Oh. See that?" Alison picked up the digital tablet on the table next to her. "I just got a jump on the monitor here that shows you two were talking with your minds."

"So it does that every time?" I asked as she showed us the spike on the screen.

"No. It's only because you're sitting right next to one of our portable energy field devices. Normally, like in your room, we only notice it when you're having a conversation between your minds. A single sentence or two doesn't usually create much of a response."

"Speaking of our room, why don't Erik and I have separate beds to sleep in? I mean, if you're keeping us in the same room, couldn't we at least have two beds? And maybe some more clothes to sleep in?"

Erik's thoughts filled my head. *"What are you doing? Why are you asking them this? Who cares about the bed and the clothes?"*

I didn't answer him. He knew why I was asking. He knew that I was trying to resist him, and sleeping next to him was making that very difficult.

Alison and Haden seemed confused. "Why would you want separate beds?" Haden asked.

"Well, obviously, it's kind of awkward to be in the same bed as Erik." They stared at me like I was speaking a foreign language. "Don't you agree? I mean, Alison, would you wanna sleep in the same bed as Haden?"

She laughed. "Well, of course not. I'm married for one. And we're coworkers."

"Yeah. And Erik and I are just friends. So it's weird."

Alison looked at Haden, then back at Erik and me. "Um, you two are much more than friends. You were designed to be."

" . . . designed to be . . ." The words sat in my head, but I couldn't make sense of them.

"What did you just say?" Erik asked.

"She said that you were designed to be more than just friends," Haden replied, in a matter-of-fact way. "Didn't anyone tell you that?"

"Uhh, no." Even when Haden repeated the words, I couldn't wrap my mind around what he was saying.

"Well, you must have figured it out on your own," Alison said. "I mean, come on. You have this insane chemistry going on between you. Did you think that was just natural?"

Erik and I froze. Neither one of us answered.

"Really? You really didn't know?" Alison was finally noticing our shock. "Well, I guess I should tell you then. You two were designed to be attracted to each other. And I mean really attracted to each other. Not just a 'oh, he's cute, I should go meet him' kind of way. I mean more like 'I can't keep my hands off this person' type of attraction."

"How can you force a person to feel attracted to someone?" I asked.

"There are several ways. For you two, the attraction is due to the software we put in your cells. Basically the software tells your brain to identify those people who have the enhanced genes. Once you find those people, the attraction begins instantly," Alison explained. "It's simply a tool for genetic preservation. Think about it. You wouldn't want people with enhanced genes getting together with people without those genes, right? It would water down the superior gene pool that we've been working so hard to create."

Haden stepped in. "For now, you two are the only ones with these enhanced genes. So your attraction to each other is off the charts. If you were in a room full of people with these enhanced genes, that attraction would be tamped down a little. But still, you would be much more attracted to the people with enhanced genes than you would be to regular people with regular genes."

"That's not true. I'm attracted to regular people. I have a boyfriend." I instantly regretted saying it. Even though Colin was safe, I knew that I should never mention him. I didn't want them even thinking about him or where he might be.

Haden didn't seem to notice or care. "You were attracted to your boyfriend because Erik wasn't there. You didn't even know Erik existed. But I'm guessing that once you finally met Erik, it was hard to keep your mind on that boyfriend of yours."

He was right. It was a constant struggle to keep Colin front and center in my mind when Erik was around. Now I knew why. It finally made sense.

"But before you arrived here," Alison said, "when you temporarily lost your abilities, your attraction to Erik probably wasn't as strong. In fact, you were probably feeling close to your boyfriend again, right?" She didn't wait for an answer. "That's because the software was disabled. When we went in and restored your abilities last week, we fixed the software, too. Updated it to the latest version. And look what happened after that? You two couldn't keep your hands off each other. Your attraction to each other was probably even stronger than before you arrived here."

I didn't try to deny it because what she had described was true. Which meant that the attraction Erik and I shared for each other was simply a product of some computer software. It was all engineered in a lab.

I glanced over at Erik, who was still too stunned to speak.

"So you've engineered us to what? Fall in love?" I asked, trying not to let my growing hatred for GlobalLife show.

"Well, love is tricky," Haden said. "It's hard to engineer. There are so many factors to consider with the whole love emotion. But physical, or sexual, attraction? That's much easier. It's basically a mix of hormones, visual appearance, fantasies, things like that."

Alison explained. "You don't have to be in love with someone to be attracted to them. And there are many ways to build attraction. We can do things like alter hormone levels or define what characteristics you find attractive in the opposite sex."

"How would you do that? I understand the hormone levels being changed, but the other part?"

"The characteristics? We'd just rework the software. At this point, all we've had to do to make you and Erik attracted to each other is to let the software identify your unique base codes. Again, it works because you two are the only people who have these enhanced genes. But in the future, when there are more people like you, we hope to engineer attraction based on more specific characteristics. We haven't defined those yet."

"Well, your technology doesn't work because I'm not attracted to Erik that way," I lied.

Alison smiled. "There's no need to pretend, Samantha. We've seen it for ourselves."

I remembered the cameras in our room and felt my face blushing.

"Didn't you feel yourself drawn to Erik the instant you met?" Alison asked. "Maybe even before you met? You might have even had a premonition or dream about him before you knew he existed."

It was all true. But I didn't answer, not wanting to prove their point.

"And Erik," Haden said, "didn't you want to . . . you know . . . the second you met this girl?"

Erik didn't respond, so Alison continued. "What's interesting is that we've noticed your attraction to each other gets stronger the more your minds connect. So the more you talk telepathically, the more attracted you become to each other. And that waltz you did?

Well, you two were so connected on that night that you basically couldn't help what happened later."

What happened later? I thought. What exactly did she see? *I* still didn't even know what happened that night.

Haden turned to Alison. "But they do seem connected on a more personal level as well, don't you think? They seem to have more than just this physical attraction."

"Yes, you're right. I noted that earlier." She jotted something down in her digital notepad. "That's actually a good thing. I mean, if you're engineered to be that physically attracted to someone, it'd be nice if you also liked them as a person." She laughed, but I didn't see the humor in it.

Erik finally spoke. "Alison, you mentioned that Sam and I were made to have a physical attraction to each other. And that you don't care if we actually like, or love, each other. If you want us to be a couple, why wouldn't you at least try to engineer that as well?"

Haden answered. "As I said earlier, making someone love someone else is very difficult. We haven't yet figured out how to do that. But for the purposes of this project, love doesn't matter. Sex does. And physical attraction drives that."

Erik moved to the edge of his seat. "Wait a minute. So was that your goal? You engineered us to have sex with each other?"

"Well, of course," Alison replied. "Are you still not getting it? We need you two to mate."

26. NEWS

"Could you say that once more?" Erik looked even more shocked than before.

"We need you two to mate." Haden repeated it as if it were no big deal. "We need you two to have a baby. We need to see what happens when two people with these enhanced genes procreate. And we're hoping we can use the new genes to—"

"What? No!" I jumped up from the sofa. "You can't make us have a baby. I won't do it." I yanked Erik up from his seat. "WE won't do it."

"She's right. Forget it. We're not doing that. You may have made us attracted to each other, but we're not animals. We don't mate when put in confinement. We can control ourselves."

"So that's why we're in that room together? Because you want us to have sex?" I wanted to scream at them, but I knew it would interfere with our goal of getting information.

"You might as well go ahead and give us separate rooms because that's not gonna happen," Erik assured them.

Haden looked at Alison and smiled. "Are you sure it hasn't already?"

I suddenly felt light-headed and sat down. "I don't feel so good. I need to go back to the room."

"Oh, she's white as a ghost," Alison remarked.

Haden motioned to one of the lab workers on the side of the room. "Ridley, could you come check on Samantha for me? Hurry, please."

A young man walked over with a wandlike device in his hand. I had seen a similar device at the lab in Minnesota. He waved it over me.

"Everything seems okay," Ridley said.

"I'm fine. I'm just tired. Do you think we could take the rest of the day off?"

Alison got up. "We'll postpone our activities for today and resume tomorrow."

She walked us back to our room, then left. I collapsed on the bed. Erik sat next to me, not saying anything. After a few minutes, he leaned down and put his arm around me.

I immediately pushed him away. "Get off me!"

He sat up. "What did I do? Why are you screaming at me?"

"Didn't you hear any of that? Weren't you listening? This is what they want! Us! Together! This fancy room, the fireplace, the clothes, the lingerie. It's all part of their sick plan!"

"Why are you getting mad at *me*? I didn't do this!"

"Because you're acting like we're still—like we were before. And we're not!"

"So you hate me now, or what?"

"No, I don't hate you." I sat up to look at him. "I don't know how I feel about you anymore. Obviously everything I thought I felt wasn't real. It was all engineered."

"Really, Sam? You think that's all we have here? Fake feelings for each other?"

"Yeah. I do."

"Real nice answer there, Sam. So now you don't even like me? You don't care at all about me? Is that it?"

I didn't answer. I was too confused. Rejecting Erik meant I was rejecting GlobalLife's master plan for me. And I had to do that. I couldn't let them continue to engineer my whole life, especially who I was attracted to or who I had children with.

Erik went across the room and sat on the chair. He started mind-talking. *"You're just letting them win, Sam. They want to drive us apart. They don't want us building an alliance. Like they said, they don't care if we like each other. They just need us to have sex. And I'm sure they have ways to force us into doing that. They'll send our hormone levels through the roof. Or drug us so we don't even know what we're doing. But if you let them break apart our friendship—or whatever type of relationship we have—then we'll never escape. It's exactly what they want!"*

I wasn't ready to talk to him. I needed time to think it over. Maybe Erik was right. Maybe they *were* trying to break us apart. Maybe they suspected we were up to something. Alison and Haden had said that talking telepathically made Erik's and my attraction to each other stronger. But they knew I didn't want that. They knew I had a boyfriend. I kept insisting that Erik was only a friend. So why would they tell us that? Probably to get us to stop mind-talking. They didn't want us saying things they couldn't hear.

So was any of what they told us true? Did the attraction software really exist? Were we really engineered to be together? Or was their whole speech some type of mind game meant to manipulate us into doing what they wanted us to do?

Erik wouldn't talk to me for the rest of the afternoon. I stayed in bed, pretending to sleep. I felt horrible for yelling at him. None of this was his fault. And I hated pushing him away. I needed him. We needed each other. Or, as he said, we'd never get out of there.

Dinner arrived as usual and Erik went over to the table to eat. I got up and joined him. "Hey, I'm sorry about how I acted earlier. And I'm sorry for what I said to you."

"It's okay. I understand," he said coldly. "I'll keep my distance from now on. I'll sleep on the floor tonight. On the opposite side of the room."

"You don't have to do that, Erik. Like you said, we're not animals. We can control ourselves no matter what they did."

"No. I thought about what you said and maybe you were right. Maybe we just need to stay away from each other."

"Erik, I was just upset earlier. I didn't mean to yell at you like that."

"Well, you meant the other stuff."

"What other stuff?"

Erik went into mind-talk mode. *"Like the fact that nothing you ever felt for me was real. You just bought into that whole GlobalLife crap without even giving it a thought. It's like you were relieved that you didn't really have feelings for me."*

"That's not true." I paused, considering how much to tell him. *"Okay, maybe a part of me was relieved. But that's only because I've felt so guilty since meeting you. I've been trying to understand why I have these feelings for you when I already have a great boyfriend. I mean, Colin is back in my life now and since being here with you, I've been acting like he doesn't even exist. So yeah, it's nice to be able to explain that."*

"And what if they lied? What if we really weren't engineered like that? How would you explain your feelings then?"

"I don't know. Before we found this out, I tried not to think about it. And obviously, if Colin wasn't in the picture, things would have gone further last Saturday night."

"Well, according to Alison and Haden, things did go further."

"Let's not talk about that, Erik. It's bad enough I don't remember, but then to think they were watching it all. I can't even think about it."

"They probably just said that to see our reaction. I'm sure we didn't do anything. I would've known."

We finished dinner and went to bed early. I insisted Erik sleep in the bed despite his protests. The room was more frigid than normal. Another way to get us together, I thought. Make us huddle up for warmth.

In the middle of the night, Erik woke me up. "Sam, I can't sleep."

"Because of me? You can't move, right?" I was curled up next to him trying to keep warm. "I'll just go to the other side of the bed."

He kept hold of me before I could move away. "No. You're fine. I just can't stop thinking about what they said."

"What about it?"

He switched to mind-talk. *"I don't think it's possible to engineer a person's feelings like that. I don't think it would work."*

"Some of it had to be true. How else would you explain our instant attraction to each other?"

"Yeah, so maybe the software in us can recognize that we have enhanced genes, but how much more could it really do? It can't think for us."

"What do you mean?"

"Think about when Colin came back. It was like you two were never apart. You didn't tell him to get lost, then come running back to me. You were able to overcome whatever they put in us and make a decision for yourself."

"Yeah, that's true."

"So why are we just accepting that some software program has so much control? We still have brains. And free will."

"What are you trying to say, Erik?"

"I'm saying that our genes and the software are just a small part of us. They don't have to dictate who we are. We can still think for ourselves. We can make decisions. We can change outcomes. We can't forget that, Sam. We can't get so hung up on the idea that we can only act the way we're programmed to act. Or engineered to feel."

"But sometimes I feel like the genes and the software really are controlling me. Like they've controlled me my entire life."

"Because you're letting yourself believe that. Or you want to believe it so you don't have to face the truth about how you feel, or why you made a certain decision. But if you think that way, you'll never overcome the outcome they've picked for you. They'll always control you."

"Wow. You've really given this some thought, Erik."

"Yeah, because what they said today—and how they said it—it just really pissed me off. They act like they control everything about us. Like we'll never have choices. But they're wrong! I was thinking about this whole attraction thing, and you know what? I would have been attracted to you even without their stupid software. I like you, Sam. You're different than other girls, and not just in a genetic way. I have fun with you. I can talk to you about stuff. And none of that has to do with physical attraction."

"But if it weren't for the software drawing us together, I don't think we'd be as close as we are now. I wouldn't have been so open with you. And I wouldn't have let things get as far as they have. It's just not me."

"I'm not saying that the software doesn't work. It's affecting me now and I'm doing all I can to control myself." He kissed me.

"Hey! Don't start!" I kidded.

"I'm just saying that we need to think for ourselves. Take control of our actions. And however they try to brainwash us, we need to ignore it and not let them get to us."

It was a good reminder and I needed to hear it. I kept telling myself that I couldn't change what GlobalLife had done to me. But of course I could, at least somewhat.

"We need to work harder to get out of here, Sam. No more nights off. We have to spend every free minute planning our escape."

"And figuring out how to open the globe," I added.

"Speaking of that, I'm done working on the cipher. I couldn't sleep so I worked on it and finished it like an hour ago. I know the password now."

"Erik, that's great!"

"It's just one piece, Sam. We still need to get that word or phrase figured out. And we have to learn how to copy brain waves."

"I was thinking about that earlier. I think we were focusing on the wrong thing before. As we heard today, brain waves are just energy waves released into the air. We need to focus on the energy waves that are released when the phrase is said or thought rather than the words themselves. I'm too tired to try it now but we'll do it tomorrow."

The next day, we went to the lab again and asked tons of questions about how brain waves worked. Alison wasn't there but Haden was, and he answered everything we asked, not suspicious at all. We even got him to describe in detail how Erik and I were able to take the brain wave energy from the air and use our minds to interpret it. Haden's explanation was exactly what we needed for our practice session later that night.

"So remember what he said about paying attention to the frequency," I said.

"Yeah, I got it Sam. Just go."

I said a phrase out loud and Erik tried focusing on the brain waves being released. Then I said several more, first saying them out loud, then thinking them in my head.

"I can't get any of those to work, Sam," Erik thought to me after an hour of trying.

"All right, I'll try."

Erik and I pretended to read while he made occasional statements about something in his book. Then I would repeat those statements in my head. It was a difficult process. First, I had to learn to tell the difference between energy from a brain wave and the other energy in the room. And once I found it, I had to focus on the various nuances of Erik's brain waves as he said each word. Then I had to try to re-create those same energy waves in my own head. It was much harder than just letting my brain listen to his thoughts.

After a few hours of trying, Erik said it still sounded like me talking in his head. *"It's really late and we've been doing this for hours. Let's just try later. Give your mind a break."*

"Just a few more times. Come on, Erik."

He said another phrase. I decided to try focusing on Erik as well as the energy coming from his thoughts, remembering what Alison had said regarding the waltz. If I focused on Erik, I might be able to harness the energy in his mind to help me replicate his brain waves.

I thought Erik's phrase back to him. He gave me a strange look. *"Hey, it sounded like you except for the last few words."*

"Let's try it again, Erik."

He said another phrase and I thought it back to him.

He looked excited. *"Three words this time, Sam! I got three words!"*

We tried again and again until I could mimic up to six words all in a row. I needed more practice, but at least we knew it could be done.

On Wednesday, we headed back to the lab. They took several vials of blood and ran the scanning wand over us. Then they did hearing and vision tests. After lunch, they strapped some helmet device to our heads and made us look at different images.

They let us leave the lab early that afternoon. Haden took us back to our room. "I need to talk to you both." He sat down, so Erik and I did as well. "Ever since we told you about your engineered attraction to each other, we've noticed that you haven't been as, um, affectionate toward each other."

Erik and I remained quiet.

"We can't have that," Haden said, in an almost threatening tone. "You need to resume that behavior or we'll need to take more drastic measures. And we really don't want to have to intervene like that."

"What behaviors exactly?" I asked.

"You know what I mean, Samantha. You know where babies come from."

"What's the rush?" Erik asked.

"We're on a schedule. And we don't know how these genes will affect a pregnancy. Could make it shorter, longer—we just don't know."

Hearing the words "baby" and "pregnancy" and having them relate to me was making me feel light-headed again.

Haden punched Erik's shoulder. "Come on, Erik. Be a man. Just get the job done." He turned to me. "And Sam, look at this handsome young man. You don't even need the software to be attracted to him, right? Well, I'll let you two get down to business."

"Tonight?" I asked. "We have to do this tonight?"

"You don't have to," he said, getting up to leave. "But if you wait much longer, we'll take measures into our own hands. So it's up to you."

He left. Erik and I looked at each other. "Well, I wasn't expecting him to say that," I said.

"Me, either. Guess they've really been watching us."

Erik switched to mind-talking. *"So what are we gonna do?"*

"We're not doing it, Erik, if that's what you're thinking."

"Well, I don't exactly like the idea of them 'intervening,' whatever that means."

"Maybe we could pretend. Put on a show for the cameras."

"I think they'll know, Sam."

"It's worth a try." I got up and took a book from the shelf, then sat down pretending to read.

"And if they find out we faked it, then what happens? I guarantee it won't be good." Erik grabbed a book as well.

"So you've just decided we're doing this?"

"Maybe just once, to get them off our backs."

"They won't accept us doing it just one time, Erik. And what if I really get pregnant? No way. Forget it."

"You won't get pregnant the first time. That never happens."

"Are you kidding? It happens all the time! I can't talk about this right now."

"Okay, but like he said, we can't put it off much longer, Sam."

"Then we need to get out of here before it comes to that."

Erik sighed. *"Yeah, but we haven't spent any time figuring out how to do that! All you want to do is focus on getting that globe open!"*

"Because we need those base codes! Owens said he'd get us out of here. So let him worry about the escape."

"And what if he doesn't? What if he can't? Then it's up to us to find a way out."

"Okay, but let's talk about that later. We need to practice the brain wave thing again. Say a phrase."

Since I was having better luck mimicking brain waves, I kept working on it rather than have Erik try. I focused on his mind again, along with the energy coming from it, as I had the night before.

After several hours of practice I heard Erik shouting in my head. *"Sam! You got it! Just now. Every word. It sounded like me talking in my own head!"*

I wanted to hug him, but I didn't since it would look odd with us not talking aloud. *"We're getting closer, Erik! We might actually get the genes!"*

"We still have a ways to go, but yeah, this is a huge step."

"I'm exhausted, Erik. I'm going to bed."

By morning, I felt a rush of optimism. By learning to mimic brain waves, I'd accomplished what I thought was impossible. And that gave me hope.

At 9, there was a knock on the door. It was time to leave for the lab. But instead of a lab attendant coming to pick us up, Allie's mom walked in.

"Mrs. Taylor," I said. "You're taking us to the lab today?"

"No, no. I'm just here to give you some news." She seemed way too happy and way too excited.

"What news?" Erik asked in a suspicious tone.

"Well, we got your lab work back from yesterday. It showed that Samantha is pregnant! You two are going to be parents! Congratulations!"

27. LAB VISITOR

I thought I was having some awful nightmare. But then Erik grabbed my arm in case I passed out, and I knew it was real.

"Is this a joke?" I asked. "Because it's not funny."

"Of course it's not a joke. I wouldn't joke about a thing like that. You're going to be a mother, Samantha. And Erik, you're going to be a father. Isn't this marvelous?" She gave us a loose hug, then stood back again.

Mrs. Taylor was loving this far too much. She knew this was the last thing I wanted to hear, and knowing that, she insisted she be the one to tell me. And I hated her for it.

"So what do you think, Samantha?"

"This isn't possible. How could this happen?"

"You do know how babies are made," she said in a condescending tone.

"Of course I do."

"Then you know how this happened."

"Are you sure about this?" Erik asked.

"The blood work doesn't lie," she said.

"But it's too soon," I insisted. "How could you possibly know that soon?"

"Our equipment is far superior than some drugstore test or whatever a doctor's office would have."

I looked down at my stomach. "But I don't feel pregnant."

"You were feeling kind of sick the other day," Erik whispered to me.

Mrs. Taylor noticed him whispering. "Well, I'll let you two lovebirds celebrate. Someone will be in shortly to take you to the lab."

I went over and sat on the bed. Erik followed. "I guess it *can* happen the first time."

I punched his arm. "That's the first thing you're thinking, Erik?" I punched him again. "You said we didn't do anything! You said, 'Oh, I'd know if we did anything, Sam.' Were you just lying to me?"

"No! I really don't remember doing anything that night. Honestly, Sam. I don't."

"There's no other way this could have happened, Erik!"

"Yeah, I got that. But I don't see how it's possible. Why can't I remember anything?"

I stood up and started pacing the floor. "I can't be pregnant. I'm only 18! I don't even want to get married until I'm at least 30! And I don't want kids."

"Really? Huh. I would have thought you were a kid person."

I stopped pacing. "What gave you that idea?"

"I don't know. You just seemed like you'd want one or two."

"Maybe someday, waaay off in the future I might *consider* it. But at 18? No way!"

"I'm sure they won't let us keep it, Sam. They'll take it and raise it in a lab. I probably shouldn't say 'it,' should I? Let's assume it's a boy. I'll say 'he.'"

"No, I don't want a boy. What am I saying? I don't want a baby! And if I'm really having a baby, I definitely don't want it raised in some GlobalLife lab." I sat down on the bed again.

"They could be lying about it."

"Why would they lie about that, Erik? They know we don't want to be forced into having sex and if I'm pregnant, we don't need to do it anymore."

"I guess. But how could it happen so fast? You think it's because of our genes?"

"I don't know. But I can't go to the lab today. You'll have to go alone. Tell them I'm sick." I pushed the covers back and crawled into bed.

Erik switched to mind-talk. *"Sam, we need more answers. You have to go. We need to get out of here as soon as possible. The sooner we get out of here, the sooner we can see my dad and Colin again."*

I sat up, yanking on Erik's sleeve. *"Oh my God! Colin! He'll completely freak out about this! And he's gonna kill you, Erik! He's never gonna believe that we don't remember doing anything. He'll never forgive me!"*

"Relax, Sam. Colin will forgive you. He won't forgive ME, but that's all right."

"No, Erik. Colin will never look at me the same way. He'll always think of me with you. He'll see me as a cheater and a liar and—"

"I shouldn't have brought it up. Let's just focus on today and what we're gonna do at the lab."

But before we could make a plan, Walter came through the door. "Apparently, I'm supposed to take you to the lab now. They're waiting for you."

Erik gave me a look, trying to convince me to go. He got up as I lay back down in the bed, pulling the covers over me.

"What's wrong with her?" Walter asked Erik.

"She's um, not feeling well."

"Ah, yes. Morning sickness, perhaps? I heard that you're expecting, Samantha. Congratulations to you both."

Erik gave me another look, begging me to go, but I wouldn't move.

"Well, I guess it's just me today."

"You should really go with him, Samantha," Walter said. "This is one of your last chances to get out and move about. Next week you'll be transferred to a different room and confined to bed rest. There will be absolutely nothing to do. And no visitors."

I sat up. "How do you know that?"

"I've seen your schedule for next week. And I won't be attending to you in your new location. You'll have someone new." He smiled. "Oh, but I'll still be attending to you, Erik."

"Why do I need bed rest?"

"Because of your condition."

"I'm barely pregnant. I feel fine. And why can't I have visitors?"

Walter sighed. "I don't make the rules, Samantha. I just follow them. Now can we go?"

"Wait," Erik said. "So are you saying that I can't see Sam anymore after this week?"

"Correct. Now we really should be going. Are you coming or not, Samantha?"

"Yes. I'm coming." I got up and met them at the door.

Erik and I knew that if we were no longer able to see each other, we'd never escape. He took my hand as we walked to the lab. *"Stay calm,"* he ordered me in his thoughts. *"This is bad news, but we can deal with it. It just bumps up our timeline a little. We need to stay focused and get as much information as we can today. You okay?"*

"No. But I'm determined to get out of here so I'll do whatever it takes."

When we got to the lab, Drew Chamberlin was waiting for us on the orange sofa. He got up and extended his hand to Erik. "So I hear you're going to be a father, Erik. You must be thrilled."

"Yes. I'm thrilled," Erik replied, playing along.

Drew came over and hugged me, making my skin crawl. "Samantha, you must be so excited to be a mother." He stood back and looked at Erik and me. "Congratulations to you both. This is such wonderful news. We're hosting a special announcement event for the Founders to let them know."

Dr. Siefert, the head of the lab, came up to Drew. "Are you still planning on staying for part of the testing today?"

"Yes. Absolutely. But I don't have much time. Let's get started."

Dr. Siefert called for Alison to come over. "Why don't you have Samantha and Erik try reading your thoughts? You haven't done that yet, correct?"

"No. We've been doing the image response exercises the past few days."

"I think you'll find the telepathy very entertaining to observe," Siefert said to Drew. He turned to Alison. "Perhaps you could even let Mr. Chamberlin give it a try, if he's up for it."

"Yes, I would enjoy that," Drew said.

"Very well, then. I'll let you get to work." Dr. Siefert went to a different part of the lab.

"Go ahead and have a seat, Mr. Chamberlin," Alison said. "I'll have Sam and Erik demonstrate how the telepathy works on me. Then you can try."

Alison turned off her brain wave scrambling device. Her thoughts were all about our surroundings. *"The man behind you is wearing a green shirt today,"* she thought. I repeated it back, hoping she would come up with something more interesting than that. But she didn't. Her thoughts were all descriptions of things in the room.

Drew wasn't impressed. He wanted to see if Erik and I could interpret more complicated thoughts. Alison tapped on her digital notepad, trying to find something more challenging for us.

"Okay, I've got an idea," she said. "Erik, I'm going to imagine a diagram in my mind, and I want you to describe it. This will show Mr. Chamberlin how you're able to interpret images. It's a much more complex skill than interpreting words."

Erik closed his eyes, as if really concentrating. A minute passed. "Sorry, but I'm not getting any type of image or diagram." I knew Erik was lying. He'd seen and memorized maps of the building and the surrounding area from Owens' mind. We both had.

"Samantha, did you try as well?" Alison asked.

"Yes. And I didn't get anything, either."

"Hmm, that's odd. I was sure that would work. We probably need to tweak the software."

Drew glanced at his watch. "Alison, although I've enjoyed watching this, I would like to give it a try before I have to leave."

"Certainly. Go ahead and disable your scrambling device and then think whatever you would like."

Drew turned the device off.

This is it! I thought. My one and only chance to get Drew to think, or even just say, the words needed to open the globe. Even if I could just get a bunch of words, I might be able to string them together to form the necessary phrase.

I could tell that Erik had the same thought. We remained calm, acting like this was just another routine exercise.

In my head, I listed all the possible phrases Drew might use to open that globe. I tried to quickly think of anything he had said before that might be significant.

"Sam, did you hear Mr. Chamberlin just now?" Alison's voice woke me from my thoughts.

"Um, no. I'm a little out of it today with the baby news and all." I looked at Drew. "Sorry about that. Try again."

"I can't wait to tell everyone about the baby," he thought. I paid close attention, memorizing the pattern of his brain waves as he spoke each word.

I repeated it back to him. "I can't wait to tell everyone about the baby."

"Yes! That's incredible!" Drew said to Alison. "Much better than just observing it. It's so amazing to have them actually read my thoughts. It's like some type of carnival act!"

I smiled to hide my anger toward his comment. Next Drew sent some thoughts to Erik and he repeated them back. The exercise allowed me to memorize Drew's brain waves for several words, but the words didn't seem like the ones that would open the globe. I felt hopeless again, considering how stupid it was to even imagine that he would say those words aloud or even think them. I wondered if I could somehow trick him into saying them.

"Does GlobalLife have a motto or something?" I asked, trying to sound completely innocent.

"Yes. Why do you ask?"

"Well, it just seems like if you're sending us your thoughts, they should be more, I don't know, impressive sounding. Rather than just random thoughts about what's going on in the room or other everyday stuff."

Erik picked up on what I was trying to do. "Yeah, like if you really had this power, you might use it to transmit a secret message or something."

"Yes. I see what you're saying." Drew's mind went blank for a second, then I heard him think a phrase. *"We're only as strong as our weakest link."*

That was it! It had to be it! The motto for GlobalLife Genetics. The phrase Drew said all the time. And it was engraved right on the marble globe.

"I've got this one, Sam," Erik said. As he repeated the phrase out loud, Drew thought it again in his head, giving me another chance to memorize his brain waves.

"Isn't that the GlobalLife motto?" Erik asked.

"Yes," Drew answered. "It's the motto for GlobalLife Genetics. Just our division, not the entire organization. Well, that was fun! But I should get going now."

Erik sensed my excitement, but I didn't sense his. He didn't seem to think those were the right words.

As Drew got up to leave, Rachel walked in and came over to where we were sitting. She was in a tight black dress and heels, looking gorgeous as always.

Drew smiled and gave her a peck on the cheek. "Darling, what are you doing here?"

"I had this announcement for you to look over. Do you have a minute?"

"Why don't we go back to my office." His tone implied that he wanted to do more than just discuss the announcement.

"No, I really need to get this sent out. Can you just review it quick?"

"All business today? Well, then I suppose. Give it here."

Alison's cell phone rang. She got up to answer it, leaving Erik and me sitting there with Rachel and Drew.

As Drew reviewed the announcement, Rachel talked to Erik and me. "I heard about the baby news. You two must be so excited!"

"Yeah. It's a little unexpected. But you can't always plan these things." Erik smiled, putting his arm around me as if we truly were the elated couple. I wondered if these people really did think we were happy about the news.

Erik kept the conversation going so I could listen to Drew's thoughts.

I could hear Drew reading the announcement in his head. *"And that's why we're so thrilled to announce that Samantha is expecting a child. This child will be the first offspring of a new generation. As you know—"*

Drew's cell phone rang, interrupting his thoughts. He answered it, setting the announcement aside. "Yes?" Pause. "I'll be there shortly. I'm just reviewing something and then I'll be over."

"Who was that?" Rachel asked.

"Eve Taylor. She met with Preston this morning. She wants to go over what they discussed. I could look at this later, right?" He held up the announcement.

"No, Drew. It really can't wait. Can you please just make your changes?" She smiled at him flirtatiously.

He smiled back. "Oh, all right. But it's sad how I let you control me, Rachel."

She laughed. "Oh, Drew. Don't be silly."

For someone who claimed to be breaking up with him, she sure played the girlfriend role well.

"So, Rachel, when is this big announcement?" Erik asked.

"Friday night. Since so many of the Founders were just here for the gala, few people will be able to attend in person. We're hosting a live teleconference at 7. Drew will make the announcement and then we'll send out more information following the event. For those people who are still in Iceland, we'll be hosting a cocktail party."

As she talked, I listened to Drew again as he reviewed the announcement. *"As you know, Samantha Andrews, Subject 46A, has been our biggest success and we're so proud to—. Wait. I can't say that."* I watched as Drew crossed out a small section of the announcement. *"Oh, I might as well get rid of the whole sentence."* He crossed it out and kept reading. *"This news puts us one step closer to achieving our goal. We will now truly be able to take the human race to a higher plane of being. Your generous support of this project allows you to be the first to reap the benefits of this technological breakthrough and join a new class of humanity. You will be part of an elite group that will rise above ordinary human weaknesses and frailties. And your future generations will become royalty—a new royalty chosen not by ancient bloodlines but by cellular superiority. Perfection above all else. The future has arrived. The time is now!"*

Drew handed Rachel the announcement. "Splendid job, Rachel."

"Thank you, Drew." Rachel leaned over and gave him a long kiss on the lips. It was very odd and even surprised Drew.

"Not around the workers, Rachel," he muttered to her.

"Oh, yes. I'm sorry," she said, getting up. "I was just so happy that you liked it."

Drew got up as well. "I couldn't have written it better myself. It's like you can read my mind as well as these two."

As soon as he said it, a panicked look came across his face. He started searching his belt for the brain wave scrambling device. "Dammit! I had this off and I forgot to turn it back on."

"Relax, Drew. It's already on," Rachel assured him. "See the green light? You must have turned it on without even thinking."

"Yes, I see that now. All right. Well, I just had one change to the announcement. You'll provide me with a revised version this afternoon?"

"Of course." Rachel gave him a peck on the cheek. "You should head over to your meeting. I'll see you at dinner."

Drew raced off. I sat there wondering how I could have heard his thoughts with that scrambling device turned on. Did the device not work? But it worked when he first arrived. And as he left I couldn't hear his thoughts, so it was working then.

"Sorry for the interruption, Alison," Rachel said as Alison came back.

"It's no problem. I had to take that call anyway. I'm getting the room prepped for next week. I have so much equipment to order. We weren't expecting this so soon."

"I'll see you all later." Rachel left. Alison sat down with her digital notepad.

"What room are you getting ready?" I asked, already fairly certain of the answer.

"*Your* room, Samantha. Yours and the baby's." She casually tapped on her notepad, not looking up. "We're moving you on Sunday."

I shot Erik a look. *"Sunday? Walter said next week! Sunday is only a couple days—"*

"Just stay calm and act normal," Erik thought back.

"So why does Sam need to move to a different room?" Erik asked. "I thought you wanted us to stay together."

She looked up. "No. We didn't *want* you to stay together. We *needed* you to stay together. Simply for mating purposes. But now we don't need that anymore, so she's moving out."

"But I need to be with Erik," I insisted. "Don't you think I should be with the father of my child?"

Alison took out her phone and began texting. "He's a contributor of genetic material, Samantha. Not a father. In the future, we won't be tied to such antiquated terms and conventions. You don't need Erik now. His role is done."

"But I need him for support. I can't go through this alone."

"Don't be ridiculous. Of course you can. What decade are you living in, Samantha? Women have children on their own all the time."

It was no use arguing with her. There was no way they would let me stay with Erik. The decision was made. I would be moved on Sunday. Just two days away.

28. PREPARATIONS

"So what happens after you separate us?" I asked Alison. "Will I ever see Erik again?"

"We don't know our plans for Erik just yet. I would think they'd still want you two to make a few public appearances together, given the whole golden couple thing. You could ask Rachel about that. She's head of public relations, so she would be the one planning your appearances. As for you, Sam, you'll be under constant monitoring because we're not sure what to expect with this pregnancy. But that new equipment I ordered will allow us to run a variety of tests."

A throbbing pain filled my head as she talked. I wasn't sure if it was caused by my stress over the pregnancy news or all the energy I'd expended trying to memorize Drew's brain waves.

"I'm sorry, but could I go back to the room? I have a really intense headache."

Erik put his arm around me. "What's wrong? Did you just get this?"

"Yeah. It came out of nowhere. I need to lie down."

"I'll have someone take her back," Alison said. "Erik, you and I will continue with the tests."

"No. I need to go with her. She shouldn't be in the room alone."

"I'll have Walter sit in there with her. She'll be fine. It's probably pregnancy hormones kicking in." Alison waved for one of the lab techs to come over to walk me back.

I heard Erik in my head. *"What's wrong, Sam? Are you okay?"*

"I don't know yet. I think so."

"I'll go with you. I'll make something up."

"No. Stay here. She'll get suspicious if you go. Just stay and see if you can get more information from her."

Erik reluctantly agreed. I went back to the room and slept until Erik got back later that afternoon. "Hey, how are you feeling?" He was sitting next to me on the bed. Walter had left.

"I'm better." I switched to mind-talking. *"Did you find out anything?*

"No. She made me wear some headset thing. Then I had to repeat these phrases that different people were thinking. It was just like we did earlier. Now tell me what happened to you. Was it just a headache?"

"Yeah. I think my brain was on overdrive trying to memorize what Drew said."

"Well, it wasn't worth it. The guy didn't even think anything that we could use."

"What are you talking about? He said the GlobalLife motto. That's gotta be it. It's written right on the globe."

"Yeah, so it couldn't be that. It's too obvious."

"That's why I think it's the right phrase. Think about it. Drew is arrogant. He put the alien genes right in the lobby to prove that his security system was so brilliant that nobody could ever access the vials. And then he puts the phrase that opens it right on the globe, knowing that it only works when he says that phrase. I'm sure he loves hearing people read it out loud over and over again, knowing that the globe only opens when he says or thinks the phrase."

"It's a good theory, Sam, but I still don't think that's it."

"Well, we have to try something. I don't know what else to try."

"When you were listening today, did you hear any other words or phrases that he might use to open it?"

"I'm not sure. He said that phrase about taking the human race to higher plane of being. So that might be it. I need to replay his thoughts in my head. I think I might have to combine words to come up some of the other phrases he says."

"Well, you need to have several options ready to try. If we ever get a chance to."

"Yeah, I'm getting worried about that, Erik. Owens said he'd get us access to the globe, but we haven't heard anything from him. And soon it'll be too late."

"We can't let them move you, Sam. We've got to find a way to delay it somehow."

"They won't delay it. We just have to get out of here before Sunday. Otherwise, we're never leaving. Or at least I'm not. I'll be locked away on bed rest. What do you think Alison meant when she said they don't need you now?"

"She just meant that they don't need me for 'mating purposes' anymore. But I'm sure they still need me."

I didn't agree. It sounded more sinister to me than that.

After dinner, I practiced thinking Drew's words in my head while Erik listened.

"You sound just like him, Sam, at least in my head," Erik thought to me.

"Then we just have to hope that I can figure out the right phrase. And that Owens can get us access to the globe."

We went to bed, but I didn't sleep. I kept thinking of the pregnancy. I couldn't imagine myself pregnant and I definitely couldn't imagine myself as a mother.

The bed moved as Erik tossed and turned.

"Erik, are you awake?" I whispered.

"Yeah. I can't sleep."

"Me either. I keep thinking about being a mother. It's so weird. I can't imagine myself taking care of a baby."

He switched to mind-talk. *"I don't think you'll have to take care of it, Sam. I don't think they'll let you see much of the baby. Maybe you won't see it at all."*

"No. They can't take the baby. I don't want our baby growing up in a lab, like—"

"Like I did? Yeah, I know. I don't want that either." I sensed Erik's anger building as he thought about it. GlobalLife had taken him as a baby. They locked him up in a lab and experimented on him, as if he wasn't human.

"It's not happening, Sam. I won't let it. I won't let this baby grow up in a lab like I did. We have to get out of here, whether Owens helps us or not. No second guesses. No doubts. I need you to be 100% on board with this. You can't hesitate, no matter what."

"Okay. So how do we get access to the globe without the guards around and cameras watching?"

Erik sat up in bed. *"Forget the globe! Forget the damn alien genes! I need to get you and our child the hell out of here! We'll worry about getting the genes later."*

"What? No! You're almost out of time, Erik. We have to get them!"

"You have almost two years left, Sam. You'll be able to get the timer turned off by then. I know you will."

"But we need those genes now! For you!"

"If we can get them in time for me, great. But if not, then—"

"What are you saying, Erik?"

He laid down again and stared up at the ceiling. *"I'm saying that our priority needs to be escaping. We've been too hung up on getting the alien genes when we should have been focusing on how to get out of here. Getting the alien genes is way too complicated and risky. We have no idea if we'll even be able to open that globe. Trying could mean getting caught. We have a way better chance of escaping than getting those vials."*

"We're getting them, Erik. I'm not letting you—"

"You need the password to open that globe. If I refuse to give it to you, then it's useless to try opening it by yourself."

"But Erik, we have all the pieces now! We have to try!"

"We don't have all the pieces! We have one piece. We're just guessing about the other one. We won't have much time to escape, Sam. And I don't want to waste even a second trying to open that thing unless we're absolutely sure we can do it. And as of now, we're not even a little bit sure."

"We're getting those vials, Erik. If we don't, you'll run out of time. You'll—" I couldn't say it. Letting his timer run out was not an option. At least to me it wasn't. *"Why would you even consider this, Erik? This is your child, too. You need to be here for him. Or her. And I can't raise a baby on my own."*

He turned to face me. *"Sam, you know my dad would help you and—"*

"Stop talking like that! I'm not going along with your plan, Erik. If you want to run and try to escape, go ahead. But I'm staying behind and opening that globe. If you won't tell me the password, then I'll just have to guess."

"Why are you being so stubborn about this? Do you want to risk being a prisoner here forever? And having our baby raised by GlobalLife?"

"No! Of course not! But I've lost enough people to GlobalLife. I can't lose you, too, Erik. We have to get those genes."

"We'll find another way to get them. I still have months before anything happens to me. It's not like my timer is running out tomorrow. We'll figure something out, okay?" He paused. *"Would you just think about this some more? If we try to open the globe we probably won't escape. Don't you get that? We can't risk it. I need you to be safe, Sam. And now we have a baby to think about."*

I kept quiet. I had nothing more to say to him. It was true that trying to get the globe open would slow us down, lessening our chance of escape. But I couldn't have Erik's timer run out. I couldn't let him die.

Early that morning while we were still in bed, someone came through the door. It was Walter. "Mr. Owens has requested to have breakfast with you this morning in the executive dining room. You need to be ready in a half hour. Wear your normal dress attire, not your lab uniforms." Walter left without waiting for a response.

"Sam, Owens is meeting with us. Get up," Erik thought to me.

"Yeah. I heard. He better have his part of the plan ready."

"I'll talk to him and you listen to his thoughts. I'll just make small talk about what we've been doing in the lab this week."

We got dressed. Walter walked us to the dining room. Owens was waiting there with Allie's mom.

"Well, I hear congratulations are in order, young lady," Owens said as soon as we entered the room.

"Yes. Thank you." I took a seat at the table.

"Eve, I know you have plenty to do to get ready for tonight. I think these two can keep me entertained." He smiled and stood up, encouraging her to go.

"Oh, all right then. Phone my office when you're done and I'll send Walter to come get them."

"Don't bother. I can walk them back." Owens waited for her to leave, then sat down with us again. "And how are you two this morning? Tell me what you've been up to all week."

Erik talked while I listened to Owens.

"Do you have what you need to get the vials?" Owens thought to me as he kept his eyes on Erik. *"Pick up your spoon for 'yes.'"*

I picked up my spoon as Owens glanced over at me.

"Are you certain? Put your spoon back down for 'yes.'"

I kept my spoon in my hand.

"We've run out of time, Samantha," he thought. *"If you don't think you can open it, we'll have to forget that part. We'll have to get the genes later."*

The cameras in the ceiling were pointed right at us, so I tried to act natural. But I had to let him know we weren't giving up on the globe. "Erik and I have really been working hard this week in the lab," I said out loud, "and we're ready to try—" I struggled to find the right words so as not to give anything away.

"Whatever they need us to do next," Erik said, finishing my statement. "Sam loves a challenge." Erik kept talking out loud while also listening to Owens.

"Are you sure you want to try?" Owens thought. *"It could mean you won't get out of here. And I only have one chance to get you out. If I try again, they'll suspect you're getting help."*

Erik gave me his "I told you so" look, trying once again to convince me to give up on the globe. I smiled at Owens to indicate my continued determination to get the genes.

"All right. Then here's what's going to happen. I have several people positioned in building security and maintenance. When it's time, a gas will be released through the ventilation system that will temporarily knock out anyone in the building. It's the same as that floral-scented gas they pumped into your room the first day you were here except without the scent. After that, I have someone taking down the power for the building and the surrounding area. That means no lights, no security cameras, no locked gates. But the backup generator will kick in within minutes. My guys will try to delay it from coming back on to buy you time, but we need to assume they won't be able to. That means you'll have a maximum of 4 minutes to get the genes, get out of the building, and get off the GlobalLife property. After that, you'll go to the meeting place that I showed you on the map."

Erik was talking but still heard what Owens said. We both looked at him, wondering when all this was going to take place.

"This is happening tonight at 6 sharp," Owens thought. *"We have to get you out of here, Samantha, before they make that announcement. If the Founders find out about the pregnancy, they'll make sure you're locked away for good. Being pregnant, you're even more valuable to them than you were before."*

I wanted desperately to be able to say something out loud to Owens because we still weren't sure how to get out. The maps we were given showed exits located on the opposite side of the building. It would take too long to get there. So would we use the air ducts? Sneak out the underground garage?

Owens continued. *"For your escape tonight, forget about the exits on the map. I want you to simply run out the front door."*

I glanced at Erik, who seemed to be losing confidence in Owens. Run out the front door? Was he crazy? It seemed too easy to get caught.

Owens must have noticed the looks on our faces. *"With the power down, you don't need to worry about the cameras. The doors will be unlocked. The guards will be unconscious. We've also taken care of the perimeter guards. You can just run right out. You don't have time to go out a different way. The power will come back on, locking every exit and you'll never get out. That's why you have to work fast. If you can't get that globe open in a minute or less, forget it. Just run out of the building. Run as fast as you can away from here before the lights and cameras come back on."*

Eve came into the dining room just as Owens was finishing up. "I thought I'd stop by and see how everything is going. These two should really be getting to the lab, if you don't mind."

Owens got up. "Certainly. We had a lovely talk. Will I be seeing them tonight at the announcement?"

"Yes, of course. We have people coming in to get them ready for the event."

"So we'll be leaving the lab early today?" I asked her.

"Yes. You'll be done by 3. Natalie and Kendall will be by your room at 5 to get you ready. Our guests will arrive for cocktails around 5:30. The announcement follows at 7."

Owens raced to send some final thoughts to Erik and me. *"Don't worry about what she said. All those people will be in the dining room. And they'll be unconscious once that gas hits. I'm sending you pills to take so the gas won't affect you. Make sure you take them! And remember. Power is out at 6. Generator will be on in 4 minutes, maybe earlier. Don't waste even a second!"*

29. THE GLOBE

Walter came in and escorted us back to our room. We changed clothes, then went to the lab for more testing. Neither one of us could concentrate, which annoyed Alison. I blamed it on the pregnancy. Erik told her he was upset about us being separated on Sunday. Luckily she bought both our excuses and was happy to get rid of us by 3.

"Sam, forget about the globe," Erik thought to me when we were back in our room. *"There's no time. 4 minutes! That's nothing. And Owens said the generators could come on even before that."*

"We have to try it, Erik. I'm not backing down on this. We'll give it 1 minute. If we can't open the globe within that time, then we'll leave."

"That minute could be the difference between escaping and being a prisoner here forever."

"Yeah, and that minute could also mean saving both of our lives. We need to get those vials, Erik."

"Dammit, Sam! You're driving me freakin' crazy with this! What's wrong with you? You're always the cautious one. I'm the one who's all about taking risks. And now I'm being cautious for once and you won't listen to me!"

"I'm not arguing about it, Erik."

He gave up trying to change my mind. We spent the next hour playing out the escape plan in our heads. Then I practiced mimicking Drew's brain waves again.

Right before 5, I hugged Erik tight one last time, just in case our plan didn't work. I knew if it didn't, I would never see him, or anyone else I cared about, ever again.

"We'll get out of here, Sam," Erik thought to me, but I could feel that he wasn't confident.

I wouldn't let go of him. Erik and I had been through so much together since meeting at that diner in Texas, but the past couple weeks had brought us closer than ever. *"If we screw this up, Erik, I'll never see you again. They'll keep us apart so we can never escape."*

"I know. That's why I need to tell you this before we go. And it's not because of some stupid software, either. I know how I feel. I—"

Natalie and Kendall walked in and Erik let go of me. He didn't continue his thought, but I wasn't sure I wanted him to. I couldn't get sidetracked with emotions. I had to stay completely focused on our plan.

Natalie whisked me off to the bathroom for hair and makeup. She had a new dress for me to wear for the announcement. It was pink and flowing. Very girly. Erik wore a gray suit and light blue tie. The pink and blue were obviously picked to go with the baby announcement theme.

Erik and I didn't mind-talk until 5:50, after Natalie and Kendall had left. *"Okay, one more time. Just to be perfectly clear,"* I thought to him. *"As soon as the power goes out, we'll run to the globe. I'll try thinking the phrases while you time me."*

"Right. But wait a minute. Is the gas being released at 6 or is the power going out at 6?"

"Crap! I don't know! He didn't say. And the pills! We never got them!" I was panicking. The plan was falling apart before it even began.

"Shit! Where are the damn pills?" Erik yelled in my head. *"Sam, what if Owens isn't helping us after all? What if it's all been some elaborate game that GlobalLife's been in on all along to see if we'd actually try to escape?"*

"No. Owens has to be helping us. He's already helped Colin and Jack. In that dream I had, someone got Colin and Jack out of the airport and into a car. They were safe, just like Owens said."

"You don't know if they were safe. You just saw them get picked up. Owens is the one who told you they were safe. He could have been lying about the whole thing."

Erik was right. I was relying on what Owens had said. A man we'd just met. Why were we trusting him? Because he let us hear his thoughts? What if he *was* working for GlobalLife?

It was 5:58 and we still had no pills. Erik began pacing the floor. Suddenly the door opened and Walter walked in.

"I'm here to take you to the dining room." As always, he walked in slowly, seeming completely uninterested in us. "Come on. We don't want to be late."

We followed him to the door. He stopped suddenly and pulled a small round container from his pocket. "Oh, yes, I almost forgot. I was supposed to give these to you. One of you has a headache?"

He handed me the container. Inside it were two small capsules. I took one and gave the other one to Erik. "We both have a headache," I said.

"From all the testing in the lab today," Erik added. He went over and poured us some water. We swallowed the pills, trusting they were meant to help us and not harm us.

"Very well, then. Let's go." Walter held the door for us as we walked out. We went down the hall and to the lobby. Nobody was there except for the guards and the woman at the front desk. The guests were already in the dining room having cocktails.

A platform with a podium had been set up in the lobby. A GlobalLife Genetics banner hung behind it.

"The announcement is being made in the lobby?" I asked Walter. He didn't answer.

Suddenly, I heard a loud thump. Erik and I turned back to find Walter had collapsed on the floor. More thumps echoed in the lobby. We looked to find the guards unconscious on the floor. The lady at the desk was slumped over sideways in her chair. Then everything went black. Pitch-black. Even the lights outside had gone out.

It was time. Erik and I could see perfectly in the dark thanks to our enhanced vision. We ran to the globe.

Erik stopped before getting there. "Oh, shit! What if it needs electricity to open? Let's just leave, Sam. Forget this."

"No! Get over here and start timing me!" I stood right in front of the globe. *"We're only as strong as our weakest link."* I focused all my energy into replicating Drew's brain waves when he said the phrase. Nothing happened.

"Ten seconds," Erik called out.

I thought the phrase again. Nothing. Then again. Still nothing.

"Thirty seconds," Erik called out again. "Just try something else!"

"To take the human race to a higher plane of being," I thought. It was the phrase Drew had used when describing the goal of the Founders. He had also thought it in his head when he was reviewing the announcement. I waited but the globe didn't move.

I tried the phrase again, tweaking it. *"The Founders' goal is to take the human race to a higher plane of being."* The globe remained still.

"Forty-eight seconds. Forget it, Sam! We have to go!" Erik grabbed my arm.

"No! Not yet!" I closed my eyes and thought of all my encounters with Drew. First at dinner, then at the gala, then at the lab. He hadn't said much at the lab because of that announcement he was reviewing. Then it hit me. The announcement! The phrase I'd just tried had been in the announcement. And the announcement was apparently being made in the lobby. So if Drew was reading the announcement in the lobby next to the globe, he couldn't say that phrase. If he did, it would open the globe. So that phrase couldn't be it!

But there was something in that announcement that Drew had crossed out. He'd made a change because he said he couldn't say something. What was it? What couldn't he say when he was next to the globe?

"Sam, we're leaving. Now!" Erik pulled on my arm.

I tried to remember that day in the lab. What were the words Drew crossed out? He was announcing the pregnancy and said—

"Sam!" I heard Erik yelling. "Come on!"

"Samantha Andrews, Subject 46A." I closed my eyes and put all my energy into mimicking Drew's brain waves.

As Erik dragged me away from the globe I opened my eyes. "Erik, wait! Look!" I pointed to the globe. It was slowly spinning and splitting along invisible cracks. We watched as it unfolded into pieces, like petals on a flower. We ran up to it. Inside was a small box. It looked like a tiny safe with a keypad on top.

"Erik, the password! Put the password in!"

Erik reached inside the globe to get the box. But the box wouldn't move. It was permanently attached to the inside of the globe. Erik punched the password into the keypad. Nothing happened.

He tried the password again. Still nothing. "It's not working." He checked his watch. "Sam, there's less than 3 minutes! Just go!"

"What? Without you?"

"Yes! Get out of here. Run!"

He reached back into the globe, trying the password again. Still nothing.

The lights in the building started to flicker. The generator was trying to start.

"Sam! Get out of the building!"

"I can't! I can't go without you!"

"Sam, I have to keep trying! We're so close. We'll never get a chance like this again! Get a head start. I'll catch up. I'm faster than you. Just get to Owens' car and tell them to wait."

"But you won't make it in time!"

"Sam, listen to me! I'll meet you there! Now go!" His voice echoed in the lobby.

I hesitated. "Okay. But hurry!"

I bolted out the entrance doors and took off down the hill. Suddenly I heard Erik in my head.

"Sam, it opened! I got the vials! I'll be right there!"

"Hurry, Erik!" I stopped to wait for him. I looked around but couldn't see him anywhere. *"Erik, where are you?"* I heard nothing back. *"Erik, can you hear me? Where are you?"*

He didn't answer. The unexplained silence was making my heart beat so fast that I felt like I couldn't breathe. Where was he?! Why wasn't he answering me?! I ran back toward the building.

"Sam, keep going!" Erik's voice filled my head. *"Get to the car!"*

"Erik, where are you? Why aren't you out here?"

"The doors locked as I was trying to leave. I can't get out. Just go!"

"What? No! I'll come get you!" I sprinted back to the entrance doors. I yanked on them as hard as I could. They wouldn't budge. *"I can't open them, either! There's gotta be another way in."*

"Sam, what are you still doing out there?! I told you to go! You're running out of time! Don't worry about me! I'll find another way!"

It was the last words I heard. He cut his thoughts off from me.

The outside perimeter lights were flashing on and off. I raced down the hill to the large steel entrance gate. I tried to climb it, but it was too slippery and there was nothing to hold on to. I pushed on the gate. It didn't move.

I closed my eyes and imagined my brain and muscles connecting, just as Erik had taught me back in Texas. Then I used every ounce of strength I had and pushed on the heavy, steel gate. It nudged a little, just enough to squeeze through.

I quickly reviewed Owens' map in my head as I continued to run. The map led me to an area of old abandoned warehouse buildings. It was the location Owens instructed Erik and me to go to once we escaped. Owens said a car would be waiting for us. But there wasn't a single person or vehicle in sight. I hid in an alley between two of the buildings and waited.

As I caught my breath, I was hit with the realization that Erik hadn't made it out. I slumped to the ground. Why didn't he leave with me? How could he stay behind like that?

Sirens began going off, waking me from my thoughts. Soon they would be searching for me. I had to get away from there. I was too close to GlobalLife. Where was Owens' car? It should have been there waiting! Where was it?!

My head began to ache terribly as scenes began flashing in my mind. I recognized it instantly. The scenario streaming. It was an ability I'd first experienced when I was in Texas. But I hadn't experienced it since then. I figured I didn't have the ability anymore. To make it work, high levels of stress hormones had to be released into my bloodstream. And despite all the stress I'd experienced at GlobalLife, this ability hadn't turned on. Until now.

The scenarios came to a halt and I could see a pathway telling me where to go. I took off, racing down an abandoned road, trying to stay focused. But my mind couldn't stop thinking about Erik. I should have refused to leave, I thought. If I'd refused, he would have come with me. Why did I listen to him when he told me to go? Why did I even consider leaving him there? What was I thinking? Now I would never see him again and—

I hit something, knocking myself to the ground. "Sam!" A hand reached out to help me up. I recognized it instantly.

"Erik!" I hugged him tight, then stood back to confirm that he was actually there. "Erik, how did you get out of there?"

"Sam, we have to go. I'll tell you later." He started to head back to the original meeting spot.

"Erik, wait! We need to go this way."

"No. That's the wrong way. The map said to go to that area with the old warehouse buildings."

"Yeah, I already went there but Owens' car never showed up. Something must have changed. I can see where we need to go, Erik. It's all in my head. Just follow me!"

I heard Erik's voice as I ran in front of him. "You better be right about this, Sam."

The pathway generated from my scenario streaming had us run down a narrow, deserted road. Snowy fields surrounded us on both sides. After a while, I could see the pathway running out. It ended under an old stone bridge.

"Erik, the bridge. That's it."

We ran under the small bridge and waited. Off in the distance, we could see helicopters hovering over GlobalLife, surveying the area from above.

"There's nobody here," Erik said. "Maybe we should keep running."

"Just wait a minute." I knew this was the right spot. I could feel it.

"This doesn't seem like— " Erik was interrupted by the rumble of an engine racing up behind us. But it wasn't a car engine. And it wasn't just one engine. It was two.

Two large motorcycles stopped right next to us. They were driven by large figures wearing helmets that hid their faces. "Get on," the one yelled at me. The other one ordered Erik to do the same.

"Sam, no! We don't know who they are. And we have to stay together."

"I'm going, Erik. I feel it. This is right." I got on the back of the motorcycle, ripping my dress to get my leg over.

Erik hesitated, then hopped on the back of the other one.

The motorcycles sped off, going farther and farther away from GlobalLife. We slowed down when we got to a remote area near the ocean. I could hear the waves breaking on the rocky cliffs. The driver stopped, then suddenly sped up. I held on tight as he drove almost to the edge of the cliff but then turned sharply down a long and steep incline into some type of underground garage, which opened as we approached.

Inside, the bright lights of the garage blinded me for a second. As my eyes adjusted, I looked for Erik. He was right behind me with the other driver. We parked near a door and both drivers jumped off. The driver who'd been with me removed his helmet and held out his hand to help me off.

"Hi, I'm Vince. I work for Mr. Owens."

I climbed off the motorcycle. Erik came over and stood beside me. "What is this place?"

"It's a safe house. We're deep underground. There's a whole complex right through this door."

"Owens said a car was picking us up by some old warehouse buildings but it never showed up," Erik said.

"Yeah. We had a change of plans," Vince explained. "That generator kicked in sooner than we expected. With the power back on, the original meeting spot was too close to GlobalLife. They would have seen us."

"How did you know we'd find you?" I asked.

"Owens knew that one of you would figure it out. Let's go inside. You can clean up."

I looked down to find that my dress was not only ripped but also covered in mud from the motorcycle ride.

Vince led us inside to a long hallway that opened up into a large seating area. It had modern, high-end furniture and concrete floors. Off to the side were several other rooms. One of them looked like a control room. It had computer monitors lining the wall and people were working on digital touch screens that hovered in the air.

"This is the common area," Vince said, leading us over to a large leather sofa. "It's a place where people come to have meetings or just hang out. Have a seat. We'll be right back." He and the other driver disappeared down a hallway on the other side of the room.

A soon as they were gone, I hugged Erik. "We did it! We really got out of there!"

"It was close. But yeah, we made it. It's kind of hard to believe."

"Wait—how did you get out?"

He smiled. "The garbage chute. It was in a maintenance room off the lobby. I remembered seeing it on the building map Owens gave us. I'm guessing that room's usually locked. But when I went to check, the door was open. There was a cleaning cart wedged in it. The maintenance guy was wheeling it out when he got knocked out by the gas. I didn't know where the chute would take me, but I tried it anyway."

"Where did you end up?"

"In a dumpster outside the back of the building. I got out, then ran and climbed the fence just as the alarms went off." He brushed his suit off. "I didn't even get that dirty. I don't smell, do I?"

I laughed. "No. So what was the deal with the password? Why wasn't it working?"

"I don't know. It's like you had to put it in multiple times. I was ready to give up, but I punched it in one last time and the box popped open." He showed me the two vials tucked away in the inside pocket of his suit jacket. He grabbed my hand. "We got what we needed, Sam! We can turn off the timer!"

"Yeah, but I shouldn't have left you behind like that, Erik. And you shouldn't have told me to. I thought you were gone forever." I hugged him again.

"We both made it out, Sam. That's all that matters. Hey, what happened with the globe? I was so busy keeping time I wasn't listening to what you were thinking."

"The first two phrases didn't work. I was in a total panic and then you were yelling at me to leave."

"So what was the phrase?"

"It was my name. And my, uh—my number. Subject 46A." I told Erik how I'd remembered Drew reviewing the announcement speech and how he crossed out the part with my name and subject number. "Why would that even be in his speech? Isn't that weird?"

Vince came back in the room. "There are some people who want to see you."

Erik and I stood up, expecting to see Owens and whoever else played a role in our escape. But instead, we saw Jack and Colin coming out from behind Vince.

"Colin!" I ran over to him.

"Sam, I told you never to leave me again," he said, not letting me go.

Jack went over and hugged Erik. He looked like he hadn't slept since we'd seen him last.

"Colin, I didn't think we'd ever get out of there. You wouldn't believe what happened when we—"

I stopped, almost passing out when I saw another person coming down the hall.

30. SECRETS

"Uncle Dave!" I yelled.

Colin let me go. I ran up to Dave, tears streaming down my face.

"Uncle Dave! I can't believe it's really you!"

"Hi, honey. I'm so happy you're safe." He gave me one of his big Uncle Dave hugs that I'd loved since I was little girl.

"What happened? How did you get up here? Was that letter really from you?" I had so many questions for him.

He smiled. "Sam, just slow down. We'll get to all that later. But first, tell me, are you okay? Did they hurt you at all?"

"No. I'm okay. What about you?" I stood back and looked him over to see if he'd been harmed by GlobalLife. But he looked just as I'd remembered.

"I'm fine, Sam. I got away from them before they could do too much damage."

"Uncle Dave, I was so worried about you."

"I know, honey. I've been worried about you, too. But it sounds like you've been taking pretty good care of yourself. Getting out of GlobalLife not just once, but twice! Making it down to Texas. Finding my old friend, Jack."

Jack came over and gave me a hug. "Hey, Sam. I didn't even get to say hello when you came in."

"That's okay. You need to be with Erik."

Jack turned to Dave. "Dave, I need to introduce you to my son, Erik."

Dave shook Erik's hand. "Nice to meet you, Erik. I've heard a lot about you."

"Yes. Dave and I have had some time to catch up while we've been waiting here for you two," Jack said.

"Well, sorry we took so long, Dad," Erik kidded. "See, Sam? I told you we should have escaped sooner."

"Let's go sit down," Dave said. "We have a lot to talk about."

Jack and Erik sat down. Dave and I sat across from them.

"Colin, get over here and sit by your girl," Dave said. "He's talked about you nonstop," Dave whispered to me.

Dave moved over and Colin sat down, putting his arm around me. My heart ached as I sat next to him, knowing I was pregnant with Erik's child. How could I ever tell Colin that I was pregnant? I felt sick just thinking about it.

"I have to admit we were surprised you were able to get out this soon," Jack said. "Owens didn't think the plan would happen for another few weeks. And then all of a sudden it was tonight. What happened?"

"There was gonna be an announcement about—" Erik stopped before mentioning the pregnancy. He looked at me for permission to continue.

I got in his head. *"Please don't tell them yet. I need to tell Colin myself. And Dave. Let's just wait. They don't have to know this second."*

I could feel Erik's mood change from excited to sad as I waited for his response. It was almost like he couldn't wait to tell them about the baby.

"What announcement?" Colin asked.

"Oh, just some announcement about the project," Erik lied. "But the reason we had to get out tonight was because they were gonna move us to separate rooms on Sunday."

"And being separated would have made it impossible for us to escape," I added.

"You were in the same room together?" Colin asked. "The whole time?" He glared at Erik and held me closer.

I started to say something to change the subject when I suddenly realized that we were missing someone. "Where's Brittany? I want to see her."

Jack's face changed from happy to disappointed. "I'm sorry, Sam. They haven't rescued her yet. According to Owens, GlobalLife moved her to a different location about a week ago but now they've moved her back to the facility you just left."

"What? Why do they keep moving her?"

"We don't know," Jack said. "Owens overheard them saying she was supposed to be moved to the GlobalLife headquarters in Sweden. But then at the last minute they decided to keep her here in Iceland."

The pregnancy, I thought. It had to be. With my enhanced genes, GlobalLife would worry that my pregnancy might have complications. And that meant they'd want Brittany close by in case they needed her as a donor.

"We've got to get her out of there."

"Owens has people working on it, Sam," Dave said. "There's nothing we can do. He'll get her out."

"I don't understand why this Owens guy is helping us so much. Who is this guy?"

"I actually met him years ago at a genetics conference," Dave said. "We really hit it off. But we didn't stay in touch. After he learned of the explosion at the GlobalLife facility in Minnesota, he contacted me. It's long story, but basically that's how I ended up here."

"But Owens never even told me you were here. Why didn't he tell me?"

"He probably just wanted you to stay focused on getting out of there. Anyway, that was Owens' private plane you took here to Iceland. This is his underground facility. Few people know about this place. That's why we're staying here."

"Maybe we should talk later," Jack said. "You two probably want to clean up and change clothes. By the way, what's the story with the fancy clothes? A suit and tie, Erik?"

"They made us dress up every day. Suits for me. Dresses for Sam. And for tonight's event, we had to dress up even more than usual."

"It's an odd color choice," Dave commented. "Pink and blue?"

"Well I don't know about Erik, but I would love to take a shower and put on some clean clothes," I said, trying to get everyone's mind off of Dave's statement.

Colin got up. "I'll show you where everything is." We went down the hallway to the bathroom. "Towels are in the cabinet. I'll grab you some clothes and leave them outside the door."

"Thanks, Colin." I waited for him to leave.

He smiled. "That's it? Sam, we haven't seen each other in weeks. And I knew you wouldn't let me give you a real kiss out there with everyone staring at us. Come here." He kissed me, then hugged me tight. "I'm so glad you're okay."

"Colin, I'm covered in mud. Let me clean up. I'll be right out."

Colin left and I heard him stop Erik in the hall. "Hey, Erik. Tell me. Is she all right? She's really quiet. And she's not acting like herself."

"Give her time. I'm sure she'll tell you everything eventually. Is there another shower around here?"

"Yeah, just down the hall and to the left."

After I cleaned up, I went back to the common area to find everyone waiting for me. We had some food, then Erik and I told them about our escape and how we got the genes.

Owens never appeared. But Vince came by later and reported that Owens had stayed at GlobalLife after Erik and I escaped. He offered to assist with damage control, helping Drew and Rachel come up with a story to tell the investors about why the announcement was postponed. I had to give the old guy credit. He did an excellent job playing double agent.

Later, Jack gave us a quick tour of the place. Dave explained that it was a safe house for people acting as spies for Owens in his efforts to stop GlobalLife. We still didn't know the whole story about Owens. And we didn't know why he was working so hard to help us. There was so much that Erik and I had to learn. But it was late and we were exhausted. Jack and Dave would have to catch us up later.

That night, I decided to stay in Colin's room. After everything I'd been through, I didn't want to be alone. I was actually afraid to be alone. Part of me still thought this wasn't real. I worried that I would wake up in the middle of the night and find myself back at GlobalLife.

Before heading to bed, Erik caught me in the hallway. "So you're staying with him?"

"I don't want to be alone tonight, okay?"

"So what happens now? You just go back to him and that's it?"

"Please don't make me talk about this. My mind is a mess right now, Erik."

He switched to mind-talk. *"When are you telling him about the baby?"*

"I don't know. I don't think I can tell him."

"You have to tell him. You want me to?"

"No! Don't say anything. And don't drop hints."

"What about my dad? I have to at least tell him."

"Please don't. He'll start acting weird around me. And then Colin will know."

"I can't promise you that I won't say anything to him."

"Sam, are you coming?" Colin was calling me from his room.

"Yeah, just a minute." I turned back to Erik. "We can talk tomorrow. Goodnight, Erik."

I went back to the room, and got into bed next to Colin. "I'm so tired. I barely slept at that place."

Colin turned off the light. "Sam, is there something you want to tell me? Do you want to talk about what happened there?"

"No. It's too soon." I turned on my side, away from him.

"Because you can tell me anything. You know that, right?"

"Yeah. Of course."

"If something happened while you were there—"

"Like what, Colin?"

"I don't know. Anything. It doesn't matter what it is. I'm just saying that you can tell me."

"Colin, could we talk tomorrow? I'm really tired."

"Sure." He put his arm around me and moved in closer. "I love you, Sam."

"I love you, too. Goodnight."

I did love Colin. But part of me also loved Erik. And now Erik and I shared this secret. As much as I tried to sleep that night, my mind wouldn't let me. A scene of me telling Colin the truth kept playing over and over again in my head. Each time, I imagined him never speaking to me again.

When I wasn't thinking of Colin, I thought of Brittany, all alone, trapped at GlobalLife. And I could still hear that timer in me, ticking away. What if the alien base codes didn't work?

Although I was relieved to have escaped from GlobalLife, there were so many more challenges yet to face. And so many more secrets to be revealed.

Made in United States
Orlando, FL
03 March 2022